The Very Annoying Jew

About the author

Michael Kretzmer was born and brought up in Bulawayo, Southern Rhodesia (now Zimbabwe). He moved to England in 1976 and became a journalist and film-maker, eventually writing for the London *Sunday Times* and producing television documentaries for the BBC, Channel 4 and overseas broadcasters, including *J'Accuse!*, a film about Holocaust denial in Lithuania. His career has included many digressions, including building a small media company, busking across Europe and creating a tiny farm producing vegetables, fruit and smug chickens. *The Very Annoying Jew* is his first novel. Michael is a husband, father and grandfather and enjoys motorbikes, reading, Torah study, gardening and travel.

The Very Annoying Jew

a novel by

Michael Kretzmer

30

ENVELOPE BOOKS

Published 2025 in Great Britain and the USA by
EnvelopeBooks
A New Premises venture in association with Booklaunch

12 Wellfield Avenue, London N10 2EA, England
116 West 73rd Street, New York, NY 10023

www.envelopebooks.co.uk

Cover design by Stephen Games | Booklaunch

A CIP catalogue record for this title is available from the
British Library.

Edited and designed by Booklaunch
EnvelopeBooks 30
ISBN 9781915023629

This is a work of fiction. Names, characters, places and incidents
are either products of the author's imagination or are used
fictitiously. Any resemblance to actual events, locales,
organisations or persons, living or dead, is entirely coincidental.

To Joanna

Dear Olivia …
April 2, 3:35 am

Olivia, this is for you. David Britton on David Britton. The unvarnished truth. A final plea from the ridiculous man who became your husband, loves you and wants you to come home.

The ridiculous man. That's me. It's what I've become, Olivia. You'll agree, of course. Enthusiastically, no doubt. But maybe you'll also agree that it wasn't always this way and that the speed of my descent from leftish cool to right-wing fool has caught all of us off guard. From celebrity to laughing stock in, what, ten seconds? Because it wasn't that long ago, was it, Olivia, that I was not just not ridiculous but highly prized—a B-List celeb: the educated older woman's Mr Sexy, perched languidly on the TV couch with his white shirt, grey-flecked curls and ironic patter.

And then last night, just before the Pain Fairy laid into me with her new set of tools, I ran a census which revealed that apart from Ronny the Runner, there isn't a single person alive who does not find me ridiculous. And not just ridiculous. Annoying too. Honestly, we're talking hundreds of thousands —refreshingly from all races, cultures and walks of life—who loathe me with a singular passion. Everyone despises me, Olivia. I've become a sort of human blood sport.

You could probably populate a whole nation just from People Who Find David Britton Annoying and Ridiculous. Last week I got about two thousand tweets from total strangers, all over the world, who find me so painful that many want to kill me, often in highly inventive ways. The consequence of my *Newsnight* disaster, of course, but more of that later.

And that's not the worst of it. The worst of it, Olivia, is that the people who find me most ridiculous and most annoying are the people I love most: You and Moose.

1

Look, I know it's all my fault. From the Pain Fairy drilling into my neural pathways to my beloved wife leaving me, I deserve it all. But I want you to know that something else is going on here. Something unnatural. Supernatural, even. Forces I can't control. Like demons coming back to punish me for all my sins.

I'm not saying God sent them. God forbid! More like an Eastern karmic thing, but engineered by some weird angel with a personal grudge against me. Of course I couldn't tell you this to your face because you'd think I was insane as well as ridiculous and annoying.

But I'm not insane, Olivia—merely on a spiral that I cannot stop, a malevolent rollercoaster that turns everything I touch these days into whatever the opposite of gold is. Lead. Everything I touch turns to lead.

Like this morning.

Brace yourself. It concerns your cat. And the news isn't good.

This morning I had the most important meeting of my life. The. Most. Important. Meeting. Of. My. Life.

I woke early, showered, shaved, pruned my increasingly rebellious eyebrows, put on a new white shirt, polished my shoes, checked myself three times over, examined my teeth, ears and nostrils, prepared some drop-dead lines, typed them up, printed them out, grabbed my bag and keys, and headed purposefully to the door … and what happens?

Your cat decides to stage its own death. Again. But unlike its previous 387 attention-grabbing suicide attempts, this time I know that Sylvia Plath isn't gagging for ratings; she's actually gagging. It starts with histrionic choking, then moves on to jerky pirouetting and the issuing of froth from orifices I didn't even know she had.

I scoop her up, rush her into the kitchen, extract some ageing smoked salmon from the fridge—everything's old since you left, by the way—and shove it into her mouth, the way you do when she's sick. But she won't eat. Instead, she's rolling her eyes back into their little pink sockets and convulsing in terrifying tiny spasms.

Naturally I panic at the thought that animal torture and

2

other feline crimes will be added to my tally of Unforgivable Inadequacies, so I try dropping her onto the living-room carpet to shock her back into life (it's worked before) but this time she lands like a sack of wet laundry.

I hold her boney chest to my ear. She's breathing! I grab my phone, dial the vet and finally get through to a Spanish girl of about four who tells me to bring the cat in. This will mean missing The. Most. Important. Meeting. Of. My. Life. but I know how ardently you love that cat and so it's worth it.

But when I race back, Miss Plath is unresponsive, no matter how much I shake her and shout at her to wake up.

Dead as a dodo.

I did my best, Olivia. I really did.

I rush back to the bedroom, wash again, throw on a fresh shirt, grab my bag and keys, and race down into the garage —still smelling of dead cat. I clamber into the Merc, rev the engine in that way you hate, lurch out into the streets of London and almost hit a cyclist who tells me he's going to knife my kids.

This of course reminds me of the corpse. I've forgotten to bag the cat.

So now I'm thinking: What happens if you do, miraculously, come home and discover Sylvia Plath dissolving into your favourite living room rug, the Afghan blue one? It isn't a difficult question to answer, is it? It would definitely, absolutely, hopelessly be over between us (you see I still have hope, Olivia). So I prepare to execute the most dangerous U-turn ever performed on the Euston Road in rush-hour traffic.

Then my phone rings.

Angela. You remember Angela, I presume? Her fourth call in an hour.

'Angela,' I say pleasantly.

'You're twenty minutes late!' she barks.

I tell her she should relax and it immediately becomes apparent that this was the worst thing I could possibly have said.

'Relax? Did you say relax? Where the fuck are you?'

'Euston Road. Be with you in fifteen,' I say, chirpily.

'Euston Road? More like forty if you're lucky—which you aren't mate, you really aren't.'

She's so obviously in the right that it's painful, so I'm about to suggest a face-saving twenty-seven minutes rather than forty, not really as a compromise but more to annoy her (I know you find this childish but I can't help it, Olivia, I really can't) when her voice snaps back. 'I feel violated, David.'

Believe me, Olivia: Angela's always feeling violated.

I put on my Celebrated BBC Announcer Is Obliged to Address Idiotic Pleb voice: 'Angela, please rest assured that the last thing on earth I'd like to do is violate you. It really doesn't matter if I'm a few minutes late. Just tell people there's been an accident at home. Which happens to be true.'

'Now listen to me, yeah?' As usual, her sense of violation has morphed into an uncontrollable teenie rage. 'When you come in late, yeah?, and all over the place, and looking stupid and old, you'll need to have a good excuse, yeah?'

I can hear Matilda—you remember sidekick Matilda?—fussing in the background, trying to calm her down.

'And I mean a fucking good excuse, yeah?'

'Actually I have an impeccable excuse—'

'Accident, dead kiddy, cancer—I don't fucking care. You cannot be late for a meeting as important as this!'

'Actually there's a very good reason—'

'And I'm really pissed that you've done this to me—'

'Angela, my cat—'

'—because to be honest, if you do fuck this up, I will walk out and never return and everything I have done over four years and seven months will have been a chicken-foxing waste of time.'

'Chicken-foxing', incidentally, is her new expression, which she has been deploying whenever she's really angry or really happy. I gave her the word before her last boozy girls' weekend to Berlin. *Fickungsfotze*. That's right. Our word *Fickungsfotze*. Now kidnapped and serially abused by Angela.

And yes, I know that at that point I should have just shut

4

up and let her get on with it, or killed the call, or something like that, but I couldn't, Olivia. Like all young people, she's just too irritating to be allowed the last word, and especially if that last word is *Fickungsfotze.*

So I said, '"We", Angela. It's what *we* have done over four years and seven months'—and I'm about to remind her of the alchemy of our respective skills and talents—my pedigree, experience and, above all, credit line combined with her menace, self-love, idiot-cunning and deadly ambition, not to mention the gigantic opportunity I gave her for self-advancement when she was nothing ... and the line goes dead.

And you know what happened? Suddenly I feel this wave of scalding sadness. I'm bawling, Olivia—for the cat, of all things. The malodorous, cantankerous, man-hating cat. Because SP was our cat, our cat which waited for you every day by the door and curled up in your lap every night and slept on our bed, and her death breaks another link in our chain and that breaks my heart, Olivia: it breaks my heart.

So I'm kinda howling now in the feral traffic but mid-howl it gets worse.

A lot worse.

Because, dimly at first but then like a sucker punch, it hits me.

Sylvia Plath didn't just die. She was poisoned.

I am afraid I have to reveal yet more bad news. We have a stalker. I think he only wants to kill me, so you should be fine. But he's been in the house. I can explain. But not right now. The pills are kicking in and the angel of narcoleptic sleep is upon me.

Just don't forget where I got up to: this was just the start of my day, Olivia, and before me lay The. Most. Important. Meeting. Of. My. Life.

Olivia, I wish you'd get back to me. I want you to come home.

The. Most. Important. Meeting. Of. My. Life.
April 5, 7:30 am

And now let me tell you about The. Most. Important. Meeting. Of. My. Life (and quite possibly yours too, by the way.)

I arrive forty minutes late at the ridiculously-named Hungry Dog offices—I mean, what sane human being actually decides on a company name like Hungry Dog? Who are these imbeciles? Actually I can answer my own question because, unbelievably, they're all waiting for me in reception: Angela, Matilda and three clients all under the age of five.

I've taken Angela's advice and gone for the accident excuse. I've rucked my jacket, smeared some dirt onto my cream trousers and rubbed some dead cat scent behind my ears and on my wrists, the way you do, and it seems to do the trick.

They freeze.

'Hello, everyone,' I say in my TV-smart baritone voice, my handsome studio smile fully unfurled, my hand extended in a gesture of Victorian exuberance. 'I'm really terribly sorry to have kept you all waiting. Had a little accident.'

'Poor you,' says Angela, patting my arm. As ever she has her hair slicked back, has daubed her eyes an oceanic blue, and manages to look like a giant spider. This woman has a ghastly power, no doubt about it.

'Ja, so zat is bad luck,' Matilda confirms. 'But you're obviously okay now, zank God, so I guess we can start, ja?'

I really love Matilda. She's like a cross between a Labrador and a recreational drug.

'What happened?' says a thin client in a skin-tight black suit.

Weirdly, the question takes me by surprise. I say, 'I hit a cat' and instantly regret it. I do that a lot these days, you know—say things I instantly regret.

'A cat!' exclaims the thin one. To my surprise he and the other kiddies are intrigued.

'Yes, definitely a cat.'

'Whose cat?' says an even thinner one. He's also in black.

'My cat.'

Now nobody's breathing.

'We called her Sylvia Plath,' I say, to lighten the mood, but the opposite happens. They look devastated in a primary-school sort of way and now gaze at me with a fresh adolescent intensity, both terrified and hungry for lurid detail. I'm about to tell them not to look so worried, because the cat was ancient and stank and I loathed it anyway, but then decide that this might traumatise the young folk further, so I pull back sharply, and it sounds like I'm sobbing.

I really don't know what to do so I cover my eyes with my hands and gently rock.

'So sad,' the thin kid says.

'Totally sad,' says the thinner kid.

'Indeed,' sniffs Angela.

'Ja, so *zis* definitely sad,' Matilda confirms.

'More than sad,' says the third client who hasn't spoken yet. He is fatter and older than the others, because he's American, and wears jeans and a check shirt—because he's American. His eyes are glistening. 'We can set this meeting back if you like.'

'I'm okay,' I say, offering up my handsome studio smile again. 'She was very old and sick, to be honest, so in a way it's a mercy.'

'Oh good!' cries Angela.

'Ja, *zat* is good,' screeches Matilda way too loudly, then shrinks back.

The short guy is standing firm. 'Are you sure?' he says, staring at me with watery eyes.

'Oh, yeah, the cat's definitely dead,' I say.

'No, that you can do this meeting.'

I feel Angela's arachnid fingers tightening on my back. 'Of course I can,' I say, 'but thank you for your concern. Really appreciated.'

'Good,' says Angela, marching us all towards the entrance.

'Ja, we should begin,' says Matilda, starting to march.

The short guy hesitates, then nods, and leads us through security and up the elevator to the famous Hungry Dog boardroom on the seventh floor.

LET ME EXPLAIN WHY THIS WAS THE. MOST. IMPORTANT. Meeting. Of. My. Life. Because if it went well, Olivia, I'd finally be free. We'd finally all be free.

Free of the unbearable Angela. Free of the financial worries that keep me awake every night—the idiotic juvenile frenzy of Mee!Zee!'s expansion. Free of that grotesque East London office, that purple-and-black four-storey dungeon rat hole of rooms so cramped and crowded that I sometimes have to literally crawl on all fours to get around. You know, it was barely tolerable when there were six teenies working there, so now there are twenty million, there isn't room to breathe, let alone move about.

Allow me one quick, angry digression, okay? Everything about my company, absolutely everything, is awful, but nothing is quite as awful as its name, don't you think? Mee! Zee!—with two illiterate exclamation marks! Of course the name was Angela's idea. She squealed for a week when she first dreamed it up and when I told her I thought it was the dumbest name I'd ever heard, and anyway what was wrong with David Britton Films Ltd, she went predictably beserk and shrieked, 'It's in sync! It's karma! It's what we are! It's Us!'

This surreal but rather entertaining disagreement went on for weeks because under no circumstances was I going to allow my unexpectedly revitalised BAFTA-award-winning company to be called Mee!Zee! with two illiterate exclamation marks—but what happens? Her idiot series *Crip Trips!* —you know, the twelve-parter on the sex lives of cripples and amputees—went viral. You probably read about it in the papers. Topped every chart, all over the world.

And just as I'm reeling from the humiliation of being up-staged by a teenie moron, in my own company, and by a grotesque show built on prurience masquerading as social inclusion, what happens? The abysmal *Guardian*, your favourite newspaper, identifies her as one of the 'Twenty Young Women Who Will Change Britain'.

How does she do it? You tell me, Olivia. You like young people, don't you, so I'm guessing you understand them a little and have some ideas. You tell me how anyone as thick, uneducated (a 2:2 in Media Studies from Manchester Met) and appalling as Angela Sutton can be qualified to change Britain? She can't even change a light bulb, so how does this undernourished, fizzing, nasty freak of a girl—twenty-two when she arrived here as an unpaid intern—transform my accoladed but admittedly narcoleptic documentary film company into a multi-million-pound kiddy-social-media-and-TV powerhouse with software that's apparently going to re-make the world?

Of course, any normal man would see this as good news. The house is mortgaged to the hilt, as you know, so Angela may yet not only dig us out of the financial shit but actually make us rich. The problem is that if I remain at this company, I may end up killing her, as well as Matilda and an awful lot of children.

But there is light at the end of the tunnel, Olivia. The good news is that Angela wants me out. I know this because she told me. Well, actually, she told a young electrician who'd popped in to fix a circuit in her office last week. She was explaining to him that the last thing a young, brilliant, world-changing web company like ours needed was old men who did nothing but sit on a controlling share of what she now calls the 'Youth Genius Dividend'—and just in case I missed it, she stared at me for about a minute while touching the ceiling with a prosthetic leg, left on the set after filming the last episode of *Crip Trips!*

Since *The Guardian* pushed the boat out further by identifying her as one of the Women Who Will Change the Universe, Angela has morphed into something truly dangerous. Her aggression has become very targeted. She is no longer content with just the occasional insult and instead has launched an active campaign to edge me out of every one of my remaining professional functions at work—even my motivational sessions, you remember: the 'Win Your Own Oscar!' lectures. Summarily scrapped; no reason given.

So as things stand, all I am left with at Mee!Zee! is to keep the company afloat, by putting our house on the line, and to finish what I think you know will be my last prison documentary for the BBC (more of this disaster later). That's why when Angela broke the news about Hungry Dog, I almost cried with relief.

'They wanna meet Oscar Man!' she says, cheekily. Oscar Man, by the way, is the pet name she gave me when she first spotted Oscar on my shelf. She couldn't believe it. For about half an hour she kept repeating 'so ... you—you won an Oscar?—you?' and when the message finally got through that, yes, I had indeed won an Oscar, she kept shaking her head in a sort of disabled way, while shrieking 'Chickenfoxer! You chicken-foxer!' This went on for days.

I suppose that at this point, this apologia should include a note about Oscar, because you and I know the truth, don't we? —that, as usual, I fluked it, becoming, I think, the only man in history ever to have won the International Short Documentary Newcomers Award. (The following year the category was axed.) Still, *Love Killing* wasn't a bad film, was it, Olivia? Who doesn't enjoy sugary sagas about one-armed killers, doe-eyed borderline imbeciles, blind best friends, abusive uncles, deaf prison doctors and, of course, one-eyed pharmacists with dodgy fingers? Especially when told by a smirking Englishman with perfect ironic timing? But how strange, don't you think, that *Love Killing* was the only time I strayed out of my pompous little worthy-but-dull filmmaking ghetto into the garish world of populist TV.

I know what you're thinking, Olivia. You're thinking, 'that jammy David Britton: how does he get away with it?' You're thinking that only David Britton could be lucky enough to take a schmaltzy TV car crash of forgiveness, handicap and incest and use it to kickstart not one but three dazzling careers: as a director and producer of sensitive prison documentaries; as an elegant TV pundit on the vagaries of the penal justice system; and as a passionately telegenic campaigner against the death penalty. And you're right. I think so too. Only David Britton. And look how he squanders his luck.

But let's return to Hungry Dog. This buy-out could change everything, Olivia. Angela's strategy—and I think I interpreted her bark correctly—is to fight like crazy for 14.5, take 13.8 with a share slice for her, and then I can retire and 'do what the fuck I like, like make little vids about cons'. Angela says the deal's a cert because 'how can the dickheads refuse when the contract value alone of the *Crip Trips!* sequels makes it a chicken-foxing flier, and that was before you took Wang into account!' Wang, as I think I've mentioned before, is the spectrumy weirdo who leads our web team and laughs at me whenever I see him. But apparently he's a genius when it comes to coding for adolescent morons so I am under strict instructions not to hurt his feelings in any way.

So that's why today's meeting really was The. Most. Important. Meeting. Of. My. Life.

WE GO UP TO THE SEVENTH FLOOR WITH THE FAT CAT-guy making eyes at me, and eventually the elevator opens into the Hungry Dog boardroom. It's like a huge flight deck for infants on acid. Absurdly large screens on curved walls; tiny, shifting, piercing lights set into the ceiling; and soft-lit recessed cavities displaying vintage stuff: you know—computers, TVs, telephones, audio gear, that sort of thing. Every chair has its own console bristling with tech.

I troop in, rehearsing the Hungry Dog names, which fortunately all rhyme. The skinny black suits are Ken and Ben and the chubby old guy making cat solidarity eyes at me is Len. Still won't take his eyes off me.

So we're sitting around this giant aluminium and glass table and the infants are extracting armouries of phones, tablets, laptops and piles of spreadsheets. Me, I'm copying what I see, putting my own old iPhone with the cracked screen onto the table, and everyone's staring at it when it suddenly buzzes and starts crawling across the glass like a legless cockroach.

I snatch it up.

It's your text, Olivia.

—*We can't be fixed. I've decided. It's over, David.*

I'm staring at the message, desperate to reply, to say "No! No! No!" But you know what? I can't. Because there really isn't much a man can say or do when his wife catches him with her life-rival on her knees, unzipping his zipper, in a closet room at a dinner party while she's downstairs, is there? It's not a situation they rehearse you for in the English public-school system.

And after that, I just don't remember. The. Most. Important. Meeting. Of. My. Life. rumbles on, in a surreal storm of chattering memes bouncing around on a tide of sugar-rush adolescent excitement, acronyms, concepts and, worst of all, jokey spasms that I don't even vaguely comprehend but which leave everyone else either sneering or guffawing—in concert.

So I'm sitting there, pressed into my kiddy-adventure chair with a frozen smile, reading and re-reading your message, sinking my nails into my wrists until they're bleeding, because it's all I can do to stop myself from howling, while braying Ken's saying something about 'bang on demographic positive-bombs' and smartass Ben's adding 'definitively' and Angela crowing 'which is why we came to you' and Matilda's shrilling 'Ja, *zat* is why!' when I suddenly observe that they've all gone silent and they're staring at me.

Maybe I'd howled.

'I'm sorry, I have to go to the bathroom,' I say.

They all agree.

'You okay?' the cat guy asks.

'I am okay, Ben, thanks.'

'I'm Len.'

'That's okay,' says Angela. 'We'll press on.'

Len is now squeezing himself out of his chair. 'I'll show you where to go. Come.'

We leave the room and, outside, it's open-plan—a bright carpeted orange field of chattering teenagers sitting on cushions around big white plastic desks, playing with phones and screens.

'It's over there,' Len points. 'Just behind the ping-pong table and Big Dinosaur. You see it?'

Big dinosaur is located in the middle of the expanse, a giant fibre glass brontosaurus thing extending to the glass roof, with a demented, phosphorescent smile.

'I get why you call Big Dinosaur "Big Dinosaur",' I say, in a dim attempt to curry favour.

'Our mascot,' says Len. 'The Boss's idea. Intersectional product evolution. Survival, long term. A genius.'

'Aren't dinosaurs extinct?'

Len chortles, clicks his fingers and points. 'You got it!'

I chortle and click my fingers too. But of course I don't get it, Olivia. This rich-kid nursery, its language, its frantic algorithms, its technologies—none of it makes sense. Angela makes no sense. Matilda makes no sense. Ping-pong, Big Dinosaur, the skeletal teenagers with their tight black suits and tricksy haircuts—none of it.

'You're struggling, I can see.' Len's looking at me weirdly, like a girl in love.

'I am struggling,' I say.

He's fixing me with big watery eyes and suddenly can't contain himself and blurts it out.

'I have three cats. They're my kids. Especially since Juan left. And one of them is very sick.'

His teary eyes say the unsayable.

I don't know what to do so I hug him. This goes on for an uncomfortably long time during which I try but fail to work out how to extricate myself, but eventually he pats me on the shoulder, wipes his eyes and returns to the meeting.

I make for Big Dinosaur and locate a disabled toilet. Inside I stagger to the sink and examine my reflection in the mirror. It's an awful sight, Olivia.

Where has your beautiful man gone? The sensual lips, the sulky Levantine eyes? Both in retreat, apologetic in the way they hang in their sacks. And that skin under the sodium light, sallow as sickness. But worst of all, the ridiculous hair, still promiscuously curled but going to grey and falling out in patches. And that nose! When did that get so prominent?

13

This is me today Olivia: your handsome, clever, witty, urbane, Oscar-winning husband, metamorphosed into a beaky, ageing, ugly Dorian Grey: despised, ridiculous, shrinking with fear and scavenging a living from a pack of infant hyenas who rob him and laugh behind his back.

And now, alone.

I am on my knees, Olivia. I am so sorry.

Emile Gets On My Nerves (1)
April 6, 11:30 pm

Why do I do it, Olivia? Why do I always get into fights I can't win?

You remember Emile, the pretty-boy editor that Angela dragged out of the local Weirdo Zoo and deposited on my lap just to annoy me? Well, just in case you don't, Emile is my new editor for the tiresome BBC documentary I've yet to finish, and although Emile may have a degree in Applied Make-up and Grievance Studies, he is demonstrably unqualified to help me finish this ghastly film that eats at my body and soul like a giant leech.

Essentially, the film's about a talentless white rapper with the ridiculous name of Killa-Jah, who makes his living by pretending to be a brilliant black rapper called Killa-Jah. As executive producer, I am expected to view the nonsensical final version, gasp at how brilliant it is in every way, and vigorously stroke the pecker of the director—a morose, dyspeptic, narcissistic juvenile rodent called Mark Shapireau.

Well, you know what's coming, don't you? I'm afraid that this morning, I made Emile-the-Editor cry.

By way of background, you need to understand that my irritation with Emile has reached the point where I can no longer be polite to him. Everything about him annoys me: his preachy politics; his nursery-school lisp; his stupid haircuts (he gets coiffed roughly twice a week); his moronic slogan t-shirts and virtue-signalling badges; the cute way he says 'it's only me'; and the portentous way he ends every sentence with 'I guess', as if he needs to ratchet down his startling depths of thought. My itemisation of what drives me nuts grows with every encounter, and today's conversation took me to new levels of loathing.

But you like young people, don't you?—so I'll let you judge.

We're talking on the phone.

'We've had a call from the Beeb,' he tells me in that tiny, bleating, victim voice that makes me want to victimise him. 'They're unhappy.'

I tell Emile it is no surprise that the BBC are unhappy and I'm about to ask him if he'd be happy if he lived inside his own rectum but he presses on and warns me that Marc is not just unhappy but 'traumatised'.

'I guess he is, Emile,' I say. 'But what has traumatised him? Is it haircut-based or beard-design based?'

'No. It's about Killa-Jah.'

I've been expecting this, of course. 'No? Gosh. What about Killa-Jah?'

'It's the way you're re-editing the rushes and presenting him, and especially his kid. It's, well, sort of racist. I guess.'

I tell Emile that there are indeed intrinsic editorial difficulties in cutting a film about a white man pretending to be a black man, who has taken the name Killa-Jah, and who wrote a music track called 'Me Wanna Splat Da Whiteboy Popo' to accompany a sequence in which his tiny son dances around with a loaded gun.

'You see, Emile,' I tell him, 'what I've done is stripped out the adulatory horseshit commentary that Marc attempted to write and allowed the actuality to run without a voice-over. What I've offered is unvarnished truth rather than vacuous interpretation. What's the problem?'

'Oh, I get you,' says Emile even-handedly, 'but it does come across as, like, decontextualized racist finger-pointing.'

Emile learned the word 'decontextualized' last week and it may be the word that tips me from patrician critic to throat-slitting murderer, because now he uses it all the sodding time, though not as often as he uses the word 'racist'.

'Emile, Killa-Jah's not black,' I explain. 'He's as white as a Nordic ski jumper.'

'David!' Emile squeals. 'We've talked about this before. He says he's black, so he's black, okay?'

'Does he look black to you, Emile?'

'*Looking* black? Looking isn't what matters, David,' he

scolds down the phone. 'Being black isn't to do with skin colour! That's so racist. Killa-Jah feels black. So he's black. And Mace-Z said he was black!'

Mace-Z, incidentally, is the Brixton rapper who was shot in the head a few weeks ago in a drug deal that went wrong and is now well on his way to BBC beatification. They're planning an eight-parter on him for the summer. With Shapireau in charge.

'Ah, yes,' I tell Emile. 'The late great Mace-Z, world expert on racial ordination.'

'He was a great rapper,' says Emile gravely, 'so he'd know better than anyone, right? And the BBC agrees.'

I groan as rudely as I can, and tell Emile I'm not really in the mood for a lecture. Then, quite innocently, I ask him to send me Marc's email address, because I suddenly feel like being rude to Marc as well.

'I'm sure you've got it,' Emile says breezily. 'I am kinda busy. Sorry.'

It's the annoyingly cutesy 'sorry' that floors me, Olivia. Call me old-fashioned and a fascistic slave to public-school etiquette but the truth is, I want to get in the car, drive to the office, clamber down the stairs to Emile's kindergarten office, grab him by his newly coiffed hair and remind him that I am his Bafta- and Oscar-winning boss. I want him appreciate that I pay his salary by mortgaging my house to the hilt and to agree that if he doesn't do what I ask, I shall be fully justified in picking him up and dropping him a few times until he resembles Sylvia Plath.

'Do it or I'll pull your painted fingernails out, you *Fickungsfotze*!' I scream and slam down the phone.

It's so exhausting, Olivia. I lie on the floor and breathe deeply—mindfully, as you suggested in the days when you still more-or-less cared—but of course I can't because my mind's racing, my head's starting to throb and I now want to pick up and drop Marc Shapireau onto the floor, perhaps ornamenting my actions in the inventive sort of way that Pol Pot might have done.

Then it starts. The Pain Fairy. He's limbering up, I can sense it, preparing for tonight's cheeky fun with a new range

17

of garish tricks. A thorny tongue perhaps, yawning and slopping a tiny gratis mist of acid down my neural pathway towards my groin. Always towards my groin. Odd, don't you think?

So I limp into the bathroom and throw the usual handful of pills down my throat, go back to bed, lie down and count to a thousand and eventually the pain recedes. But I can't sleep, and that's why I'm writing to you now.

The time has come for Yet. More. Bad. News.

The Stalker.

I've been meaning to do this for a long time but after the groping in the closet incident, I figured you've got enough on your plate and that additional news of a stalker trying to kill us would not be helpful in bringing you back home, which is what I so desperately want. But then I start thinking: What if you do return home and find me stabbed on the couch and putrefying on your favourite throw—the blue and yellow one we got in Sardinia? So you do need to know. I'll be brief.

There is a stalker who says he wants to kill me. I have no idea who he is or what I have done to arouse his hatred, but here are the facts.

It started six months ago with a hand-delivered birthday card bearing a crude sketch of a man hanging by his neck from a gallows: big limbs, big feet, big eyes, big nose. It was childishly drawn in wax crayon and came with a childish scribble, also in crayon, conveying a not-so childish message.

'JEW!'

Yes, I laughed too. David Britton, a Jew. Ho ho.

But then the same thing happened the next month. And then every subsequent month, every time with one word: JEW! So now it's not so funny or wittily ironic. As you know I'm used to anonymous hate mail but never before has it been about my invisible Jewishness.

Then two weeks ago, I started getting threatening letters. Some came through the post: single sheets of paper with a swastika drawn on them or empty registered packages with a shaving blade. Others came by email or text, with inexplicable but threatening emojis. And now, Sylvia Plath.

I know it was him.

Things are happening so quickly, Olivia. All the screwed-up strands of my life suddenly releasing and snapping at once. You, Moose, the Cat, the BBC, The Stalker, Hungry Dog … oh, and my damned father.

Yes, you read that right. Last night I got a call last night from Maurice Cohen House to tell me that my father had had a stroke and had been taken to the Royal Free Hospital. It's serious Olivia. I think this is it.

I have to tell Moose, a task that I dread.—

My Father
April 7, 11:50 pm

How does my damn father do this to me? Still! At my age? When I get the news I don't even hesitate. I run to the car, drive like a madman to the hospital, and find when I park that my fingers are white on the wheel and that my chest is thumping. I just don't get it, this fear. Because let's face it, Olivia, he was never a father. Never a man I could love. But I'm a quivering wreck when I get there.

A receptionist guides me to the Stroke Unit. At the end of a long corridor there's a room buzzing and flashing with machines. I look through the window and there's my father, tubes and pipes protruding from his nose and mouth and arms, palpitating and gobby, blood everywhere, and next to him two frowning teenagers in white coats, shaking their heads.

I hover by the door. The bigger boy spots me.

'That's my father,' I tell him.

The boys exchange a serious look.

'I'm Dr Patel,' says the big boy. 'And this is Dr Smith, the junior registrar.'

'Hello,' says the small boy in a surprisingly adult voice.

'Is he going to live?'

The boys exchange another serious look. 'Come,' says the big boy. 'Let's have a quick chat in my office.'

'I'll come too,' says the little boy.

'May I talk to my father first?' I say.

Dr Patel nods. 'Oh of course. We'll be waiting for you outside.'

I enter the room and kneel to face my father. He's sunk to the bone, Olivia, bizarrely small and frail. But it's unmistakably him: his stone head, his thick lips. And you know, even as I gaze at him and take in his humiliation and diminution, there's that old feeling, that shard of anger. But this time there's something else too, Olivia. Guilt. No, I can't believe it either.

He's been ringing me a lot lately, you see—all hours of the day, pestering me to come and visit, so we can have what he calls the 'showdown'. And I've ignored him.

I take his hand and lift his arm: it's limp and soft. I shake him. I bend over and yell in his ear. 'Dad! Dad!'

And I'm suddenly thinking: Who is this man? And the known facts just tumble out my head: I can't stop them. Ben Britton, born in Vilnius, Lithuania, circa 1918 (he never knew his birth date). An unaccompanied orphan arriving in Hull in 1924. Taken to a Jewish orphanage in London, from where he embarked on a life of spectacular achievement: East-End barrow boy, RAF war pilot, trade-union scrapper, vice-chairman of the Stepney Communist Party (three times), Marxist pamphleteer, millionaire property speculator, bankrupt, millionaire property speculator again, dog lover, failed independent candidate for Parliament, loudmouth atheist, loudmouth communist, loudmouth capitalist, loudmouth hater of all religions but especially Judaism, and loudmouth resident for the last five years at the Maurice Cohen Retirement Home in Hendon, London NW4.

Veteran also of three wives and many more mistresses.

And father of me, his only child.

I'm kneeling at his bedside, Olivia, desperately searching for a flicker or a sigh and unaccountably I'm suddenly blubbing—again!—not for him but for my poor mother, the seventeen-year-old orphan Rebecca Goldschott, painfully thin and tall, with my own lachrymose eyes and lustrous curls. And I'm remembering how this son of a bitch ruined her life too.

You know, he wouldn't tell me a thing about her, the mean bastard. Just refused. All he'd say, with a disgusting snort, was that she was 'a silly girl'. I'm left wondering how this 'silly' girl felt when Ben Britton abandoned her and me within a year, leaving fifty quid in an envelope and a twenty-three-page note extolling sacrifice and Marxist necessity, and headed off to South America with the stacked young Bolivian secretary of the Stepney Communist Party to start

21

a revolution. Was he the reason my mother got breast cancer and died within two years of their departure? Probably, because everything my father touched turned bad.

And the big puzzle of course: why did Ben Britton come back to claim me after her death? And why couldn't he ever let me go? It wasn't love, because Ben Britton was incapable of love, at least for me and my mother. What was I then? A possession, maybe? All I can say is, Thank God my father got rich because, honestly, if I'd lived with him, I'd never have survived. I owe my life to the British public-school boarding system for teaching me a self-consciousness and manner of projection that he entirely lacked.

It was his acquired wealth that allowed me to go to boarding school, and what irritates me is that I know I'm beholden to him for giving me the means to detest him. You know, I actually remember the precise day my father got rich. The day he sold his first big building in the West End. That very night he arrived home in a new car. It was a huge grey Pontiac with pink leather upholstery and electric windows. He was wearing a ridiculous new pin-stripe suit and a fedora and he climbed out so the neighbours could see. I died a little that day and I continued to die a bit more every time he appeared in my life.

And he was always appearing. Even at school, where I should have been able to get away from him, he was somehow always intruding, with his out-of-hours phone calls, despotic postcards and, worst of all, unannounced visits, advertised by his dictatorial voice booming down the polished parquet-floored corridors. That ludicrous, booming, Jewy accent! God, I loathed that voice, Olivia. I withered with embarrassment every time my father opened his trap—especially when others were around—and, as you know, my father opened his trap all the time, usually at full throttle and never with any sense of shame or recognition of the virtue of self-restraint. How can he not have been offended by the sound he made or the impression he left on others?

If his impact on my life at school was bad, holidays offered no relief. I was of course compelled to return home but there was never anywhere that felt like a home, just a chaotic procession of impulsively-purchased trophy houses with tennis courts, jacuzzis, statues and fountains, all of which I loathed.

You know what else I loathed about my father? His size. His bulk. Six-foot-four in his socks, that massive head on that thick veiny neck, those blubbery lips and rheumy eyes – sensual and gross. And he had the nerve to be intelligent too. Never missed a thing, the bastard.

But that's not the worst thing. The worst thing was his anger. My father was always angry. And violent too.

Did you know that, one day, he hit me so hard, my ears rang for a week? He bribed me to lie that I'd fallen down the stairs and of course I obeyed. But I never really spoke to him after that, just answered his bullying questions as brusquely as possible, in my poshest public-school-acquired voice. It was sweet revenge, and I know he got it.

You changed all that, Olivia—you and Moose. You let my father back into my life and it all worked out for the best, I guess. After all, that's how we got our expensive St John's Wood house: do you remember how he flung the keys in my face and reminded me that by my age he already owned three houses and would never let his granddaughter grow up in a south-London slum? And the funny thing is, he loved you and Moose. About that, I have no doubt at all.

I join the boys outside. The big boy wants to know if Ben had made a living will.

'I doubt it,' I tell them. 'I don't think my father ever thought he would die.'

'Are you the closest relative?'

'His only relative.'

'We'll have to discuss how to proceed when the results come through next week. I'm afraid I'm not hopeful for a recovery, Mr Britton.'

Olivia, the story alters course at this stage in a wholly unexpected and surreal direction. Another intervention by the Dadaist Angel who got my gig. Because just as I'm leaving the room, I spot something out of the corner of my eye.

A man. A Jew. One of those Hasidic Jews. Big hat, bushy

23

beard, side curls, black suit, the works. And there's no doubt about it: he's smiling and waving extravagantly. At me.

I walk past quickly, take a swift corner and speed up but astonishingly, he's following me. Not just following me but sort of yelping. 'David? David Britton?' he's saying. 'Ben's son, right?'

And before I can untangle the words from the accent, he's set upon me with his shining eyes.

'I've been looking for you,' he tells me, 'and here you are. *Azoy!* It's fantastic we should bump into each other now right because, actually, I'm here for a completely different reason, in fact I wasn't supposed to be here at all, but I filled in for a colleague who's not well—but that's another story and here you are! It's amazing but not a coincidence, because there are no coincidences, you know that? That's what's important to understand. No coincidences. Everything happens for a reason, *Boruch Hashem*, but we can talk about that another time. How's your father?—that's the important thing.'

I blink theatrically and scowl in a manner calculated to make him back off, but the Jew's not budging. In fact he's putting out his hand. 'I'm Menachem.'

'I dare say you are,' I sneer and turn on my heel.

And he doesn't buy it. Instead he chuckles, as if admiring my performance. 'This is important, David. I need to talk to you.' He's right there in my face, short and smiley.

I say, 'Look, I don't know who you are, or what you're selling, but I'm not interested, okay? I don't do Jew.' And with that I turn on my heel.

He laughs again. Louder. He thinks I'm funny.

Around us, people are starting to stare.

I find myself balling my fists, wanting to punch him, Olivia—and, noticing this, he slowly retreats, still grinning.

'Okay okay okay,' he says. 'You're upset. Your father's very ill, and I'm very sorry, I really am, but this is important, so please listen, *oyf rega*. I'm a good friend of your father and please God I've got something important to tell you.'

'You aren't a friend of my father and, no, you haven't got anything to tell me because I'm not buying,' I yell.

He laughs again. 'David, please, I spoke to him only yesterday and—.'

'Just bugger off!' I warn him.

He backs away, hands up in comic surrender. 'Okay okay okay. So don't worry. Oy, it's a stressful time, David: I know, I know. I should have waited. I'm sorry. Go see your Dad, please! It's a mitzvah. I'll catch you another time, *bli neder*. I'll text you or call you, maybe. I've got your number but you're wrong about your *tateh*. He's a good friend of mine, a blessed man, wise and generous, and I have something to tell you, something important. But we'll talk, *nu? Boruch Hashem!*'

And with a little bow, he's off, bouncing down the corridor, punching a number into his phone.

You see? It's happening again, Olivia. My mad-as-rabbits Fate Demon up to her tricks. Yes, I know you'll be taking his side against me but please remember who approached who, and how grubbily, bossily and inappropriately. But at least I wouldn't be seeing the Jew again.

Well, I will now take a handful of pills—tramadol, codeine, naproxen and a couple of others which I can't identify—and lie down and try to sleep. The Pain Fairy's waiting, I can feel her, and I think she may have my sphincter in her sights tonight.

And you know what I'm thinking? I'm thinking, what's the point, Olivia? Without you, what's the point?

A Really Bad Email
April 9, 2:34 am

Olivia, I plead guilty, guilty, guilty. Because, let's face it, there's not much a man can say when his wife catches him in a closet room with a fellow dinner-party guest, of whom she herself is not enamoured, but who is about to take hold of his exposed penis, I know that.

But dammit, I'm gonna say it anyway. I want you to know that you helped put me there. In the built-in closet. And it was you who put my penis into another woman's hand. Almost.

Yes, you heard me right. It was YOU who led me to the closet wherein Janice Toybeen hoped to bare all. Sort of.

Oh, I hear you now. The trademark gasp of offended breath—which reminds me, incidentally, of the night itself: no shortage of offended breath there, as one might reasonably expect of a North London social gathering in aid of Oxfam. But maybe you didn't even notice it, what with your being pawed at by that hyper-ventilating Scotsman (McDonald? McIntosh?) You know the one: the one who said I was 'worse than a Nazi' for backing Brexit. Or that fawning anorexic (Xenia? Xanthe? Xenophobia?) weeping over the refugees of Syria. (By the way, did she ever take a refugee into her house, as she said she would, and, if so, has the poor sod re-applied for sanctuary in Damascus in order to get away from her?) Not to mention your other 'great pal', the halitosis-ridden dilettante priest Rupert, who thinks Jesus must have been a Hamas activist and targets black guys in toilets as an act of holy repentance.

Certainly one thing you won't remember is the contempt hurled in my direction throughout that night. And not just because of my views on Brexit or social workers or the nuclear deterrent or immigration or the nanny state or even my car-crash *Newsnight* interview. Now, of course, since I was once very much of the Islington Lefty parish, I'm possibly a tad hyper-sensitive, but occasionally, just once in a million years maybe, it would be nice, really nice, if you'd support me a little. And who knows, had you been able to do so that night, you might even have realised that I was as drunk as a skunk, and while you and McBellend were exchanging views (identical, naturally) on the patriarchal fascism of middle management in War on Want, your sister-in-the-struggle Janice Toybeen was running the tip of her stiletto'd shoe slowly up my arthritic and varicose-veined leg, under the cover of the wooden table-top.

What do I do? I flee. Run upstairs, throw some cold water on my face, squeeze out a prostatic piss, throw down another co-codamol, and prepare to extract you and me from the throng below, even if McVulvahead hasn't quite finished his monologue on how he had no existential option but to become a militant fem. But just as I'm exiting the bathroom, who should limp up the stairs to meet me? Why, none other than Janice herself, who promptly offers me a line of the best cocaine this side of Broadcasting House (yes, I concede the BBC has its uses).

'Hurrah!' I say—anything to escape the downstairs gulag —whereupon she leads me into the closet room. We snort a line and I'm about to leave, emboldened and determined, when she gets this kinda funny look, releases the bouncy contents of her bra, draws my face into her chest and before I can say 'I am a worthless white man,' has unzippered me.

Which is precisely when you appeared.

But I want to point something out, and this is important. It concerns the state of my penis (which I presume you recall from long, long ago). What about it? Well, it was flaccid from start to finish. As soft and bendy-pure as an over-boiled rhubarb.

And this, dear Olivia, is my alibi, which declares, as loudly as only a soft dick can, that nothing was further from my mind than having sex with Janice Toybeen. This was, in other words, the very opposite of sex. And the truth is, however weird it sounds, I felt a little sorry for Janice, as I've always done, as it happens, for wanting so much and getting so little. Yes, you interrupted us, but really there was nothing to interrupt. In some way I was actually grateful that you turned up because you provided me with an excuse.

But now, of course, you will have moved from the disgust of Chlöe's Feminist Bookstore to the rage of the Arab Street. No need. Calm down. Breathe. And listen, because you need to hear this and you need to hear it now.

I know it's over. Maybe I can find some solace somewhere and—who knows?—maybe you can too (hey, maybe you'll find it with McFarthead, especially when he describes how he weeps at the sight of young Afghan girls cradling Barbie dolls: he actually did say that, didn't he?)

Because really, Olivia, this whole charade of rage has little to do with me and my limp dick and everything to do with your little power struggles with her at uni and the fact that she became famous and beloved, twenty-five years ago, and you didn't—and I agree that you should have, but that's life.

What you got was me.

Well, now that the unmentionable has been mentioned, I guess that's it.

I hereby give up. Do what you like.

David.

HAVING DICTATED ALL OF THAT, I PRESS SEND.

And it is only after doing so that, in the manner of things, reality starts to take hold and I feel myself gasping.

Fickungsfotzen! Fickungs—fotzen!

I am standing by the bedroom window, naked, peering into the wet smudge of the night, listening to my thumping, ridiculous heart and wishing, with all of it, that I could turn back the clock, because it is quite obviously the stupidest email I have ever written, and you will loathe me for it.

Then your text reply pings back.

> —*Yeah whatever. Youve probably forgotten that Moose is arriving next week, have you told her about Ben yet like I asked? We need to talk … can do tues 6–7pm pls confirm asap*

Yes, of course I'd forgotten. And no, I still haven't told Moose about her grandfather. I can't. She'll break apart.

—*Of course I haven't forgotten!* I email. *I'll be there.*

And then, pathetically, before I can stop myself:

—*I love you Olivia.*

I stand there inert for the next half an hour, with the phone in my hand.

Emile Gets On My Nerves (2)
April 11, 12:05 pm

I'm in my office, slouched in the Hollywood chair, flicking elastic bands at Oscar while miserably reliving the incomprehensible events of the last hour.

Today was Beeboid D-Day. I'd arrived prepared, sneaking in early to avoid the infants. I'd closed my door, turned off the lights, switched on the computers and, just as the screens configure with that reassuring bong of the Avid software, what happens? There's a tiny knock on my door. I yell 'Yes?' as rudely as I can, hoping to repel any lurking infants—and who walks in?

Emile, pretty as a picture and instantly getting on my nerves.

Okay, I say to myself, make this brief and painless. Emile looks strikingly different today. Maybe it's to do with the silk blouse, or the multiple layers of labial pink scarves that enwrap his narrow shoulders and neck, or the startling paleness of his angelic face. Or the hair, which looks heavier and wavier on top, like a fifties starlet. Or the staggering, annoying beauty of those aquamarine eyes, jewelled in shades of purple. Or maybe it's because there's another vaguely familiar child right beside him, staring and swallowing angrily like a tiny boxer before a fight.

They stand there, the two of them, silent and oddly resolute. Eventually Emile breaks the silence. 'It's only me,' he says.

'Technically incorrect but carry on,' I say in my rich, mellow, all-knowing BBC veteran voice. 'How can I help you both?'

'I need to speak to you urgently,' Emile says, lips trembling.

The other child nods firmly and punches a little fist.

I tell him to speak away.

'It's about our phone call the other night,' he says.

The other kid nods.

I can barely remember it. 'Okay, what about it?'

Emile's choking tears but spits it out. 'You called me a chicken-foxer.'

The other child is nodding vigorously. 'I heard it too,' he cries. 'I was there.'

'Well, I don't remember specifically,' I say, as pompously as I can, 'but if I did say something like that, it would have been to take the opportunity of articulating correctly what Angela so frequently gets wrong. It's not chicken-foxer, it's *Fickenfotze*, and I don't think there's anybody I haven't called a *Fickenfotze* in the last month or so, because it's one of the few ways left to me of abusing Angela without letting her corrupt a word I generously lent her and which is one of my favourites. Understand?'

All four eyes are like saucers and there's a bit of aggrieved snivelling. 'This is … about … dignity,' Emile whimpers. 'It's not a joke.'

'Yeah!' says the other kid and pumps the other little fist.

'As a transgender person—'

'Yeah!' says the other kid, screamily.

'Who are you?' I demand.

He tells me he's Madden.

'Did I call you a *Fickenfotze* too?'

'No,' he says, disappointed.

'Do you want me to?' I ask him. 'Because I'd be happy to if you like, but right now I'd like to speak to Emile alone, if that's okay.'

'It's Emily!' cries Emile. 'Not Emile. And I want Madden here with me! He's my friend.'

'Well I don't and I'm your boss,' I say. 'There's the door, Madden. Scram.'

The little shit hesitates, pumps his stupid little fist again, then saunters out languidly, to piss me off.

I turn to Emile and ask him to explain calmly why he's so upset. People let rip all the time in the media. Why is he suddenly such a sensitive flower?

'You called me a chicken-foxer!' he cries.

'Well, not quite, but—yes?'

'You know what it means?'

'I do indeed.'

Now he's trembling and about to blub.

'Would you call a Jew a Nazi?'

'Huh?'

'To refer to a transitioning person in terms of a body part—and not just a body part but THE body part, the one thing they long for and lack, and to debase it in rudeness'—he struggles to say the word—'is very aggressive.'

Now he's not just weeping but shaking in little bursts. And it's all so strange, Olivia, because I'm suddenly seeing him as never before. As female, I guess. I'm observing the fetish-like care he's taken with each garment—the two pale-pink silk scarves, the delicately embroidered shirt, the jeans meticulously ripped at the thigh. And that face! Such stupid grief and despair. Like a translucent Geisha beauty, and—you're not going to believe this, Olivia—I suddenly feel a deep sadness for this wretched, beautiful boy or girl or whatever the fuck he or she thinks she or he is or isn't, and all I want to do is to take him into my arms and hug him tightly, because he reminds me of our fucked-up daughter.

'Sorry I called you a *Fickungsfotze*,' I tell him.

He's so surprised, he's gaping. 'Really?'

'Yes. I'm really sorry to have hurt your feelings.'

'Are you ... crying?'

I am. And then, God knows why, I tell him everything. And I mean everything. About you. About me. About Moose and Masaai. About my father, the Nazi Stalker, Hungry Dog, the Pain Fairy and everything in between.

He blinks when I've finished. 'Wow.'

'Yeah.'

'You actually mean it, don't you? You really are sorry.'

'Yeah.'

'Oh. Well, that's all I wanted.'

'I really have started to call just about everyone I know a *Fickungsfotze*,' I say in my BBC veteran voice.

We gaze at each other for a while, then awkwardly shake hands. He leaves. I crash back into the Hollywood chair and try to make sense of Fate's David Britton Circus. Then my phone rings.

I snatch it up, as ever hoping against hope that it's you, but of course it isn't. It's Shapireau.

'Hi David, it's Marc from the BBC,' he says, and that's enough to send me over the edge. I don't know why, Olivia, but something happens when I hear the words 'from the BBC' that just tips me over into the purest of maniacal loathing.

'Mark who?' I growl. 'Never heard of a Mark.'

'Marc with a C. Shapireau. You know, from the BBC.'

'And you are … ?'

There's a long, pleasurable pause.

'From the BBC? You know, from *Black and Brilliant and Buzzing Behind Bars*?'

'Oh, the *Black and Brilliant and Buzzing Behind Bars* Marc!' I exclaim. 'Hello, Marc!'

'I was wondering if this is a good time.'

I cut in sharply. 'It isn't, Marc, I'm afraid. I'm just on my way to an urgent meeting with the plumber. Have to choose new taps. Have you any idea how much choice there is out there?'

'Oh. Yes. Of course. Look, we need to meet up to discuss your proposed re-edit. I kinda see there were maybe structural weaknesses with my initial edit—maybe too Nineties classic pop video in some of its contextual visual sub-grammar. I was actually going for the Seventies Kreuzberg feel, which you may be unaware of—but there are, uh, serious issues that need addressing with your proposed re-edit.'

Serious issues. I'm insulted he's put it so mildly and hate him a little more. 'Are you sure?'

'To be honest David,' he says gravely, 'India's worried.'

I ask why a huge powerful country like India should be worried.

'No, India Abercrombie-Paton. The Exec Producer.'

'Oh, India Abercrombie-Paton, the Exec Producer!' I cry. 'Well that's a relief. At least she doesn't have nuclear weapons.'

'No, she doesn't,' says Marc portentously. 'But she does want an urgent meeting.'

'Great. Exciting. Send me dates,' I reply. 'Is that it?'

'Uh, I guess for now.' Marc sounds deflated. 'Is Emily with you?'

'No, she's not, sorry. Bye.'

I kill the call and after a short recovery period splayed on the carpet during which my spasm of hatred for the BBC dissipates somewhat, I recall the conversation's surreal denouement and the fact that at some time over the weekend, Emile has become Emily.

I inhale deeply and wonder if I can scream without attracting teenie attention. I decide the answer is no and scream into my jacket.

I Screw It Up With Moose
April 14, 3:30 pm

Well, I did it, Olivia. Told Moose about Ben. Did it today. Disastrously, as you've probably heard.

It's the same every time, you know. I pick up the phone and stretch out on the sofa. Then I stare at the phone for a long time, fighting my worst instincts. I know I shouldn't call her—not in the mood I'm in and certainly not after everything that happened last call, when I forgot Masaai's name not once but three times. As I lie there in torment, I'm fully aware that this call could rank in that special league of catastrophic calls that will require an eternity of damage control afterwards. I know that and press the green button anyway, because I just can't stop myself.

'Hello,' she says. Her bored-to-death voice. Terrifying.

'Hi Darling, it's Dad!' I cry. I hear my voice echoing across the Atlantic, booming and needy and—far worse—identifiably and embarrassingly Jewy. The attempt to dampen it with a hammy laugh fails epically.

After a clammy pause she says, 'Oh hi'.

'You okay?' I sort of shriek. 'How's America?'

'How's America?' she sneers. 'Big.'

In the background I hear Masaai's donkey laugh and I find I want to hit him on the head with something extremely heavy.

'You okay, Darling?'

'What? Yeah. I'm okay.'

'Great. Well, I'm okay too,' I say and cringe. 'Busy. Really very busy.'

'Oh,' she says.

'Yes,' I say brightly. 'I think I may be selling the business. Lotta lotta lotta moolah.'

Our old gag. Not any more. 'Great,' she says narcoleptically.

35

I want to reach across the Atlantic and slap her, especially when she and The Idiot start whispering, donkey laughing and sucking.

'You sound American,' I say.

'Do I?' Now she's angry. 'Well, yeah, I guess I do, cos I been here, like, three years.'

I tell her it wasn't a criticism and eventually she relents. There's the sound of braying and more sucking in the background.

Olivia, I barely recognise our daughter these days. Snippy or bored, no in-betweens. The polar opposite of the bubbling, baffled, curious, beautiful child that never left our side for years and brought such wild joy into our lives. Where on earth has that child gone? Do you know?

'How's the course?' I say and immediately realise it's the last thing I should have said.

She tells me it's terrible and her one lecturer's a real piece of shit who's gonna hate her big semester paper. 'Worked my ass off for it,' she tells me. 'He's a fascist. Well, a kinda Maoist fascist.'

Maoist fascist? The contradiction's so dumb, but I stay silent, bite my privileged, baby-boomer tongue and ask her what her paper's about, and she tells me I won't get it, so I say try me, and when she tells me its title—'Juggling as Revolution'—I really wish I hadn't asked.

'You know, *juggling* as political metaphor,' she says. 'I'm using the ideas of Barthes and Foucault. I love Foucault. Adore him.'

'Me too,' I say and hear her and The Idiot groaning.

You see, Olivia, I'd love to crack a few jokes at this point. About juggling. About Barthes and Foucault. About radical street theatre. About spending eighty grand a year on a stupid course that couldn't possibly benefit our amazing daughter who in any case, let's face it, is too dim and indulged to follow a boiled egg recipe without screwing something up. I know that anything I say will catastrophically bomb but unfortunately I panic and ask if they actually learn to juggle in order to earn a living.

Is that so bad? Yes, it is. In fact, it's possibly the worst thing I could have said because there's the long, lethal silence. You know the one.

'No, of course they don't teach us how to juggle,' she eventually sneers. In the background I can hear The Idiot groaning in solidarity with her pain. I mumble 'thought not' but the silence persists for about a year.

'Dad, like, are you like calling for a reason? Cos we were, like, just on our way out?'

'Oh sorry! You must go. How is—' (stupid fucking name's on the fucking tip of my tongue; had it only a second ago; should've written the damn thing down)—

'Masaai,' she says, in that very, very disappointed voice.

'Masaai!' I cry. 'Masaai. Masaai! Of course. I'm really looking forward to seeing Masaai next month.'

There's more mumbling and sucking and I am left debating with myself whether I'd like to stab, drown or shoot Masaai.

When exactly did he appear, Olivia? Three years ago? Four? I miss the old Masaai, you know?—the sweet, tactile, hairy boy—I think he was called Simon Scholnik—whose father owned large bits of San Francisco and who'd come to England, evidently to park his absurdly athletic tongue more or less permanently in our daughter's mouth but was nonetheless always polite and engaging, remember? It all changed after sweet, hairy Simon Scholnik took that mail-order genetic test and discovered a black gene. After that, as I recall, he dropped out of uni, joined a radical black political group, grew a huge fuzzy beard and changed his name to Masaai.

I continue to whimper and apologise to Moose for forgetting Masaai's name and eventually our daughter relents, sounding scarily adult and businesslike. 'Hey Dad, would you like to sponsor a great adoption app thingie?' she asks.

'What?' I ask, relieved to the point of panic that the Masaai thing has passed and she's still talking to me.

'An app to help people adopt babies with interactive sponsor-participation community engagement stuff, or something. It's something Masaai's working on.'

Her voice trails off, there's a squeal and she disappears. When she returns to the phone, she's breathless. 'Sorry, what were we talking about?'

'An adoption app that Masaai has created,' I tell her.

'Oh right.' Thank God she's bored. 'Look, Masaai will tell you himself sometime, okay?'

'Okay.'

'Is Mom there?'

'Uh, no.'

'Surprise, surprise.'

Spotted it immediately. Tell me Olivia, do you also find it amazing that the only genius cell in Moose's brain is the one entrusted with discerning rifts in our marriage?

I tell her that you had to see your sister and of course it sounds like the lie it is.

After an agonising pause I take a deep breath and go on.

'Sweetheart, it's about Grandad. I'm afraid he's had a stroke.'

There's a terrible, long silence. I can see her: stricken, breathless, hands knotted in her luxuriant hair, eyes wide in panic—and I want to hug her.

'Oh God! Oh God! Is he going to live?'

'He's very ill darling. It was a very serious stroke.'

'I can't believe you just did that?' she sobs.

'Did what?'

'Made all that bullshit small talk before telling me why you'd called.'

'It wasn't bullshit small talk!'

'You're so horrible to Grandad. Why do you hate him?'

'I don't hate him, Moose.'

'Don't call me Moose!'

Olivia, I need to draw your attention to this new and important development. As a result of a new course called Colonial Nomenclature and Empowered Choice, our daughter no longer wishes to be called Moose. It's banned. No discussion possible, I'm told.

'Sorry, sorry—' I start to beg, as is often the case in the latter stages of phone calls with the daughter whom we used to be allowed to call Moose.

'Poor Grandad,' she wails. 'Why do you hate him?'

'Sweetheart, I don't hate him!'

'I gotta go. I gotta speak to Mom. I'll call soon. Love you!'

And that's it. Click. She's gone.

So I do what I usually do after a chat with our daughter and the Imbecile. I collapse onto the bed, heartbroken at a loss that I do not understand, and stare at the ceiling for about an hour.

Olivia, I need you.

Samuel Rings Me!
April 13, 02:30 am

You'll never guess who called: Sam! He wants to see me tomorrow night.

Weirdly, I'm so nervous when I hear his voice, I feel like throwing up.

The thing is, Olivia, I have become a recluse. Can you believe it? Now tell me: am I entirely deluded in imagining that it was just yesterday that I was the most popular man in London? I was, wasn't I? I dazzled, didn't I? I was the guy everyone wanted for their dinner party and big night out, right? Well, you'll no doubt be amused to know that today I have not a single friend left, with the obvious exception of Ronny the Runner.

And now Samuel.

A strange thought assails me at 3:54 am (I always look): it's the realisation that, even at the apex of my media fame, I only ever had one true, trusted friend and it was Sam. But after all these years, meeting him is another story. What will I tell him? What will he tell me? We become repositories of private secrets and, these days, I really don't want to share. And it's been so long—eleven years I think. Also, it's so unlike him. Perhaps there's an agenda. Maybe he's getting married? Maybe he's dying?

Dear, dear Sam. We go so far back. I know I've bored you many times with my tales of life at the *Maidenhead Evening Post* and the unapologetically posh Samuel with his first-class Cambridge MA in PPE and preposterously gay mien, and the feral news editor Jerry Hewinson and his malevolent chortling at Sam's homosexuality (though even he, I recall, eventually succumbed to Sam's charm). I suppose four years of reporting on flower shows, magistrate-court low lives and small-town politics bonded us in a way that I have never experienced with another man.

And we were close when we returned to London: Sam to the *FT*, me—with my third in History from the LSE—to the BBC. Do you remember we briefly shared a flat in Islington? I think you also know why we parted: Sam was in love with me. And I, of course, was grotesquely hetero and already in love with you.

So what will I find tomorrow night, Olivia? And what will I say? I've so many questions to ask him. Why he suddenly left London. Why he suddenly stopped emailing, dropped off everyone's radar and disappeared. And other things too.

Actually, I think it was you who identified his 'innate secrecy' (your words). I liked that phrase and was thinking about it last night. Of course we all have private lives and secrets, but Samuel's otherness was—how shall I put it?— intrinsic. We never really knew what he thought or felt, did we? But I do remember the clues: his strange childhood in Buenos Aires; his homosexuality; his curious compulsions; and of course his concert pianist mother who hanged herself in the garden when he was a kid.

You know, just writing this makes me wonder how Sam seemed to get through life with such apparent ease. How, in spite of all those blows, secrets and separations, he was always so ... well, assured. He was the most socially adept of us all, wasn't he? Always at the centre, managing conversation and mood with that light, polymathic, gossipy warmth. And everyone loved him, didn't they?

Well, I hope he's meeting to say he's found someone to love. We're meeting at The Kings, our old Islington hangout.

Of course I'll let you know how it goes. He sends love. Lots and lots of it.

My Friend Sam
April 14, 11:30 pm

I walk into the Kings on Essex Road and there he is, perched at our strangely unchanged table by the fireplace, the table we sat at every Thursday evening for years. He's beaming and, of course, there is our usual order: the best single malt for him and a JD packed with crushed ice for me. Both doubles.

We say nothing, just hug for about a minute. Embarrassingly it makes us both tear up, and we laugh.

Sam looks good, you'll be pleased to know. Older, of course, weary about the eyes, but emphatically the same. Attentive, curious, his fleshy lips drawn in that ironic cupid smile, dark eyes prickling with mischief.

As soon as we're seated I chastise him. 'You've been worryingly quiet, Sam.'

And he explains. Years of diagnosed depression, to sum it up. Just couldn't face anyone.

'An interesting journey, in its dark way,' he says, 'so I thought I'd spend it on the other side of the world, where nobody gives a damn. I think that was the right choice. I'm stronger now, I really am. And, golly, it's nice to be back and seeing you, David.'

He squeezes my hand. 'I've missed you,' I say. 'But really, not even a congratulatory note after my *Newsnight* adventure?'

And in a flash, joyously, he's back, the old Sam. 'Ah, that. Yes, I did hear something about it—actually, who knows? I may even have spotted it on YouTube a few dozen times and even noted, I think, 2.5 million views, was it?'

'Hit ratings at last,' I laugh. 'And not even a call from my old friend Sam in my moment of triumph.'

'Thought best not to intrude on private grief. But, dear boy, was I imagining it or did you really say that every young

42

black man in London should be routinely frisked for knives —whether they wanted to be or not?'

'I did indeed, as an *ad-absurdum* joke coming off the back of the presenter's fraudulent outrage over objective statistics, and her snide and stupid allegation that anybody with a rational view on knife crime was a closet Nazi.'

'Brave boy. And has the BBC invited you back into bed?'

I say 'Sort of' and tell him about *Black and Brilliant and Buzzing Behind Bars* and we laugh into the second and third rounds.

Then he tells me I look like shit, so I sigh and collapse on the table and tell him he's got a point but that I don't really want to bore him with the details right now.

'I want *your* news!' I cry.

'Well, since the *FT* let me go, it's been mainly puff pieces for sheiks, oligarchs and emirs,' he sighs. 'Shameless trash, but it sure pays the bills.'

'Where've you been?'

'The East, dear boy. All over. Jakarta, Mumbai, Shanghai, Taipei, Singapore, Saigon, Seoul, Mindanao. Now I'm based in Dubai. Ghastly but convenient, and home to a rather lucrative PR contract or two.'

'And any distractions in the souk?' Of course, I'm hoping for some hilarious tales of wild homoerotic adventure but his reply is disappointing.

'Nothing dear chap, absolutely *nada*. The old body is starting to fail. Though, come to think of it, there has been a modicum of bowing, scraping and sucking up.'

'A man's gotta eat,' I say and we laugh.

'Talking of which, I hear it's all *foie gras* and champagne *chez tu*? I gather you're something of a social media sensation these days, whatever that is.'

I try to explain how my company, the stupidest on earth, is soaring in value because of the world's most vulgar TV hit show, *Crip Trips,* and how my psychotic, infant partner called Angela may or may not be the next messiah.

Sam blinks. 'Congratulations, dear boy! That must lift your spirits?'

'Have you seen *Crip Trips*?'

'Not really, though I have heard that it was marvellous.'

'Really? And who told you that?'

'Antony, of all people. Called out of the blue just to tell me.'

Ah, Antony. Knew he'd put in an appearance at some point, Olivia.

'Antony! OMG, as they say,' I say.

'Indeed. I was as surprised as you that he should notice news of such slight cosmic importance—'

'Well indeed.'

'—especially since it didn't involve Antony.'

'Quite.'

'He actually called me up to tell me about *Crip Trips*, which did seem strange, since we hadn't spoken in, what, twelve years?'

I can visualise Antony enunciating the programme's title, in his most spitefully elegant manner.

'So Lord Antony's a fan?' I say. 'Well I never!'

Sam is wearing his rascal smile. 'He was always a little envious of you, I think. I suppose we all were, in a way. Nobody was as dashing as you.'

'Well, Sam, I don't know how Antony expressed it but the fact is that my new company produces some of the biggest shite on TV and is now spreading its curse worldwide across the web. We're targeting the youth, of course, making them even dumber, angrier and cruder than they already are, and because of this I'm up to my balls in teenagers and debt—but who knows, it may just work out and make me as rich as Croesus.'

'How exquisite! Please buy a superyacht!'

'I promise. Trouble is, if it fails—and believe me, businesses based on the transient enthusiasms of low-intellect children on a collective sugar rush do have a tendency to fail—it will leave me very, very poor and homeless, because my house is hocked up to the sky. Crazy times, dear chum of my past.'

'They certainly are.'

I'm thinking of Antony and how much I'd like to stab him. 'So what exactly did Antony say? Go on, indulge me.'

'Oh, I don't know, something about the mighty having fallen.'

'Antony thinks I was mighty?'

'Can't tell. I think he meant *quite* mighty, to be honest. Not mighty like Antony mighty, okay, but … slightly mighty.'

'Antony is mightily mighty these days,' I say.

'He is. A Peer of the Realm, no less.'

'Indeed. But I've heard rumours that he's already restless. Trying to sort out a possible messiah appointment, apparently. Did you hear that?'

'I heard something.' Sam is laughing now. 'But let's face it, darling lad: you too were an early contender in the Do-Gooder race. I mean, you're the guy who made *Daily Mail* readers weep for murderers.'

His expression, lips puckered like a Victorian prude, makes me want to screech. Those dark-ringed almond eyes, like a perplexed Disraeli.

'Peaked too soon,' I tell him. 'Story of my life.'

'You did indeed, dear boy. But what really made you different from St Antony, I think, is that you really did care about people, whereas he did not. Like all professional socialists, he just pretended to. Ooh! Sorry if that sounds venomous.'

'Thank you for truthing up, Sam. And, no, it didn't.'

'And do you still save people, David?'

'Definitely not!' I say, and he roars, throwing out his hands in a gleeful flourish. We squeeze hands again. Then his expression changes.

'Now, please concentrate,' he says. 'I'm having a dinner party and would very much like you to come. I'm turning sixty-five and, as I explained earlier, I'm trying to reconnect and make sense of the loose ends of my life. And before you ask, yes, it will include His Lordship Antony, our Future King and possibly Overlord.'

'Who else?'

He reels off the names. The old gang. Antony and Lydia, Angus, Gareth and Ginny, Jean-Paul and his new boyfriend and of course Alan and Josie.

'And now you and Olivia,' he says, freezing a little when

45

he sees the darkening in my eyes. I tell him you probably won't make it, and for that reason, nor will I.

He takes a slow sip and drops his head and tells me how desperately sorry he is to hear this news. He loves you, Olivia, but of course you know that.

I ask him if he's heard any rumours about Janice Toybeen.

'Oh, David, really?' he queries.

'Uninvited, after a line of coke and pissed off my head,' I tell him. 'She attacked me. And no actual genital contact was made.'

Sam is keen to change this deeply distasteful subject so he asks about Moose. I tell him she's fine but shacked up with America's stupidest millennial, doing a financially crippling university course guaranteed only to render her ineligible for any useful work and that she hates me, along with the name Moose.

'Kids.' He shakes his head sadly and over the fifth round we reflect on the different shades of shit that life can turn. Then Sam draws himself upright and pierces me with a purposeful stare.

'Now hear me out, loveliest fellow. You worry me, to be frank. Your negativity is dangerous. The world really isn't as bad as you think.'

'Olivia's gone,' I say. 'And it's my fault.'

'I can't tell you how sad I am to hear this David. But I'm sure you can rescue this relationship—and you will if you wish to. You two have been through stuff before and overcome your problems, so be positive!'

'Potential *coitus* was well and truly *interruptus*,' I say. 'And Olivia was almost the interrupter.'

'Almost?'

'In the sense that there was nothing to interrupt. We never actually made contact.'

'Difficult,' he concedes. 'Dear boy, you need to re-engage with life, not sit out life's second act while all your relationships collapse around you. I've seen you with your family. I know how much love is there. You have to win it back. Re-engage with your old friends too. I promise you,

you're not alone. We're all here. Waiting for you. And suffering in our own ways, too.'

I am momentarily cheered by the idea of my friends suffering.

'Even Antony?' I ask, needily.

'Maybe not quite as vividly as that but, I assure you, we all have our moments. But you know what? I like to think we've all become a lot nicer as we've grown older. A little less judgmental and much more forgiving.'

I tell him I'm not so sure and he asks me where the harm is in trying, and we're now on round six and seven and things get blurry and at some point I break down and start bawling and tell him that although I'm a paper boat in a storm, capsizing with every tiny current and wave, it's also true that Fate has decided to play a part, conspiring against me at every turn, which was why there was no way on earth I could come to any dinner party, with or without Antony, because it could only ever end in disaster.

I have no idea how I got home, but I did.

Sam sends you his love, Olivia. And we're meeting again in a month.

Yippee!

Angela Is More Powerful Than Henry Kissinger
April 18, 11:07 am

What worries me more than cancer, the Taliban and the super-volcano under California is the terrifying prospect that Angela may indeed be the genius everyone except me thinks she is. I can't begin to tell you how depressing this thought is.

This week the company hit the media Big League when we snagged two very prominent articles in the press. The first, in the *FT*, was a piece about software which I abandoned after two seconds because Wang's even more incomprehensible in print than he is in real life. But the second was worse. Far worse. Actually, you may have seen it because it was in *The Guardian*, a vomit-inducing two-page homage to Angela, celebrating her as one of 'Twenty Millennials Who Will Save Humankind'. They ran this massive photo of her trying to look mystical. She'd painted her eyes orange and cut her hair into a stupid spiky helmet and they snapped her on Brighton Beach, looking very sulky, with a procession of broken wheelchairs behind her. The headline: *Voice to the Voiceless—Britain's Millennial Queen of the Downtrodden.* Gawd.

And if you think this is terrible, as you should, it's even worse on social media. Apparently Guardianista hyper-ventilation is as nothing as compared with Angela's IR. The IR, in case you don't know, is the social media Influencer Rating and last week Angela's went ballistic. She is now a WI (World Influencer), which means that she's more powerful than Henry Kissinger. She really could change the world, a prospect that is ghastly beyond words.

To make matters worse, and as a direct result of Angela's genius, the company is flying. The most ghastly consequence of this is a new infestation of kids in the office. About twelve million more joined last week and consequently they are now everywhere, in every room, corner, cupboard, bin and stairwell. The place is a pheromonal zoo and I cannot escape it.

Naturally I have tried my best to make my office a Child-Free Zone. I have stuck warning signs on the doors and new locks, and have acted sufficiently old and weird to warn stragglers off, but even I have occasionally to venture out into the building for water or excretory purposes, an experience that frequently leaves me wanting to hurl myself out of a window while projectile vomiting.

However, there is some small consolation in the fact that amusing power struggles seem to be breaking out all across the nursery. Just today Ronny the Runner told me about a fist fight in the meditation room last night. Apparently Oscara (Tribe FatZ) started it but Ivana (Tribe GinG) ended it by knocking Oscara's tooth out. Someone found the tooth. An incisor, Ronny says, and apparently it's not easy to knock out an incisor. Ronny says things are going to get worse.

Ronny's take, by the way, is that the fight was 'a metaphor of stresses in the zeitgeist utopia of Angela and Matilda,' and it's no longer just video v web or paid v intern or uni v street or straight v bent or lefty v ultralefty or veggie v vegan or tranny v swinger v fattie v ginger and so on. No, according to Ronny, what we're witnessing is 'a fundamental breakdown of national and personal identity and all of this is a prelude to the re-emergence of nativist politics because that's the natural order of things in a pure identity sense.' Ronnie blames globalism and says that what we are seeing is the end of the Enlightenment, whose fraying values and beliefs are now creating weirdly neurotic alliances across all boundaries.

I tell you all this, Olivia, not because I imagine you care what Ronny the Runner has to say about anything but because I wish to point out that this kid whom I took under my wing two decades ago has turned out to be incomprehensibly clever; and, as a charity worker, you have to concede that Ronny is a huge success and should be on all your soppy posters about under-privilege. Please remember that just twenty years ago he was just starting five years for assault with an imitation firearm and couldn't read or write.

In fact, the other day, I came across that little film I made about Ronny—*Wild Boy*. Do you remember it? What a story, Olivia. Fourteen-years-old, homeless and running weed across Birmingham for a biker gang, with his Marlon Brando sneer and his shoulder-length black locks. Remember how the tabloids snatched him up after that film? Poor kid. I promise you, had it not been for his very articulate albeit physical attack on that member of the paparazzi on live television, Ronny could indeed have become a contender and possibly even a national treasure. (Good punch, though!)

Anyway, because I am convinced that Ronny knows everything about everything, including money, I recently asked him if I stand a rat's arse of a chance of getting back the money I am investing in this company and the good news is that he thinks I will. Millions, he says.

Another good reason to come home, Olivia.

Unfortunately the key to it all is this Taiwanese weirdo called Wang. It is his software, I am told, will guarantee these millions, possibly billions, or even trillions. I've never had a conversation with Wang but he does always point at me and laugh when he sees me. I always point back and smile.

I gotta go. Today's The Cum, Olivia (you do remember The Cum, I hope?) and Ronny has instructed me not to miss it under any circumstances for three reasons. First, because it's the official welcome for two new communities— FatZ and GinG. Second, because of the fight and the incisor. And third, because of a new girl called Ariella who Ronny says is going to have his babies. You may recall the inevitable dramas that follow every time Ronny falls in love. Can't wait.

I got twenty minutes before the infants start stampeding.

Over and out.

The Cum
April 18, 10:47 pm

Even though I have told you ten thousand times, I still don't
think you get how gruesome my life is, and this is why I'm
going to tell you about today's Cum.

The Cum, of course, is another brilliant invention of The
Woman Who Could Make Gravity Go Upwards. It's her
Holy Day, I guess, when her two million deranged teeny
followers get the chance to pay homage to her. They know
that she is also The Woman Who Could Cure Cancer and
End Death If She Could Be Arsed.

It starts at three, every month on a Wednesday, but for
the whole of the previous week there's a kind of anticipatory
hysteria when the place buzzes with kiddy birthday-party
frenzy. At around lunchtime everything stops. The kids
begin gathering in their respective tribes—more of that later
—and start their pilgrimages up the stairs onto the large
landing on the third floor, where The Cum takes place.
There they wait, chattering and scoffing free food (courtesy
of yours truly) while the tension noticeably builds, as the big
Gothic clock, placed there for this purpose alone, edges
towards three.

Angela always arrives late. These days Matilda follows
two paces behind and for some reason has started wearing
white kaftans. Her main job, I think, is to sway in maniacal
adulation at key moments during Angela's deranged address
and of course to photograph everything Angela does for
social media—and I mean *everything*. I am told she is a
genius for 'getting the moment' (usually Angela with her leg
slung over stupid things and looking bovine) and uploading
her images within seconds so that kiddies across the world
can gasp and bask in Angela's genius for the rest of eternity
(i.e. till the end of the week).

I have to admit that Angela's entrance has a scary

51

glamour. First, the drums—bongos, no less—which arouse an anticipatory gasp from the nursery. These get louder (the drums and the gasps) until just as it all becomes unbearable, Angela appears, sinewy and iron-toned, dancing her way up the stairs, a sea of teenies parting before her. Then, after a bit of meditative scowling, backed by an Avecii techno track ramped to eleven, she looks at the teeny-screamers and gives a punchy wave. They go crazy every time, and once they've reached Peak Scream—Tribes FatZ and AmpZ are usually hyperventilating by now, which adds a sense of incipient medical drama to the excitement—Angela twitches and offers them a voodooesque grin that arouses yet another volley of screaming.

The cheering finally subsides—this can take several minutes, Olivia—and then the great moment, the moment when The Woman Who Could Outsmart AI slowly raises her hands, Moses-like, and says something short and profoundly inane, at which point everyone starts ululating with renewed hysteria.

And today, as Ronny the Runner predicted, Olivia, the show was epic.

First we had the formal welcome of the 'new communities'. I'd noticed them trooping in and blinking, shining with excitement, large cohorts of ostentatiously obese and ginger children getting so thrilled-out that some could barely breathe.

Now some background. I've already told you it's been a tough week. According to Ronny it all started with the ACMs—Amputee Citizen Moderators—threatening boycotts because they'd heard a rumour that the FatZ were getting bungs at the expense of the VegZ, and the GinG were getting the best office in the building after it had been promised to the TranZ, which meant that the FatZ had to climb four floors, which many felt—and I have to say, I kind of sympathise—was a flagrant attack on their human rights. Apparently, a hastily convened meeting of the 'Revolutionary Committee' threatened to leak it to *The Guardian* and it was this that ignited the Meditation Room fistfight. I actually spotted the girl who lost the tooth and she did look furious. Even worse, Ronny told me he'd seen Angela screaming at a Vegan on the staircase until the lovely Natalie calmed her down with a glass of soya milk and Matilda was called to do a quick Instagram interview on the stairs, which soothed everybody down (except for the Vegan, who got sacked).

So that's the background. I'm sitting in my usual half-hidden place, observing the kiddies swooning and screeching, when I feel my phone buzzing. It's a text from Ronny the Runner. Ronny sits on the other side of the room, as far from me as he can, because he says there's a good chance that I'll ruin his brand if we're seen together.

Wang, the text reads. Ronny does not trust Wang.

I look up and there's Wang and the software team taking their reserved seats, wordless in T-shirts with cryptic slogans. Wang imperiously chilled in the middle, wearing sunglasses. He spots me and points and giggles.

> —*Ronny, why does Wang point and giggle*
> *whenever he sees me?*
> —*To be honest dude lots of people do that*

I want you to understand all this, Olivia, because The Cum explains Mee!Zee! better than I can in mere words. Actually, it's pretty clever. What Angela's doing is simply applying the lessons of *Crip Trips!* to the web. You may not know this but *Crip Trips!* very quickly developed a fanatically loyal amputee fanbase. Every week this massive army of armless and legless people would log on to share emotional, professional, dietary, sexual and toilet habits and The Woman Who Will Make The Messiah Feel He Came On The Wrong Day somehow managed to turn this thriving online community of more than a million usually angry people into a huge market and it's right here they do their meeting, buying, advising, flirting and complaining. And with every exchange Wang's software somehow manages to turn data into dollars.

Can you imagine the potential? Well, The Woman Who Can Bring About World Peace Or World War Depending On Her Mood can. She is building an empire of aggrieved communities—Fatties, Gingies, Trannies, Vegans and Cripples—

53

each one pumped full of angry entitlement and every partici-pant addicted to a non-stop drip-drip-drip of personal media, beamed in across every smartphone, smartwatch, smarttoothbrush and smart any other device. And with all of them tripped with Wang's tiny monetised margins on every interconnected strand of social and commercial exchange—well, you can't *Fickungsfotzung* fail, can you?

But back to The Cum. Today, Angela doesn't waste time with excessive scowling. There's the tiniest prance, and a little leap, and, before you can say 'Oh Fuck, it's The Woman Who Could Resuscitate Bambi's Mum,' there she is, writhing like a snake on the platform, with Matilda dropping to the floor to get the fanny snap.

'Hello!' Angela screams.

'Hello!' the kids yell back.

'I can't hear you! Hello!'

'Hello,' they roar.

'What's it all about?' she yells.

'Co-mmu-ni-teeeessss!' the kids scream.

'Okay, we gonna do things differently today!' she yells. 'First we gonna talk about the AmpZ!' Everyone cheers and claps. 'Rosie, darling, over to you.'

Rosie—Amputee Community Commissar and local legend—is a zero-armed red-faced girl with florid make-up and hair that sticks out everywhere. You'd love her: she's a gift to all charity workers.

'Amazing week,' screams Rosie, and everyone screams back, including me (I adore Rosie).

'Absolutely, totally amazing! Twenty thousand new stumps, six thousand in America alone!' Everyone hoots, including me. 'New retrievals, algo-uptakes running at 10 per cent, byte ducks and whole big pink fucking instagrub avatar meltfest on fucking stilts with a click to pay arbitrage of 27 per cent, yeah! Yeah!'

The room explodes into mad cheering.

I text Ronny.

> —*What did she just say?*
> —*That its going well, dude*

I look up. Angela's prowling across the stage, Matilda in hot pursuit.

'Wow!' she says, sticking out a leg like it lacks a knee.

Everyone's breathless, waiting.

'How's growth?' she says softly.

Rosie's waiting for it, beaming.

'Eighteen per cent last month!' she squawks.

'Eighteen per cent!'

Everyone cheers wildly and The Woman Who Could Stop Bears Defecating In The Woods If She Felt Like It extricates the leg from its ludicrous position, takes an extravagant bow and glows.

'Rosie you've got a new girl champ. Yeah?'

Rosie's exploding. 'Yeah, I have! Everyone, I want you to meet Carey. Stand up, Carey!'

Carry's a stout, shouty, legless girl with orange hair and vivid tattoos. She's so excited, she's crimson.

'This girl,' says Rosie against the deafening applause. 'This little lady's got us twenty-three-thousand inter-sectionals!'

More cheers.

'Tell 'em how, Carey. Go on, tell 'em.'

'I live here, it's all I do, literally. I been sleeping in the corridor in a sleeping bag—' she's actually crying with joy '—I'm an unpaid intern. And I love it!'

Everyone's whooping.

'And tell them about your new champion, Carey honey.'

'Her name's Jazza!'

Everyone yells Jazza! Jazza!

'And Jazza don't mind what we do, she loves it all being live online all the time, even when she poos and ain't got arms and ain't even got elbows!'

The kids are shrieking.

Angela raises her arms. Everyone goes quiet.

'How does she wank?'

'Mouth. She got a mouth thingy. And she does WhatsApp stump groups.'

The kids' adoration explodes into the maniacal cater-wauling of devils administering the last rites.

'Is she on contract?'

'Not yet.' Carry looks scared.

'Well, do it! Get her on contract! Now! Do it!'

The delighted Carry hobbles out of the room amid a storm of applause.

'You see, Ladies and Gentlemen,'—just so you know, Olivia, the expression 'ladies and gentlemen' signals a big line—'this is why it works! Because people need to speak to their communities. We need to hear their voices. We need them to get angry. And that's what we're doing. And it's beautiful!'

I catch Matilda shrieking '*Ja*, epic! *Ja! Ja!* Epic!' and she blushes. Meanwhile Angela's pointing at some kids. 'VeganZ!'

A statuesque girl rises.

My phone buzzes.

—Ariella!

Fresh out of Cambridge and prime-pumped with heroic wrath after her well-publicised arrest at last week's vegan riot in Hampstead, Ariella is throwing her head back, black curls crashing about her face.

—Aint she a darling?

'I was in jail last weekend!' Ariella's yelling, and the kids erupt into a storm. 'In jail I learned a fuckload of stuff. More than I ever learned, getting a stupid first at Cambridge!' More wild cheering. Ariella throws back her mane again and shakes a fist. 'The war's on! It's on! It's on! And we're ready!'

The kids go insane but shut up when Angela looks doubtful and raises her Moses-like arms. Matilda is squirming on her back for the shot.

'I'm loving ya, Ariella, but we gotta be careful, yeah?' She stretches a sinewy leg over a chair and Matilda snaps it. 'We must never think old politics, yeah? No left, no right. The new politics ain't male, yeah? They're female!'

The cheering is now uncomfortably deafening and a few kids are sobbing.

'Absolutely!' shrieks Ariella, clenching both her fists. 'Not left or right but round! Oval! Fucking spherical!'

'And fat!' Angela booms. 'And crippled! And Ginger! And Tranz. And Vegan!'

Each of the cohorts takes up the shrieking.

> —*What are they talking about, Ronny?*
> —*aint Ariella a darling!!!*

And she is. Tall, full, flashing dark eyes, thick tresses flowing off her shoulders. I'm about to tell him that he doesn't stand a chance, but the room suddenly goes dead quiet and I look up.

The Woman Who Will Out-Moses Moses has got her Moses arms up again.

'Now for the really great news!' she announces. 'We have new friends! Welcome Tribe FatZ!'—the cheering explodes as a phalanx of obese people rise—'and welcome Tribe GinG! Yeah! Stand up, people! Stand up and be angry! Stand up and be proud!'

Below me, rows of obese children are rocking on their fat legs and cheering. And across the room a forest of ginger children are jumping up and down.

Angela stretches out her arms.

Silence.

'I wanna tell you something,' she says. 'I know we've had a difficult week. I know some of our people are unhappy. I know there's been arguments and bad energy. So we're gonna fix it.' There is a ripple of faint applause. 'And this is how and why. Rosie, stand up again, darling.' Rosie stands up. 'Now you all know Rosie!' Rosie waves a triumphant stump. 'Rosie was nothing before *Crip Trips*! Isn't that right, darling?'

'A piece of handless shit,' she laughs.

'And *Crip Trips* made her a star! Fifty million on Insta! Go on Rosie, wave those stumps!'

'*Ja*, wave those stumps! Wave those stumps!' Matilda yells until people start to stare.

Rosie's still waving her stumps for the roaring crowd when the Moses arms go up.

'And that's it!' Angela intones. 'And why is Rosie so positive? Because she has a community. A community where she can thrive. A community that gives her equality. And dignity. And strength.' The kids are screeching. 'A community that makes her realise she can survive anything, whatever the rest of the world thinks or does. A community that allows her to tell everyone else to fuck off! A community where she can be herself, entirely with people who are JUST LIKE HER! Now I wanna hear what you think!' she yells.

A forest of hands shoot up. Angela chooses a boy at the back who is weirdly familiar. Eventually, I remember. It's Madden, Emily's sourpuss little mate who I kicked out. Well, today he looks transformed, as if jolted into angry adulthood by a horse steroid.

And he's glaring at me. 'My name's Madden,' he says. 'I'm new in the TranZ community and we're in a revolution!' There's a round of applause. 'The world is changing! The powerless now have power. The poor can take on the rich. The young can take on the old. And you, Angela, have made this possible. Thank you so much!'

Angela is showing her gratitude by almost kicking the ceiling with an outstretched toe. Matilda, on her knees, gets another fanny shot.

'So my proposal is to integrate what we do into the political landscape,' Madden cries. 'If we examine voting and opinion blocs and work out where political pressure and influence is exercised at every level, and gather these communities in our protective and life-affirming software, we can change the world.'

'To achieve what?' Angela's prompts.

Madden doesn't hesitate.

'Power,' he says. 'I want you to take over the world!'

As the kiddies shriek, Angela modestly bows.

And then Olivia, as ever, Fate makes its entrance—in its usual spooky way. Because now Madden has turned to stare at me again, but this time everyone—and I promise you, everyone—is following his gaze.

'It's time for the old, stupid and weak to go!' he yells.

And beside him, there's Emily, head down, weakly nodding like she's about to drop. And the infants are cheering.

I text Ronny.

—Did you see that?
—Yeah aint she a poppet?!!

I've had enough, so I get up and make my way through the infants to the stairwell. But pretty quickly I'm becoming aware of this echoing silence.

I look around, Olivia, and everyone's staring at me.

And fucking Wang is pointing and giggling.

I Tell You I Have Fucking Had Enough
April 21, 4:00 pm

Olivia, I have made a decision. I have decided you can fuck off. Really. Because you can't do this. You can't blank me after thirty years of marriage! So damn you. I'm coming to find you.

I know where you're hiding. With your weirdo sister and that Martian husband of hers. And I don't care what you think. I don't care if you call the cops and have me sectioned. I don't care if you shoot me as I storm the building (I'm sure the Martian has a stash of shotguns next to his chorister porn collection)—and you know what else? I'm not even scared of your psycho sister.

So this is what I'm going to do, Olivia. I'm going to drive to that Hobbit village where you're hiding, I'm gonna park under the trees on that Hobbit road, I'm gonna stride over to the Hobbit front door, ring the Hobbit bell and if there's no immediate answer, and by immediate I mean thirty seconds, I'm gonna break the Hobbit door down before you have time to flee.

I will then enter, either by force or invitation, pinning your plump, squealing sister or the Martian or both to the wall while threatening them with enormous violence until you—no doubt hiding upstairs and listening to the screams below—come downstairs and talk to me like a normal human being.

That's what's gonna happen. See you in two hours.

A Mad Drive To Hobbitland
April 22, 4:53 am

Okay, okay, I get it. You're angry. Disappointed. Almost certainly violated. But just so you get the whole picture—and believe me, there are two sides to this, Olivia—let me tell you my take on what just transpired at your sister's house.

I'll start at the beginning. The drive. Two hours it took, and I spent it screaming. Screaming at you, mostly, but also at our daughter, her Imbecile, Angela, Matilda, Emily, Madden, Marc, the BBC, the Mee!Zee! infants, Lord Antony Fuckface, Killa-Jah, my father … and yes, even God, just in case.

I screamed the entire A40, the B6854, the B3481 and all those stupid muddy ox-paths that your sister crawls around in. I screamed so much at one stage, I felt I was fainting, so I pulled into one of those stupid mud lay-bys and started screaming again and then I sort of did faint a little and when I woke up and blinked, there was a clear night and a sky-full of stars, the sound of an owl, and insects crackling in the moonless air, so I inhaled deeply and screamed again. And when that was done, I screamed once more—and you know what happened then?

I felt something I haven't felt for weeks.

Hope. Or at least, the possibility of hope.

Hope that you'd be there at the house, Olivia. That you'd see me arriving. Turn on a light. Watch me, in that laconic way of yours, maybe from the shelter of the porch. Walk slowly across the sloping lawn and sit with me in the darkness on the low wall. Who knows, maybe, eventually, smile at the absurdity of my sad, limp penis about to be toyed with by Janice Toybeen's arthritic hand.

I'm never giving up on you, Olivia. This also gives me hope.

So I park at the end of that stupid rutted road and start

the walk towards the Frankenstein house, wondering how I am physically going to restrain your sister and the Martian. How the hell did she end up there? I mean, I know that Eleanor is the true family weirdo—pipe smoker at school, army recruit and combat nurse, willing partner to Martin the Martian, fifteen years her senior and about ten foot taller, and choosing to live in a creaking Hobbity house that's always freezing because the Martian considers it healthy—and as a headmaster he should know, yeah. Pretty weird for a Jewish girl from North London. Even I know that much about Jews. And North London.

And now a drippy confession. I cried when I got out of the car, Olivia. I cried because it was right there under those ash trees and sycamores—you remember them, don't you?—where we taught Moose to ride a bike, and I remembered you, suddenly, like it was yesterday, running behind, crazy with delighted panic.

That's why I'm marching towards you like a soldier. I will not give you up without a fight.

The Gothic Horror Home looms in the country night and I walk quickly because I know you'll try to escape if you see me, and I'm afraid you'll hear the gravel crunching under my shoes.

The gate's open. It's dark: not a single light. Then I see it! By the garage: your Citroen!

You *are* here!

Olivia, I'm so pumped, I can barely breathe. I don't hesitate for a second. I stamp across the porch and press the doorbell once, twice, then twice more. Then I knock. Loudly. Then I kick the door just a little.

A light goes on. Then another. The sound of doors flinging open, the sound of doors slamming closed, the sound of footsteps on staircases, footsteps on floorboards, audible muttering. A voice from behind the door.

'Who is it?'

'Martin, it's David. I'm sorry if I've woken you up. It's an emergency.'

'We've always found the phone a rather useful device in such circumstances,' Martin brays as he opens the door to

62

stare at me, censoriously of course, through his thick spectacles. He's loving it, the prick. 'Do you have one, David? A phone?' He's in his dressing gown.

I begin to apologise. He's sighing theatrically and crossing his arms, the dick.

'Come on then, David, come in!'

So I lurch into the living room and flop onto the big red sofa. The Martian is gazing at me with his most reproachful frown. I've never seen him so happy.

'You okay, David?' he asks.

'No, Martin, of course I'm not okay,' I tell him.

He becomes the beleaguered headteacher, stern but controlled, with the tiniest hint of conditional kindness.

'I see. And how did you imagine we could help you in the middle of the night?'

'You know very well,' I tell him. 'I can't get hold of Olivia. I'm worried about her. I need to know she's alright. Is she here?'

'No. But as far as I know, Olivia's fine. Nothing to worry about there,' he says chirpily.

I'm about to insist that Martin explain why he said that so chirpily when Eleanor comes crashing down the stairs like an affronted hippo. She's in a bulky dressing gown and halfway through one of those extravagant yawns she sometimes deploys to indicate extreme disapproval.

Martin says he'll make tea, and springs away, glowing.

Eleanor's yawn gradually runs its course and she blinks at me accusingly.

'You do know that I work, David?'

I tell that of course I know she works.

'That I'm an ICU manager?'

I tell that of course I know she's an ICU manager.

'And you do know that tomorrow I will be managing fifteen critically ill patients?'

I tell her that, yes, of course I know that tomorrow she will be managing fifteen critically ill patients.

'And that any one of them could die at any time?'

'Yes, I realise that any one of them could die at any time,' I say, and I do, I really do, because every time I meet Eleanor, she mentions at least once but usually twice and sometimes three times that she's an ICU manager and that her patients can and do die at any time. Maybe I should report her.

'I need to speak to my wife,' I tell her. 'Is she here?'

'No,' she yawns.

'Well her car is parked by your garage!' I yell triumphantly.

She responds with a shorter, angrier yawn.

'She left it here. It's a nuisance, to be honest. Why don't you try calling her?'

'I've tried calling her. She doesn't pick up.'

'Then maybe she doesn't want to speak to you.'

The nursy censure is momentarily crushing but I recover and prepare to launch myself at her throat before rushing up the stairs to the guest room where I know you are listening against the door.

'Eleanor, I need to know she's safe!' I yell, hoping you'll hear.

'I'm sure she's fine,' Eleanor says and starts to pick her teeth the way she always does. But just as I'm about to punch her in the throat and rush the stairs down the Hobbit corridor, I hear Martin pleasuring, a sort of low grunting accompanied by kettle-and-mug sounds, and of course the question arises: should I kill Martin before punching Eleanor in the throat and rushing the stairs?

Actually, it would serve him right. Because even though I've always been nice to him, never once mocking his Hobbitness or inadequate height or secret collection of chorister porn, which I've no doubt lies in the no-doubt huge attic, he is always rude to me. Every time. I'm not sure why but I think it may have something to do with my metropolitan wit, my saturnine good looks, my telly fame and of course my money (ha-ha!) but, whatever the case, I know that behind my back he calls me the 'Show Pony'. I know this because one day he confidentially told me he called me the Show Pony behind my back.

Sadly, instead of killing Martin and punching Eleanor in the throat and rushing the stairs to find you, I resort to begging. 'Please Eleanor, please! Tell me where she is!'

'How would I know?' Yawn.

She's lying, the bitch, but because I can't punch either Eleanor or Martin in the throat I start to cry. It is beyond humiliating, especially when your loathsome sister sits down beside me and starts to pat me in a ghastly nursy way. 'Now stop that,' she commands. 'It's complicated.'

'Sugar, David?'

I look up to see Martin bending into the doorway with the most ludicrous grin I've ever seen. He's so cheerful, he's in danger of exploding.

'No,' I snap and glare at Eleanor. 'What's complicated? She's my wife and I need to know she's safe. And I need to talk to her about our daughter and her cretin of a boyfriend.'

'No need for rudeness,' sniffs Eleanor. 'Olivia's safe.'

'How do you know?'

'Because I do.'

I'm about to karate chop her in the thorax for more information when the Martian reappears, beaming. 'Well, this is a first. You haven't visited for ages,' he says.

'I'm not visiting, Martin,' I yell. 'I'm desperately trying to make sure my wife is safe.'

'Enjoying the sunshine, I shouldn't wonder,' he trills, vanishing back into the kitchen.

Then I spot it: Eleanor's tiny grimace.

I demand to know where you are enjoying the sunshine.

Eleanor tells me to stop harassing her, because unpleasantness like that is actually *illegal*.

'But how do you know she's safe?' I cry.

And then it gets really scary, Olivia, because Eleanor turns all soft and gentle. And why do you think that is? Because she's feeling sorry for me, Olivia. Isn't that ugly? Your mad sister and her Martian husband have decided to humiliate me with their concern. That's not their role; it's yours. Of course I blame you.

'I know she's safe because I spoke to her yesterday, David,' your sister confesses. 'I'm not saying where she is because she asked me not to but she's fine.'

I'm back to begging. 'At least tell me what continent.'

And then the answer, courtesy of the Martian who's

bringing in the tea, because when he hears the word 'continent', he's so tickled by my despair that he puts the tray down and starts doing a weird dance with his forefingers pointing up and singing '*oyoy-oyoy-oyoy-oy*'.

It takes me a while to register. 'What are you doing, Martin?' I ask politely. 'Are you dancing like a Jew?'

'Just dancing,' says Martin enigmatically.

Then it hits me. 'Israel? Is Olivia in Israel, Martin?'

Eleanor cuts in sharply: 'My sister does not wish to share this information,' she snaps, skewering the celebratory Martian with her stare.

Israel? Why in Jesus's name would you be in Israel, Olivia? What's with you? A few years ago you and every other Jew I regret knowing was boycotting Israel.

'Now, David, the bed's made up in the spare room; you know your way around. I won't have time to see you in the morning. Come on, Martin!'

Eleanor kisses me bossily on the cheek and rounds up Martin, who leaves with a grin that makes me want to vaporise him.

Israel. Why, Olivia? Why Israel?

And then, from somewhere, the answer emerges. Small and tentative at first, then exploding with an unstoppable, grotesque clarity.

I know where you are, Olivia! You're with fucking Ivan! And all those *fickungsfotzen* blind people.

I jump in the car, adrenaline crazy, drive like a lunatic, but somehow make it home, flop onto the bed and lie there staring at the ceiling, furiously awake, heart pounding like a fucking gun and thinking of ways to kill Ivan that I haven't thought of before.

That's how I fall asleep. Thinking of new ways to kill Ivan.

Crossbow, I'm thinking.

Fucking Ivan
April 22, 6.53 pm

Ivan. Fucking Ivan.

Okay, I know I'm on dangerous ground here. I know you like him. I know you find my hatred for him excessive, ridiculous and disappointingly revealing of a man who is not just morally retarded but also your husband. I also know you think I'm envious of Ivan because—and I'm going to be very blunt here—it was he and not me who snagged your gorgeous sister Suzie, who you've always imagined I was really in love with, which I wasn't. Ever. It's always been you, I'm afraid.

But you're right, I do hate Ivan to an excessive degree. And I admit to being curious about how such a dreary little suit could walk away with your undeniably gorgeous sister. How is such a thing possible, Olivia?

Okay, I'm going to talk about your sister now, since her name has come up, and I'm going to get psychological, and for once you're not going be able to stop me.

I did love Suzie, but really, who didn't? But there was always The Mystery, wasn't there? The mystery of Suzie remaining single. You remember how we tried to fix Suzie up with someone—or more accurately, anyone? And how quickly all of us, Suzie included, came to expect that nothing would come of it and that beautiful Suzie would be left on her own, again. You know, I even remember when the looming prospect of there being no prospect for her became a settled fact. It was when Suzie started making gags about preferring dogs. And remember her thirty-fifth? The party she threw for her first dog, the awkward toast we raised to it and the bitter realisation we all shared that lovely, sexy Suzie, who so wanted kids and a husband, would for some unknowable reason remain single and childless.

And then it happened. Fucking Ivan.

I know you'll find it weird but I really remember that

evening as if it was yesterday: Suzie bursting into our flat, flushed with idiot joy. Remember how she actually seated us on the sofa, poured a glass of bubbly and vivaciously announced that she was embracing not just the idea of marriage to her boss—a man fifteen years her senior—but orthodox Judaism? And how she then brought him in. Remember?

Well, there he was. A small, neat, ridiculous little man with a black suit and a little black yarmulke pinned to his grey hair with a little girly hair clip. I hated him from the moment I saw him, as I think you know.

You often tell me I am 'obsessed' with Ivan. You may be right. I also acknowledge that anyone meeting him would probably agree that he is, technically, a very nice man. All I can say in my defence is that there is something about Dr Ivan Greenberg, consultant ophthalmologist and full time Pious Prick, that just gets on my wick. It's not just his fun-less bourgeois fortitude and charitable piety. There's something else, something super-Jewy—an almost contrived inoffensiveness—that I find offensive. There's nothing about him. He just isn't there. That nothingness arouses in me a special, inexplicably furious anger.

I know you think I have a problem with Jews, Olivia. You're right. I do. I will happily concede that I prefer the company of Mexicans, Swedes, Abyssinians, Greenlanders, Torres Straits Islanders, Pygmies, Texans, Geordies, Albanians, Matabeles and even Afghani tribesmen who do terrible things to wives and goats. And why? Because they're normal, and Jews are not.

Okay, I'll spell it out. I never asked or wanted to be born a Jew. All I want is the elementary right to be a free man, liberated from ancestral forms of oppression and tribal stupidity, and this has been denied to me. From the moment of my birth, without my having the slightest say, I have been imprisoned with a label that, however much I try, I simply cannot understand or escape. And this identity was literally, brutally, carved into me when, at the age of eight days, my stupid father, for reasons I cannot even begin to understand, engaged some bearded lunatic to mutilate my poor defenceless penis (you remember him, I presume? The

68

penis, not the bearded lunatic) and consign me to the ranks of the most despised and weird people on earth.

That badge of shame has followed me everywhere, Olivia. And not just because of my languid black eyes and Oriental lips. No, I was always identified and separated out because of my wicked father. At each of my schools, he made sure that every headmaster not only knew I was a Jew but insisted that I take no part in the normal, Christian life of the school. And so I frequently found myself alone, cut off from the world and largely disliked for it. And why? I asked him one day. He said: 'I want everyone to know you're a Jew. It'll toughen you up. You need it.' And because of this, from the age of eight, I was mocked, isolated, humiliated and, on at least two occasions, beaten up.

Even worse, this forced me into keeping company with people I had nothing in common with. Looking back, the few Jews who washed up in my schools were pretty much like me: sad, abandoned kids despatched to fancy, hostile institutions by wealthy parents who just wanted to get rid of them. I became the go-to guy for these rejected Yid kids. They'd cleave to me as if I was their long-lost brother and introduced me to this incomprehensible tribal world of over-familiar nicknames, guttural expressions and primitive rituals. I still remember them: Martin Biderman from Leeds, who sucked my oxygen for three years. Geoffrey Kremer, a plump, lachrymose maths-, Holocaust- and chocolate-fanatic who wouldn't leave my side until I one day threatened to strangle him. And Pablo Friedman from Mexico City, who insisted on wearing a stupid little yarmulke on festival days and pretended to be surprised when people laughed at him. All of them assumed an immediate intimacy with me that was both invasive and repulsive.

Why do Jews do this? Why do they make this assumption of ethnic buy-in? Even after I made it perfectly clear to all of these boys and headmasters that the unhappy coincidence of my having Jewish parents did not and would not make me a Jew, nothing changed. It was a despised and incomprehensible identity, a sublime punishment from my sicko father that would follow me to the grave.

You tell me, Olivia: you tell me how a normal, free man should respond to this unwanted, primitive identity?

Well, I'll tell you how I responded. I coped by telling jokes. Jewish jokes. Gags about noses and money and circumcisions and the Holocaust (I was young) and yarmulkas and holes in sheets and phylacteries and mumbling men in beards rocking with weirdo incantations and cries. I mocked it all.

And you know what? It paid off. People laughed. They loved my Jew put-downs—because, you see, as a Jew, I was obviously best-qualified to deliver them. That gave me authority. It became my fail-safe route to making friends. And not only did I survive socially—I prospered.

Same thing at university and even more so at the BBC. There, it required just a little more subtlety, but it was the same pantomime. You know, Olivia, I'd go so far as to say that my Jew-shtick was the undeclared factor that got me through childhood and made me successful and acceptable.

And then what happens? I fall in love with you. A Jew, dammit, or 'Jewess', or do we not use that word any more? But I was right about Ivan, wasn't I? Remember all those Jew problems, right from the get-go? How Ivan the Meek became Ivan the Terrible? Wouldn't eat this, wouldn't eat that, so Suzie couldn't either. Wouldn't drive on Saturdays, of course, or any other day that God had circled in His holy calendar, so Suzie couldn't either. Couldn't go to restaurants, or parties, or even to dinner with friends in their own homes, so Suzie couldn't either. Our beautiful, witty, scabrous Suzie suddenly silenced by the million idiot rituals that came to dominate her life. And it was Ivan who prised our families apart shortly after their wedding because they then fled to a Jewish district in Essex where your beautiful sister devoted her life creating the kosher home that Ivan demanded for himself, and in turn for their two gawky sons, and their ten million prognathic cousins from Manchester.

And there she remained until the end, but as vivacious and cheerful and gorgeous as ever, which I admit annoys me more than I can understand.

Then that dreadful prickly cough of hers that turned out to be a cancer. Guess all that praying and kosher food didn't

70

come good after all. And you began to spend all the time you could at your sister's home.

With *fickenfotzen* Ivan. And that's when you started to pull away from me, Olivia.

Look, I haven't slept for two days, it's six in the morning, I'm still revving from the Martian visit and I'm shredded from a handful of Pain Fairy pills … so what do I do? I do what any lovestruck lunatic would do. I pick up my phone, scroll through the numbers until I find the prick's number, and press.

To my amazement, he picks up immediately. 'Hello?' he says.

He sounds sleepy, which for some reason enrages me.

'Hi Ivan. It's David Britton,' I yell.

'David? Oh dear. What's wrong? You okay? How can I help?'

Not a trace of shame, the little shitbag. Anyway, I demand to speak to you, this moment, even if he has to wake you up.

After a pause he says 'What?'

'Olivia. I want to speak to her.'

'I don't see how I can help you.'

'Really?'

'Yes, really.'

The one thing I hadn't counted on was outright denial. Clever little shit.

'Okay, is Olivia in your house right now?'

Feeble, I know, but at least it gives me a moment to think.

'Of course not.' And the little shit's got the gall to sound angry!

I plough on. 'Are you in your house right now?'

'Yes!'

'In England?'

'Yes of course in England!'

'Not in a hotel?'

'No, not in a hotel. In my house. In England. In my bedroom. Alone and, until this call, asleep.'

'And you say you don't know where Olivia is?'

There's a long pause.

'I'm saying she's not with me and nor would she be, David, because she's married to you. And, frankly, it's impertinent of you to say otherwise.' I must say, the quiet fury in Ivan's voice is a novel, bracing experience.

I crack. 'Ivan, I really need to speak to her. Please can you help me? You did offer.'

His kindly sigh is worse than a medieval axe. 'No, David, I can't help you. But you do need help.'

The phone goes dead.

So I lie there for ages, frozen with exhaustion and shame, and I'm finally drifting in and out of sleep when I hear my phone buzzing.

I pick it up in the dark. Your name pulses in the black.

—*Will call tomorrow morning now ffs stop annoying everyone!*

I'm flying, Olivia. So happy I could scream.

Wild With Joy And Hope
April 23, 9:53 pm

This morning, after your promised call, I walk to work and replay our conversation in my head, Not a complete disaster, I'd say.

Undoubtedly there are positives. The fact that you called at all. The fact that you said *hello* nicely. Your insistence that we meet, which suggests you think we can hammer out a shared strategy together for dealing with Moose and the imbecile ... and therefore who knows what else?

And of course the collegial way we discussed our daughter's latest academic challenge. I know you think I maybe went too far in critiquing the spring assignment of Moose's that bombed, but '*Juggling as revolutionary theatre: a Foucaultian dialectic*'—I got that right, didn't I? Of course I laughed!

'If you carry on laughing, I swear I'll put the phone down on you right now,' I think you said, and I stop laughing. Then you instruct me not to talk about anything academic to Moose. Why? Because, to quote you, I lack 'the emotional and intellectual awareness or skills to say anything that could possibly help her'. Not nice, Olivia, but I took it. See? I'm capable of growth.

Then we discuss the Moose-Masaai fight and the fact that she'll be coming home alone to see Ben next week. I haven't heard you so happy for years. And then this: 'David, if this is the last thing we do as a couple—'

Do you know how much that hurts? You plough on.

'—we need to help our daughter get rid of Masaai. Her life depends on it. And now we have a chance! A real chance!'

I say I will do whatever I can to help get rid of the Imbecile. And I will, Olivia. I promise.

Then, having staked out what I had considered refreshingly shared ground, you turn and deliver an ice-cold blast. 'As for Ivan, are you insane David? He's seventy-eight! You're such a fool! See you Tuesday.'

I am wild with humiliation, joy and hope.

Ronny The Runner
April 23, 11:53 am

I arrive at work early, shaved, clean, prepped in that Old-School way, because today, Olivia, is an important Old-School Day. Today I finish my last-ever film for the BBC, though the word 'finish' may require elaboration at a later stage. They're gonna hate it. It's so exciting!

But right now there are other matters that need dealing with. Ronny the Runner's outside my door and, before we're through it, he's asking me if I've heard of Quantum Displacement Theory. No, of course not, I tell him but when Ronny's on one of his mind-benders, there's really no point in trying to stop him.

'So try getting your head round this,' he says, and now he's commanding the central space of my office and raising both his forefingers in the air. 'Two electrons can be a million miles apart in the universe but come together the moment they're observed.'

I say gosh.

'I know, it does my fruit proper,' he says.

I ask if he got my message. Stay with this one, Olivia; it's about The Stalker.

'In other words,' he goes on, 'it's the *observation* that creates the event, yeah?' and I take a seat, because sometimes you just have to let him run his engine. 'That's insane, Man, and contradicts all our notions of physics— quantum too! Dude, you do realise that Newtonian and quantum physics contradict each other, yeah?'

I tell him that, when it comes to news about electrons, what he said is actually quite interesting.

Ronny's got that eager grin, his big green eyes wanting to play. How the fuck can you not love Ronny, Olivia?

'Interesting?' Ronny goes on. 'It's fucking epic. See, Dude—and now you gotta concentrate, yeah? These electrons can be light years apart and nobody can work out why it happens—'

And before I can bring up The Stalker, he's using random objects on my desk to model all the connected elements of the universe.

My phone's buzzing.

It's a text from Angela. She needs to speak to me pronto. Whenever she uses the word *pronto* I know she's going to be more annoying than the last time.

'No, Man, you gotta get this, Daveman! It's life-changing!' Ronny's kind of yelling. 'What it means, yeah?, is that there is no fixed idea of reality and therefore—let me get this right, yeah?—no objective basis for science or, at least, the model of science that the post-Enlightenment world's come up with, yeah?'

I'm transfixed by Ronny. Believe me, Olivia, my ex-prison pal in this space is an astonishing spectacle.

'You know, Dude, I came across a great word yesterday. You wanna hear it?'

Go on, I say

'*Ontological.*'

He says it reverentially, on-to-lo-gi-cal, like a Brummie incantation. 'I guess a posh boy like you knows what it means?'

'Nope.'

'It sorta means, seeing ourselves seeing the world.'

'Are you becoming religious, Ronny? I hope not, cos I'll not only have to sack you but have you shot.'

'Nah,' he laughs, 'don't do that us-and-them shit.'

'Good!' I cry and then try to bring him down to Earth. 'More importantly, Ronny: was that Ariella climbing onto the back of your bike last week?'

'Yeah, Man. You saw her? Cool! Man, why you laughing?'

I tell him that a Cambridge dilettante jailbird half his age and four times his social class would make a very unlikely bet for future harmony, even if she hadn't been arrested at the vegan riot in Hampstead.

'That's it, Man,' he grins. 'The jailbird thing.'

'You didn't mention you had a common interest in prison, did you?' I groan.

'That's about all I mentioned.'

I say *Oh Dear!* in my prim ex-prison-adviser way.

'Dude, her call. Seriously, she was only arrested for three hours but, since then, that's all she's into. Obsessed with the nick. Manna from heaven, Dude. Worth every one of my days inside … and the rest. Worked a dream. I told her everything. Made her cry an' all. We was there till closing.'

'And then?'

'Nothing, Dude, nothing. Told her I was over the booze limit and it wasn't right for her to come on the back of the bike. Got her an Uber, paid for it, little hug, proper gentleman-like, no funny business. Left with a beautiful wheelie in her honour.' Then he pauses. 'Dude, I'm in love.'

I shake my head sternly. 'No you're not,' I tell him.

'Yes I am,' he says. 'She's the one. Though I gotta say, for a proper educated lady, she's got some really screwed-up ideas. Real uni-horseshit, Man.'

'Like what?'

'She wants the whole fucking world to just walk into little ol' Britain. No passports. Nuffing. I'm serious!'

'What did you say?'

'I agreed, Dude—what do you think? Don't want dumb politics blowing my chances with her. I'm telling you, she's the one.' Then he glances at his phone. 'Man, I gotta fly.'

He's got his helmet and is heading for the door when I remember.

'Ronny, I've got a problem. Someone's attacking me at home. Letters, phone calls …'

'No way, Man.'

'They poisoned Olivia's cat, Ronny.'

'No way!'

'I'm telling you. Died in my arms.'

'Man!'

'Been going on for months. Quiet for about two weeks now but I don't think it's the end.'

Ronny's sitting down now, alert as a snake.

'Any ideas?'

'No. Can you think of anyone?'

'Could be anybody, Dude,' he says.

I ask him what he means by that.

'Well, to be honest, you're pretty widely disliked,' he explains. 'People don't get you, if you get me. You're kinda Old-School White-Man Tosser, if you wanted me to put you in a category.' He says it in a kindly way.

'I get you but really, Ronny, the kiddies here don't dislike me to the point where they would actually get off their lazy, ginger, fat, vegan, crippled arses and poison my cat, would they?'

After some reflection, Ronny agrees probably not.

I tell him I want to sort it out without having to go to the police and he agrees with that too.

'And, obviously, I don't want you to get your hands dirty —you know that.'

'Yeah, Man, too old for that shit.'

'I just want your advice, is all. Your opinion. Your thoughts. This stays between us and you don't talk to anyone, yeah?'

'Yeah, Man.'

Ronny the Runner gravely shakes his head and gets up.

'Daveman, I gotta fly for my Lady, but we'll talk soon, yeah? I need everything: letters, messages, everything. You still got them?'

'Yeah.'

'Okay, bring 'em in. We'll find this motherfucker. Thursday?'

'Okay. Where you going now?'

'Brighton. On the Ninja. She's gonna melt.'

He hesitates at the door and turns around. 'Poisoned your cat? Man, what kinda screwball does that?'

So that's where we are, Olivia. I'm using Ronny the Runner to find The Stalker. And yes, I hear you sighing.

My Last Film For The BBC (1)
April 23, 11:02 pm

An epochal day has passed, Olivia. A milestone in the life of the once-famous film maker, David Britton. His last-ever film for the BBC. I finished the edit this afternoon. It's good. They're going to hate it.

But I'd love your opinion …

> OPENING: *Tight shot of child (aged six, beautiful, cherubic boy).*
>
> CAMERA PANS DOWN: *Child is clutching a heavy gun. Male laughter in background.*
>
> CAMERA PANS UP: *We see father of the child, a laughing oaf called Khallija, the subject of this ridiculous documentary (one of five programmes in the absurd Black and Brilliant and Buzzing Behind Bars series). He's snorting coke with his equally oafish pals. They're screaming with laughter, finding the kid hilarious.*
>
> TIGHT SHOT ON KID: *He's cute as hell, big brown teddy-bear eyes lovingly seeking the person holding the camera.*
>
> CAMERA PANS AND SLIPS INTO SLO-MO: *A tight shot of the gun, so heavy it's flopping about in the kid's tiny hand. You can see it's real by the weight.*
>
> OAF OFF CAMERA SAYS: *'It's loaded' and there's screaming laughter*
>
> TIGHT SHOT OF KID: *The kid's laughing and twisting the gun*
>
> FLASH TO BLACK: *Mute, no commentary, just oafish cackling*

Good, huh?

Naturally it's also the opposite of what they want. What they want is the vacuous trash served up by the maniacally ambitious and cliché-ridden director, Marc Shapireau. His version, which I am expected to sign off as executive producer, is very different: a twenty-eight-minute slobbering pop video uncritically sanctifying the 'artistic genius' and 'moral heroism' (I kid you not) of Killa-Jah, whom I call Olaf the Fraud because he is just not BLACK! Yes! Another one!

What the BBC want me to do is lie: to say that Olaf is black (which, like Masaai, he isn't); that he is talented (which, again like Masaai, he isn't, apart from that uncanny ability to say stupid rhymes very quickly while making finger guns); and that he is culturally 'significant' (which he isn't because he's a talentless fraud).

Olivia, I know that, at this stage, you will be raising your eyebrows, bored to death by yet another of David Britton's anti-BBC rants, but I need you to know that I tried. I really did. I took this exec producer gig thinking of you, hoping it would signal a new maturity, a symbolic rapprochement with the BBC. I mean, what could be more persuasive of moral growth, right? That's the truth. I honestly never anticipated another war. I honestly thought it was what it seemed: a gracious farewell wink from the Beeb, thanking me for past efforts and slapping me on the bum after the *Newsnight* disaster. All I had to do was nod the horseshit off, collect my severance pay and leave with my head held high.

But what happens? I'm innocently looking through Shapireau's rushes, one idle moment, and what do I stumble upon? A little kryptonite folder called *Lol!* which naturally I explore, and what do I find? A tiny kid with a loaded gun and a dickhead of a father whom the BBC has decided to canonise. I just can't do it, Olivia.

Fate, again.

Olivia, I know you'll be groaning and pointing out the obvious truth that it was my decision to use hidden and probably illegally obtained rushes to fight the BBC in a battle I simply cannot win. But please allow me a defence. Let me try and explain why it became impossible to watch Marc Shapireau's idiotic film, impossible not to be outraged by its woke dreariness and pop vacuity and impossible, therefore, to sign it off.

If you were with me now, right next to me, you'd

understand. I'm watching Killa-Jah now as I write these words. He's on three editing screens in front of me, screaming idiot platitudes, prancing around with that stupid finger gun, a gangly, veiny, angry, violent, white-blonde Swedish tosser whose alleged one black grandparent made him ludicrously eligible for the accolade of having a whole programme in the idiotic *Black and Brilliant and Buzzing Behind Bars* series.

You know when I first laid eyes on Killa-Jah, I actually called Marc to ask for proof that he had a black grandparent. Marc found this allegation 'unimaginably offensive' and pointed out that that matter was beyond question, because some Brixton rapper who'd been elevated to sainthood the week before, after being gifted a bullet in the head, had declared that Killa-Jah was as 'black as any niggah', a position firmly upheld by a several top BBC execs whom I informally approached.

I have to tell you about Shapireau, Olivia. One of the BBC's up-and-coming. He's made the Killa-Jah film in the customary epileptic manner, you know? Twitchy cuts and unhinged sojourns into pompous, monochromatic nonsense, all of it backed by Killa-Jah's thumping moronic soundtrack and a troupe of bovine porn dancers gyrating like they were auditioning for a snuff movie only available on the dark web.

But you know what? In spite of all this, I was just about to approve it—for you, remember, to prove I'd reached adulthood—and was about to sign the compliance forms, about to send Marc a foolish thumbs-up and get the fuck out, when what happens? I'm holding the mouse and something literally grabs my hand and forces me to drag the cursor across a vast and busy screen to that fatal anodyne folder called 'Lols!' Which is why, for the last few days, I've been re-editing Shapireau's film into a professionally suicidal letter of resignation. The whole story told from the kid's point of view. It will be the last film I ever make, my suicide coda after a lifetime at the Beeb.

And if you feel that's enough Weird Fate for one man, think again because you'd be wrong. Because just as I'm preparing for the BBC showdown, a text arrives, a text that I hope will demonstrate how surreal my life has become. And this one has nothing to do with stalkers, Mee!Zee!, Angela, my father, Moose, you or the million other catastrophes that absorb my time.

This one's from my new stalker: the rabbi by the name of Menachem Katz. Remember him? The one from the hospital? Well, this annoying lunatic now phones and texts me regularly—three times this week, in fact—with the demand that I see him immediately, in bold caps, just in case I missed it. So I reply:

> —*Stop trying to contact me, Katz, because you have nothing to tell me that I want to know. I am not interested in hearing your religious claptrack and, no, my father did not give you a message to say that I should, and no, I do not intend to give you all his money—nor mine. Now stop pestering me or I'll call the cops and sue you for harassment and I mean it. Just FUCK OFF!*

Sent!

But now I gotta go. The gorgeous Natalie has just informed me that my lovely peeps from the Beeb are here and she's bringing them down.

My Last Film For The BBC (2)
April 23, 10:28 pm

Things went as planned, I'm afraid. Please try remain unbiased.

First, I want you to picture it. We're sitting there in my untidy office, Oscar leering from a dishevelled shelf, the Hollywood chair set iconically before the three-screen Avid editing desk, and Shapireau and India (exec producer, not country) hostile, curt and crammed soundlessly into tiny kiddy chairs I have specially selected for the viewing.

I ask if everyone's sitting comfortably (yes, it amuses me too) and without waiting for a reply I dim the lights and hit the button. The film rolls.

It takes only twenty seconds before Marc starts squealing, and India, her neck churning, instructs me to stop the viewing immediately and turn on the lights.

I switch off the film. We're at the point where we've just seen the kid waving the gun and heard Killa-Jah's fabulously stupid machine-gun riff, *Me Wanna Splat Da Whiteboy Popo.*

In the silence that follows, I can hear my heartbeat. The Beeboids are sitting like statues. I cheerfully ask if they're liking it so far.

India's neck is like a python processing a small deer. 'So, thank you for your efforts, David. Marc warned me, and I think we know where this is going. I know Marc's original vision—which you seem to have ignored—and that will work very well. We'll take over from here, okay?'

She ignores my guffaw and starts to pack her things into a bag.

Shapireau is managing to look both heartbroken and homicidal. 'You do realise the series is called *Black and Brilliant and Buzzing Behind Bars*, David?' he intones mournfully.

'He's not black,' I say.

'He is!' Shapireau yells.

'Does he look black?' I smirk. 'He looks like a bulimic Norwegian ski jumper, right?'

'Well, not according to fucking IzZaxeTdfs%q!' Marc yells.

'Whoever the hell he is,' I say.

This makes Marc shake violently. 'Killa-Jah is a black man, David!'

'And a pretty bad one, don't you think? He has three children by three women whom he calls *bitches* and *whores* in his songs, if you can call them songs—'

'Do not attack his art! I will not permit you to attack his art!'

Marc has actually roused himself from his chair and is waving his hands in a vaguely threatening manner. I can't help laughing. From there, things go significantly downhill, especially after I suggest a spin-off show, also featuring Killa-Jah but called *Blond, Bubbly and Bullshitting Behind Bars*, which frankly I still find quite funny.

India tells me I'm embarrassing myself. Marc wants to agree but is so offended he can't breathe.

I know I should stop, Olivia, of course I do, but I'm on a roll and you know my rolls. 'Leaving aside his abysmal music,' I hear myself saying, 'what about his lyrics? What about his crime record? His violence? His lack of moral restraint? His parenting? The man behaves like an animal and there is nothing about him that is either admirable or a role model. As for your film, it says nothing, other than that the Beeb is so desperate to curry favour with black teenies, presumably to give its pompous, horrifically White uberclass the sense of a little 'edge'—itself a grave disservice to black people!—that it is willing (that is to say, *you* are willing) to put something out that's fawning and servile and offers no counterbalancing critique.'

I know I sound like an offended drunk vicar and I feel a little ashamed but, on the bright side, I note that Marc is now so offended that he may actually explode, and when he sweeps off his little wire specs and calls me a racist, I feel an adrenaline high and merrily return to battle.

'Racist? I'll tell you what racist is,' I gleefully shout. 'Racist is dropping your expectations to rock bottom because you don't dare demand any meaningful level of achievement from a black performer, or not being able to tell the difference between black artists who are doing sensational work and those who aren't even getting by. Racist is not giving a shit about this man's wives and children and the way his music abuses them. A three-year-old with a loaded gun and the daddy writes a song that celebrates it? And you know what's funniest of all? It's all a lie. The daddy's not black and you're letting him make a fool of you because you don't dare call him on it! That's racist!'

India's glass voice cuts through Shapireau's growling. 'It's very simple David,' she says calmly, getting up to leave. 'The gun footage has to come out. It's unusable.'

'Yes, because you want to protect the blond, bubbly bull-shitter from being seen for what he is.'

'No, David, it's unusable for legal reasons of child protection. On other questions, I will seek advice. There may be scope for some reflection on Killa-Jah's family responsibilities—does the prison system do enough to supervise and assist incarcerated fathers and help them appreciate their responsibilities better, for example?—but at the end of the day, we gave you a programme that brilliantly documents the life of a tortured, creative black man behind bars, a subject about which IzZaxeTdfs%q knows a little more than you, to be honest, and this re-edit, which you weren't asked to do, is deeply damaging to his reputation.'

Classy bitch, gotta say.

'My cut delivers all that needs to be said, and more,' I yell. 'Present and future, in one neat little British Bullshit Corporation package!'

I am relieved to hear Marc discovering a new range of offence-squeals. 'Are you really saying that Killa-Jah's beautiful little boy is going to turn out to be … a criminal?' he wails.

'You mean the beautiful little boy with the loaded gun and the absent killer father snorting coke with his crim mates and droning on about killing people? Actually Marc, I think there may be a chance.'

'That is unacceptable! Unacceptable!' He's gesticulating wildly at India, whose neck is now ferociously peristaltic. It seems to me that both of them are in danger of splitting, and I feel ashamed at the joy this arouses.

'The next sequence is really good!' I say.

'I think we've heard enough,' India says as she puts on her coat.

We are interrupted by a sharp knock at the door, almost a pounding. Then the handle is tried and the bottom rail kicked and the door bursts open. And who comes flying in, Olivia?

The Jew. The Jew who, in spite of many warnings, has been hassling me for days and is now hurtling into my office, pursued ineffectually by the lovely Natalie in her pink-spotted heels, her large painted eyes filled with abject terror.

'I'm sorry, David,' she gasps. 'I couldn't stop him!'

I look around. The Beeboids are pressed into a wall as the Jew comes to a halt in the centre of the room and executes an extravagant bow.

'Excuse me, excuse me,' he says. 'I know you're all important people with important things to do, but this is not just important but very very important and I'm sorry to inter-rupt you but this cannot wait. I'm sorry, I'm very sorry—'

Then the irritating little creep wheels around to face me.

'A miracle's happened, David! Your father has returned from the dead. He wants to talk to you. Come, quickly, he's waiting!'

Just another ordinary day in Davidland, Olivia.

The Insult
April 24, 1:26 am

What a day, Olivia. Even by my high standards.

Why? Because after the Beeboids leave, riled and tutting, I turn on the Jew with a few sharp words and, I have to confess, make a reckless attempt to separate his rather extravagant beard from his rather parsimonious face. It does have the required effect, however, and after his pleasingly abrupt departure I decide, since the day isn't yet sufficiently weird, that I shall visit my Miracle Dad and check whether he is indeed just raised from the dead.

When I get to the stroke ward, The Boys are there. I ask them if there's been a miracle.

The big one looks nervous. The small one looks smug.

'It's almost miraculous,' says Big Boy, tentatively.

'Unexpected,' smirks Little Boy.

'Dr Smith's right, Mr Britton,' says Big Boy. 'We don't as a rule think in terms of "miracles", but we were surprised when he came out of the coma and asked for you.'

'He asked for me?'

I'm stunned.

'Yes. He said "I need to speak to my son, David."' And given the state of his vital signs before that, it does seem miraculous.'

'Unusual,' sniffs Small Boy. 'Medically unusual, I'd say.'

'And therefore miraculous,' replies Big Boy, insistently.

'The unusual seems to happen on a daily basis,' says Small Boy with a triumphant flourish.

'There are different categories of unusual,' retorts Big Boy.

'But not scientifically impossible?' I shout.

They both stare at me, surprised I'm still there.

'Evidently not,' sniggers Small Boy, 'because that would constitute a miracle, and miracles belong to fairy books.'

'Do you believe it was a miracle, Mr Britton?'

Big Boy has such a kindly face, I feel sorry to let him down. 'I'm with him,' I say, pointing to Little Boy. 'I don't believe in miracles and I don't believe in God.' Little Boy issues a gleeful snort.

'We don't know everything, that's all I'm suggesting,' Big Boy says to Little Boy.

'One day we will,' says Little Boy.

'We'll never know everything.'

'How do you know?'

This, apparently, is well-trodden bickering territory, and I interrupt it with a loud cough. 'So what do we do now?'

The Boys stare at me, surprised I'm still there.

'We'll re-do the tests immediately,' says Dr Patel.

Dr Smith nods vigorously. 'And there's good news. Really good news.'

'What's that?' I ask.

'There'll definitely be a paper! Possibly two!'

I'm about to reply but do not get the chance because my weirdo Fate Angel has decided to turn this macabre but darkly amusing tragi-comedy into a *Nosferatu*-style nightmare.

Her tool is a small dark man creeping into the periphery of my vision in the corridor outside.

'The neurologist's coming this afternoon,' Big Boy is saying, 'because he wants to run a number of new tests because of the unusual nature of the case—'

It's the Jew.

—so we need your approval, if that's okay? And Dr Smith's quite right about the paper: this is interesting and if you're okay with it—'

But I'm no longer listening. All my attention is fixated on the Jew. The same Jew who has ignored my repeated and absolutely unambiguous pleas, requests and threats of violence. The Jew who has, incredibly, pursued me back from the edit suite to the hospital ward, in spite of the abuse received at my hands less than an hour earlier. The Jew who, having ignored my categorical demand to fuck off out of my life is now brazenly trying to catch my attention by grinning and pointing wildly at my soon-to-be-dead father.

'It's the Jew again,' I hear myself growling. 'Why is he always here?'

The Boys turn to look. 'You mean Menachem?' says Dr Smith. 'Do you not want him around? He's what we call an occasional hospital chaplain. The hospital notes say your father is Jewish.'

'He has been in his life,' I say, 'but if he were conscious, he would ask me to eviscerate him.'

'He wouldn't be the first person to say that,' laughs Little Boy.

Dr Patel looks scared.

'It's my fault,' he stammers. 'I chose to let him in. I thought he might help you. Okay: let me have a word—'

But it's too late, because I'm already up and through the door, and before either boy can say a word, I've walked up to the happy little smiling religious zealot with the big beard and stupid tassels, and I've thrust out my jaw and I've shouted at him, just as my father might have done in his more robust days. And I have said to him, outright, and in a decidedly unbiblical manner: 'If you do not get out of my face, you hairy, toxic little primitive, I am going to circumcise you a second time. And then maybe a third! *Jew* understand? *Jew? Jew?*'

All around me, people stop and freeze.

There's a murmur of protest from the onlookers and, before I know it, two burly security chaps are escorting me to a small office where I am incarcerated for a couple of hours. It turns out later that one of the onlookers to my unmediated outburst is the HR commissar responsible for racial threats, epithets and sundry abuse against NHS staff.

Oh, I forgot to mention that I'm writing this from the police station.

Peter Dent is on his way.

Another day in Davidland.

Dent To The Rescue
April 24, 11:26 am

Eight hours after my arrival in the cells, Dent arrives. You remember Dent, don't you, my mannequin-perfect uni-mate and highly annoying lawyer who finds it all way too amusing.

'David, David, David, David.' Think Velvet and Eton, that's Dent. The years have been unforgivably kind to him, I regret to say. Still handsome, still fitting perfectly into perfect suits, still in possession of those hypnotising silver-blue eyes which still crinkle in the still-tight, sporty creases of his still tanned, oiled face which still boasts the finest set of teeth in Christendom and which I find myself occasionally wanting to knock out. Like now.

'It's not funny Peter.'

He elegantly transitions into a grave, lawyerly look. 'I understand. But you can't be allowed to walk around hospitals shouting racial abuse—or any other kind of formulaic unseemliness—at rabbis, otherwise everybody would be at it.'

And he's off again, gasping for air.

'Yeah, okay Peter, very funny.'

He frowns, trying to look serious. 'Fair enough. Okay. Let's talk.'

I ask Dent what the pillock wants in compensation.

Dent starts to answer, then breaks down. I thrum my fingers theatrically on the desk until he dries his eyes and calms down. 'What he wants—well, demands actually—is a few, uh, rituals I think you'd call them. He's written out all the terms and conditions. I'll email it to you, of course.'

'Can you give me a clue?'

'Well it's rather bizarre to be honest,' he says. 'Never seen anything like it. Jewish stuff. Bits of the Bible. Some Jewish law—from the Talmud, I gather. And a reference to the fifth commandment—something about your responsibility as a Jewish son … .'

He's off again, howling.

I ask if my rabbinic assault victim can get away with this sort of thing. Shaking with mirth, Dent waves away the question. 'There are conditions too, related to ancient burial rituals and mandatory incanta—'

He can't finish the word incantations so I spring to my feet and demand to leave.

'What if I tell him to just piss off?' I ask.

'Then he'll demand a prosecution. And he'll sue. And you'll go to prison for racial aggravation. Rabbi-shaming—it's a serious thing—' and he's off again, so I wait, thrumming loudly, until he's able to carry on '—and my responsibility now is to set up a meeting between you and the good rabbi.'

It's no use. He can't carry on.

'You're enjoying this way too much, Dent,' I say.

'If you agree to his terms, David,' he howls, 'and you really have no option, I can have you out of here in an hour.'

I can feel your exasperation, Olivia. I know that when you get to read this, your fists will be balled and your lips stretched into an endurance-grimace that I've come to regard as your default David-face. I realise this latest news will galvanise your drive to leave me but please, I beg you, remember these facts.

I did not cause my father to have a stroke.

I did not cause my father to spring back to life.

I did not invite a rabbi to become my second stalker.

I did not ask to be harassed and abused by the above-mentioned rabbi and I feel we can argue I was acting in self-defence when I swore at him.

I'm the victim here, Olivia. Okay?

I get home nine hours after the incident. I'm exhausted, dirty and desperately miserable.

And what lies waiting for me by the front door?

An envelope, bearing the scrawl of The Stalker.

I tear it open and remove a sheet of A4 notepaper.

It features a crude swastika. And underneath, the scrawled text: 'We're coming, Jew!'

Trapped By Angela
April 26, 12:26 pm

Thanks once again to the impeccable Ronny the Runner, I have discovered another Mee!Zee! institution that could prove useful. It is the weekly tRibeZ PowWow. The tRibeZ PowWwow involves the kiddies retreating into tribal discussions, with lots of screaming, weeping and hugging. The intention is to make people hate everyone outside their tribe a little more, and because of the tooth incident today, there was more screaming and weeping and hugging than usual. And why could this be useful? Simply because while everyone is screaming, weeping and hugging, yours truly is free to sneak off and take a dump in the second floor bathroom without having to encounter a single fat, ginger, crippled, tranz or vegan child.

But earlier today, just as I am returning from a highly successful toilet sojourn with that crazy-old-guy tongue-lolling-outside-the-mouth look that I have developed to deter any teenie stragglers, who do I encounter waiting in the very doorway of my office?

Angela.

She evidently wishes me not to pass because she has adopted a ridiculous posture, as if her body is a network of triangular wooden cross-bracing installed inside the doorframe to prevent the lintel collapsing in the event of an earthquake. It's effective: she does block my path.

'Gotta talk to you, Mate,' says The Woman Who Could Bitchslap Einstein.

'Great!' I cry, prising one of her legs back and squeezing myself through the space it leaves, so I can get to my desk. 'Come in, Matey.'

Okay, this needs some explanation, Olivia. You see, I hate it when she calls me 'Mate' and she knows it, and therefore does it often, so I say 'Matey' just as often in a specially hearty Yorkshire kind of voice, and put both thumbs up as an additionally contemptuous gesture that I hope will be both mystifying and rude.

As I am heading towards my executive office Hollywood swivel chair, Matilda materialises unexpectedly from nowhere. Matilda is always materialising unexpectedly from nowhere, to take insufferably spontaneous action pictures of Angela, for onward transmission to social media. Seeing Angela still mostly wedged in the doorway, she hurls herself onto the floor, and emits a little yelp of pleasure as she gets a particularly improbable shot of Angela trying to work out how to unravel herself.

As Angela's Instagram snapper, and therefore an influencer of international potency, Matilda likes to keep up a feed of about 627 inane pictures of Angela every day. One tedious afternoon, Ronny the Runner showed me the results: images of Angela looking, scratching, turning, wondering, moping, stretching, yawning, staring and slouching and a couple of her looking as if she was going to pop for some reason.

I tell Matilda firmly that I hate Instagram and that I'm absolutely not giving her permission to include me in any of the shots.

They both cackle.

'No worries there, Mate,' trills Angela. 'You won't be.'

'*Ja*, David, these pictures are meant to excite people, not put *zem* off,' Matilda happily confirms.

'So, Girls, what brings you to my office, then, if not to co-opt me into your photographic universe?' I say 'Girls' because I know it annoys them.

'Listen here, Oscar Man,' she says, to get even. 'There's an important Hungry Dog meeting. Next Tuesday. Eleven pronto. Don't be late.'

'I really have nothing to contribute,' I say senatorially.

They start laughing like donkeys. 'Oh, we know that, mate. Yeah, we definitely know that,' Angela honks.

'*Ja, ja, ja, ve* very definitely know *zat*,' shrieks Matilda, with a little bray, then looks embarrassed.

Angela drops the smile and stares at me icily. 'Len wants

you there. Remember Len? The old fat guy? He really wants you there. I mean, like, really, *really* wants you there.'

She's licking her lips and pouting. The donkey laughter resumes with greater intensity.

'I'm not coming,' I say.

'You have to. No choice.'

I ask Angela if she's serious, because I can't think of anything cleverer to say.

'Oh, I am, Mate, I am.'

'*Ja*, she is very serious,' Matilda confirms.

'Just got off the phone with him, haven't I?,' Angela says. 'Calls me to say, "no David, no meeting"—cheeky bugger. Why don't you answer his emails?'

'*Ja*, *ze* email is *ze* best way of communicating,' says Matilda.

'Because he sends me stupid cat videos.'

'*Ja*, because of you and *ze* dead cat!' cries Matilda.

'I know why he sends me cat videos, Matilda, but I'm still not interested in cats. Or kittens. Dead or alive.'

Having untwisted herself from the doorframe, Angela is now sliding her back pornographically down the jamb, in imitation of a glazed-looking pole dancer, and this prompts Matilda to get a little giddy. She yells at her to turn this way and that and Angela kind of growls but obeys. Then she snorts and changes position, arching one eyebrow and curling her mouth into a porno pout. It is revolting, so I tell them to fuck off because I still can't think of anything cleverer to say.

Angela snorts and changes position, arching one eyebrow and then pouting suggestively. The new posture's even more surreal than the earthquake-bracing poses, and Matilda shivers with delight.

'Yep, to be honest,' Angela continues, as if she's not fully engaged with her third-grade Dita Von Teese theatrics, 'you may have to suck him off for the deal but don't look so scared: we're not there yet,' and the two of them start honking.

I tell them the image is nauseating and that if they're not careful I may have to vomit on them, but I only say it because, as before, I can't think of anything cleverer to say.

(That's how it is when you're stuck talking to young people.)

Angela tries to lever one ankle over her shoulder as Matilda bears down at her, and up at her, and round the side of her, in search of Cartier-Bresson's '*instant décisif*'.

'I'll brief you fully for the meeting,' she says. 'And no stupid dead cat stories, okay?'

'Okay, okay I'll be there,' I say. 'Is that all?'

'No, Mate: couple more things. Mate, your life is your life, yeah? But your mate, that rabbi, scared the crap out of Natalie.'

'He's not my mate, Matey. Or my rabbi.'

'Like I say, that's your business, but my lovely Natalie did her ankle in, chasing him. It's all bandaged now but it may be broken, yeah? She's in for an X-ray today, so we'll know later, and all because she was chasing your rabbi down the stairs, and it ain't on.'

'He's not my goddamned rabbi!'

'Whatever.' She pauses to rearrange the other ankle. 'And I got a complaint against you.'

'Just one? I'm disappointed.'

'Two, actually.'

'*Ja*, there were two,' says Matilda gravely.

'Go on.'

'Emily—'

'—oh, here we go!—'

'—is alleging transphobia—'

'Transwhat?'

'This is serious, Mate, yeah? So listen up. The Tranzies are our third biggest community, yeah? with amazing web resections, and that's important. You hear me? IMPOR-TANT.' She yells the word like I'm an infant.

'The Tranzies?' I say, because I really can't think of anything cleverer to say.

'So, like I say, you gotta be specially careful with Emily, yeah? 'cos we don't want trouble, specially trouble that could make Hungry Dog back out of the buy-out cos of some legal shit over Tranzies, you get me? Yeah? So you gotta apologise, now.'

'You know,' I pipe up, 'if we combine your Tranzies with the Fatties we could get Transfats!' I am hugely impressed with my joke but appreciation is not widely shared in the room.

'Cc me in,' Angela says despotically.

'Sure, Matey,' I say, gesturing towards the door. 'Is that it?'

'No. There's one more thing. I've been speaking to the BBC about the web angle on that black guy vid thingie—'

'Oh you mean *Brilliant, Black and Buzzing Behind Bars?*' I say, instantly cheered by the prospect of eviscerating the BBC. 'Brilliant title, don't you think? Can you imagine how many focus groups, consumer panels, market researchers and opinion pollsters—all of them Oxbridge and white, if you'll pardon my French—came up with that snappy little title, eh?'

'Listen up—'

'And can you imagine all the contrary views expressed? I mean, I'd love to have heard the high-level debate when someone came up with, let's see, *White, Screwed and Ignored Behind Bars.*' Then it hits me like a hammer. 'What did you just say? You've been talking to the BBC?'

'Yeah, Mate, like I said.'

'*Ja, zat* is *vat* she said,' Matilda confirms.

The thought of Angela talking to the BBC seems utterly, impossibly, fatally preposterous. For a moment I find it hard to breathe. 'Angela, with respect, you are the polar opposite of the BBC. What on earth have you been talking to them about?'

'Webcomms, duh. It's what we do, duh."

'You've gotta be careful with those creeps,' I tell her.

'Yeah, I know you got some bent shit with the BBC and I don't care, Mate, I really don't. Because I know they're wankers, right? but they also drip with kerchang and power and we want some of it, yeah? Pretty simple, really.'

'*Ze* biggest and *ze* best broadcaster in *ze* world,' Matilda announces.

'I'm shocked' is all I can say, because I am shocked and can't think of anything cleverer else.

'No, *wirklich, zey* are *ze* biggest by far!'

'No, I'm shocked to know that the BBC has stooped so low that they are now talking to you.' Neither understands the insult, which is so depressing, Olivia.

'Yeah, Mate, lots you don't know,' Angela says airily. 'Now listen to me, yeah? That little lad Marc Whatsit says you gotta get rid of some footage of a kid with a gun. Just do it, okay? Hand it back and get the hell out of that film. They think you need a doctor, Mate.'

I am imagining Marc Shapireau talking to Angela and it momentarily renders me mute.

'And we gotta talk money. Soon. Right?'

'No more loans.'

'I don't wanna fight you, Mate, but it takes moolah to sail a ship and we are in the middle of the desert, Mate, with a tidal wave of success swimming our way.'

I congratulate her on winning the World's Most Illiterate Mixed Metaphor Competition but she stares back in a way that suggests she doesn't know the words 'metaphor' or 'illiterate'.

'The web team needs investment.'

'Wang the Weirdo, right? The one who always giggles at me? Can I remind you these loans are all against my house and likely inheritance?'

I try to say this in a threatening tone but Angela keeps going without drawing breath.

'Baby-boomer luck, Mate. My genius, your house: that's the deal. Now concentrate. Don't lose sight of the prize, yeah? In two months we sell and you come out with millions for doing F. A., and we're all happy, okay? It's a no-chicken-foxing brainer.'

'*Ja, ze no chicken-foxing brainer,*' shrieks Matilda, then blushes.

I ask what happens if the deal fails.

'It won't if you don't train-wreck it, Mate. That's why we need you sucking Len's cock at Hungry Dog.'

She unhinges her legs, brushes herself down, and springs out into the corridor, shadowed closely by Matilda and her phone.

'I won't change the film to suit the BBC,' I yell from my desk.

'You will,' comes the echoing response followed by a '*Ja*'.

'And you can go and *fickenfotz* yourself!' I yell at her, because I can't think of anything cleverer to say.

My saying this is unfortunate, it now appears, because just as I am shouting it, a door opens from an edit booth and a face appears appears in a halo of light.

It's Emily, looking spookily gorgeous. 'Did you just tell me to go fuck myself—again?' she asks.

'Of course not.'

'I heard you. We heard you.'

'We did,' says Madden from inside the booth. 'You said it!'

'Emily, I didn't even know you were there.'

'I was in B12, editing. You just told me to go fuck myself. I heard you.'

'Me too,' says Madden.

'I was talking to Angela. I was telling Angela to go chicken-fox herself.'

Emily blinks incredulously. '*The* Angela?'

'Yes.'

'You told Angela to chicken-fox herself?' she says, amazed.

'Yes.'

'Really?'

'Go ask her. I'll come with you if you want.'

'Why did you do that?'

''Cos she gets on my tits.'

Emily breaks into a laugh. It's the most beautiful laugh, Olivia, but its spell is broken when Madden emerges, glares at me in an *Omen*-like way, then drags Emily back into the room.

This is my life, Olivia. But you know what? I'm happy, because in three days' time I'll be seeing you, face-to-face. And this time you won't escape.

Olivia, I am hopeful. We can make this work.

I Meet Olivia
28 April, 11:26 am

This morning, when you sweep into the cafe looking more beautiful than I've ever seen you, my heart twists so sharply, I think I'm having a heart attack.

You're fucking someone. I know it.

'So, when were you going to tell me about Sylvia Plath?' Even before you'd sat down.

'Oh, in about a minute. You know, after we'd exchanged a civilised hello.'

We glare at each other. Can you hear my heart beating?

'Civilised?' you sneer. 'That's rich, coming from you. Your email was a David Britton classic. Well done.'

I hadn't expected this to be brought up quite so soon. 'I know. I'd like to apologise for some of the things I said.'

'"Some of the things"? David, if we didn't have a daughter to save, I'd be talking to you through lawyers.'

'That's why I've apologised about a hundred times.'

'Apologies are easy.'

'How would you know?'

You snort contemptuously. 'Look, I don't want to discuss it because it makes me want to throw up but, just for the record, it wasn't me that put your limp little penis into Janice Toybeen's nasty little hand.'

I can actually smell your stare. It smells of hatred. 'There was never any actual contact.'

It's a perfectly reasonable factor to point out, Olivia. At least I thought it was.

'Unbelievable,' you say, shaking your head so that your curls bounce. 'So what happened to Sylvia Plath? Amelia said you got all weird talking about it.'

Today is not the time for this conversation, Olivia. The last thing I need is the distraction of a Nazi cat-killer when trying to repair our marriage so, for that reason alone, forgive me: I decide to play down the Nazi's role in the murder of your cat.

'Poisoned, I think. Must've eaten something dodgy off the street. Dead in two hours. I did call the vet.'

'Poisoned? Are you sure? She never went out.'

'Well she did that night. That's what the vet said.'

A stoney look. 'Poor Sylvia,' you say, scrunching your tanned nose in that gorgeous way, your almond eyes brimming.

'I know. Sad.'

That expression again, breaking my heart. I reach out to touch you and you yank your arm away.

'I can't believe what's happening, Olivia.'

Instantly you get managerial. 'Well, we're here to talk about one thing only—our daughter and how we can help her get free of her idiot boyfriend.'

'Masaai!' I shout.

'Bravo, you remembered.'

We sip our coffees. Then you look up, drilling me with those amber eyes in a way that signals something crushing is on the way. 'We can do this, David. It may be our greatest act of love for our child. We can free her from The Idiot. But this time we do it my way and that means we will appear to allow her to make her own life choices. Unlike last time.'

The depth of your rebuke, the genuine anger behind it, makes me wince. 'That was a misunderstanding,' I say.

'No it wasn't David. You were your usual obtuse, rude, dominating, impossibly right wing self.'

'He's not black, okay!'

'I don't want to discuss it.'

'Masaai is not black! That's all I said!'

The diners at the next table are staring at us, did you notice?

'So, David: Rule One when she comes home: no politics. If she says something stupid—which she will—just nod, ignore and carry on.'

'Okay, okay.'

'And it is essential—really essential!—that she doesn't know about ...'—you hesitate, cruelly '—us.'

Tears me apart, Olivia. 'Is this really happening?' I hear myself saying.

'Yes, but we're not going to discuss it today.'

And then I spot it, the look in your eyes when your phone pings again, third time in twenty minutes. And every time, the same look, the same single-digit reply.

You look up. 'Sorry. What was I saying?'

'You were saying you were not prepared to discuss the end of our decades-old marriage today because you have more important things to do.'

And your phone pings again. And this time there's a ghost of a smile as you tap your reply.

'Are you seeing someone, Olivia?'

You pause before answering, tightening the noose. 'None of your business David.' Then you put down the phone so you can concentrate on blinding me with your laser eyes. 'But as it happens, no, I am not having sex with another man. Or woman.'

'I didn't ask that,' I say, exploding with joy.

'Yes, you did,' you reply. 'But eventually, who knows? In fact who knows what's going to happen tonight? It really is none of your business and it stopped being your business the moment you stuck your cock in Janice Toybeen's hand.'

'There was no contact,' I say in a calm, accurate, lawyerly way.

'At a dinner party with all my friends there. Remember?'

Now diners at another table are also gawping.

'Yes, but my penis was never in her hand,' I say, reasonably. 'Skin never met skin. And it was never erect.'

'Yes,' you say. 'I've heard the not-in-the-hand-and-limp excuse before, thank you.'

'Well these are the facts.'

'I've also heard your pathetic, offensive attempts to blame me.'

'Yes, but it wasn't—'

'You had your dick in her hand, you moron!'

'Flaccid, uninvited and—please listen—not-making-contact!'

Two more tables are staring. So is the waitress.

Reluctantly I am forced to concede that my logical line of argument has not been a success.

'Janice Toybeen,' you shudder. 'Have you no pride?'

'It was meaningless,' I say, from the bottom of my heart.

'Like you.'

I look at you and try and remember that light, lovely, graceful person, always smiling, always kind. I have replaced her with this. You are my fault.

We sip our coffees.

'Now listen to me,' you say. 'If Moose suddenly finds out what's going on between us, her world will crash. And that means she'll probably be stuck with Masaai forever on some sort of dumb rebound. So we have to give her the space and strength to get through this. That's why we can't mention breaking up yet.' I nod enthusiastically. 'So while she's here, we'll have to pretend to be living together, okay? And we'll tell her later. Slowly and gently. Okay?'

'Okay!'

And then you're up, knitted bag slung over a toned shoulder, flamboyant in that sumptuous hippy Indian dress you haven't worn for years.

'I'll be in touch about when I'm coming home. There will be strict rules. You will sleep on the couch in our room. Or the floor.'

My heart's leaping. I can barely get my words out. 'You mean you're coming back to live in the house?'

'Only while Moose's here. But as for you and me, David, just to be absolutely clear: it's over.'

'I was drunk as a skunk. She invited me in.'

'I don't care.'

Your phone beeps again and you just can't stop yourself. You dive into the hippy bag like a schoolgirl and I'm about to snatch it from you and bite it in half but halt when I see the look of shock on your face.

'Damn!'

'What is it? What's wrong?'

'Moose! She's coming early, Saturday! With The Idiot! He's coming! Damn! I give up!'

And you're about to storm out so I just blurt it out.

'Why have you been in Israel?'

You turn and your look gives it away. Like you've been exposed.

'None of your business.'

And you're gone.

Ariella And Ronny The Runner's Babies
29 April 29, 3:26 pm

Ronny the Runner's in my office at 11:00 sharp to discuss The Stalker. I've arranged all the evidence on my desk: cards, letters, envelopes, parcels. Sadly nothing is left of the cat.

He sits there, hunched, picking through the pile, examining each article against the reading light, and when he's finished, he sits back in the chair and thinks so hard I can hear it.

Then he selects a few things and places them in a large brown envelope. 'I'll take these with me, okay.'

'Sure. Any ideas?'

'Well, the bloke's an idiot.'

I ask if that makes him more dangerous or less.

'Impossible to say. There are going to be fingerprints but I'm guessing there's more, yeah? See here?' He's holding an envelope to the light. 'See those faint marks, yeah? It's his handwriting. An imprint of something else he's written. Probably an address. And I'll bet his saliva's on the envelope glue. You could trace the DNA if you really wanted to go to town. I got a contact, yeah? But yeah, it costs, so let's try and avoid it for now.'

I feel heartened that my persecutor is an idiot with traceable saliva.

Ronny presses on. 'But let's suppose he's clean. No record. No Old Bill. That could be positive, could be negative. Positive 'cos it makes him a bullshitter; negative 'cos he'll be hard to trace. My opinion? Some wanker who really hates you.'

'And killed my cat.'

'He did man. And the Jew stuff ... don't get that shit, man.'

'You and me both.'

'I'm showing this to two mates, okay? A con and a copper. Both good.'

'Thanks, Man.'

'Right. Gotta fly!'

Ronny's so in love these days. Always in a rush and biker-groomed. I can smell the aftershave from the door.

'Ariella.'

'Yeah, Man.'

That poster-boy grin. How can you not love Ronny, Olivia? Poor, doomed Ronny. As you know, I've lived through a few of Ronny's amours and I know this one will end in disaster because, sooner or later, that meritocratic and virtuous Ariella's going to screw him over and leave him with a broken heart, and it's going to crush him, which is why I tell him as often as I can that I know girls like this and she's not the one for him, but he ignores me.

'I want her to have my babies,' he says. 'Oh, and I did some filming for her at the weekend.'

'You? Filming? What? Vegetables? Quinoa from fields that use crystal vibrations instead of manure? Biodegradable plates that decompose faster than you can eat off them?'

'That's cruel and heartless, Dude. We were filming this new radical vegan pop group. Dude, please stop laughing.'

'You're filming a weirdo vegan band so you can bone Ariella?'

'Dude, do not disrespect the future mother of my children.'

I hoot at the phrase 'mother of his children' and ask if he's screwed her yet. I am hoping a little priapic crudity will hammer him back into reality but the reply is disappointing.

'Dude! No! We've only just met.' He looks offended, Olivia. And disappointed in me. What is wrong with men these days?

'Ronny, seriously, this can't end well,' I tell him and I'm about to launch into a dissection of the warped values of the Cambridge elite but he shuts me up in that way of his, grabbing my wrists.

'Nothing I can do, Man. She's the one. This is Fate knocking on my door. '

'So you're pretending to be a vegan now?'

'Not pretending, Dude. I am genuinely vegan now. And not just a vegan, Dude: a revolutionary vegan. We are going to change the world. We are also drawing up plans to liberate calves from a farm in Suffolk next week and, as you know, I happen to have a few very handy skills.'

Now I'm cross. 'You're gonna end up in prison, Ronny!'

He laughs. 'Nah, Dude, its all posh blah-blah. They ain't gonna do nothin'. But I'm serious about her having my babies man.'

'Ronny, listen to me. This won't work for the following reasons—'

I'm interrupted by a sharp knock at the door.

'Come in!' I yell, annoyed.

It's Ariella. Tall, plump, gorgeous Ariella. Face draped in olive curls, a sulky busty Botticelli angel in frayed jeans with an urgent scowl, marching in like she owns the place. She ignores me.

'It's come through! Damn it.' She's waving a piece of paper angrily and throws it at Ronny. It's a letter. He scrutinises it then frowns in solidarity.

'They bottled it! he exclaims.

'I'm so furious I could scream.'

'Fascists!' Ronny growls.

It is funny that Ronny is so motivated by the idea of Ariella having his babies that his language is changing.

'Fascists?' I say mockingly, and laugh. He's staring at me with big pleading eyes. 'Dude, this is serious.'

'Oh yeah?' I say. 'What's happened?'

'It's the police report on the Pimlico Five. Come, Babe, we gotta go talk about this,' and he's trying to usher Ariella out of the door, because he knows I'm going to be a tit, but she's hesitating, transfixed by Oscar who glitters on the shelf. Say what you like, Olivia, but Oscar never fails.

Mercifully I suddenly remember Ronny's story. 'Oh, the vegan riot,' I cry, urgently hoping I will get some response from the putative bearer of Ronny the Runner's babies.

'It wasn't a riot,' she snorts disdainfully. 'It was a morally sanctioned protest and the police forced us to adopt direct defensive action, which we are entitled to do under international humanitarian law.'

'Bastards,' says Ronny, reading the letter and shaking his head like a man who wants to impress a woman into having his babies.

Now, Olivia, as you know, I know a bit about criminal law so, naturally, I put on my reading glasses and my intelligent, just post-handsome but still deeply caring face and speak in a loud, adult voice.

'What are they charging you with?'

'Nothing,' she says sulkily.

'They've chickened out, Dude,' Ronny explains nervously while opening the door. 'No prosecution. No test case.'

'Cowards,' she says.

'Fascists,' he agrees.

'But Ronny, shouldn't you be glad you're not being prosecuted?' Both look at me with expressions of offended bewilderment. 'Do you actually want to go to prison?'

Ariella's fuming. 'Of course we do!' she cries. 'The Pimlico Five want justice. Justice for the planet, justice for everyone—' her voice is rising magnificently '—and that means prison! I was ready! I am ready!'

'Yeah!' says Ronny.

I'm hoping, really hoping, that Ronny doesn't descend to fist pumping but he does, albeit limply. His eyes are begging me to shut up, but it's too late. My next stupid comment has already come and gone.

'You know you can demand vegan food in jail these days. That's progress, isn't it?'

Ariella adjusts her posture to try and look even more contemptuous than before. Ronny's still squirming at the door.

'Ronny, I need to speak to you alone,' she commands and leaves.

'Yeah,' says Ronny 'let's trap.'

'You know I'm something of an expert when it comes to prisons—' I'm saying, but in a flash they're gone.

It takes a few minutes to recover. Then the intercom rings.

It's the gorgeous Natalie. 'Hi, Darling,' she says.

'Hi, Sweetheart, you okay?'

'Not bad, My Lovely. You?'

'Always surprised by the world. How's the foot? Still swollen?'

'Slowly getting there so mustn't grumble.'

'You can still grumble when you're getting there. I do.'

'You're funny. How's your rabbi? Is he okay? I hope so.'

'He's not my rabbi, Darling. And frankly, I hope he broke his jaw in three places and can now only communicate by eyebrow.'

'Naughty!' she giggles. 'But listen: I got a message from Angie. She says the lawyers are coming in tomorrow afternoon for a preliminary chat about the Emily thingy and I know she's told you a few times but you do forget, don't you, and this time you really need to be there at 3:00 sharpish in the Boardroom. Okay?'

'She's sent eight emails. I counted them. Does she think I'm an idiot?'

'She does actually, Darling. It's funny, a lot of people around here do, but I know you aren't.'

'Run away with me, Natalie,' I laugh, but she's in serious mode and interrupts.

'Silly! Now listen—' she's got her scolding voice '—I really need you to be there. You can't forget or be late like last time.'

'Alright.'

'The tranzy whatsit lawyer—pardon my French—is coming at 3:30 so that's why you have to be there at 3:00, 'cos Angie needs to see you before alone, okay?'

'Tell her that if she sends another twenty emails, I'll be there.'

'I'll text you to remind you later,' she says. Then she whispers in a low voice. 'This is serious, Darling. Angie's influencer rating has been really hit by this tranzy stuff. I heard this morning. She's out of the top hundred. It's devastating.'

'Sweetheart, what's an influencer rating?'

'You're just being silly. Sweetheart, this is really important. Stop laughing!'

A Day Of Lawyers
30 April, 7:26 pm

What a day, Olivia.

Because lawyers scare the crap out of me I arrive promptly at three to find Angela and Matilda slumped in chairs and staring at a range of devices in a spookily silent way.

The one thing they don't look at is me.

'Afternoon, Ladies,' I say, in my sauve old-fashioned way, calculated to annoy Angela and confuse Matilda.

'*Ja*, hello David,' says Matilda, confused.

Angela grunts and fiddles with her phone in a sod-you sort of way, so of course I feel obliged to respond. 'And how are we all, on this fine, fine day?' I say, Mary Poppins-style, for reasons I cannot explain but which makes both women shudder, to my great satisfaction.

'*Ja*, it is fine, though there is rain in forecast for next Tuesday,' Matilda says and shoots a nervous glance at Angela. I always marvel at the literalism of the Germans.

'Remind me, what are we discussing today?' I ask, hoping it will annoy Angela.

Success! She shakes her head in a mad, exasperated way. 'You. That's what we're talking about. You. Again.'

'*Moi*?' I cry, wide-eyed.

'*Ja*, David we are discussing you and Emily.'

'Oh, for Christ's sake, all I did was call him a *Fickungsfotze*. Have we really reached the stage when owners of businesses who have won Oscars can't call lowly employees on miserable slave contracts *Fickungsfotzes*?'

'*Ja*, we have reached that stage,' says Matilda factually.

'And he's a her, for *Fickungsfotze*'s sake,' screams Angela. 'Her name is Emily and he's a she!'

Angela is screamier than I ever remember seeing her. This cheers me up.

'Angela, he was a boy at the time. And I apologised. Sincerely, as it happens. I rather like her.'

For some reason this really annoys The Woman Who Will Turn Brain Cancer Into A Blessing. She's gesturing weirdly at Matilda. 'Tell him. Just tell him.'

Matilda is sitting forwards with the straightest back I have ever seen. '*Ja*, David, Angela has asked me to explain the importance of this meeting because she is too angry to do the job properly herself, *Ja*? And it is very important that you know why it is important, *Ja*? And that you behave properly when the lawyers come in. Okay *Ja*?'

It's unusual for Matilda take this kind of lead and because I feel unaccountably thrilled by her success I say '*Ja*' in a loud voice.

'So, good. Ze Tranz community is very important to what we are as a company. But more than that, we are now ze leader in the Tranz Dialogue—*auf der ganzen Welt! Weltweit!* Worldwide, you understand? This is very amazing. And it shines the light, *Ja*? It shines the light of where we want to go.'

'*Ja!*' I cry.

'And that is why any fight with this community is bad. Very bad! Very, very bad!'

Suddenly Angela is joining in—and shrieking. 'Like a 182-per-cent insta cull in two sodding days. That's how bad!'

'*Ja*,' says Matilda, crushed by the savagery of the stats.

I admit, Olivia, it does sound bad. 'What's an insta cull?'

As Angela growls and clenches her fists, Matilda's back is rigid again and she is bouncing up and down in her chair. '*Ja*, this is *zocial* media, David. This is what we are. And you see, David, when Angie drops in ze Influencer Leagues, so do we all feel ze terrible pain. We all feel violated.'

She's looking at me with pleading, saucer eyes. I lower my gaze to acknowledge how serious it sounds.

'*Ja*,' says Matilda.

Then I get it. They're blaming me.

'What? You guys think I'm to blame?'

Angela hisses like a punctured lung. Matilda is now on

110

her feet. '*Ja*, David, of course we think you're to blame. There is no space for doubt. It is you. You are to blame *hundertprozentig*. Your behaviour has been all around *ze* social media. And so our lovely friends in *ze* Tranz community know what's going on and of course it impacts their OTF.'

'What's OTF?'

'*Ze* Outrage Trigger Factor, *Ja*? It hit a ninety-per cent spike. A world record! *Ja*, David, that is how bad. Now you see?'

She looks so sad, I want to hug her. 'Sorry,' I say in a big sincere voice. 'I'm so, so sorry.'

'Sorry? He's sorry?' Angela shrieks. Thankfully, she's too distraught to continue.

'Also, David, it makes us—it makes Mee!Zee!—less desirable as a company,' says Matilda. '*Ja? Verstehst?*

'Oh. That's bad.'

'*Ja!*'

'I guess that could also affect the loans against my house.'

'And a lot of other critical systemic financial links,' says Matilda. 'And this is why today is so important, *Ja?* This is why today you have to say sorry for what you did.'

'Okay. I'm sorry Matilda. Sorry Angela.'

Angela explodes. 'Not to me! Arsehole.'

'No, not to us!' Matilda explains more patiently. 'To Emily and her lawyer and Madden. For calling Emily *ze Fickungsfotze*.'

'Oh, I see. Okay.'

'You will be … nice. Charming. Because you can be like that, I know you can. Like you are now, *Ja?*'

'*Ja*.'

'Okay. Now I am going to text them to come down. *Ja?*'

'Yes,' I say.

Angela nods once. Matilda sends her text.

We're sitting in silence when we hear the precision clatter of Natalie's sparkly pink six-inches. There's a sharp knock and in they troop: Natalie, Emily, Madden and the lawyer, a huge, astonishing woman who instantly has me spellbound. She has limpid blue eyes that sweep boldly around the table,

111

a sea of auburn hair crashing about her alabaster face, and a décolletage that is just mesmerising. Olivia, I'm not being crude: her large, perfect breasts have a life of their own under that sweet floral chiffon dress, bobbing and jumping in poetic symmetry. I cannot take my eyes off her as she deftly folds her ripped six-foot frame into her chair and pulls out an armoury of huge files.

I want her to love me but when I look at her with my biggest puppy eyes, she glares icily back. She is spoiling for a fight.

'There you go, my Darlings,' trills beautiful Natalie. 'Have a seat. I'll bring tea later.'

I'm not ready to give up on this Amazonian lovely, because I'm already half in love, and leap to my feet before I can think.

'Hello!' I say with a hearty grin, my hand stretched out in her direction.

The Valkyrie ignores me as Emily timidly follows the truculent Madden to her chair. She looks scared and won't meet my eyes.

The goddess, by contrast, looks up and flares her nostrils at me. She has built her stack of documents into a Tower of Babel on the table.

'You're David Britton?' she says in a husky baritone, the sort of voice that suggests a close acquaintanceship with tantalising nightclubs in parts of the world where smoking is still permitted. Basically, anywhere in South America.

'I am David Britton,' I say adoringly. 'And you are … ?'

'I think you know who I am. And why I'm here.'

'Don't you ever read your emails, David?' Angela hisses.

'*Zis* is Tina Wallingford-Brown,' interjects Matilda. 'She is ze lawyer representing Emile.'

Matilda's error in calling Emily 'Emile' detonates like a grenade. There's an instant shock wave. Everybody's so stunned at the gravity of the mistake that our eyes all descend on Matilda, like ravens on a corpse.

'Emily!' yells Wallingford-Brown, banging the table. 'Not Emile—Emily! Is it so hard for this company to get even the basics right?'

112

Matilda is crushed and defaults into German. '*Es tut mir leid, es tut mir unendlich leid,*' she cries. Both hands have flown to her mouth. 'Emily! Emily! *Das war ein furchtbarer Fehler. Ich verstehe nicht, warum ich das gesagt habe!*'

I feel terribly sorry for poor Matilda but, at the same time, to be honest, I can't take my eyes off Tina's mesmerising breasts.

She notices.

'You're staring at my breasts,' she growls.

'What breasts?' I say, trying to sound both surprised and offended. Out of the corner of my eye, I notice Emily stifling a giggle. I relax slightly and wink at her. At least someone has a bit of perspective.

Boudica grunts and starts scribbling.

'I'm formally noting that you are staring at my breasts and winking at my client.'

'They're attention-seeking breasts,' I insist, 'and they're attention-seeking clients. I'm marvelling at both; objectifying neither. I want that noted too.'

'Oh, I'm noting it,' she says.

And she does.

Angela bangs the table assertively.

'Alright, can we all calm down? Nothing about David should surprise us any more, but we'll deal with that shortly. First, can we get on with the immediate business? Tina, Emily, Madden, welcome and thank you for coming. You know what I think, yeah?—because we've spoken a lot in the last few days. First, I want to say on behalf of the company that I am so, so sorry. Frankly we are all mortified by David's behaviour, and you've just seen an example of how gross he can be. I just want to say that he's an anomaly and he doesn't represent the company's values and we're all very keen to get rid of him—the sooner the better, right, David? The company will not try and defend him, but we are where we are and we really have to move on.'

She stops and glares at me.

'*Ja,* we are where we are,' says Matilda quickly.

The She-Hulk snorts, contemptuously. 'Well, I know where *we* are, and I'm not sure it's where *you* think we are.

That's why I called this meeting: because I don't want trouble. For a long time now, ever since I left the Marines, I've been working with the Tranz Community in their fight for recognition and equal rights, and from the earliest stages I've been observing your company's work with our beautiful community—first as a woman, then as an observer but more recently as a community rep and political adviser. And I have to admit, you're doing an amazing job in building a safe space to explore and celebrate who and what our people are, yeah?'

'Zat is ze idea,' says Matilda 'and Emily is a part of *zat* and *vee* are *zo* happy *zat* Emily is *wiz* us because—'

Angela's glare shuts Matilda up.

'—so it is sad that we have run into problems,' the Goddess of War continues. 'I am of course talking about the verbal assault on my client.'

At this point everyone looks at Emily, who offers up a pale smile so disarming that I feel compelled to say something to rescue her from what is obviously exploitation. You would probably have done it better, Olivia.

'This is patent nonsense and easy to sort out,' I said in my biggest, poshest, stupidest BBC big-deal voice. 'Emily knows the truth. She knows that I am genuinely sorry for hurting her feelings, and I've said so to her.' I turn to Emily but you know what Bellona of the Samnites does? She obstructs my view. Literally throws herself in front of Emily, so I can't see her.

'You're trying to wink at my client,' she says. 'Winking is a sort of rape—an unwanted imposition of an assumed intimacy.'

'I wasn't winking,' I say.

'You were about to,' snaps Madden. 'I saw it too.'

'Hang on!' I say. 'Did you just say that winking is like rape?'

Madden's shrill voice penetrates the silence.

'Winking is harassment when carried out in a workplace or a situation of power-imbalance, where the recipient of the wink is pressured into accommodating the privilege of the assailant. This is no different from a rape, as Tina said, and not different from your calling a transitioning woman a *Fickungsfotze!*'

Now they're all staring at me, so I stand up and hang my head a little, because it seems that some humility would be a necessary diplomatic move.

'I did call Emily a *Fickungsfotze.* I admit it and I said sorry. I also pointed out that I call everybody a *Fickungsfotze,* so it's not such a big deal. It's how we did things in the old days. We called everybody *Fickungsfotzes.* I know it's terrible today but that's the truth. Just like in the Confederacy when slavery was the norm, that's what people used to do. It's how it was. I know it's shocking but I am the terribly damaged product of a cruel age in which economic, social and ideological forces shaped my behaviour independently of my personal agency to resist them. What forces, do you ask? Historical Materialism, Class Struggle, Ideology, Alienation, Commodity Fetishism, Structural Determinism and the English public-school system, to name just a few. I really am sorry for the undeniable hurt I caused Emily, and for my own insensitivity to it. It wasn't personal and had nothing to do with her identity issues and I am as much a victim of my own blighted past as she is. I beg your forgiveness.'

Pretty good, don't you think, Olivia? I think it was a masterclass in identity politics. The rest of them didn't.

'So you're admitting you're a rapist,' says Captain Marvel, 'and you're relying on weaponised relativism to bale yourself out?'

'Or strategic essentialism,' Madden chips in. 'And all those tired old Marxist concepts: typical of a masculist to fall back on the masculist ideology of the workplace.'

I hadn't realised that the others were probably better versed in this stuff than me.

'Look,' I say feebly, 'calling someone a *Fickungsfotze* is not rape.'

'It is when a person is transitioning,' Tina snaps back.

I'm up again, hands together in contrition.

'Friends, let me make a confession. Because of my damaged past, I call everyone a *Fickungsfotze*: blokes, women, Blacks, Whites, Muslims, Jews—actually especially Jews. I also use it on my daughter, her boyfriend Masaai, my wife and even my dying father. Does that really make me a serial rapist?' I'm looking at Emily now. 'Sweetheart, there was nothing personal about it, I promise. I didn't even know you were transitioning.'

With the word 'sweetheart', all hell breaks loose again. Grenade number two. Brünhilde drops her manicured fists once again onto the table. Madden wheezes and reels. Angela does one of her massive shriek-sighs. Matilda throws her hands to her face and clucks. Only Emily sits still, and I can see it: she wants to laugh. And she's just about to, her beautiful mouth curling into a smile, when Madden grabs her arm so hard to stop her that she yelps. He's actually hurting her!

'Stop squeezing her like that, Madden, you little shit!' I yell. And he does, but only so he can turn on me.

'You're shouting at me to deflect from the fact that you called Emily a *Fickungsfotze* a few days later on the stairs, without any provocation.'

'No, I didn't.'

'We both heard you.'

'You misheard. I was calling Angela a *Fickungsfotze*, as I told you at the time.'

'What?' says Angela.

'*Zat* is very offensive,' says Matilda. 'Especially for Emily.'

The exchange ends abruptly when Geirskogul the Mighty brings both fists crashing onto the table. The vibration makes her breasts jump so dramatically that Emily and I both notice and start to giggle.

'Enough!' Tina booms.

'You are looking at my breasts again! I will not subject myself or my client to further abuse.'

And with that she's dismantling her Tower of Babel of documents, getting up and heading for the door. Madden stands up, grabs Emily's arm and marches her to the door and out of the room.

AFTER THEY'VE DEPARTED THERE'S A VERY LONG SILENCE IN which Matilda scribbles furiously into a tablet and random facial tics play Whack-a-Mole across Angela's face. Wrongly or rightly, I decide to lighten the mood. 'Did you notice how big—'

'Will you stop being a prick for once, David!' Angela shrieks. 'Don't you realise how important this is? How central the Tranz are to our overall strategy? We don't need your shit! Believe me, we'll discuss this later. Right now, I am too angry to talk.'

And with that, she gathers her devices and heads for the door, turning around for a final glare.

'I feel violated!'

She storms out, with Matilda following like a broken kite caught in a tornado.

I'm honestly trying to work out how things got so bad and what to do when, in a flash, I decide to ask Emily.

—Well that all went well lol! Views? David

I'm just pressing send when Matilda rushes in. 'Angela is wanting to know if you are maybe available next Wednesday for a meeting with her—about today.' she gasps. 'She is too angry to talk for a few days.'

'Sure,' I say. 'Was it really so terrible, Matilda?'

'*Ja*, I think it was so terrible. I must go.'

She canters off wildly.

I'm on my way to close the door when my phone buzzes. I'm hoping it's a reply from Emily but it isn't.

It's from my lawyer.

—11am Wednesday at my offices. Rabbi Menachem, you and me. Important! Will buy bagels! Don't be late.
Peter Dent

There's a smiley face too.

I Take On The Jews
3 May, 3:56 pm

Another surreal day, Olivia, for which I have my treacherous lawyer Peter Dent to blame.

I'm sure you'll remember Peter Dent. My faux-hippy roommate from university. The deadhead with whom I shared a dealer. The guy who knew every Robert Hunter and Jerry Garcia song by heart, and had four theories to explain each one of them, all of which were completely bonkers. The guy who tripped on LSD every weekend for a year and danced like a flailing electrified marionette and is today one of the most successful lawyers in London. That Peter Dent. Well, today, I had a meeting at his office. Me, him and the Jew.

What a place. Two entire floors of the rhomboid skyscraper that overhangs the Thames at Canary Wharf. From Dent's chrome-and-crystal office you can see both. Everything about it screams 'success'. Dent is my private lawyer because, weirdly, he refuses to let me go. There's no other explanation. I am Dent's only case unconnected to the City and this reinforces my belief that Dent does this as an amusement because he finds Jews funny and I'm the only Jew he knows.

I arrive optimistic, with high hopes that we'd finally nail the Semite legally and relieve me of my civic obligation to destroy him in one-to-one combat. I'd even texted Dent twice to let him know I was coming in early to discuss strategy. But as soon as I get there, I know that something's up.

He's waiting in reception with a guilty, lawyerly grin. 'Ah, my dear Old Chap. There you are, there you are. Come up, come up. They're here. They're here.'

'Who's "they"? The Jew? Who else?' I yell.

'"Plaintiffs" is a better word,' he says, quietly. 'Menachem

118

and his lawyer are here. In my office. I wanted them to come in early, you see.'

'Menachem's got a lawyer?'

'Yes. Hymie.'

'He's called Hymie? You're joking.'

'No, I'm not joking and, yes, his lawyer's called Hymie,' Dent says. 'Rather oddly, Hymie doesn't speak English. Only what I take to be Yiddish. Anyway I've been learning about Jewish death rituals from your rabbi friend. He's just told me—'

'He's not my rabbi and he's certainly not my friend!'

'Of course not, of course not! Silly me!'

I cannot get over the fact that Dent has been talking to the Jews without me.

'Wait a minute. You invited the Jews in early without me?'

Dent stops me with a powerful grip on my forearm and that ray-gun saintly stare ramped to the top. 'Now calm down, Old Chap. I know this is all rather emotional for you, for all sorts of reasons I don't understand, but that's why I'm here: to forge a rational route ahead. All you have to do is stay calm and trust me. And of course try not to insult anyone racially along the way or use expressions like—' his distaste is clear '—"the damned Jews". Okay?'

'Okay.'

'And let me do the talking: it's what you're paying me for.'

'Can't help feeling you should be paying me, what with all the entertainment you're getting.'

'Nonsense, David,' Dent laughs. 'What utter rot.'

WE ENTER DENT'S OFFICE AND THE JEWS ARE EMPHATI-cally there, black-coated, fiercely bearded and totally ignoring us because both are yelling into their phones. They spot us and use their free hands to tell us to wait, sit down, maybe have a cup of something if we want, and don't worry: they won't be long.

Eventually their conversations end.

'Peter!' exclaims Menachem 'Peter, Peter, Peter—I'm sorry, really. A problem came up with a *chasseneh*—a wedding—and the *kashrus* certificate and a million other things, and you can't ignore these things—they have to be done yesterday—but, thanks God, we got it sorted and it'll be a wonderful affair: actually it's Hymie's cousin, so *Kol HaKavod*—now I'm all yours! And a very good morning to you, David!'

I stare at him with lofty theatrical disgust, resolutely refusing to acknowledge his cheerful greeting. He finds this hilarious and turns to Dent. 'A man of few words!' he says, laughing. He translates what he's said to Hymie, and Hymie laughs. Then Dent laughs, until I scald him with a stare.

'Might I ask what language you and your counsel were talking in?' Dent enquires sycophantically.

'Yiddish.'

'Fascinating,' says Dent.

'Really?' I say, looking witheringly at him. 'Fascinating?'

Menachem grins and turns to me, delighted.

'Yes, fascinating. *Du reden Yiddish, Dovidl?* You speak Yiddish?'

I reply with a snort.

'Your father didn't teach you Yiddish?' He's amazed.

'Of course not.'

'Why of course? What, nothing? Not a word?'

'Crazy guy—my father doesn't speak Yiddish.'

Menachem laughs. Then he tells Hymie what I have just said and Hymie laughs. Then Dent joins in.

'What are you all laughing at?' I hiss.

'Nothing, nothing,' says Dent, chastened. 'Gentlemen, please sit down.'

This inspires another urgent conversation that makes me want to push either Jew or both of them out of the window. I mean, why does the simple instruction to sit down at a table necessitate a long discussion—in Yiddish—before sitting down at the sodding table? Isn't that why we're all here? What's wrong with these people, Olivia?

Eventually the Jews finish their lengthy discussion about sitting down at the table and sit down at the table.

'Right, Gentlemen,' says Dent in his deliciously suave way. 'Thank you all for coming. We all know why we're here —to thrash out the details of the agreement we made verbally to the satisfaction of all parties and—'

'You know something, *Dovidl*,' Menachem interrupts. 'Of course your father speaks Yiddish.' He's smirking.

'I think I'd know that, Mate, don't you?'

'I'm not so sure you would,' he says, triumphantly.

'What do you mean by that?' I demand.

'*Dovidl*, I'm sorry to be direct but when was the last time you visited your father?'

'None of your damn business!' I yell.

'Can we please start, Gentlemen!' Dent says firmly.

'Okay, okay, okay,' says Menachem.

'Did you even hear what he just said?' I ask Dent.

'The agreement that we made verbally—' Dent begins, but Menachem butts in again. 'Hang on, hang on, hang on.' He hands his phone to his lawyer who fusses with it and then hands it back.

It's a video. Menachem turns up the volume and puts it on the table facing me and Peter.

A tinny babble buzzes from the device.

I look closer. It's my father. He's singing. In a foreign language. It sounds very much like Yiddish.

'What's this, *Dovidl*?' Menachem asks, teasingly.

'Basque,' I say. 'Or Breton. Maybe Frisian? Votic?'

Menachem smiles. 'Mr Lawyer,' he says, 'please carry on.'

But of course I now can't stop myself. I seize the phone —and there he is: my stupid father, an idiot grin on his fat, totalitarian face, not just warbling away in Yiddish but wearing a big fat freaking yarmulke.

The two Jews across the table are lustily joining in with the warbling chorus.

> '*Ikh vel aykh, bashvern,*
> *Ir muzt mir dos oys'hern,*
> *Vayl ayer toyve lign dokh nor dorin ...*'

It's a catchy melody, if you like that kind of thing. Myself, I don't, but regrettably my lawyer does. He has started to thrum his fingers and hum along.

'What the fuck are you doing?'

'Nothing, nothing,' says Dent, embarrassed. 'Gentlemen, Gentlemen, please.'

121

The Jews stop warbling and Menachem triumphantly closes the video.

'A beautiful song,' he says. '*Dovidl*, your *Tateh*'s got a lovely voice.'

Dent notices my fingers gripping a heavy glass paperweight and forcefully removes it from my grasp. 'May I take that, David?' he says in a calm, lawyerly manner, and then continues, 'Thank you, Menachem. And may I suggest that whether Ben Britton knows Yiddish or has a lovely voice is not relevant—'

'—You mean, whether he can sing a little ditty that they probably groomed him into singing post-stroke.' I'm glaring at Menachem, who grins back at me.

Dent intervenes with surprising determination. 'Gentlemen, please! This meeting now needs discipline. Ben Britton's knowledge of Yiddish is immaterial. We are here to discuss the terms agreed verbally at the police station and in subsequent conversations with Menachem. I intend to review the conditions we agreed.'

'Okay, okay,' sighs Menachem, Jewishly. He translates to his companion, who sighs in return. Then they all look at me.

I grunt. 'I want this stupid matter dealt with,' I say poshly.

'That's why we're here,' says Menachem, translating for Hymie, who strokes his beard, nods thoughtfully and starts to rock.

Dent resumes in a loud voice. 'Okay: the first of the four conditional terms. *Tef-i-llin*?'

'*Tefillin!*' says Menachem.

'*Tefillin*,' recites Peter Dent.

'Perfect!' Menachem says, peering meaningfully at me. 'Not just because it is good for my friend here to lay *tefillin* but because it is good to do it at his father's bedside. Why? Because sometimes there are miracles.'

I turn to Peter and speak loudly. 'I haven't a clue what this nutcase is talking about. Can you organise a translator, or a spirit medium, or a social anthropologist or a witchdoctor with warthog tusks in his nose or whatever is required—'

'Please David,' Dent says in his exquisite City of London tones.

'You've never seen these?' Menachem interrupts. He's dragging a velvet bag out of his case.

'Of course I have,' I reply. 'They're called phylacteries. They're like Christmas bunting for medieval religious fruit-cakes. You wrap them around your arm. Or your head. Or whatever. So, are we done? Now can I get back to work?'

'You know,' says Menachem with a giggle, 'your father told me about you.'

'Really? Did he tell you I really need to be back at work?'

'He gave me a very beautiful message for you, but only to be delivered after his death—*may he live to be 120*. What is important to discuss now are the terms, as this very nice man, your solicitor, says—and the terms are stated in the document; and the first of those terms is for you to lay *tefillin* in the hospital next to your dear father, with all your family there, and me supervising, and that's all we need to say. Next point, Mr Lawyer.'

'Is he serious?' I turn on Dent, who is smiling nervously.

'Please David,' says Dent. 'Can we just get through the terms? Then we can discuss them. Right. Second point: fixing a … *moo-zoo-zoo*—?'

'*Mezuzah*,' says Menachem.

'*Mez-u-zah*!' cries Dent.

'That's right. You'll put up a *mezuzah*,' Menachem says and nods at Hymie, who pulls something about the size of a finger from his bag and waves it in the air. 'Fix this to your front door and then everyone in your street will know you're Jewish. *Dovidl*—for the first time in your life! What a joy!'

'Why would I want *anyone* in my street to know I'm Jewish? I sneer, as nastily as I can.

'To bring honour to your people. It's a privilege.'

'You guys are freaks,' I say. 'You need locking up.'

'Next, Point Three,' says Menachem: 'to have a proper *Shabbat* at home. With your wife, but if your daughter Moose and her not-so-smart boyfriend Masaai came too, that would be even nicer.'

I can't believe my ears, Olivia. How does he know about Moose? And Masaai?

I rise, fists balled.

123

Dent is panicking. 'David please—' he beseeches.

'How the fuck does he know I even have a daughter?'

'I don't know,' says Dent.

'And how does he know she's called Moose?

'I really don't know that either,' says Dent, reasonably.

'And how does he know her boyfriend's an idiot and that he's called Masaai?'

'I know, I know,' sings Menachem. 'That's all that matters. Now sit down, *Dovidl*: it's more comfortable. You called her Moose because you thought she wasn't so quick. Right? But she's the one with the heart, the one who calls your father. Every week—every week!—without fail.'

I turn to Dent, who looks hypnotised. 'Peter, this is intrusive. Have you been stalking us, you and Hymie here?'

Menachem finds this hilarious. He translates for Hymie and they both laugh. 'Why would I want to stalk you?'

'So how the fuck do you know about Moose and Masaai?'

'Your Dad told me.'

'My father?' That takes the wind out of my sails.

'Yes! I keep telling you, we're friends. Good friends.' Then he changes the subject and holds up three plump fingers. 'So, one, *tefillin*; two, *mezuzah*; and three, a *Shabbat* meal at your home with the whole family, as described.'

I slump back into my chair and watch Menachem unfurl a fourth finger. 'And finally—' he's sort of singing this, as if praying '—finally, and this is not easy to talk about but it is necessary to talk about, and that is why I am going to talk about it. Finally we have to discuss what happens when your dear father goes to his eternal rest.'

I'm holding my breath. Whatever he says, it's going to be unspeakably dreadful. 'Go on,' I say.

'*Kaddish*.' says the rabbi. 'You will say *kaddish* for your father when the time comes. I will teach you. And that's it.'

And before anyone can say a word, the Jews are gathering their things and heading purposefully for the door.

'Gentlemen, Gentlemen,' Dent pipes up, desperately. 'A cup of tea before you leave? Maybe a bagel? I picked up some very fine bagels on the way here. Kosher. With smoked salmon. The best.'

The Jews shake their heads, shake Dent's hands and shake themselves out of the door before either of us can say a word.

When they've gone, Dent takes a seat opposite me and we stare at each other for an uncomfortably long time.

'A bagel?' Dent asks, at last. 'With smoked salmon? I'll ring my assistant.'

'Please don't tell me you're going to let those fanatics get away with this?' I growl.

'Get away with what, David?'

'They're blackmailing me, Peter, or were you having such fun you didn't notice?'

'Blackmail is a very serious and specific charge,' Dent replies.

'Then how would you put it?'

'I would say they articulated what Menachem agreed at the police station after you racially assaulted him. But with a little more detail.'

'I barely touched him.'

'That's not what the police report says, David.'

'We're not going to agree to all that religious horseshit, are we?'

'It's entirely up to you, dear chap.'

'I'd rather go to prison than let him take his pound of flesh.'

'Going to prison is certainly an option, Old Pal, but I'm not sure it would be in your best interests.'

I extract my phone. 'You know what? I'm calling him now and I'm going to tell him where he can shove it. I'll go to prison. I don't care.'

'I really wouldn't do that if I were you.'

'Oh—and why not? Because you're having such a laugh?'

'No. Because I did some important research and discovered that your father has changed his will.'

'Because frankly I've had enough and—.'

I stop dead as the words sink in.

'What?'

'I called your father's lawyers,' Dent says. 'Menachem is now the executor of your father's will. It appears that he acts as executor on behalf of many poor Jews who die without wills, but also of rich Jews like Ben who, to quote Ben's lawyer, do not see much of their children.'

'*Fickungsfotzes.*'

'It gets worse.'

'It can get worse?'

'Much worse, dear chap. The bequests in the estate now depend on the terms set out in Menachem's document. If you don't comply, you'll come away with nothing. Except a term in chokey.'

There's a knock at the door. A young woman wheels in a tray of bagels.

'Ah, thank you Kristina,' says Peter, walking over to the tray. 'I said they looked good, didn't I, David?'

'Peter this is unbelievable.'

Peter elegantly wipes his mouth with a napkin.

'We're old friends. We've known each other since university. I like you very much; always have. But you're—' he hesitates '—impetuous. You always were, when we were students, and you still are, especially with your father—and, surprisingly, with this Judaism thing. But David, speaking purely as your lawyer, I need to impress upon you that impetuosity is not your strongest card. We have here a simple case with a simple, inexpensive solution. It will take up some time but it won't use up your money. Do what he says. It's not so bad. It could even be rather amusing, if you approach it in the right way. Because, frankly, Menachem has you by the balls. And I think you should be grateful he's asking for so little to release them. Now then, have a bagel: they're really rather nice.'

A Discovery In My Father's Bedroom
3 May, 9:36 pm

I spend today simmering and when my emotions finally reach boiling point, I jump into the car and drive like a lunatic to my father's flat.

I want proof. Proof that my damned father did not speak Yiddish. Proof that in his angry dotage he did not become a ghetto Jew. Proof that 'Rabbi' Menachem 'Katz' is a fraud, a blackmailer and a thief, and that his lawyer accomplice, the so-called 'Hymie', is a criminal retard.

I park in the almost-empty car park, pace through the security doors and emerge into that huge macabre reception area, set off with ornate mirrors and sprays of plastic flowers. It gives me the creeps. The place smells of cleaning fluid, toilets and death.

The Filipino nurse at the reception desk looks familiar. His badge identifies him as Stan.

'Good evening, Stan,' I say.

'Mr Britton.' he says.

'You remember me?'

'I 'member you.'

'Wow. I don't come often.'

'Maybe that why I 'member,' he laughs. 'You know your father in hospital, right?'

'I do.'

'How your Dad condition?' He looks genuinely sad.

'Not good. In a coma, without hope of recovery.'

'I hear that. So terrible. Especially for he so strong a man.'

'Stan, can I ask you a favour. I want to go to his flat. I'm looking for something he'll recognise, you know—something to take and show him.'

Stan says 'Sure,' and off we go down the long polished corridors. As we walk, I casually ask him if he knows Rabbi Menachem Katz.

'Menachem? Oh sure,' he says. 'Real live wire. Full beans. Come here often. Take the Shabbat service, sometime. Why you ask?'

'I met him recently. He says he knows my father well.'

'Oh sure. They big mates.'

'More than mates, actually. Apparently he's also executor of my father's will. I hadn't known that.'

Stan thinks about it for a while. 'I'm not know that but I'm not surprised. Menachem always here. He help our residents when they need help. And you know—' he hesitates, but decides to go on '—it's been a while since you been here.'

I tell Stan that Dad and I had had a row.

'I know.'

'He told you?'

'He tell everyone. Your father have loud voice. So, here his flat.'

As he's unlocking the door I ask: 'Long shot, this, Stan, but did you ever hear my father speak Yiddish?'

'I don't know, Mr Britton' he says. 'Some of the old ones do but not many, these days. Well: I leave you here. You lock up, please, and let me have key before you leave.'

'Sure. Thanks. But … can I ask you one more question? Did my father ever mention me?'

Stan turns to face him. 'Oh sure, Mr Britton!' He's choosing his words carefully. 'He so proud of you!'

The shockwave hits me like a bullet, Olivia.

'Really?'

'So proud. Always telling me about you being on TV.'

'He told you that?'

'He told everybody. Your dad have very loud voice.'

INSIDE, IT SMELLS OF HIM.

Of course he's bought the best flat that the Maurice Cohen Retirement Home for the Elderly can provide, '*Le grand appartement*', a name I'm quite sure my old man would have gobbled up. It's like a miniature mansion. Stunted columns, a preposterous chandelier, a lush, velvety entrance and the very best in hoists, handles, alarms, buttons, intercoms, screens, exercise devices and weights.

I close the door. The air's warm and still in the capacious, carpeted lounge, the heavy net curtains emitting a sepulchral haze as if the sky was wrapped behind a shroud. But it's creepy so I turn on the lights, then sit on the sofa, and smell him again.

The big new television. The other armchair—new, dark, expensive, silky of course. The great oak desk and the ornate brass reading light glowing emerald above it. Slippers peeking from under the Georgian oak desk, the fancy laptop unused on top. The big glass Victorian walnut cabinet, covering an entire wall. I remember that cabinet: He used to boast how much it cost, so he could watch me cringe, I think. He must have told me that a million and two times.

And what's that in the centre of the wall? Oh, the Tarzan shot of course: handsome, muscular Ben Britton emerging from the Cape sea. And arranged around that photo, in little crystal panels, a miniature museum telling the triumphant story of his life. Ben in sepia, a wide-eyed, unsmiling infant. Ben the scowling schoolboy with his boxing gloves on. Ben in the RAF, in Soho, in Bolivia distributing bags of corn. Ben towering over a bench of tiny bespectacled Mile End Trots. Ben's first property. Ben's second property. Ben's first block of flats. Ben's first factory. Ben in his bathers on Clifton Second Beach in South Africa. Ben with Dora. Ben with Krystina. Ben with Nadia. Ben with Bridget. Ben in Beijing, New York, Rio, Cape Town, Cannes, Moscow, L.A.

Really, the infantile vanity of the man! And you know, I'm about to laugh—when I spot it. An entire new shelf of photographs of you, me and Moose. And in the middle, a photograph I don't remember, that takes my breath away. Maybe you know it?

I'm about fifteen. Lanky, bored, black curls draping heavily across my face, my posture one of sullen rebellion. And the reason it takes my breath away? Because I remember the day, Olivia, as if it was yesterday. It was one of those Commie Weekend Specials I've told you about—you remember?—when the bullying bastard dragged me across the East End all weekend, from one turgid Commie landmark to another. Well, when this photo was taken, we were almost at the end of the day, the sniff of escape in the air. But unfortunately, I timed it catastrophically.

We were readying for the climax, you see: the very moment when Ben Britton would reveal to his only son the biggest Ben Britton story of all, bigger even than his fighting with the RAF in the skies.

His heroic Cable Street battle.

I know what's coming because I've heard the story a thousand times since I was two. I also know that my pedantic father's been leading up to this sugary moment all afternoon. So what do I do?

I yawn. Like a hippo. An open-mouth fuck you.

He punched me, you know that? I remember it so clearly, I can still feel it. The jolt. The pain. It knocked me to the ground, left me half-conscious and bleeding. And honestly, if Bridget hadn't been there' I'm pretty sure he'd have killed me.

But you know what this photo revealed, Olivia? It revealed that I'd won. I'd carried the day and nothing would be the same after that. It was the day my relationship with my father came to an end. From then on, I was free. I knew it. He knew it too.

Now I'm on my knees, in his bedroom, scrabbling under his bed. Nothing.

I get up and rifle through cupboards, through bags and cases in the closet, through the medicine chest in the bathroom. I go through his bookshelf, its yellowing parade of Marxist dross, flipping the pages for hidden letters. Nothing.

And then, out of the corner of my eye, I spot it.

Under the armchair. A small, dark bag.

I know what it is even before I pull it out. The deep purple velvet has ornate Hebrew letters sewn into the fabric and, as I unzip it, I can feel the weight of its contents.

Tefillin. Fucking tefillin.

And then something weird happens. I suddenly remember what's been bugging me for the last few days, ever since my surreal encounter with the Jews in Dent's office. It's a lost memory—and it drops, like a sudden stone, leaving me breathless once again.

It's the puzzle of my father's accent, terrifyingly resolved.

He talked like the rabbi. My father talked like Menachem Katz.

I Get To Know Emily
4 May, 11:36 pm

I love Natalie, Olivia. I love her for the same reason that everyone loves her. I love her because she's perfect.

In she comes today, with her signature cartoon-rhythm knock on my door and the crooning 'Hellooo' as she trips in on her red six-inchers and a wave of exquisite scent. And even when she says 'I'm afraid I've got bad news, Darling'—our code for an unexpected meeting with Angela—'three o'clock next Monday with Angie and you have to be there!', it still does not affect my love for her. Which is entirely pure, I might add.

She's shaking an impeccably manicured finger at me, blue eyes shining amid a halo of seraphic hair, and teeth and goodness.

'You can't be late for this one!' she scolds. I howl loudly. 'The Hungry Dog chaps are coming in. Okay?'

I cry 'Not Okay' a few times, then suggest that we run away, pointing out there's only thirty years between us, which is nothing in Earth time, and that she can trust me because I'm a failed chat-show celeb with a history of feckless but always entertaining behaviour. I then give her several socio-economic reasons why we have the perfect age difference and suggest we go to a desert island and have twelve babies pronto.

She's delightfully unleashed with laughter.

'And don't be late!'

And off she goes, clickety-click up the stairs, spreading sunshine. But of course this brief sojourn into utopian Natalieland does not last long because, just outside the door, Fate's got his Surrealist hat on and wants to call me in for another round of Texas Hold'em. Stay with me, because you will not believe what follows Natalie's fragrant departure.

A quiet knock at the door. I yell, *Come in.*

It's Emily.

'It's only me,' she whispers

I'm so overjoyed to see her, I start yelping. 'Emily! Come in! Wow! This is so great. Sit down, sit down.' I elaborately present the Hollywood Chair and when she's seated I ask her a few times if she's comfortable and whether she got my text, just in case she's come round for reasons of her own.

'Yeah. Madden went out so I thought I'd drop by.'

'Madden's welcome too,' I growl.

'To be honest, he doesn't like you.'

I tell her that surprises me and that I'm sorry to hear it, and she laughs.

'Actually a lot of people around here don't like you,' she says and, to my delight, looks a little surprised.

'So I've heard. But I'm really glad you've come. I want to sort things out between us, you know?'

'I know. So how did you meet Lance Schlewin?'

I'm so stunned, I actually have to sit down. Olivia, I'll wager the house that you don't remember Lance Schlewin, right? Nor does anyone else. Even I struggle to remember him. And who was Lance Schlewin? None other than the hero of my first big doco, *Love Killing*. And here's little-big beautiful Emily asking about him.

I ask her if she's actually watched the film.

'Three times! I watched it again last night,' she says. 'I love prison docs. Madden thought it was shit but I thought it was great. So how'd you meet Lance?'

'Well, I was in America making a dull film on judges and I met him in a bar, and that's the truth. Then he put me in touch with Al: you remember Al?'

'Oh yeah!'

'And so it went on until I got to meet them all.'

'Wow! I liked Al.'

'Hey! You and me both. You know, I think you must be the only other person on Earth who remembers that film.'

'You know that Tony Rivero?'

'One-armed Tony, the angry D.A.?' I growl in a bad Tennessee accent.

'Yeah,' she laughs. 'Was he in love with Ruby?'

'You know, I think so. I thought so then. But what you don't know, 'cos I couldn't put it in, was that he *was* having the affair.'

'With Al's daughter?'

'Yes! And that's why it all kicked off.'

I tell her she's remarkably perceptive, because she is. She beams.

'I like prison docos,' she says. 'You know, my dad's inside.'

I tell her I'm sorry to hear it. 'For how long?'

'Oh, life. Murder.'

'Oh dear! That's tough Emily. Do you see him?'

'Her. She transed.'

'Oh. So it's a sort of family thing?'

'I guess.' She laughs, beautifully.

'Do you see her often?'

'Never. I've never seen my dad. Or "other mom", I should call her, I guess,' she says.

'I'm sorry,' I tell her.

'I'm not. She's nasty. So why did you make films about prison?'

'I dunno.'

'You gay?'

'No, it just sort of landed in my lap. And the subject sort of interested me. And there seemed to be a market for it.'

After a short silence Emily says. 'Can I trust you?'

'I hope.'

'I'm booked.'

'Sorry?'

'For the op.'

She looks at me, Olivia, large eyes burning against the white skin. She lets the tears run down her face in vivid mascara streams.

'You okay?' I take her hand. It's freezing.

'I'm scared.'

'Are you sure you want it?'

A slight pause. Then: 'Don't have a choice.'

'You have a choice.'

'I don't. I'm a warrior,' she says in a tiny voice. 'I'm invested in it.'

I'm about to ask what the fuck that means when the door swings open. It's Madden: small, angry, flushed, spoiling for a fight.

'Next time, knock,' I tell him.

He ignores me. 'You okay?' He says it like a threat. I notice Emily's wilting.

'I guess,' she says.

'I said I'd appreciate it if you knocked next time!' I declare in my 'angry BBC' voice.

He ignores me. 'You've been crying!' Then he looks me in the eye, tiny gangster-style. 'You've made her cry!'

I tell him to fuck off and ask Emily if she's okay, but she's already disappearing out of the door.

'Yeah. Bye,' she whispers.

Madden's standing his ground, the impudent little shit. Glaring at me. 'Piss off, Madden or I'll throw you out!'

And then get this: the little snake shakes his pink, spikey head, retrieves his phone, clicks off the record button, clenches his little fist and leaves with a grin that even the director of *The Omen* would have found excessive.

I'm reeling back in the Hollywood Chair, wondering if Ronny the Runner knows anyone who might kill Madden slowly, when I am enveloped in Emily's scent—and I get it, the tragedy I've been handed.

A poor, sweet-natured boy-girl called Emily is having her penis chopped off for reasons that may be more political than personal.

I really don't want any of this shit in my life, Olivia. But can you see now how it follows me? How I have no choice? How my Dark Angel seeks me out for special cruelty? It fills me with rage, exhaustion and dread, but I have no choice, I have to fight for her.

Why? I guess because, amid the anger, shame and grief of the Emily melodrama, I see our daughter, clear as day, and almost as screwed up. The daughter who, I suddenly remember with a shiver of anxious delight, will be arriving in London with her idiot boyfriend in a few hours.

Well, I want a world where good people will protect her too, Olivia, if she needs it. That's why I need to protect Emily.

135

Moose And Masaai Arrive
6 May, 12:36 pm

You've cleaned and dusted, changed the sheets and towels, and swept, vacuumed and polished every corner of every room, cupboard, nook and cranny. You've made the bean stew and the crème brûlée that Moose has loved since childhood, and now, after a day of unrelenting labour, you're wandering around our bedroom discarding shoes and bits of underwear, to make it look like you hadn't left me. And it's driving me crazy.

'Won't work,' I say from the door.

You wheel round. 'Got a better idea?'

'Yes. My idea is that you come home for good.'

'And why isn't that going to happen, David?' You're drilling me with that stare, hands on your hips, eyes blazing. 'Go on. Remind me why I'm no longer sharing your bed. You want a clue? Okay. Janice Toybeen. Get it yet?'

I get it, Olivia, but there's no chance to tell you so, because you're on a roll. 'And in case you haven't noticed, I'm doing this unpleasant charade for our daughter, because if we cock it up tonight, David, if we cock it up—.' You're sobbing now, and it breaks my heart, Olivia. 'If we cock it up, our beautiful girl will be lost forever.'

All I can do is collapse over-dramatically on the big soft chair and sigh loudly in solidarity.

'Now listen to me, David. Please! Tonight I need some space to talk to her alone okay. A brief moment when that moron doesn't have his tongue in her mouth.'

'I saw it fully extended once—' I start to say, because I did and it was frightening.

'Shut up! Be serious! I need to know she's okay. *We* need to know she's okay!'

'I know that, Olivia.'

'So give me some time. Look after Masaai while I have a

good talk with her. We haven't much time because they're leaving right after dinner to visit Ben in hospital, and then that collective—'

'The Hackney Black Zion Roots Consciousness Collective,' I say, accurately.

She knows what's coming. More rightwing fascist crap, as my daughter would say.

'Stop it! Just stop it! I know he's an idiot, David—a stupid white boy who thinks he's black—and I don't need further proof of this—'

'Okay, okay.'

'—but I do need our daughter to fall out of love with him, and only she can do that. Believe me, I understand such things. So just behave tonight. Please!'

You breathe the word so soulfully, and you look so beautiful that I wish I could pounce on you. 'Okay,' I manage to say.

'That's all I'm asking, David. Just don't be a prick. Not tonight. Okay?'

'I am a prick. This is my existential condition.'

'I know, but I also know you can pretend not to be a prick when you need to. Make a proper adult effort tonight, alright? You can chat to Masaai politely for thirty minutes without screwing it up.'

'Thirty minutes alone with that moron?' I gasp.

You don't smile back.

'Be calm, David. Nice. Relaxed. Amiably indifferent. And not obsessed about his racial confusion. After all, who cares? All we want is for them to break up.'

'I don't want us to break up.'

'We've already broken up. We're finished.'

And before I can say a word, you've grabbed the keys and headed off to pick up Moose from the airport.

No, Olivia. We are not 'finished'.

This, I promise.

I HEAR THE CAR TURN INTO THE GRAVEL DRIVE, SEE THE headlights sweep like sirens across the walls and my heart starts to gallop.

She's home! Moose is home!

She barges in first, of course, enveloped in a storm of luggage, bags, gifts, scarves, shrieks, tears, hugs, kisses and sobs and melts into my arms. I can feel her heartbeat through her hug, her fragrant hair and her angel embrace, and it fills me with a delirious joy that makes me want to scream: Moose still loves me!

This is what I'm thinking when Masaai shambles in, hunched and hairy, fuzzy head encased in enormous headphones that look like sneakers.

I see your urgent look. Time to look after Masaai.

'Hey, Masaai!' I coo and stride off in his direction with a cartoon posh-boy grin and a ludicrous outstretched hand. 'You're looking good! Welcome to London, My Man—can I call you that? It's been too long!' And all the time I'm saying this, I'm watching you shrinking at the doorway. I think you're telling me that whatever schtick I'm trying to sell him, it ain't working.

But Masaai loves it. 'Hey,' he says, boxing my handshake. 'Cool space, cool space. How y'all hangin'?'

Then he tells me I remind him of Basil Fawlty, and donkey laughs to prove it, and he's off, sniffing around.

I follow him into the living room where he's sizing up the bookcase and sort of grunting. The sneaker-headphones are buzzing loudly.

'Thing is, this is quite a white area,' I say loudly.

Masaai turns and, after a pause, takes off his headphones.

'What you say, Man?'

'This area. Where we live. It's quite white. Very worrying. Wish it was more black. Like—more real, you know?' I shake my head mournfully.

'I get it, Man. I was looking out for brothers on the streets—right?—as we was driving here but there wasn't much going on.'

'I know, I know,' I say, and tell him I feel a little ashamed. Here I am, braying like an Islington liberal to please a certifiable moron, and then I hear myself exclaim, 'But one more brother is here tonight, and that's fantastic!'

Masaai's looking confused, so I set about helping him.

'Your DNA test. I heard about your DNA test! That you're officially Black. Congratulations!'

'Yeah, Man.'

'What a fantastic result,' I say. 'So, err, how black were you? What did the tests show?'

'Whoaaa, Dude!' he says, collapsing into the large sofa. 'That's kinda personal shit, you get me?'

'But it's marvellous!' I continue, with a crazed determination that frankly puzzles me too: 'to have science signal who you really are. It must be like finding your soul.'

Happily the expression 'finding your soul' brightens Masaai visibly.

'Yeah, Man. You know, that's kinda what it was. I like that. Finding my soul.'

'Of course, of course,' I purr and for some reason decide to lie. 'I had my genome thing done, you know and found I was a fifth Scandinavian. And it's really weird—you know? —'cos I've always had thing about Viking culture.'

'No way!' says Masaai. He's on the edge of the chair.

'Like, whenever I see a longboat, or an axe, or a herring or even a big wild blonde beard—honestly it's as weird as that—I get this inner feeling. It's a very precious thing: probably too hard to communicate.'

'No, Man, I'm getting you!'

'So, what would you like, Masaai? A beer? A whisky? Something with coconut in it?'

'Viking!' Masaai giggles to himself. 'That's tight! Yeah, Man, a beer'd be cool.'

You and Amelia have disappeared into a bedroom. I get the beers and settle back into the armchair.

'So, according to the test, how, uh, how black were you? Between ourselves. We're family: we should talk openly.'

'Twenty-one percent,' he says proudly. 'They said that made me a statistical abnormality. How 'bout that!'

'Fantastic!' I cry. 'And the name "Masaai"?'

'Yeah, so listen up. My gene was traced to West Africa. That makes me one of the Igbo people. Masaai is a popular Igbo name among the priestly castes.'

'So you're an Igbo Jew?'

'You got it,' he chortles, 'but, Man I don't do, like, shit that divides me from other brothers. We black people, Man, we're all equal, ain't that right!'

He throws out a weird fist.

'And that's where we're at—you get me?—me and Moose. We wanna do some good in this world, yeah? for our people: not only Igbos but all black people, yeah? And white people too, you know, because their liberation depends on ours. It's kinda a triangle that kinda intersects, you know what I'm sayin'?'

'I know what you're saying, Masaai. Oh, I've been waiting for someone to come into our family and say stuff like this. It expands who we are, right? So has Moose become Igbo?'

He looks puzzled. 'Moose? No. Not, like, officially.'

Masaai's taken off the sneaker headphones and is about to say something confidential when Olivia and Amelia walk back into the room. Amelia's saying 'yeah, right' in that way that signals the small chat idea hasn't worked.

'David, where are my bedside books?' You sound shrill.

'What?'

'My bedside books. Our bedside books. Have you taken them anywhere?'

'Yes, yes of course,' I say, instantly realising that Moose, once again, has rumbled us. 'I took them back to the library, Darling,' I say. 'Sorry: I thought you'd finished them.'

I feel proud of my swift response, and it amuses The Idiot, who honks, but looking back, I realise it was ludicrous.

'"Library"? "Darling"? Euwww! I'm not stupid guys. Okay?'

'We know that!' we say together.

'And we have an excellent library,' you add, heading for the kitchen. 'Anyway, I better get supper together.'

As you leave, Moose is putting on the traumatised child face we both know and fear. But this time Masaai's there to cauterise all anguish by thrusting his tongue deeply into our daughter's mouth. To be honest, Olivia, the distraction is useful.

I flee to the kitchen. You're there.

I love that moment, pressed against the wall, you and me

together, holding our breath and listening, first joyfully as our daughter and The Idiot start a tiny row but less cheerfully as they resolve it by joyously exchanging fluids on the sofa.

We're in this together, Olivia.

Moose Is No Longer Moose
6 May, 10:38 pm

I spend the meal watching you watching Moose and Masaai. Observing how you flinch when, instead of tucking into her all-time favourite tarragon bean and tofu sesame bake, Moose gets up and makes herself an ongoing avocado and Bovril sandwich with a half pack of pastrami and a plate of raw onion fisted on the top. Raw onion, for God's sake, which she used to hate with a passion. I glimpse your near collapse when you witness Masaai tearing through several trough-loads of the bake—his own helpings and Moose's—signalling his approval with loud burps and two double fists across the table.

As usual I am rendered mute by Moose's gorgeous proximity at the table and it is at this moment of weakness that I make the rookie mistake of telling her she looks beautiful, because she does.

'I know—I'm fat, okay! No need to bang on about it.'

'I didn't,' I say.

'You're not!' says Olivia.

And suddenly, from nowhere: 'And I don't want to be called Moose any more.'

She glares at us, to signal that she really, really means it. 'I'm not a kid.'

'Of course you're not!' we chant.

'Fat is cultural, Baby,' Masaai croons, eyes only for Moose. 'The elders are right. You look fantastic. My beautiful Igbo girl. Sexyyyy!' When he starts pinching her nose and puckering those stupid lips, with his giant tongue about to emerge, I see you instinctively reaching for the knife.

'Sorry, what's the Igbo angle?' I say hurriedly.

Masaai looks at me, surprised I'm still there.

'Oh. Our people like their women big,' he says. 'Not scrawny.'

'Honey, you look gorgeous,' you tell our daughter 'and I mean it. But I don't get why you don't want the bean dish. It used to be your favourite. What's with the avocado and Bovril? And onion?'

'Can you just drop it?' Moose cries. 'Enough colonisation. I eat what I eat, okay?'

And then, just as we're wondering how to deconstruct this ideological car crash of foodie rejection, Masaai chips in with a paradigm-changing observation. 'She threw up this morning. And yesterday. Gotta eat what the body tellin' you, Man.'

I look across the table. Your eyes are like saucers.

I panic and resort to the old gag about Dad liking whatever garbage food Moose liked. 'Avo and Bovril! Sounds delicious,' I hear myself saying, and thank God that there is a reluctant flicker of a smile from our daughter, enabling us to segue smoothly into less troublesome waters.

'Actually, Mom, you've given me an idea,' she says, brightening up. 'Parental signalling as integral to the decolonisation paradigm. That could be my Fall project.'

Is that what she said? Who knows? Who cares?—because whatever it was, it has you and me beaming. Let's face it, our daughter's never more loveable than when she's using those big university words. Almost worth the 100 grand a year my old man is paying to her little Californian college.

Right on cue, Masaai enters the fray with a big donkey laugh. 'Derriiiidddaaa! White guys talking about Black guyssss!'

And out comes about a quarter of the feared tongue. 'Derrida is God' Moose shoots back, and pulls her own tongue out. At which point, you and I exchange a glance of terror occasioned by the terrifying prospect of Masaai unleashing the full lingual package but, once again, he pulls a blinder and sticks out only the very pink tip, which he waggles at an astonishing speed.

You flee for the desserts.

'So where are you Wonder-Kids going tonight, after the visit to the hospital?' I ask loudly.

Masaai withdraws his tongue from our daughter. He looks surprised to see me there.

'The Hackney Igbo Black Zion Collective.'

Irresistible. Sorry.

'Is that, like, a movement, or a college, or a band, or maybe an ashram?'

'You know, Man, I don't really know,' Masaai chortles. 'I found it online, yeah? I explained my situation and they seemed to get it.'

'Your situation?'

'That I'm a black man who's only just discovered he's a black man. And the dude there said they do race re-orientation and reclamation, and not just that—and this is really cool—but his wife is also an Igbo.'

'As a film-maker I'm interested in human journeys,' I say in a studio-couch way. 'And you, Masaai, are on a human journey. This is what life is all about.'

Human journey. Masaai loves it. I've got him eating out of my hands, and I decide to keep him there. 'Tell me more.'

'I was always *black*,' he tells me. 'You know? Even as a kid. Literally *black*.'

Our daughter nods reverentially and fists more onion onto her plate. 'He's been *black* ever since I knew him,' she says. 'I mean, I thought he was *black* the very first time I saw him. I mean, like, *black* black.'

'I am *black* black,' says Masaai testily.

'That's what I'm saying,' says Moose defensively. 'I mean, like, not *white* black. I mean like *black* black—*black* black black.'

'I am *black* black black.'

'Yeah, I know, but you're *black* black black from a *white* black black background,' she says frantically.

I intervene to save her. 'But you were raised white, Masaai?'

'I was,' he says, nodding thoughtfully. 'Very white. *White* white. Very *white* white.'

'Very white, like Jewish middle-class white?' I suggest.

'Worse, Man. The whole whitemare. I'm not even gonna lie. It was difficult and, like, kinda alienating, you get me? Because I was like *black* black black.'

'Alienation is shit,' says Amelia, disappearing into the kitchen.

Masaai's got his head in his hand, probably to show he's thinking hard. 'There was always, like, something kinda wrong with me,' he finally says.

I tell him I'm sure there was.

'An' I never kinda knew what it was but, you know what the funny thing was?' I confess to not knowing. 'I had this poster, yeah, of a black man. Against the sun. It was a Nike advert. On my bedroom wall. But he was the first person I saw in the morning and the last person I saw at night. And I used to talk to him. Every day.' He pauses to stare enigmatically at me. 'Can't be a coincidence.'

I tell him I guess not. 'But when did you actually take the plunge and become black in your brain?'

'It's a whole process, Man,' he says meaningfully and starts nodding and swaying, to show just how meaningful.

'A very long process,' says Moose brightly, returning from the kitchen with a jar of capers and a spoon. She's so beautiful I can't stop gaping. 'What are you looking at?'

'Nothing, nothing,' I say, turning again to the still-nodding-and-swaying Masaai. 'But was there something specific that made you know, with absolute certainty, that you were black?'

I'm leaning in, sultry studio smile on full. Me: The Interviewer. This: A BBC Special. He: Putty in my hands. I can feel it.

'It was everything, Man,' he says. 'Everything.'

'Absolutely everything,' Moose agrees. She's got a large pickle in her mouth and I can't stop staring at it. 'Why are you staring?' she demands.

I transfer my gaze back to the nodding and swaying Masaai. 'So what does "everything" mean?' Can I keep him going?

'The music, the food, the dance … Man, it was everything. I came home, Bro.'

At this point Moose crashes down on his lap and giggles when he grabs her nose and starts to suck it.

'And your family?' I ask loudly.

He's surprised to find me still there and withdraws suction. 'Don't talk about them no more.'

'I don't either,' says Moose.

'But surely, genetically, they're also black?'

Masaai and Moose guffaw and shake their heads and say 'No, Man' over and over again.

'They're, like, totally *white*,' says Moose. 'I mean, like *white* white.'

'No, they're *white* white white,' corrects Masaai.

'That's very white,' I say, to rescue Moose, and I'm about to return to the tricky subject of sub-categories of white when I notice you skewering me while carrying a tray with the fancy desserts you'd been working on all day.

'Crème brûlée!'

And they are as brilliant as ever, Olivia, creamy and delicious, the brown sugar burned to perfection.

After Masaai has demolished his third portion, he scrapes the bowl with a long boney forefinger which he then triumphantly sucks, but you miss this show because your attention is of course entirely focused on our daughter's refusal to have even a tiny taste of her favourite dessert.

I know what you're thinking, so I quickly change the subject. Catastrophically.

'So you're going to see Grandad this evening?' I say.

And of course Moose starts wailing.

'Grandad! Poor Grandad!'

As you know, I've never got it, this relationship between Moose and my father. I knew it was weird from the moment she was born. Every single thing she did, from crapping to sleeping, filled the old man with a wonder that made me think he was going senile. I still can't believe it. The old bastard still never misses a birthday! I mean, even when she was in her most unpleasant adolescent stage and we were history, there was still room in her life for my father. They'd talk for hours, quiet conspiratorial chats, mainly, about you and me, with sudden bursts of freakish hilarity.

In his eyes, she can never do wrong, which I guess is why he bought us our house and why to this day he finances Moose's horseshit degree. Radical Street Theatre Studies! And he does it cheerfully!

Moose is still howling and it's starting to get on my

nerves. 'Grandpa's not in pain, Darling,' I tell her. I glimpse across the table at you but you're texting. Again.

'I know … but … it's … so … so … sad,' our daughter wails.

And once again it's Masaai to the rescue, enveloping her in a ursine hug.

Who are you texting, Olivia? Third time in one meal. And always with that ghost of a smile.

Suddenly, pandemonium. Moose is up and dragging Masaai to the door.

'We gotta go!' she cries. 'I gotta see Grandad before it's too late!'

'He's in a coma, Darling,' I say.

'You've told me,' she snaps.

'So he won't be able to respond to you.'

'I know what a coma is, Dad. I'm not stupid.'

'We know that, Darling!' we exclaim together.

'She knows what a coma is,' adds Masaai. 'We were like googling it. Heavy.'

And then, do you remember? She suddenly turns from Masaai and looks at me with those Moose eyes? 'Why do you hate Grandpa so much?'

'I don't hate him, Darling,' I protest lamely.

'You stopped visiting him. He told me.'

'Well, yes, I did. That sort of thing happens.'

Evidently this is the worst thing I could have said, because she's up again and dragging Masaai. 'Masaai we gotta go now! He's reaching out. I can feel it!'

There's a vortex of activity, a scrambling of bags, tablets, cases, rucksacks and jackets and, after a quick assembly line of frantic hugs and kisses at the door, they're out the door and off to catch their Uber.

You and I are left alone in the blissful, echoing silence. We stagger into the living room, flop into the big chairs, say 'bloody hell' a few times and then sit there, silent.

It's enchanting, Olivia, and I'm drinking in your hypnotic proximity, wondering how to make this moment never end but equally frantic to discover the recipient of your texts when, as if reading my mind, you look at me, almost with pity, and say, 'I think I'm seeing someone, David.'

147

Col. Boaz Shahak
7 May, 3:48 am

I think I'm seeing someone.

'What the heck does that mean?' I reasonably ask.

'Wish I'd never said anything,' you reply.

'You mean, like, sort of going steady—'

'Oh, grow up.'

'—but he hasn't given you the nose ring—'

'Oh, piss off.'

'—or maybe you're not sure if it was a dream, that you kinda imagined, or a sort of adolescent fantasy—'

'It isn't a dream, David,' you say firmly.

'—so you kind of kissed, but without tonguing?'

'You're pathetic, you know that?'

I know that; boy, do I know that. 'Please explain. I'm begging you!'

And when you stop and say 'okay then', my heart dies a little and I sit down and await the worst.

'When I was in Israel I visited Ivan's charity' (bloody Ivan, I think: I should have killed him when I had the chance) 'and they do incredible work there with the blind—'

The *Fickenfotze* blind again.

'That's great for Ivan,' I say. 'So, who are you seeing?'

'Ivan's nephew. He helps at the charity.'

'What's his name?'

'Does it matter?'

'Yes it does!'

'Boaz.'

Boaz. Even the name's terrifying. Biblical. Heroic. Horrific.

'So Ivan got Boaz a job there?' I splutter. 'Is he special needs?'

This prompts a snort. 'He's an ophthalmologist. A professor at Tel Aviv University.'

I'm injured but plough on, because I just can't stop. 'Did you fuck?'

You're looking down at me, shaking your head so the curls bounce. Radiant. Imperious. 'No, as it happens, we didn't. But since you stuck your withered penis into Janice Toybeen's toxic hand—'

'There was no contact,' I reasonably point out for the somethingth time.

'Oh, you're ridiculous! Look, David, whatever you did with Janice Toybeen's toxic little hand, the rules have changed. From that moment, what I do with my own body is none of your business.'

'So what did you do together?'

'I'll tell you because I have nothing to hide David. We did not have sex. We did spend time together, mostly at the charity, and one afternoon he showed me Israel by helicopter. He was piloting.'

There are so many blows in that sentence, I'm reeling. You see it too and look sorry for me, which is worse than ten kicks in the balls.

'I need a pee, David, and then I'm leaving.'

I'm left alone, assailed by the image of you, naked with Boaz, who's just finished saving the sight of millions of blind Africans and is now gifting you multiple orgasms in the helicopter while hovering over the combined crushed armies of millions of cheering Arabs all singing his name.

'What will your lefty friends think?' I say meanly when you return.

And you lean forward in a 'fuck you' way, more Marlene than Marlene, to deliver the blow. 'To be honest, David, I wish we had made love. In fact, looking back, a blowjob in the helicopter would have been fun.'

Blowjob is bad enough, but 'made love' just tears me apart.

You expertly resume your packing and then, with a bit of pity, perhaps for yourself, you say: 'He's married, so nothing's going to happen.'

My heart sings!

But you haven't finished. 'But we connect professionally

149

and he's coming to London next month. And, yes, I like him.'

'Well why don't we all hook up?' I say. 'You, me, Herr General Boaz, Amelia, Masaai?'

Another pathetic miss.

'I'm leaving.'

'Olivia sit down!' I cry. 'Please. You can't go now! What if Moose comes home later and finds you gone?'

You've evidently already given your answer some thought. 'You know what David? The deception is tiresome. Amelia's an adult. She's seen right through it. And maybe she's right. Maybe we have been breaking up since she was two. So you choose. Maybe something about Janice Toybeen's little arthritic hand?'

And you're off.

I listen as you leave. The rumble of your car disappears into the night and as soon as I'm able to breathe properly I lurch to my computer and google *Boaz ophthalmologist Tel Aviv* and in no time there's the motherfucker himself.

Prof. Col. Boaz Tzahak.

Tanned, lithe, with a mouthful of white shining teeth.

The Plan
8 May, 11:35 am

Olivia, I hate young people. All of them.

Let me explain. Today was one of those HUGE meetings that have to be attended from time to time. Blessed Natalie reminds me three times in the space of an hour not to miss it and not be late, before adding that Angela's really, really, *really* in a strop this morning because she'd just heard that she's dropped out of the Top 500 Influencer League and apparently it's something to do with me.

'Darling, this is really, really, *really* serious,' Natalie says in the sweetest, kindest way. She sounds like she's going to cry.

'It's going to be fine, Sweetheart. I promise,' I say in reply.

And I'm thinking that it will be, Olivia. Because last night, in the early hours, I wrote a plan for how I, David Britton, can survive this Mee!Zee! business. I call it *The Plan*. It's a roadmap showing me how to walk away with dignity and moolah.

The thing is, if I don't leave the company soon, I will die, Olivia. Not fade out in some poetic, metaphorical, can't-get-his-cock-up sort of way but die in the writhe-around-in-agony, stop-breathing-and-start-to-stink-because-it-would-take-days-for-anyone-to-find-me sort of way. Cancer of the brain, I'm guessing. (Actually I have been getting these weird head pains lately, but more of that another time.)

So strategically, it's quite simple: what I need is to focus on selling the business and to avoid Angela and anyone under the age of thirty. That means concentrating on three directives:

1. Befriend Angela and Matilda. Be polite, whatever the provocation. Thank them. Praise them. Win their confidence.

151

2. Apologise for everything and anything I have done in the past and be *especially* sensitive to Angela's social-media ratings, whatever they are.
3. Finish that crappy BBC film and never have anything to do with the BBC again.

THE DAY STARTS PROMISINGLY. I'M TEN MINUTES EARLY (part of *The Plan*) and standing outside the Kiddy Boardroom, and inside I can hear the buzz of angry female voices. I take a deep breath and enter the room in a jolly way that I'm hoping will ameliorate Angela's distress at her ratings thingie and lighten her mood, but as soon as I enter, I realise I have underestimated the depth of teenie rage and loathing.

'Good morning,' I chirp unconvincingly.

Matilda and Angela are frozen and enraged.

Matilda utters a cool '*Guten Morgen*, David'.

Angela snorts.

I remember *The Plan* and do not snort back. 'Morning Angela, and how are you on this fine day?'

Nothing.

'*Ja, zere* is no rain in the forecast,' Matilda confirms.

Angela's shaking her head contemptuously.

'Look Angela, I need to say something,' I say in my Patrician Presenter's Last Programme Announcement After Serious Illness Diagnosis voice. My hands are spread, contrite, and I continue with my delicate little studio bow, and say: 'I'm sorry if I've annoyed you recently. And historically. Really. I'm aware that I've annoyed you for years and I deeply regret it.'

'Ever since I met you, Mate. And everyone else too.'

'*Ja*, David, it is true,' says Matilda. 'You annoy a lot of people.'

'So there you go,' I say gracefully. 'Well, I'm sorry, I really am. I know I'm not everybody's cup of tea. But we are where we are. So what I think we should do is move on positively and I will support anything you and Matilda decide to do.'

Matilda looks surprised, in a German way. 'David, *zat* is very nice. Thank you! *Zis* makes a welcome change.'

Then I turn conspicuously to Angela. 'To that end, I will finish my uplifting documentary about prison creativity among brilliant, buzzing, white men who pretend to be black men and as soon as it's completed I shall no longer come in, but leave you and Matilda, who does a smashing job, to manage the company to completion of the sale to Hungry Dog.'

Angela's looking at me in a stroke sort of way. 'Fuck me,' she eventually says.

'*Ja, und* fuck also me,' says Matilda.

'And then we can part ways, hopefully in a friendly fashion. But there is one thing we need to discuss.'

And I was doing so well.

You see, Olivia, the weird thing is that I wasn't going to do this. In fact, this was the one thing I wasn't going to do. But the word just leaps out of my mouth, and that's the truth.

'Emily,' I hear myself say.

Angela groans extravagantly. 'Here we go!'

'It's very serious,' I say 'and I just want you to be aware of it.'

Angela's staring like a cobra about to strike. 'Yeah, I know it's serious, Mate: believe me, I fucking know it—'

'*Ja*, mate,' says Matilda. 'Is definitely now serious.'

'—because you attacked Emily and made her cry in a dark locked room. Genius! As if you haven't done enough damage to her.'

'What? Who said that? That's the opposite of what happened, actually!'

'Madden says you made her cry.'

'Because Madden is a controlling little shit who wants to chop her damn cock off. That's why she was crying.'

'And he's off.'

'And her balls.'

'Blah cock blah. Blah balls blah. Will you just bottle it for once?' Angela's shrieking makes me feel strangely proud.

'*Ja*, David, we know what you think of *ze* cock of Emily,' says Matilda. 'and *ze* balls, but *zis ist kein* company matter. *Naja?*'

I can't let this go.

'So let me pin down my concerns precisely, because I don't think either of you do actually understand.' They're shaking their asinine heads but I plough on. 'In a nutshell, my fear is that Madden is encouraging Emily to have genital surgery for political purposes and that she is too weak and vulnerable to resist.'

'Her choice, Mate,' snorts Angela.

'*Ja*, Emily *ist eine* adult woman.'

'She's easily led though. You know that!'

'She's a tranny, for fuck's sake!' Angela has that mad look, the one when her eyes try to pop out of her head. 'Fuck you, David! Who are you to judge? That's what trannies do! They're always lopping things off or sticking things on. Stop being so interventionist and judgmental. She doesn't want you butting in. No one wants you butting in. No one wants you.'

'*Ja*, David, *das ist so*,' Matilda offers.

'So let's deal with Emily and then I'll go.'

'I'd love that, Mate, I'd fucking love that—' she's actually shaking now '—but we've got Hungry Dog joining the meeting and, unlike us, fat Len wants you there, so you gotta be here. I don't know why he wants you. I don't know why anybody would want you. Maybe he wants to fuck you. But that's how it is.'

A fresh wave of hatred courses through my blood, along with the clear realisation that *The Plan* may have run into potentially fatal problems.

'Gosh! Len wants to fuck me? Do I look alright?'

'*Ja*, zis is a nice shirt,' Matilda is saying when there's a bustle at the door, a brief knock and Natalie's tripping in with a new posse of skeletal, truculent teenagers.

And Len.

They're an hour early.

I Hate The Young
8 May, 10:28 am

Today I met a new team from Hungry Dog. Three ferrety teenies and my plump kitten-aficionado Len, who's still throwing me cat-related lachrymose looks.

The meeting goes badly. I think something's changed at Hungry Dog, and since my entire future now depends on one group of juvenile narcissists paying another group of juvenile narcissists a narcissistically huge sum of money, I have to watch this closely. The trouble is, I don't understand a word either side says. But I know today was bad.

For a start, nobody exchanges air kisses, which I believe in the Mee!Zee! nursery code is tantamount to a spitting attack. More significantly, none of the big-name infants is here. They're all strangers, except for Len.

We take our seats around the board table, everyone silent and frowning at their devices. Then a text pops up. It's from Len.

—see me afterwards. important!

I nod in his direction.

Discussions begin around me and stumble along in their usual incomprehensible way, but today they are laced with sarcasm and impatience. I glance at Angela and Matilda and they're nervous, taking shelter in fake laughter and long, technical speeches that make them sound like asthmatic warthogs. Things inexorably reach a tricky denouement when Angela wheezily exclaims 'You're 'avin' a laugh!' in a cartoon Cockney accent.

'*Ja, ze* technical details of our sub-comm algorithmic *spazial* social-media profiling matrix is protected information, *hein?*, and so it would be *sehr* funny for us to give that to you, just like *zat*,' says Matilda, who hasn't yet mastered the art of the pithy, ironic gag. 'So, *Ja*, for *zat* reason, is very funny.'

Xavier, a bored-looking infant with a thin moustache, sneers. 'Yeah yeah yeah, but, without that, we can't know the derivative cross-community expansion differential, can we? So what are we saying?'

'Not to mention the correlative associative knock-on chain implications for cross-platform multiversing angularities, algorithms and margins,' says a boney infant called April.

'Especially if there are sub-schematic run-on widgetisation issues,' says Xavier. 'Which there might be.'

Angela tries to grin chummily. 'All you need at this stage are the intra-community margin potentials and performance algorithms,' she smarms, in a way I find macabre.

'*Ja, das ist so alles was* you need,' says Matilda. Her grin also fails, on every count.

'Yeah, we know that,' adds a shouty young stick insect called Sudzy, 'but we also need the deep-web protocols.'

'We can't give you that information!' Angela insists, less chummily.

'*Ja*, it is impossible!' huffs Matilda.

'But if we don't have the deep-web protocols, we can't do the fringe intra-flow v. extra-flow analysis on the app-matrix contingency planning models,' says Xavier in a soft, menacing voice.

'The fringe intra-flow v. extra-flow data is all there in black and white,' says Angela, with a forced smile and a grotesque pout.

'*Ja*, in black and white,' says Matilda.

Suddenly I am seized by the overwhelming need to leave and find myself standing up. 'Sorry I have to go,' I hear myself say. 'My wife needs me urgently,' which is obviously not true, Olivia, but it reminds me of a time when you might have done, and that cheers me, momentarily.

'David: a quick word outside?' Len says, as I squeeze past him.

'Uh, sure,' I say and he prises himself out of his chair to follow me out the room.

'I've been worried,' he says when the door's closed. 'You okay?'

'No,' I say.

Len swallows. 'You never replied to my email.'

I haven't the faintest idea what he's referring to.

'About your cat?'

My cat? Sylvia Plath? Oh, right. He was upset. I improvise.

'It's too soon, Len. I'm sorry. It's just too soon.'

He squeezes my shoulder.

'I understand. Okay, I can't stay long, but read this.'

He thrusts a handwritten note into my hand and we stare at each other for a moment. He cracks first.

'David,' he says. 'The cat. It wasn't your fault, okay? It was an accident. An accident, okay?'

'I was rushing,' I say, hanging my head, 'and my cat paid the price.'

Len squeezes my shoulder. 'Now listen to me. You have to choose life. You deserve a life!'

'I know.'

'Get a kitten, David!'

Then he envelops me in a hot bear hug, whispers 'Read the note!' and rushes back into the meeting.

I open the note. It says,

—They want Wang. That's all they want.

After that, he's written the url of a website. Something to do with cats.

Ronny's Deadly Wrapper
11 May, 11:28 am

I'm back in my office. So is Ronny the Runner. He looks terrible.

'You look terrible,' I tell him.

'I am terrible. Worse than terrible.'

'Astrophysics or Ariella?'

'Cosmology,' he sighs wearily. 'Not astrophysics. But yeah, Man, it's Ariella. Oh Man, I so got that wrong.'

He slumps forlornly into a chair, leathers creaking.

This of course does not come as a huge surprise, Olivia. Almost all of Ronny the Runner's romantic escapades end in a lachrymose mess, although usually it's the woman who ends up perched on the bridge.

I do not say 'I told you so' although I had done. Instead I say, 'Ah! Ronny. I thought it was going so well.'

'Oh Man, it was!' He's holding his head in his hands. I'm terrified he's going to cry.

Olivia, in Ronnyological terms, this is epic. I've never seen him so cut up, so I ask, as casually as I can, if, as the result of a lover's tiff, he has just strangled Ariella in a motel room, chopped her into pieces, stuffed the pieces into suitcases and dropped them in a pig-feeding trough in Essex.

'Oh, Man!' He glances at me wearily and slides histrionically from the chair onto the carpet. 'We'd just made love for the first time. The first time, Man! At mine. Last night. And it was beautiful! So beautiful. Because I love her. Really love her. I mean, really love her. You know?'

'I think you've said you want her to have your babies.'

'I do want her to have my babies, Dude.'

'I know. So what happened?'

'I lied to her, Dude. Cheated. And got caught.'

'Another girl?'

He sits up, aghast. 'Dude! No! Of course not! I would never cheat on the woman who is going to have my babies!'

'You said "cheated".'

'Cheated on her soul, Dude. Her soul.' He's covering his eyes with both hands.

'Huh?' I say.

'It was terrible, man. We was making love, on my bed, and we kind of ended up on the carpet. And then she smelled it.'

'Smelled it?'

'The meat.'

'Ronny, that's overshare. Please!'

'No, Man, not me: the carton. The wrapper. The clamshell.'

'The clamshell?'

'Under the bed. The burger box from the night before. Her nose is unbelievable.'

I'm trying not to laugh.

'Dude it's not funny. She spent the night retching. Then she left and retched in her father's fancy car. Then she got home and retched on the carpet. Then she called and said I'd raped her. Raped her with two dead animals.'

'She said that?' I ask.

'Exact words. 'It's like you've raped me with two dead animals'. That's what she said.'

'Why "two"?'

'The BigBoy Beef 'n Bacon Burger. Hey, it ain't funny.'

'Oh dear.'

'I'm totally crushed, Dude. And ashamed. I lied to her. Told her I was vegan. An' I was until that burger. Man, I only got it 'cos I was passing the takeaway on the bike and I was ravenous, you get me? It's a kinda habit ... .'

His voice trails off.

'What are you gonna do?'

'Dunno, Man. I lied, you know? I betrayed her. I killed the trust. How could she possibly have babies with a liar?'

Olivia, this is Shakespearian. 'Ronny,' I tell him, in my most adult voice. 'I think you have to get off the floor, take a deep breath, look in the mirror and ask yourself if someone so judgmental is worth it. Because, Ronny: that's judgmental.'

'Are you serious, Dude?' He unknits his hands and peers through his fingers. 'I told you, Man. She's the one, the only one.'

I resort to Plan B, which involves putting my hand on Ronnie's huge shoulders and giving him a squeeze. 'Do you want me to talk to her?'

He stares and stares. 'You? Talk to her? Dude, no offence or nuffing, but she doesn't really like you.'

I tell him that that sounds harsh, and he sits up and nods, preparing me for awkward news. 'Dude, to be honest, you're widely … not really … see, a lot of the kids here don't get you like I do.'

This is why I love Ronny so much, Olivia.

'I think you're wrong,' I tell him, pleased to have shifted the subject away from Ariella. 'Some kids like me.'

'Yeah?' He's genuinely surprised.

'Emily. I think Emily does.'

'The tranny? Dude, news on the street is that she's suing you.'

'Well, I know, but I still like her.'

'Ah,' he says warmly. Then he gets a Ronny grin. 'She looks nuts.'

'I'm actually worried for her, Ronny. I think Emily is being coerced into having her cock off.'

Ronny isn't clear what I mean. 'Her … *cockoff*? Is that a uni thing?'

'No. I mean literally. You know Madden, the permanently enraged trans-warrior? He's forcing Emily to have her cock off.'

'What? Like off, off?' Ronny is reassuringly horrified.

'And her balls.'

Ronny looks like he wants to vomit. 'Fuck!'

'It's a power play. If he can persuade little Emily to cut her tackle off, it's another win he can chalk up for the movement. And himself. Manipulative little sod. He's pure evil.'

'I'm not enjoying this, Dude.'

160

'Me neither. Got any thoughts?'

'Not about Emily, Man, but I got some news for you.'

Ronny gets off the carpet and sits in a chair. 'The Stalker. Dude: we got half an address from an imprint he left on one of your notes.'

'You can identify him?'

'No. But we can locate him. Kind of. Goldhawk Road. West London. All we need now is a number.'

'So what do we do now?'

'We scout. Early next week, say Monday?'

Ronny's checking his phone again.

'She's avoiding me, Man. I gotta go.'

'Listen, Ronny, I'm having second thoughts.'

Ronny the Runner throws me a defiant glare.

'Na-ah. No second thoughts.'

And with that, he's gone. I get up to close the door behind him, because he never does, and my phone buzzes.

It's you. Your text:

—*Did you notice what she ate the other night? David I think she's pregnant! We really need to talk*

Who Doesn't Love A Baby? (1)
11 May 8:28 pm

Okay, here's the elevator pitch:

> *Beautiful young girl is in crisis. She is alone. She is with child. She is still a girl, not quite a woman. And she is Amelia Britton, a free, beautiful spirit with an inner steel that has never been tested. And she accepts the test. She has the baby and what gets her through the crucible days … is love. Love for her child, as pure as light itself; love for her parents, slightly more nuanced; and the love of those parents, whose unconditional support gives her back the home that she has been missing, and rebuilds for them the unity and harmony that they had been missing.*

'Crucible days'. I like that, Olivia. I will deploy it when you get home. Any minute now, I'm guessing.

And this is what I'm going to say to you: A baby, Olivia! A baby to bring us all together!

A baby could be the making of our daughter. It could oblige her to grow up and take responsibility for her life. It could rescue her from that pantomime university and bring her home. And it could make demands on us as carers and grandparents that will restore to us the meaning and optimism we had when we were younger. Amelia's baby could make us a family again.

Masaai, I will calmly point out, presents us all with a challenge but there's every likelihood he will flee, once he sees the baby is white, white white. The Idiot will hightail it out of London, return to his wealthy family in San Francisco and at last find his life's purpose as provider of a handsome monthly income for our daughter and grandson (I'm sure it's a boy).

The obstacle is you, Olivia. You are fanatically biased. I know that if you could, you would sneak up into Amelia's uterus and strangle her foetus with the shreds of its umbilical cord, using your teeth if necessary to tighten the sinews.

So this is the plan, Olivia. Tonight I am going to persuade you.

For fuck's sake, Olivia: who doesn't love a baby?

Who Doesn't Love A Baby? (2)
11 May, 11:48 pm

So, this is my interpretation of your response to the David Britton Baby Proposition.

It begins with the harrowing sound of you fumbling with your keys outside the front door. I nervously get up, sit down, get up again, straighten my clothing and then loosen my clothing again. Only as you're walking through the door do I think of stretching out on the sofa with my long legs crossed, in that groovy studio-couch way you know, and that's how the blue cup from Ephesus goes crashing to the floor. One of your favourites. Sorry.

I dispose of the debris and join you in the lounge.

'I liked that cup. It was from Ephesus.'

'I'm really sorry. So you think our daughter is pregnant?'

'Did you see what she was eating David?'

'I was too busy watching Masaai eating.'

'Who eats a pile of avocado, banana, onion and Bovril sandwiches? And then vomits in the morning?

'She vomited?'

'Every morning since she's been in London, she told me. Who does that? A pregnant girl, that's who. And let me tell you: she had that stupid pregnant look on her face when she was here.'

You throw your head into your hands, curls spilling out of your knuckles. You could always spot a pregnancy from a million miles. I am feeling an illicit sliver of joy.

'I think she looks unusually beautiful,' I say.

'What?' You're bolt upright, staring angrily.

'I said she looked nice. She does.'

'Are you actually happy that she might be pregnant, David?'

'Don't be so jumpy.'

'You seem happy, which is odd because I thought you

were convinced that Amelia had to be separated from her idiot boyfriend or that her life would essentially be over. Isn't that what you've always said?'

I agree that I had always said that.

'In which case you will also agree that a baby is the last thing on earth she needs and that the only solution—I repeat, the *only* solution—is an early termination. Are we agreed, David?'

You've got tears in your eyes, your hands are on your hips, your lips are full and hurt, and because at that moment I'll do anything to please you, I enthusiastically say 'yes, of course'.

Say it again,' you demand. 'I don't believe you.'

'Yes!' I say.

After a pause you say, 'That sounded Jewish.'

'"Yes" can sound Jewish?'

'The way you said it, yes. That *yes* could also mean *no*.'

'I said "yes", Olivia, so let's leave it there, okay?'

'David, we need to be on the same side now, because she's going to need our help: she really, really is.'

It's time. Now or never. I pause before elegantly rising to my feet, tossing my heavy hair in that studio way, and pinning you with my biggest, most puppyish eyes. 'I agree. I do see that not having a baby would be best for her, but ultimately she'll have to make the decision for herself, won't she? There'll be such pain, Olivia: it's a terrible decision for a young woman to make but, Olivia, we both know her inner steel, and really, if she decides independently to have this baby, to get through *the crucible days* that lie ahead, she'll need the love and support of her parents. And we have a home of our own to offer her! She has no one.'

She looks at me as if she is skewering a kebab. 'You rehearsed that, didn't you?'

'Don't be ridiculous,' I say. 'Herbal tea?'

'Thank you.'

I find your favourite cup and drop one of your weird infusions into it—then, on a whim, make another for myself, in an attempt to get on your vibe. It tastes like urine.

165

'Did you tell Moose that you suspected she's pregnant?' I say.

'Of course not. Anyway, all she's been wanting to talk to me about is *us*. I think she's aware of our separation.' I ask you to stop calling it that. 'That's what it is,' you say quietly and for a while we sip in silence. Then you say: 'You seem weirdly relaxed about this catastrophe, David.'

'I just think that until we have all the facts, we shouldn't panic. Anyway, I doubt they'll want their own baby. Masaai told me he thinks having babies is fascistic. He wants to adopt black, brown and multi-coloured babies from war zones instead.'

'What?'

'Really. Moose told me he's built an app for that very purpose.'

You burst out crying. 'You see? You see how screwy this moron is? A baby? Jesus Christ, she can't cope with making herself an instant coffee. Stupid girl!'

We sip in silence.

'You can't leave now,' I eventually say.

You start sobbing, beautifully.

'I can't stay. We're just not working together David. There's been no real relationship for years, has there?'

And I'm about to tell you how I would die for you, how I can't face life without you, how sorry I am for the Janice Toybeen dick-almost-in-the-hand incident, how I will make every effort to change and improve, when it happens.

A crash from the front door.

We both get up to investigate. A large parcel has been forced through the letterbox.

It's seeping.

Blood.

I grab it, run through the house into the kitchen and shake the contents out into the sink. You're watching from the door.

Something fleshy and dead slithers out. And there's a note, saturated in blood, with a crudely drawn swastika that's now dissolving. Underneath it, in bold, childish, capital letters:

—I'm coming Jewboy

It seems the time has come to update you about The Stalker and how I plan to handle him.

I Tell Olivia About The Stalker
12 May, 10:52 am

'So now we have Nazis trying to kill us? Well done, David. Bravo.'

'I'm not sure about the "us" part,' I reply. 'Happily, it's only me they want.'

'I don't find this funny.'

'Don't you? Really? Gosh, Olivia, I've been laughing for weeks. I just love it when Nazis poison our cat and drop a cow's liver through my door with swastika-decorated death threats. Yes, it's the best fun a bloke could have.'

'I can't help feeling you probably deserve this.'

'Oh, for God's sake: I didn't write the Treaty of Versailles!'

'Is there anyone you haven't offended recently?'

'Probably not, but I think the Nazi aversion to Jews preceded my recent bad form—'

You interrupt. 'Are we safe here? Is our daughter safe?'

'I think so,' I say. 'I'm already dealing with it.'

'You've told the police?'

'Sort of.'

'What does that mean?'

'I've told Ronny the Runner.'

You sigh extravagantly. 'Ronny the Runner. No, David: Ronny the Runner is the opposite of the police. Isn't he back inside?'

'He knows a lot of policemen.'

'He knows a lot of ex-policemen.'

'Same thing: once a cop, always a cop. And no, he's not back inside. That's how he got hold of the stalker's address.

You stare at me. 'He's got the address?'

'And we're going to find him!' I say, triumphantly. 'We're going to case the joint next Tuesday.'

Secretly I'm hoping you'll tell Boaz, word for word.

You've kept quiet about him for a while now but guess what? He's still in my sights.

'Wait: you and Ronny the Runner are going to pay a house call on a Nazi? Next week? Jesus, this just gets better and better.'

'Olivia, I didn't ask for this.'

'Yes you did. I'm sure you did. It's what you do. I'm just sorry that this crackpot of a Nazi couldn't have found himself a better Jew than you. Someone who doesn't share his loathing.'

'There's a difference between loathing, dislike and the wish to harm.'

'That's new, from you.'

'Tell you what: maybe Boaz could help me!'

'Piss off.'

'He's a general isn't he?'

'Colonel, actually.'

'A colonel in the Israeli Defense Forces, there to protect all Jews. Put my name on his list.'

'All of a sudden you've become a Zionist?'

I realise this might be an appropriate time to tell you the other Jewy news that's been burning a hole in my crisis-driven To-Do list. 'It's funny you should say that,' I say. 'I have something else Jewy to tell you.' You sigh. I take a deep breath. 'I have to put on tefillin, Olivia. They're kind of Jewish strappy things—'

'I know what tefillin are, David.'

'—and I have to do it for my father in hospital at his bedside. And you and Moose have to be there to watch.'

It's so quiet I can hear the moon.

'What?' you eventually say.

'This rabbi's been stalking me.'

'What?'

'This rabbi's been stalking me so I sort of shouted at him.'

'You "sort of shouted" at a stalking rabbi?'

'It's a long story—but the police got involved.'

You're staring madly again. 'So as well as antagonising some perfectly law-abiding Nazis, you've found time to attack a few rabbis.'

'One rabbi, who fully deserved it.'

'Deserved it! What, did he pray too aggressively?'

'Look, he claims to be a friend of my dad's and he was following me to the hospital and harassing me—and at work too—so, yes, I kind of reprimanded him.'

You're laughing but not laughing. 'And you were arrested?' I nod. 'And taken to a police station?' I nod again. 'In a police car?' A third nod. 'And charged?'

'No, of course not!' I shout triumphantly. 'Peter Dent got me a plea bargain—' your hand has flown to your forehead '—and that involves you, I'm afraid.'

'You've involved me in your plea bargain?' you growl.

'As part of the plea bargain I have to lay tefillin—the strappy things—at my father's bedside with all the family present. That's what the stalking rabbi asked for in the documents. And a few other rituals. He mentioned you and Moose by name. All you have to do is come along and watch and then I won't go to prison on a race-hate charge.'

'This is literally unbelievable.'

'I know. He wouldn't back down.'

'And I won't do it. It's humiliating.'

'Olivia! It's that or prison.'

'Good. You deserve prison. I want you to go to prison. I want you to spend the rest of your life in prison.'

'I understand that wish, and I respect it, but if you don't comply, my father will cut us out of the will. The stalking rabbi now controls my father's estate which, as you know, is worth a few bob.'

'How on earth does your rabbi get to control your father's estate?'

'He's not my rabbi.'

'Well, whoever he is!'

'He's a thief who trapped my father and turned him into a Jew so he and his mate Hymie could steal from us.'

'Who the hell is Hymie?'

'Menachem's mate.'

'Who is Menachem?'

'The rabbi.'

'Your rabbi?'

'He's not my rabbi.'

Then you lean over, your head bowed in your hands. 'David, what is wrong with you? Why are you trying to ruin everyone's life?'

'I'm not. I didn't mean to. It was an accident. Things happen. I just want you to be happy. And instead you're crying. It's breaking my heart.'

'I'm crying because of my life. What a waste it's been. And stop looking at my tits.'

Sorry about that.

'I'm crying because our stupid daughter, who's incapable of looking after a pet amoeba, let alone a baby, is probably pregnant thanks to an idiot boyfriend who thinks he's black and isn't. I'm crying because my husband thinks it's okay to endow Janice fucking Toybeen with his penis. I'm crying because I have spent twenty-eight years married to a self-obsessed idiot who annoys Nazis and attacks rabbis and who has never taken me seriously. I'm crying because the man I may be in love with lives in another country and is married with four children. That's why I'm crying. Okay?'

After a long silence I look up with my biggest possible puppy eyes and say, 'four little beautiful kids; that's lovely', but before you can respond, there's a scuffling at the door. We share a delicious moment of horrified solidarity before panic sets in.

'I thought they were at that Black Centre tonight?' you hiss.

'Me too,' I whisper, overjoyed.

In the nick of time you leap into the bedroom and lock yourself inside while I advance on the front door in a preposterously jolly, studio manner. 'Ah-hah!' I hear myself croon. 'Welcome! Welcome, one and all!'

Masaai Wants To Go Into Business
13 May 1:22 am

They stagger through the doorway, luggage, bongos and bags crashing against the walls. Moose drops what she's carrying and scurries into the bathroom, whence comes the unmistakable rumble of retching.

'Is she alright, Masaai?'

'Tired, I think. Little sick, maybe. 'Fraid we gotta crash here for a few nights, Man, if that's okay. Lotta weird shit going on. Lotta weird shit.'

'Great!' I exclaim and pump his hand. He looks puzzled.

Then you walk in, freshly made up. You look embalmed.

'The kids are staying,' I announce. 'The bed's ready, right Darling?'

You whimper assent and collapse onto the sofa. Then we all sit listening to Moose's retching.

'I better go check things out,' Masaai says, during a lull.

'Jolly good idea, Masaai,' I hear you say and, as soon as he disappears into the bathroom, you leap up, stride across the room and clamp your ear to the bathroom wall.

'They're fighting,' you whisper, signalling me to be quiet. 'They're fighting!' You're actually pumping your fists. 'I think she just told him she hates him!'

Then you prise yourself from the wall, turn to me and crease into a prayer-like pose. 'Now please don't fuck it up! I beg you! She hates him! Now's the time! And for God's sake hide the Nazi stuff!'

I hide the Nazi stuff and we both return to the wall. This time the outlook isn't so rosy. We can now hear the muffled sounds of Masaai and our daughter joyously exchanging body fluids.

172

EVENTUALLY THE KIDS JOIN US IN THE LIVING ROOM AND announce they're starving. Moose is back on the avo, raw onion and Bovril, but this time with a bucket of miso soup and liquorice. Masaai gobbles up another immense plate of the bean stew and is filling up again when I can no longer contain myself.

'So how was the Hackney Black Roots Collective?'

Yes, I notice your icy look, Olivia, but you know what? Even human catastrophes like David Britton deserve an occasional bit of fun.

'Long story,' says Masaai, masticating thoughtfully.

'Horrid!' says Moose.

'Not all of it,' says Masaai reasonably. 'There were moments.'

'No, there weren't!' says Moose.

'So, tell us, Bro,' I say, encouragingly.

'Well, it was okay at first, if you get me—'

'No, it wasn't.'

'Yeah, Baby, it was. It was interesting.'

'He's an idiot, that Oge-what's-his-name.'

'Ogewulo. No, he's not,' says Masaai calmly. He's addressing me. 'See, it's all his brainchild, right? Peter Ogewulo. He realised that people all over the world are discovering their negritude, 'cos of genome testing, you get me, Dude? I found him on the web. He did my second test.' He's pausing to think. 'Man, I love that word.'

'Testing?'

'Negritude.'

'Carry on.'

'He's, like, a genius, Man. Knows right where I am as a *white* white black man. And not just me: all of us who've just been discovering our negritude. It was like this miracle thing, just meeting him like that, online, you know.' Masaai helps himself to a few more mouthfuls of bake. 'It was a kind of fate thing, to do with the ancestors, he says.'

'The ancestors were telling you to get in touch with your negritude?'

'Love that word. Huh? Oh yeah, I guess.'

173

'How's the bake, Masaai? A spoonful more, anyone?' I think you're hoping that Masaai and I both choke to death simultaneously. And as you glare at me, serving spoon raised, your eyes plead: S*hut the fuck up, David!*

'No, Darling, thanks.' I say cheerfully, and return to Masaai.

'Darling?' Moose breaks in. 'What's with the "darling"? You never used to "darling" each other.' Moose has been watching us like a hawk all night, as you'll have noticed too.

'What do you mean, what's with the "darling", Darling?' you trill desperately.

'Since when do you two call each other "darling"? Actually forget it: I don't care.' Moose laughs bitterly and nails a liquorice.

I turn back to Masaai.

'So, Buddy, were there, like, lectures, or discussions, or something to develop your connection with your … negritude.'

'Negritude' he marvels, dreamily. 'So, mainly he asked lots of questions, Man. You know: about the genome test and what it kinda felt like … and, oh yeah, about my family. That's real important to Peter.'

'Oh. What did he ask?'

'All kinda things, Man. Business mostly.'

'That's all he spoke about,' says Moose, suddenly alive.

'He's into real estate. It's a Nigerian thing, I think.'

'It certainly is,' I comment. 'So where were you staying? At the centre?'

'There wasn't a centre,' snaps Moose.

'Well there kinda was. It was a house centre. A little house centre. In Hackney. In a room kinda centre.'

'A tiny room—' says Moose.

'—It wasn't that small—'

'—with a dead animal on the floor. It was disgusting. It stank.' She looks as though she's going to retch again.

'And he took it away?'

'Eventually.'

'I presume they were charging you?' I enquire.

'Yeah,' says Masaai sheepishly.

'A lot!' says Amelia.

'That's kinda why we came back,' says Masaai. 'I gotta organise some shit, you get me? Speak to my trust lawyer at home.'

Suddenly Moose bursts into tears.

'Oh baby!' cries Olivia and flies to her.

'Stop it, can't you? I'm not a fucking baby!' she cries and bolts to the bathroom. After a door slam there's more retching.

Masaai breaks the silence. 'Look, I know you think we're kinda weird—hell, even *I* think we're kinda weird—but you gotta understand. I love your daughter, Man. Really. There's nothing on this Earth I wouldn't do for her. She's my life, Dude.'

You looked crestfallen, Olivia—and now the retching has got louder. 'Is Moose alright, Masaai?' I ask.

'Yeah, Man. She got this little stomach thing. It's nothing. It started last week but I think she's getting over it. It's cos of all this English food she's eating: the avo and banana and white-man Bovril shit.'

'How often is she throwing up?'

'Just sometimes.' And then he guffaws in a particularly stupid way. 'And I know what you're thinking. Relax, she's not pregnant, Man. We're careful, so chill,' he chuckles.

'Oh, thank God!' you cry.

Moose returns, pale as a ghost.

'Why are you all looking at me?'

'Because you were throwing up, Darling, and we were worried,' you say.

'I'll throw up if I want to, okay? Stop trying to imperialise me! You've been using guilt as a weapon from the moment I got here.'

'Babe babe babe, they weren't doing shit, Man: just caring about you, yeah?'

'So now on you're on their side?' she screams and storms into the bedroom, slamming the door.

'Ah—just like old times,' I say.

'Oh, shut up, David,' you say and rush to join Moose.

'Ah—just like old times,' I say.

175

Masaai has stopped chewing and is grinning at me. He looks like a happy sheep jammed with an excess of cud. 'That's funny,' he says, with a surprised look.

I say thanks. 'It's how we do shit in this family, Masaai. High voltage, you get me.'

'Yeah, Man, I really like that. That's a *black* thing too,' he chuckles.

'Maybe I'm *black*?'

Masaai's happy-sheep expression vanishes and he looks at me sternly. 'Dude! Seriously, Man! You can't say that. That's, like, cultural appropriation.'

'You just did!'

'Dude, I *am* black.'

'Oh. Sorry.'

'It's okay, but never again, okay? Listen, Man, I need to talk to you about something. It's serious.'

'About Moose?'

'No, Man. About this app I've written. You know I'm a programmer? Remember I mentioned it?'

'It is unforgettable.'

'You're in the social media game right?'

'My company is. But, yes, I think I know what an app is.'

'Cool. Yeah, Man. So I'm looking for a partner. Someone to back an idea for changing the world. Save millions of lives.'

'I'm listening.'

'Okay, Man: it's like this, yeah? As a *black* man I've got a responsibility to do what I can for other people of colour, yeah?'

'Yes!' I say, and for some reason raise a fist.

'And you know that because of imperialism and racism and climate change and shit, there are wars all across the world, yeah?'

'Uh, yeah.'

'And because of that, there are millions of black, brown and divergently coloured babies who don't have parents, yeah?'

He looks like a very happy, post-cud-chewing sheep.

'I guess … '

'Well that's what this app is about, Man. It's about

finding the babies and matching them with parents who'll adopt them all over the world, yeah?'

And before I can utter a word he's whipped out his phone and drawn a chair alongside me.

'This is it. The WaZoBlaBroYeloBayBap.'

'The what?'

'The WaZoBlaBroYeloBayBap. You gotta rap it, Man. C'mon, rap it, Man: it makes sense. WaZoBlaBroYeloBayBap! The War Zone Black Brown and Yellow Baby App!'

We rap a while until it becomes embarrassingly apparent that I can't rap WaZoBlaBroYeloBayBap because I'm a white, white *white* man.

Mercifully, Masaai kills the attempt.

'So this is how it works, yeah? Sorta like Tinder. So you're walking along and you think, yeah, I wanna adopt an otherly-coloured baby from a war zone, you get me?'

'Uh, yeah.'

'And it doesn't have to be a war zone, yeah? That's what's so beautiful.'

'That is beautiful.'

He's swiping images of babies on his phone. 'So … you scroll here … and Bang! You find one you like—hey, this one's cute!—so you click here and, bim bam, it's all there: which baby, which war, which country, deets of the baby, the kid's name, its weight, the whole thing. Click here, input your own deets, and Boom! You got yourself an otherly-coloured baby!'

He's grinning triumphantly.

'That is really impressive, Masaai.'

'Thanks man.'

'And it's—that simple?'

'It's that simple. And what's so good: you could re-skin it, you know? For, I dunno, Inuit babies. Or Pygmy babies. Or, I dunno, teenagers. I originally wrote this software for selling bongos. Then I got into the *black* thing—you get me?' He looks up at me, seriously. 'It's made me a whole better person.'

'I get you. How about white babies?'

He peers at me, horrified. 'Man, that is such a white white *white* thing to say!'

177

'I was joking,' I say.

Generously, he moves on. 'So I was thinking, you and me could become partners. And Peter Ogewelu wants in.'

'Partners?'

'Business partners. I got the idea, Peter got the distribution network, you got the capital. Put them together in a three-way split and … Boom!'

'Boom!' I yell, just as you walk back into the room, shell-shocked and pale. 'Masaai, Amelia wants to speak to you.'

'Cool, Man, cool.'

When he's gone you collapse onto the sofa and groan like a wounded animal.

'You okay?'

'Does it sound like I'm okay? Of course I'm not okay!' You look tearful. 'She's probably pregnant. Can you believe it?'

'Jesus.'

'And then I hear you and The Idiot talking about babies.'

'Yes, but that was black, brown and yellow babies from war zones who need adoption. And possibly Innuit and Pygmy babies. It's the app I told you about. He wants me to go into business with him.'

You emit a plaintive howl.

Then we hear it. It's unmistakable. Muted at first but growing stronger and more groany.

Next door, they're exchanging body fluids.

178

The Beeboids Pay A Visit
14 May, 4:48 pm

Another epic day starts with Natalie's clickety-clack shoes tripping down the stairs.

They're here. The Beeboids. Right outside my door.

To be honest, Olivia, I'm not entirely sure why they've insisted on this visit. According to Shapireau, it's to sign the contract termination papers and organise the transfer of the rushes of the film. But I know it's ritual humiliation, approved by Angela and insisted upon by about 200 BBC lawyers.

I'm feeling like a naughty schoolboy.

And now comes the knock.

'Come in!' I yell loudly.

Natalie enters, immaculate on her pale green glittery four-inchers, and followed by three grey Beeboids. 'Morning Sweetheart,' she croons. 'I've got your lovely guests here.'

'Morning, Darling,' I purr back, entirely ignoring the scowling procession behind her. 'I've got the tickets.'

'Silly!' she giggles.

'No really,' I croon. 'I've booked the desert island. Just us. Love in the tropical sun, ready for us to spend all our time making lots of beautiful babies!'

'Haha!' she trills.

Behind her, India, Marc and the capacious mystery third Beeboid are squirming, which is delightful.

'You won't regret sacrificing your life for a much older, dominant man,' I coo at Natalie.

'What is he like?' she says to the gawping visitors and, with a gorgeous shake of her glistening hair, departs in a trail of perfume.

I face the Beeboids and extravagantly gesture them to sit down. 'Hi, everyone! Welcome, welcome, please, please have a seat.'

Wordlessly, the drudges take off their coats, scarves and

jackets and sit on the teeny sized chairs I have brought in specially for the occasion.

'Isn't Natalie a darling?' I say charmingly. They gape, eyes like polished pebbles. 'The beautiful girl who brought you down, I mean. A goddess.'

Nobody's breathing. To be honest, Olivia, I don't think I've been this happy for years.

'Let me tell you about Natalie,' I explain in a jolly way. 'You know, it's so great to be a famous, powerful BBC director because it makes it so easy to seduce young beautiful women. Especially the more impoverished ones. But of course you guys at the BBC know all about that! You're the world experts!'

The new fat Beeboid is breathing stertorously. I grin at her and wink. 'Hi. Sorry we haven't met, have we?'

'This is Lydia Applegate-Smith,' says India, recovering her icy verve. 'She's Series Executive Producer and Head of BEM Factual Arts Programme Legal Management.'

'Wow,' I say.

'Yes,' Marc and India say darkly.

'Hello,' she says in a low voice.

'A six-figurerer, eh?' I say, big ol' handsome smile fully cocked.

'Pardon?'

'I presume you are one of the 20,000 six-figure salary earners? Great honour to meet you. Okay, let's get started. Please, sit!'

They crease themselves into their tiny chairs and I plunge into my huge one. 'Now of course, I'm so proud to have been commissioned to exec produce one of the *Black and Brilliant and Buzzing Behind Bars* documentaries. It was an honour, truly, and I'm sorry to have let you down. So I've made up for my lapse by producing my own little tribute to the Great Man and poetic genius that is Killa-Jah, which I'd really like you to see.'

They're suspicious, and shoot glances at each other, while the maximally salaried one steps in to command obedience. 'Thank you,' she says. 'I don't think anything like that is necessary so why don't we move on.'

I interrupt. 'I realise that my first cut, with a decontext-ualized focus that could be considered homophobic, was wrong, so what I've tried to do—'

Marc is shaking his head vigorously. 'Racist, not homo-phobic,' he says firmly.

'Killa-Jah is gay, Marc,' I say.

'He isn't,' Marc says.

'He is,' I insist, with a suave smirk.

'He definitely is not.' says India.

'Oh I think he is,' I say.

'No he's not,' says Marc tetchily.

'He so is' I say with the slightest hint of a rubbery wrist. 'Oh, he just so is.'

'He's not!' says Marc, his face changing colour.

'He definitely, definitely isn't,' says India firmly. 'Like Lydia said, can we move on, please?'

'Have you seen him dance?' I say.

'He's not gay!' Marc screeches.

'Marc, black men can be gay you, know.'

'I know that, but he isn't gay!'

'My gaydar says otherwise.'

'He's not gay!'

'Bi?'

'No,' says India, with a calm, resolute authority.

'It really doesn't matter what he is,' says Lydia. 'Can we get started? David, show us your little film quickly and then let's talk.'

'Thank you Lydia. But just before you all settle down, would anyone like something to drink?—please help yourself —and here are some nibbles.' I pass around a bowl. 'This was Mandela's favourite snack.'

'What's that?' says India, peering suspiciously into the meaty bowl, her neck churny.

'Biltong. Dried meat from South Africa,' I say. 'They shoot the animal, skin it, salt and season it, then hang it out in the sun on wires. Delicious. Mandela's favourite snack, anyone?'

They look bilious.

'I'm fine, thank you,' says Lydia. 'Let's begin. I've only got an hour and there's a lot of legal stuff to get through.'

'Of course, of course. Your being—' I read from the notes '—Series Executive Producer and Head of BEM Factual Arts Programme Legal Management must keep you very busy. Okay, here goes.'

I kill the lights, hit the button. The video rolls.

It opens with the simpering music from *Love Story*. The toddler wanders slo-mo into shot—a sweet little darling in a woolly white romper suit stomping unsteadily into frame with a huge gummy smile.

The Beeboids have stopped breathing.

As the music swells, the shot widens to reveal the gun in the child's tiny hand. It dangles there, its full metal weight hanging precariously in the child's tiny grasp. Then, as the music hits the schmaltzy high note, the video cuts to a tight shot of Killa-Jah, who is laughing oafishly, as usual.

Marc's on his feet waving his hands and yelling *Stop it!*

I ignore the protest and ramp up the volume. The blistering bassy rap comes in on a rat-tat-tat loop.

Me wanna splat da Whiteboy popo.

'Love this bit,' I say, getting up and dad-dancing.

There's pandemonium. Marc is shrieking 'That's illegal! That's illegal.' India's neck has started to vibrate. She looks forlornly at the Series Executive Producer and Head of BEM Factual Arts Programme Legal Management who is scribbling something down in a very big and important-looking black book.

I kill the video and turn on the lights.

'I won't allow this!' Marc's screaming. 'I won't allow you to rape his art!'

'Calm down Marc,' says India quietly, veins pulsing across her throat.

'You're just a fucking old dead white man!'

'That's enough Marc,' says Lydia, looking squarely and coolly at me.

Olivia, I am having the time of my life, loving every fresh moment of the suicide circus, because I know that, after this, I will never have to meet the BBC ever again. I turn on Lydia's marble, bossy gaze. 'Sorry to ask: what's your name again?'

'Lydia Applegate-Smith,' she says. 'May I say something? And for once will you allow me to finish?'

'Of course, of course' I say affably. 'Some biltong before we start?'

'No thank you.'

'Mandela's favourite snack?'

'I don't like biltong,' she says.

'You don't like the snack that was Mandela's favourite snack?'

'I'm vegan. You seem to have an agenda David,' she says.

'Quite. A Reithian agenda. To tell the truth, as far as possible.'

'And what is your "truth" here?'

'To show that this "artist" is a BBC artifice, politically motivated and made possible only by an amalgam of the usual white guilt, self-hatred and sanctimony. Acceptable only because of the privileged middle-class post-imperial guilt trip that you inflict on the country's army of licence payers while extorting them to pay for it. You're promoting violence and the violence is a fraud.'

'I will not allow you to attack his art!' Marc's shrieking.

Lydia shuts him up with an imperious wave of a fleshy, jewelled hand. 'Violence is often a part of art, David,' she says. 'What this series is trying to do is explore its origins and provide context and explanation.'

'So why object to the shot of his toddler carrying a gun and Killa-Jah there giggling about it?'

'He wasn't giggling!' comes the shriek from the corner. 'He adores the boy!'

'No doubt. And is amused that he plays with a loaded gun.'

'It wasn't loaded!'

'He boasts that it was.'

'You seem to have a problem with black people,' Lydia squeals.

'I don't, Lydia. But the issue is irrelevant, because he's white. That grandparent story is bullshit.'

'You're a racist, David,' she says. 'I watched your excruciating *Newsnight* interview again. You actually said that every young black man in London should be routinely frisked for knives.'

'No, I said that knife crime figures would fall radically if every young black man was routinely frisked for knives. I went on to say—but no one remembers—that if every young white man got frisked, knife crime would also fall. It's become a national epidemic but it started in the black community, or aren't you allowed to acknowledge that at Broadcasting House? Or that it afflicts the Black community more than any other. Or that it's intolerable and needs to be called out and dealt with, urgently.'

'Oh, that is so bigoted!' India's neck is starting to convulse. 'Young people carry knives because they're afraid. And why are they afraid? Because of the deprivation we've trapped them in.'

And now there's no stopping me. It's the moment I've been waiting for. My goodbye speech to the BBC. 'Fair warning, Lydia, but you're my target here,' I tell her. 'Not you personally, although maybe you as well, but the disgusting, lying, extorting, propagandist organisation you work for—'

She cuts me off in a loud voice. 'I'm afraid we can no longer continue with you on this project, David.' She's up and packing her stuff away. 'From now on, Marc will take over.' Then she pauses. 'You don't like black people, do you David? I know a racist when I see one and you tick all the boxes.'

'The opposite is true,' I say. 'And you're a *Fickungsfotze*.'

'That says it all,' she replies, gathers her things and heads for the door. The others follow her out. I listen to their footsteps recede, then collapse into the Hollywood chair.

A few minutes later the phone rings. It's Natalie.

'Darling, what have you done now?'

'Why, what have I done?'

'We've had a call from the BBC lawyers. Angela wants to see you tomorrow.'

Ronny The Runner Discovers The Jews
15 May, 5:05 pm

Olivia, I spend last night hunting Nazis. Or rather, I spend last night trying to stop Ronny the Runner from hunting Nazis and in doing so, end up hunting Nazis.

Since it was me who involved Ronny in the first place, I now feel a responsibility to drop the whole thing, keep Ronny out of prison and go to the police, as you suggested. But this is proving harder than I imagined, because Ronny has become obsessed.

The evening starts and ends in terror and it's got nothing to do with Nazis. I'm riding pillion on Ronny's Ninja 12, slicing through the London night like a laser, dipping and swerving in sudden crazy bursts of speed, and in no time at all we're there, in the Nazi's street, and I feel like vomiting as Ronny brings his ton of gleaming black metal gliding to a feather halt in a small alley just off the Goldhawk Road.

He gets off silently and stamps his feet and fists to get the blood flowing.

He's angry. Has been all day.

I know these moods. I also know Ronny can't control them: another important reason to squirm out of this ridiculous plan. The problem is that Ronny simply won't let me. And now he's got that crazy look.

'You okay, Ronny?'

He brushes the question away with a jerk of the head and calls up the map on his phone. 'Okay, Man, now listen up. The postcode we extracted from the letters says our Nazi lives between here and here. We're here, you get me, and the road's there, just behind this building. It's about a block. Somewhere in there is our bloke and I'd venture a guess it's right there.'

He's pointing at a large squat building.

I'm taking off my helmet when Ronny scolds me. 'Keep

185

it on for now, Man. Our Nazi could be anywhere—and he knows you, probably. So the plan's this. We walk the space and clock the layout. How many shops, offices, houses, distances, that kinda thing. We're trying to find out where he lives.'

'And if we find him?'

'We won't. It's just research.'

'And then?'

'Then we act.'

'How?'

He's pissed at the question. 'Man, I dunno. Now isn't the time for questions. Maybe tell the police. Maybe give him a warning. Maybe just run him over like a dog.'

Ronny wants a fight. That's not good. Not good at all.

'Run him over? Really? Ronny I don't think we should do this while you're in this mood.'

'I'm cool,' he says quietly; then he's off, hunched into his leathers, stomping forward like a biker into a brawl.

The Goldhawk Road's a dirty slash of London, single-fronted shops and run-down offices, fried-chicken takeaways, East European convenience stores, nail-and-hair salons, a boarded-up pub and, bang in the middle of everything, a squat grey sixties block of council flats which Ronny's been squinting at for over a minute.

He gestures at them. 'Follow me.' We cross the road through a slipstream of diesel and litter and take shelter in the greasy spoon opposite the flats. It's almost empty. We take off helmets, order coffees and grab a table one away from the window.

I put on my sternest adult face. 'Ronny, listen to me. I want out. In fact, I am out. This is insane.'

He ignores me. 'Let me tell you the plan. We are doing nuffing illegal. I get my young mate Jenny with the angel face and big knockers to knock on every flat door one evening when everyone's home. She pretends to be selling something. She clocks the occupants, their names, their profiles, what they've got on the walls, on the shelves, in their rubbish bags outside. She's excellent. Ex-copper. She'll eliminate the obvious: Blacks. Asians. Chinese. Gays. Muslims. The elderly.'

'No elderly Nazis? Ronny this is crazy.'

'Plenty old Nazis but I don't reckon they kill cats. We're looking for a white man between twenty and forty.'

The waitress brings the coffees. When she's gone I grab his wrist. 'Now listen to me, Ronny. I have made a decision. This is insane. I am calling the whole thing off. I'd rather go to the police.'

Ronny firmly removes my hand with his 'you're not my father' look, tips three teaspoons of sugar into his cup and stirs it before glaring straight into my eyes. 'I got a question, Dude. Don't get me wrong, okay? Why do people hate you?'

'Not everyone hates me, Ronny,' I begin to say.

'I don't mean you, Dude, though to be honest … .' His voice trails off. 'I mean Jews.'

'What? I don't know. I'm not really a Jew, Ronny.'

'Yeah you are.'

'Well, technically.'

'You are, Dude. Everyone says so. You know, in the office, they call you "The Big Jew".'

'Really?'

You know, Olivia, that genuinely shocked me. It's possibly the first time I've heard Ronny say the word *Jew*, and it's the first time I've imagined that that's how people view me. I'd rather assumed that the special-needs children who populate Mee!Zee! wouldn't even know what a Jew is.

'I been reading up on you lot,' he says. 'an' I don't get it.'

'They're not my lot and what don't you get?'

'The hatred.'

'You and me both,' I say. 'Which is why we are going to call this whole Nazi thing off, Ronny.'

'So what do you think? I'm being serious.'

'Why do people hate Jews? I think it's our behaviour. We have annoying behaviour. We're insecure.'

'No, Man. Most people don't know any Jews, so it can't be their behaviour.'

'Maybe it's our noses.' I'm teasing, of course, but he's onto it at once.

'It can't be the nose thing, Dude. I've been scrutinising noses. Seriously. I've examined every nose at Mee!Zee!—

every one. There are eight that you'd say were in the top percentile for honk size, and to my certain knowledge, none of them is a Jew—unless Jews have started wearing hijabs and shit.'

'I'm pretty sure they haven't,' I said.

'That's what I thought,' he says. 'So, then there are another five with honks that aren't so high on the distribution curve but are still up there, and you know what? Just one Jew. Just one Jewish honker out of thirteen. And that one was only on the third quartile.'

'Plastic surgery, Mate. We're crafty like that.'

His eyes are huge. 'Really?'

'No, of course not.'

'Okay, so these are all the Jews I know, yeah? There's the kids I mentioned at Mee!Zee! There's my doc, Jonty. There's Greenie, who I met when I was doing time. And there's you. No funny big noses: not one. So I went on the web and looked at pictures of Jews and their noses seemed, I dunno, statistically normal. Maybe a bit wider but no big deal. Not big hooks, like in the cartoons. Just the one at Mee!Zee! that's on the third quartile, like I said.'

How can you not love Ronny, Olivia?

'Ronny, I have little to say about the Jewish Nose Question.'

Of course, this is all rather funny, Olivia, but I also know it isn't. Because in the absurdity of the moment, I intuit that something bigger is happening. That Fate, once again, is directing this surreal drama, and that the Ronny-and-cat-killing-Nazi thing isn't going to end well.

Ronny's still talking noses. 'So you know what I did? I looked at Italians as my nose base control group—and Dude, now we're talking noses. Right?'

'Ronny you crack me up.'

'Just listen. I'm being serious. So then I started noticing Jews. Reading about them. What people say about them. The money and power and controlling the media shit. And the Holocaust. And I went to the Imperial War Museum. They got this Holocaust exhibition. And I started reading about what happened—'

'Ronny, maybe not so loud?'

'You know what? I didn't believe it.'

'Oh.'

'So I started researching, you know, to see if it was bullshit.'

'Well, I guess—'

'—or exaggerated, so everyone feels sorry for you—'

'Ronny you're shouting.'

'—and supports Israel, whatever they do to the Arabs, yeah?'

'I hear you, Mate, very loud and clear.'

''Cos you're clever like that, get me? That's what they say. So I read more and more how people say it's all a fucking lie yeah?'

'Ronny, you're kind of yelling.'

'Fucking right I am. So I joined this online group called National Action, yeah?'

'You joined an online group of Nazis to find out more about Jews?'

'I did, Man, and I got to meet one of them an' he told me what he thought and how the Auschwitz gas chambers were physically impossible and all that, you get me?'

'I get you.'

'So I went back to the exhibition and joined this guided tour and afterwards, I spoke to the guide and at first he was kind of suspicious but it turns out he likes bikes and also had a Ninja 12 so we got talking and went through it all, and he put me right—and you know what?'

'What?'

'It happened.'

'I know it did, Ronny.'

'Everything. It's true. In fact it's probably worse. And so I went back to that motherfucker online Nazi—this was last night, Man—and I told him he was talking shit and I explained why, and you know what he did? You know what he fucking did?'

'What?'

'He laughed. He knows it happened. They all know. And I tell you what: they'd do it again. They'd do it again

189

tomorrow. And you know what else? Nobody—' he's pointing outside at people on the road '—nobody would lift a finger to help us.'

It takes a while for this to sink in.

'Us?'

'Yeah. Us.'

'Well Ronny, that's wrong on two critical counts. Firstly, 'cos I'm not really a Jew and secondly 'cos you definitely aren't. In other words, this really isn't your problem, Ronny. Or mine. Which is why I'm walking out and cancelling this operation.'

'I'm doing this for me, Man, not you,' he says. 'Go if you like.'

'For fuck's sake, Ronny: you're not Jewish!' I yell.

'You know we were talking about noses?' he says. 'And I said there was one big Jewish nose in our building?'

I nod.

'Ariella,' he announces. 'My Ariella.'

'Ariella's Jewish?'

'Yeah. With a great big fucking honker that I love, Man. And one day she's gonna have my babies—'

'Ah, the babies.'

'—yeah, the babies, and they're gonna be Jews, 'cos it goes through the mum, and they're gonna have big fucking honkers, and no motherfucking Nazi is gonna hurt them, you get me?'

Why do these things happen to me, Olivia?

'Stop laughing, Dude. It ain't funny. This is for Ariella.'

'So you're back together?'

'No Dude. But I'm doing this for her. I want her to be proud of me. So, yeah, I get that you're not in but I am, Dude. This is my war. Leave if you want.'

My phone buzzes.

It's a text from Emily! Like I don't have enough crazy shit to deal with! But at least I know why this is happening. Because my indefatigable Fate Fairy has decided that Ronny the Runner's babies and a cat-murdering Nazi are insufficiently weird so she's throwing in a Tranny who is having her cock cut off.

—seeing the doc monday thought youd wanna know. gotta be done I'm a warrior X

This is the worst of news, Olivia. For reasons I can't quite explain, Emily matters to me and because the last thing I need now is a Nazi-stalking operation to protect Ronny's future hook-nosed babies, I get up to leave.

'Ronny, this is a really bad idea. I'm out!'

'Do what you like Dude. What your conscience dictates.'

Stuff I've taught him. The very words. He's got me.

'Bah!'

I sit down, and Ronny goes through the plan.

Emily And Her Cock
16 May, 4:05 am

Olivia, it is 4:00 am and I have just had an extended nightmare featuring you, me, Killa-Jah, Madden, Angela, Matilda and the interchangeable cocks of Boaz, Tina the Giantess Lawyer and Emily. Which is why I'm in the bathroom throwing cold water on my face and staring at the brutal reflection of my face in the mirror.

I look like death. Creases have etched so deeply into my skin that my face folds like parchment. My vain hair has withdrawn to a greying coral reef around the emerging dome of my head. My eyes have silted into occluded slits, below which dark bags are starting to inflate. And, most weirdly, my whole face omelette now seems dominated by a nose I didn't think I had: not so much beaky as wide.

An old man, preparing for death.

I pad back into the living room, slump into the armchair, turn on my phone and, before I even know what I'm doing, find myself sifting through Emily's texts and emails.

Can't get her out of my head.

I'm afraid the time has come to tell you about Emily, the one-time Emile. I can't really explain it but I feel protective of her because nobody else is. And I know something awful's about to happen. The Gender Commissars are going to cut her dick off. And her balls.

No, I'm not imagining it, Olivia. The operation's booked. And when I look, there is a terror in her eyes. The language of her texts and blogposts has changed. She uses idiot phrases like 'the fight against imperialist binarism' and 'the freedom to self-define' and, most scarily, the 'eradication of capitalist masculinity'. Madden-speak, Tina-speak, every damned word of it. And you know what? It's not what she wants. She wants the stuff that goes with it, the people who go with it, the ideas that go with it, because it's all new and thrilling, but not the

192

thing itself—but they've persuaded her that she can't have the one without the other. So she's given in to it, and agreed to offer her cock as a sacrifice to another false revolution. And I'm worried that, a little way down the line, she'll throw herself off a bridge into the Thames.

So that's the reason I'm sending her a text in the middle of the night.

—*Emily need to speak to u URGENT pls pls could you drop in to my office today?*

I'm so thrilled when the reply pings back.

—*sure c u 11*

SIX HOURS LATER SHE ARRIVES, LOOKING LIKE A BOTTICELLI. I compliment her because she loves that and then get straight to the point.

'Are you really having the op, Emily?'

She looks cornered. 'There's no alternative, not if I am true to who I really am—because I'm not a man. I never have been. I've always known that.' Her trained declaration, in a tiny, terrified voice.

'Emily, tell me about your cock.'

This hangs in the air, scarily. I was also shocked when the words came out my mouth. Thankfully, Emily is giggling, her hand on her mouth like a little kid. 'What did you say?'

'Tell me about your cock. And your balls.'

'You can't ask me about that!' she laughs. 'You're so weird!'

'Alright,' I say. 'Sorry.'

She can't stop giggling now. Neither can I.

'It's quite big,' she whispers. 'People are always surprised. Me especially!'

We're really laughing now.

'What else?'

'Wanna see it? I got a photo. Or should I just take it out?'

'No! Definitely not. But I really want you to think about what you've got, what you've lived all your life with, and

193

what's a part of you, even though it may have troubled you. You know, when girls get breasts, they often feel embarrassed and self-conscious. Suddenly they're carrying this rack on their chests and they're getting looked at. A lot of young girls are afraid of becoming teenagers because they don't want to take on the obviousness of being women. It's not an unusual feeling. And lots of us have similar feelings about other aspects of ourselves. Some of us, as we age, get facelifts or tummy tucks. Some of us have behavioural features that we're not proud of, and we go to shrinks to try and iron them out. We all have stuff we want to get rid of, but very often, what bothers us doesn't bother anyone else, and what we really need to get rid of is the feeling of discontent, not the thing that causes it. To alter yourself physically, and permanently, can be done but it's not necessarily helpful. And it's not necessarily truthful. I want to be sure you know what you're doing and that you're not allowing anyone to influence you.'

'I know you think that,' she says. 'Madden says you're a Nazi. If you are one, you're a nice one.' And with that, her beautiful green eyes are suddenly spilling tears. 'I'm so scared.'

'Then for fuck's sake, delay everything. Go on holiday. I'll give you the money. No obligation. You don't have to pay it back. Just go away somewhere and think about it.'

'I'm a soldier,' she says.

'No you're not.'

'I am. That's what I came to tell you. And I'm sorry but I don't think we can meet again.'

And with that she gets up, gathers her bag and walks out.

And because today's a day that the Fucked-Up Fate Fairy has decreed should be the day when another part of *The Plan* gets crapped on, I don't even have time to say *Fuuuuuck!* I just bang my head against the door because my phone's pinging in that shrill, annoying ringtone that Natalie has instructed me sternly never to ignore:

—*Don't forget! Angela is after you, so be prepared …*
IMPORTANT!

And a tiny spray of flowers and hearts.

Another Difficult Meeting With Angela
16 May, 9:23 pm

Am I the unreasonable one, Olivia? Really? Judge for yourself. This is how today went.

Angela and Matilda arrived unannounced and this time I know it's serious because Matilda isn't throwing herself around, trying to get Instagram fanny shots with Angela angrily tugging on a new nose ring. Realising that my only hope of getting out alive from this juvenile gulag is to be obliging in every possible way, I shepherd them in with a capacious grin and allow Matilda to read her little agenda— *ze* BBC issue, *ze* Hungry Dog issue, *ze* Vang issue—all without interruption, until a little pause before *ze* finance issue.

Mention of the BBC does of course require some response but when I playfully ask if the BBC is happy with everything Angela stares at me crazily, as if I'm crazy, and shouts NO! several times, in response to which I explain engagingly that my problem with the BBC is both philosophical and autobiographical—a spurned-lover sort of thing—but all I get is the trademark shriek and a flurry of furious BBC legal letters all demanding the return of their stupid paperwork, and when I calmly reply 'Okay, relax: I'll send back all their stuff; now can we now talk about Emily?' Angela creases into a mute heap and Matilda moves swiftly onto the next item which is not Emily but *ze* Hungry Dog.

It turns out that the deal is now in real trouble, and that they've started making weird demands like a pre-merge of our software teams, and when I say 'Okay, let's pre-merge,' it's immediately clear that I've said the stupidest thing imaginable, because Angela uncreases and puts on her sarcastic face—the one with the bared teeth—and demands to know if I know anything about what we do as a company, to which I truthfully reply, 'No, Angela, of course not. We

195

both know I'm here purely for the money and my position is based entirely on luck and pedigree, so please explain,' to which she starts to howl and says, 'I. Can't. Do. This. No. More,' which is how I speak sometimes, when I'm enraged —but more grammatically.

I am stopped from forgiving Angela her double negative by Matilda, who urgently explains that the company needs more capita, *Ja*, because *ze* whole proposition is based on *ze* marginal arbitrage points built through *ze* algorhythmic comm-webbing strategy *zat* enables us to harvest micro-yields through every point of *ze* web exchange, *Ja*, in every trans-action, be it *ze* dating or *ze* purchasing or *ze* avatar shifting or *ze* many other point-of-exchange yields, before continuing that 'we have *zis* advantage because of our software and without *zis* we are very vulnerable. *Ja*?'

And it is at that point that I slice through the word soup of Matilda's babble to tell them about Len's stark warning: that all they want is Wang.

The effect is stunning. I'm suddenly back. In charge. Me, Olivia: boss of my very own company. Can you imagine?

After a stunned silence they both ask if I'm serious.

'Like, what did he say? Word for word!' Angela barks.

'He said all they want is Wang,' I repeat. 'And some stuff about rescue cats.'

'All they want is Wang?' cries Angela.

'All *zey vant* is *Vang*!? cries Matilda.

At this point Matilda turns to me with big pleading eyes. 'David, listen to me, please. *Vang* is everything. No *Vang*, no MeeZee mit *ze* exclamation mark and *zat* is why you have to invest in *Vang*. Because *Vang* is *Vang*, and MeeZee! Is MeeZee! No *uzzer* way.'

And that's it. They're up and packing up their phones, iPads, chargers, laptops and tablets and are heading for the door, so I spring up and block their exit. 'Now listen to me! We have to talk about Emily. Do you know that Madden is a psychopath who's persuading Emily to have his prick and balls cut off?' whereupon Matilda puts her hand on my arm, offers a gentle squeeze, and tells me that she asked Emily about this herself, and was assured her that it was her own choice, *Ja?*, and that Emily was a warrior in a political struggle and that we should all respect her wish for liberation, and that *zat*'s all *zere* was to say.

When I yell—and I do yell—that Emily isn't a warrior but a victim, Matilda gently pats me and asks me if I'm maybe being a little loud and a little sexist, *Ja?*, because women can be warriors too, you know. They then push past me and head out, leaving me wanting to projectile vomit myself out of the window. But I'm spared from such drama by the sudden intervention of my Fate Fairy, who decides to stage another surreal little entrance in the form of a cheerful text from Dent.

—*Don't forget. Tonight at six at the hospital. Don't be late! Can't wait!*

All of which means I've got precisely three hours to get home, wash, change, meet you and Moose and Masaai, get you all into the car, and hurry us off to hospital so that a bearded fundamentalist can bind me with leather straps beside the bed of my brain-dead father.

And now I no longer feel like screaming. Now I feel like running amok with a chainsaw.

Can you blame me? Really?

The Big Moment
17 May, 11:45 am

This is how I recall last night's events, Olivia. I'll begin at the hospital.

We arrive to find Dent in reception, smiling and waving like a toothpaste ad. He's enjoying this way too much.

'Hello, hello, hello,' he says. 'Good, good, good. Lovely to see you're all here.'

'Lovely?' I say, feeling a fresh stab of loathing. 'Bring your opera glasses?'

'Oh, don't be daft, David,' Dent laughs. 'This is business, that's all. Hello, Olivia. Hello, Young People. Nice to meet you all.'

You step forward in that elegant way of yours. 'Peter, please can you explain exactly why we're here? Every time I ask David, he loses the capacity for rational speech.'

'Yes, yes,' Dent chortles, then reverts to a lawyerly scowl. 'It is rather unusual, Olivia. We're all here because of a legal agreement. Think of this as a plea bargain.'

'A plea bargain?'

'That's right, Olivia. You see, David racially assaulted a rabbi called Menachem—not *his* rabbi, we must stress—and to avoid a trial, a civil action, a scandal, a prison sentence, an incalculable reputational loss and the probable forfeiture of his father's not inconsiderable estate, David has undertaken to perform certain Jewish rites and rituals and— unusually, I have to say—you and Moose are required to be present.'

We all stop breathing.

'Did he just call me Moose?'

Moose has been miserably passive all day, head in a droop, but now she's furiously alive. 'Did he just call me Moose?'

'I don't know, Dear. I don't think so,' you say.

'Did you just call me Moose?'

For the first time ever, Dent looks nervous. 'I'm afraid I did.' he stutters.

But Moose is rounding on you and me. 'Did you tell him my name was Moose? Did you tell the whole world?'

'No! No!'

'I'm not stupid, Guys,' she says.

'Of course you're not stupid!' we both say, and shrink with relief when she turns on Dent once more.

'My name's Amelia, okay? Amelia!'

'Delighted to meet you, Amelia,' Dent says with a desperate smile. 'And thank you for coming. And you are—?'

'Masaai,' says Masaai who's been lapping up the Moose drama.

'Ah, the famous Masaai!' laughs Dent. 'Very good, very good. Well, welcome, and thank you all so much for coming. Ah, look, they're here bang on time!'

The Jews have walked in and both are on the phone. Hymie, remember, the one who can't speak English, spots Dent, who speaks it exquisitely, and heads exuberantly in our direction.

'*Shulum aleichem*,' he says and enthusiastically shakes Dent's hand.

Then he turns to me. '*Shulum aleichem, Dovidl*!'

'*Sholom-a-whydontyougoandfuckyourself*,' I slur as he pumps my hand ingratiatingly.

'David, please,' Dent mutters. 'We're all going to have a nice, civilised meeting. Okay?'

'Relax: the dumb arse can't speak English,' I remind him. I'm about to launch a fresh attack on the mobster with the mobile but am cut off by Menachem marching swiftly up to me.

'A full house of bearded medievals,' I say. 'What a joy.'

'Oh, stop it, David,' says Olivia. 'Let's just do this and go.'

Menachem's is grinning from ear to ear. 'Hello, Everyone, hello, hello, hello! Sorry for the delay: such a nightmare, parking a big car—and you want me to be honest? So I'll be honest: I'm not such a good driver, *tsum bedoyern*, but of course you need a big Volvo when you have five children and another on the way, *Borich Hashem*, and even now it's too small, *tucker*! So, hello, Peter! Hello, Mrs Britton! Hello, *Dovidl*! Hello, Moose. *Borichim haboyim!*

Everybody stops breathing.

'Did he just call me Moose?'

The three of us—you, me and Dent—all suddenly feel the need to examine our fingernails and murmur about not having heard anything untoward.

'What did you call me?'

'Moose. I called you Moose. *Nu?* That's your name! Nice!'

'My name's Amelia.'

'Moose! Amelia! Not something to make a *farbrengen* about. Amelia's not as nice a name as Moose, if you ask me, but *azoy*, hello Amelia! And hello, Masaai Skolnik.'

Masaai starts hooting. 'Fuck, Man. You know my old name. That's weird, Man: weird.'

'Masaai Skolnik from San Francisco! Of course I know your name. I've got *mishpucha* in San Francisco—but that's for another time. Okay, so I'm Menachem, Ben's friend and rabbi, and there's no need to use bad language, anyone. Good. Shall we go up and see your beloved father, *Dovid*?'

And with a sly wink he scuttles off to the elevator, accompanied by Hymie and a florid exchange of hand gestures.

'Wow,' says Masaai. 'That's what I call a fucking Jew!'

'Me too,' I say.

We enter the room and Moose rushes to Ben in a storm of sobs and throws herself upon his inert, tubed-up body. The Boys look at each other and exchange eyebrow chat. I'm watching you watching Moose but I also notice that Masaai is glued to the sight of the Jews, now fussing with an ornate velvet bag and unwrapping two little black boxes with long leather straps dangling from them.

I whisper to the Boys, 'That's my daughter, smothering the patient.'

'Oh you mean, Moose?' says Little Boy.

'We met her the other night,' says Big Boy.

I urgently explain to them the danger of calling her Moose.

'Okay,' says Little Boy with a naughty smile.

'Actually, I saw mooses in Canada last year,' says Big Boy.

Little Boy pounces on him. 'It's "moose". The plural is "moose".'

The Big Boy is flustered. 'I knew that. "Mooses" sounded wrong the moment I'd said it. I was about to correct myself.'

'I'm sure,' says Little Boy provocatively.

'I knew it sounded wrong.'

'Yes, because it was wrong.'

'Okay, Boys, but can you please remember, her name's Amelia, not Moose.'

They're surprised I'm still there.

We resume staring at Moose straddling Ben.

'Doctors: is it okay, doing what she's doing?'

'I think so,' says Little Boy.

'I'm watching the monitors,' says Big Boy.

'How is my father?' I say.

'In himself, not so good, but there's an upside!' says Little Boy.

'Really?'

'Yes! Another paper's been accepted!'

But there is no time to discuss this because the Beards are moving purposefully to the centre of the room amid a trail of shawls, skullcaps, books and leather straps.

'Everybody, thank you for coming,' Menachem announces loudly. 'May I ask the Jewish men here to put these on—' Hymie passes around a pile of black *yarmulkes*'—and then we can begin.'

'Actually, I'm more black than Jewish,' Masaai tells Menachem.

'Black is good,' Menachem laughs. 'You know what? They call us Blacks too—because of the *kapotas*! The black coats. See? Funny! And you need a *yarmulke* too, David: here you are.'

'I'll wear one,' says Peter Dent brightly.

'No need,' I growl.

'Don't be so selfish, David.' Menachem's laughing. 'Covering the head shows respect for God and God is there for all people, not just *di Yidn!* Of course you can wear one if

201

you want, Peter. Here, take this one, it's my favourite. In fact, keep it. A present from me to you. Don't mention it. Alright, so we're all ready?'

Dent is gushing in a nauseating way but I am distracted. From the corner of my eye, I spot Hymie creeping up on me with an outstretched arm and an elaborate prayer shawl.

'So, what we're about to do is connect with our Creator, the *Eybishter*, with the words of the *Shema*,' says Katz. 'You know what the *Shema* is, David?'

'A dance step?'

'No, ' he says firmly 'it's a prayer from the *Toyreh* and it serves *Yiddishkeit's* basic creed. So, first put on the *tallit*.'

Hymie's all over me, enveloping me in the large, fringed shawl.

'Is this in the contract, Peter?' I groan.

'Oh yes,' says Dent with a stupidly holy look.

'Fucking Jesus.'

'And from this moment, no profanities!' Menachem says fiercely. 'Now, *Dovidl*, repeat after me: *Boruch atah Adonoi, Elohynu Melech Ho'olom, asher kidishonu bemitzvosov, vetzivonu, lehisatef batzitzis.*'

I repeat it, phrase by phrase, juggling and almost choking on the unattractive gutterals in my mouth, all the time conscious of the penetrating silence that has suddenly gripped the room.

'Now we are going to lay *tefillin*. These *tefillin*—' he holds out the phylacteries so everyone in the room can see them '—are the source of miracles. For 3,000 years Jewish men have performed the ritual that David is about to perform in honour of his father. Are you ready, *Dovid*?'

'Bind me, Menachem, bind me!' I cry.

'Are you ready?' he repeats.

'Yes.'

'So, hold out your left arm and roll up your sleeve as far it can go.' I do this and the Rabbi pulls the phylactery up over my bicep, tightens the strap, wraps the leather strap round my arm in seven coils and around my hand three times, and recites a prayer, which I copy. 'Now this one goes on your forehead,' and he arranges the second phylactery on my head, with the black box where my hairline once was, followed by another prayer. 'And now we go back to the arm strap and bind it around your fingers, to make the Hebrew letter *shin*—ש—and then we say the *Shema*. Okay?'

As the prayer tennis goes on, I suddenly hear another Hebrew voice. It's Masaai, at the back of the room, grinning like an oaf, reciting the *Shema*, which he knows by heart.

When it's over, I see Menachem staring at me with a predatory grin.

'I bet you get your rocks off binding men, Menachem. Is it some bondage thing you've got going on? Something you guys took with you from the House of *Bondage* all those years back!'

'Did you notice the positions of the *tefillin*?' he replies coolly.

'Actually, no.'

'So I'll remind you. One on the arm, one on the head. Can you think why?'

'It's a martial arts thing? S and M? A way of remembering the shopping?'

'The one on the arm is next to the heart and the one on the forehead is next to the frontal cortex. Body and mind. Earth and soul. You get me?'

'Now that is interesting!' says Dent, suddenly piping up.

'Peter, if I catch you putting one of those things on, I promise you will no longer be my lawyer,' I say.

'Don't be daft, David,' Dent laughs. 'I'm a cradle Catholic. But I do find all this stuff terribly interesting.'

'Well, great,' I say, stripping myself of all the loathsome fetish accessories. 'Tell you what? You stay here with your new love to explore it all further—and then you can tell me all about it some other time. I'm off.'

I turn to find you stroking Moose's back as she resumes buffeting her prone grandfather with a fresh battery of hugs and sobs. I also spot Masaai examining the phylacteries with a forensic seriousness, and decide that sidling up to him would give me some protection from being assaulted straight off by the bearded twosome. 'Did I hear you muttering away in Hebrew?'

'Yeah, Man! Yeah, Man,' Masaai chortles. 'All comes back. Fucking mad! You know, Dude, I could be an Igbo. They're the Nigerian Jews.' I'm keen to explore Masaai's rich new seam of Kantian self-reflection but Dent is loudly clearing his throat.

'Ladies and gentlemen, one moment please. Firstly I'd like to thank Menachem and Hymie—' he bows slightly '— and Olivia and Amelia and Masaai for coming along today and helping David sort out his contractual obligations. The next stage of the arrangement is a meeting at David and Olivia's house for the installation of the mezuzah. Is that right, Menachem? Did I say it right?'

'Like a born *Yid, tucker!*'

'Excellent. So, see you all in a week or two, and thank you, Menachem, for setting this all up. Goodbye.'

Dent is grinning like a lunatic so I follow him out of the room and corner him by the lifts so I can slap him. 'What the fuck is wrong with you, Peter?'

'What? Nothing! Nothing at all. You're too emotional about this, David. And to be frank, you should regard yourself as lucky.'

'Lucky? Lucky! Are you kidding?'

'Yes, lucky, because they could have had you thrown into prison, and ruined your career and reputation, and sued you for a very great deal of money, and purloined your father's money into the bargain. I think you're missing the point here. Think about it. I'll call you later in the week.'

And with that, Dent turns on his shiny heels and closets himself in a waiting elevator, without looking round.

On my way back to my father's medical suite, I run into The Boys and detain them in the corridor.

'May I ask you a question, Lads? How much longer is this bullshit likely to go on for?'

'We're still waiting for final editorial approval,' says Little Boy. 'It could come through any time now.'

'I don't think very long,' says Big Boy, a little more helpfully. 'Your father's body is deteriorating. I think we're talking days.'

'Yes, we've only just made it,' says Little Boy.

And then it happens. Moose has torn herself away from her grandfather, and hurries out of the room and into the corridor. You walk uncertainly after her, your head in your hands and despair in your eyes.

I rush to your side. You stop, grudgingly, wanting to follow and not be waylaid.

'What?' I say.

'She's confirmed it!' you hiss. 'She told your father.'

'He's about to die.'

'That's why she confided in him. I overheard. She's pregnant. She's bloody pregnant.'

The Truth Emerges
19 May, 11:05 am

I can't believe it, Olivia. We're alone together. And going out.

'I wasn't expecting you to come out with me tonight,' I say.

'Believe me, David, we are not going out. Samuel called and begged me for half an hour. He said he'd already spoken to you, and you were up for it, and I find it very difficult to say no to him. So this is Samuel's birthday party and very much not a date. Besides which, Amelia's driving me insane and I had to get out of the house. Did you manage to speak to her today?'

'She's shut me out,' I say. 'Slams the door whenever she hears me coming. And on those rare occasions when I might otherwise be able to trap her, he's there with his tongue lodged in her oesophagus.'

You look me straight in the eye and clutch my arm.

'You have to talk to her, okay? She can't have Masaai's baby. She just can't. You agree, don't you?'

And because you look so beautiful in your distress and because you're holding my arm so tightly that I can feel the sway of your breasts, I enthusiastically agree. 'I don't think you need to worry. They're aborting.'

You stop dead.

'You know this for a fact? How?'

'I spoke to Masaai.'

'Why didn't you tell me! What did he say?'

'He said it was immoral for white people to have babies. I pointed out he was black but he said there was still an unacceptably high genetic risk of the baby being white. So they're aborting.'

'Good boy! Clever boy!' You are actually pumping both fists when your phone beeps again and off you go.

Third time tonight. Bleeding Boaz.

I watch you as you walk into the shadows. The verve of your stride. The boots. The swell of your breasts. The sway of your hair. And that annoying dreamy smile as you type. Like a schoolgirl, Olivia. Like you once were with me.

Eventually you return, frowning. 'Remind me again, who's going to be there tonight?'

My heart sinks as I go through the list. 'Antony and Lydia. Angus. Guy and Ginny, of course. Alan and Josie. And that gay French academic, Yves or something.'

Then I emit a long, low groan.

'They're your friends not mine David,' you say witheringly. 'Samuel told me you told him about us. He actually begged me not to leave you. Told me how much you loved me.'

'It's the truth. What did you say?'

'I told him you demonstrate it in unusual ways.'

'You mean Janice Toybeen? I wish you could understand what a non-event that was. It had nothing to with me. At the most it was entrapment. There was nothing about it I wanted.'

It's the slow way you stop dead and turn that's so scary. And the determined look in your eyes. I guess I know what's coming. Something I've been expecting for years,

"But it wasn't entrapment, was it, David? This thing with Janice has happened before. You think I don't know?'

I can't breathe. The worst of secrets, seemingly locked away, now exposed. And with such casual disdain. 'Three times in forty years. Nostalgia fucks. All to do with the past. Nothing meaningful. That was it.'

You shrug. 'Let's go. We're late. And don't worry. I'm not going to bang on about her. But you have to get used to it. I've decided. I'm going to live by myself. And I'm going to tell Moose.'

I am struck down. Literally, can't move a muscle.

And then you smile, a beautiful *coup de grace*. 'Now man up,' you say and take my hand. 'We can do this together. It does not have to destroy us. And we'll always have the good things that we had. Come, we're late.'

In Vino Veritas
20 May, 1:05 am

This is what I recall from last night's disaster.

We arrive, wordless and avoiding each other's eyes, but Sam opens the door with a joyous smile and envelops you in a hug. 'Olivia, darling! You came! So glad!'

'Of course I came. Happy birthday, Sam!'

'And David, dear boy!' He pats me quickly, and then the two of you sail down the hallway, chattering and giggling, and that's you gone, until your rather dramatic turn which comes a lot later in the evening. I am left alone at the foot of the staircase, my wounded heart dropping another notch as I hear Antony's unmistakably annoying faux-Cockney voice notch up in volume.

He knows I'm here. He's waiting.

It's going to be torture but I've made a resolution. Tonight I will show courage for you, Olivia. I'll be quiet, responsible and sober. And under no circumstances will I break my pledge to Sam not to say anything unpleasant, not even to Antony and his yellow-toothed wife, Ginny.

My stomach is twisting as I enter the room.

The first person I see is Antony. He's occupying a large presidential armchair and grinning like a shark.

'Ah David!'

'Hello, Antony,' I say. 'Hello, Ginny. Hello, Alan and Josie and Gareth and Lydia. Hello Angus. Hi, Guy: that sounds silly doesn't it—the rhyme! Long time no see, Yves.'

I am instantly aware how much I dislike everyone. Top of the list has to be Antony and Ginny, the lord and lady millionaire socialists. Next comes Guy Morrison, whose tenth film about ugly people—ugly miners, ugly midwives, ugly labourers, ugly hod-carriers, ugly pigeon fanciers, ugly factory drudges—is now on general release, which means that everywhere I go I am assaulted by images of his fat bearded face peering out with his repulsively manicured compassion. Next to him is his fleshy wife Lydia, once a producer of drearily socialist kitchen-sink dramas, her suspicious piggy eyes blinking and her mouth stuffed with something bready. On the sofa, the skeletal Yves Monroux, infamously radical professor of Sociology at the LSE and world leader in using words no one human can hope to understand, together with his latest pretty-boy catamite, a young unsmiling Brazilian lad called Salim. Next to them, Alan and Josie Greenberg, *Guardian* columnists notable for their permanent whine of high-pitched indignation. And finally Angus McCourt, BBC grandee with a Scottish voice so hypnotisingly emollient that every time he opens his suave trap, I feel an irresistible urge to karate-chop him in the throat.

I tell myself to calm down and then suffer a pang of panic when I actually hear my distaste and wonder if others can hear it too, the way you worry about people hearing your stomach rumbling; but it appears that I'm safe, because everyone greets me warmly, some with a touch of pity perhaps, some even getting out of their chairs to give me an encouraging hug. I'm pretty sure they know everything: Janice Toybeen, the *Newsnight* car crash, my BBC disgrace, you.

Sam pops his head around the door. 'Glass of bubbly, dear boy?'

'Always,' I say, lifting the fluted glass and making for the furthest seat from Antony, who's following my every move. Finally he corners my gaze because there's nowhere else to look.

'And how is David Britton?' Antony inquires, glinting.

'Yeah, we haven't seen you in yonks,' Ginny adds.

'It must be much more than yonks,' I say, desperately. 'Wasn't it yonks last time we met? And how are Ant and Gin?' I call them Ant and Gin because I know they hate being called Ant and Gin.

'Busy,' says Antony darkly.

'So busy,' Ginny repeats. 'You've no idea. Life really changes when you join The House. And both of us! Imagine! Ridiculous really.'

On this point my mind is set. Under no circumstances will I acknowledge their stupid peerages. 'Pass the peanuts, please,' I say and decide to abandon the evening strategy and get blind drunk. 'And the bottle.'

As you know, Olivia, I've never liked Antony, not even when we were at university and floating around in the same circles. He was always tiresome, his unrequitable neediness flecked with moments of aggression. It wasn't just that he lacked humour or had studied business or had gone into the dullest recesses of industry after graduating—unlike us, the glamour pusses, who'd gone into the media. You know what gets on my nerves about Antony? It's his eagerness to outperform morally. He's shameless about it. I can't stand it. And the fact that he's never had one idea that's even marginally original or the slightest bit funny.

And today he's fabulously wealthy and a key Labour Party donor, so everyone of course finds him hilarious and brilliant.

'Still in TV, David? Haven't seen you on screen for a while.' He's not giving up.

'No, too old, I'm afraid, Ant. And definitely too right-wing.'

A nervous laughter flutters about the room.

'You know, I had a long chat with a Brexit supporter the other day,' Alan's saying. 'Like talking to an extraterrestrial from some planet we've never heard of.'

'Earth, perhaps?' I say, trying make it sound playful but failing catastrophically, to judge from the faces around me.

'The thing is, he wasn't entirely unintelligent,' Alan continues, refusing to be derailed. 'A sort of intellectual cannibal. And there are probably hundreds more like him.'

'You had a chat with someone whose views you don't share?' I say, feeling my blood rising and pouring myself another glass. 'Now that is unbelievable.'

'Oh David!' says Guy benignly. 'Always so angry!'

He's looking at me compassionately, his lachrymose face lined with benevolent pity. I want to say, 'By the way, Guy, I saw your shit little movie the other day. Well done, Mate: it's about as uplifting as a sheltered employment scheme for out-of-work abattoir workers,' but I can't because the bastard's film has just been selected for the Palme d'Or at Cannes.

'Talking of Brexit, our au pair was in tears last week,' says Ginny. 'It's so sad, all this xenophobia.'

All I remember about Ginny is that she studied Arabic, spent six months in Damascus, and then talked about nothing else for the next thirty years.

'Who's your au pair feeling xenophobic towards?' I ask, and knock back the remains of my second glass.

'No, David,' says Lydia, in that actressy voice. 'Ginny was referring to the xenophobia that Brexiteers are unleashing on migrant workers in this country. They're so vile.'

'Vile? The Brexiteers? The migrant workers? Just trying to get my bearings.'

'The poor girl was actually crying,' says his Lordship grimly. 'Real tears.'

'Sure it had nothing to do with her terms and conditions?'

Before the conversation can morph into an auction of solidarity with the put-upon nannies of London's media elite, I pour a third glass and brace myself for Antony's inevitable second wave.

'Let us move onto more important matters,' he announces. 'I think that a toast's in order, *n'est-ce pas*, David? Your great television success. First you win the Oscar and then, your crowning glory … *Crip Trips*? Is that what you called it?'

'That's it.'

'To *Crip Trips!*'

They all roar and raise their glasses.

'The show that blows the lid off tetraplegic sex,' I say desperately. 'Any of you watch it?'

'I caught a bit of it,' sneers the he-Greenberg. 'What can I say, apart from … gosh?'

They're all snorting.

'And of course we should all acknowledge that great *Newsnight* interview,' Antony continues. 'David, you really are becoming a bit of a rebel!'

There's a fresh round of malevolent laughter.

'Did you really say what you said, David?' says Angus.

'Say what?'

'What people said you said?'

'Which was what?' I say.

'That a lot more black kids should be frisked on the streets?'

'I didn't, Angus. I said that *all* black kids should be frisked on the streets—' they're staring now, mouths wide open '—because there's an epidemic of black gang crime. It might infringe on civil liberties but if everyone was frisked, there'd be fewer knives and fewer stabbings and fewer dead black kids and fewer weeping black parents. You'd think that would be obvious to any half-decent journalist. Freedom isn't always the highest good.'

'You can't possibly mean that,' says Guy, his fleshy face creased into a rictus of outrage. 'You're advocating a police state!'

'Actually, you can't possibly disagree, because it's a fact. Knife-crime rates per capita are higher among black kids than white kids. Can you not acknowledge that, Guy?'

'Now come on David,' says Angus. 'Knife crime has nothing to do with ethnicity: it's a factor of structural inequalities, youth unemployment, school-exclusion rates, urban poverty. You're sounding a little racist, loading it all onto skin colour.'

Yves is waving his hands around and yelping. 'No, no, no, no, no,' he cries; 'Angus, that's not enough! You must go deeper than crude structuralism. You must step back from any reliance on logocentrism and hierarchical oppositions. Your code words impose a nostalgic privileging of pater- nalistic pluralism—'

'So true,' marvels Ginny.

'—locking you into an artillery of imperialistic-capitalist hegemony.' Now Yves is shaking his head wildly, his tiny fists smashing gently against his lap in little spasms. 'You are the prisoner of your nuclear cultural weapons, the chosen alchemy of identity, you … '

He pauses, relishing his genius the way one might relish

an unusual fart, but lingering long enough to allow Angus back in.

'Oh, that's enough about *Newsnight*: it's for the chop soon anyway and it's far from being anyone's cup of tea any more. Now, tell us about *Crip Trips*.'

I realise that there is nothing but nothing to say about *Crip Trips* that is in any way positive, so I am hugely relieved when you and Sam enter the room.

Sam looks around in that innocent, surprised way of his, instantly discerning what's up, and says: 'You cannot be behaving yourself, David, which means that I must rescue everyone. Come, dear people: dinner is served. Can we all footle into the dining room? Thank you.'

SAMUEL HAS SPENT THE WHOLE WEEK PREPARING FOR THE dinner party and the table, as ever, is perfect. There are little bowls of the finest Aloreña and Castelvetrano olives, Ladurée crispy macarons with delicate shells and luxurious fillings, a variety of dips with Duck Rillettes, Burrata and Truffle Aioli, Caviar Butter and Lobster Thermidor, and Wagyu Tartare and Salted Caramel and Mascarpone crudités. The table is set with laced linen, antique silver cutlery and dazzling crystal. There are elegant name tags in satin and interweaved with fresh lemon blossoms and the lighting is intimate and subtle.

The food is of course sublime. The starter is sea bream ceviche with charred sweetcorn. Then we are offered a choice of Beef Wellington or truffle chicken and potato gratin but Sam, in his usual kind and careful way, has remembered Ginny's exuberant veganism and has just served her a caramelised onion tart with chicory and a vegan 'I'm Not Gorgonzola' gorgonzola.

Then everything unravels at a ferocious speed.

It's shocking because there's no warning. On the contrary, when it happens the mood's perfect. There've been no arguments or disagreements. Sam has expertly and sweetly stewarded all conversations with his subtle and wise humour, allowing everyone to take their boastful turns while steering us away from all landmines. Thus Antony and

213

Ginny have been able to mine their compassion for weeping au pairs and alzheimery lords while Guy has shown his deep love for the 'jejune' Croisette prostitute who stole his wallet and Yves has banged his tiny fists again in celebration of his new book *The Holocaust of Knowledge* and Alan and Josie have spoken of the heart-rending plight of the homeless who'll be 'teaching us so much' on those once-a-month Thursday-night meetings in a Hampstead church which they haven't attended yet but hope to do in the near future. Even I have enjoyed the evening, drunkenly talking football with the saturnine Salim and deploying my erratic Portuguese with vengeful abandon, all the time watching you, my beautiful wife, with heartbroken wonder. You're glowing on the far side of the table, the candlelight bathing you in a Caravaggio light, guffawing and gossiping with Sam.

So when, after a momentary lull in the conversation, Samuel returns to the table with two more bottles of wine from his famous cellar, the fury of the sudden storm catches everyone by surprise.

It erupts after Yves pronounces his own fabulous verdict on Sam's choice.

'This wine! Full-bodied, rich, spicey—I taste a background of dark fruit—plums, maybe blackcurrants—with a soupçon of herbs and, *oui*, oak. *Superbe! Magnifique!*'

'Thank you,' says Sam. 'I agree. Really quite special.'

'Certainly is,' says Guy relishing a dramatic sip.

'Top plonk,' says Alan. 'Top bloody plonk!'

'Ooh,' whinnies Ginny. 'What is it?'

'I'm guessing Argentina,' says Angus.

'California,' says His Lordship cannily.

'No,' Sam says affably, and holds up the bottle. 'It's a Yatir Forest Red. From the Golan, I believe. Who's for more?'

There's a sudden silence. Everyone's frozen.

'Did you say the Golan?' asks Alan.

'Yes,' says Sam.

'Golan—as in the Golan Heights? In Palestine?' asks Guy.

'Well, Israel, actually.' says Sam.

'Well it's not Israel, is it?' says Alan. 'Or Palestine. It's Syria. But it's occupied by Israel.'

'Worse than that,' says Ginny in a strident whine. 'They've annexed it, haven't they?'

'What, the vineyard?' says Sam. 'I hardly think—'

'The Zionists annexed it!' says Ginny, ceremonially slamming down her glass. 'They stole it! Samuel, I can't drink this!'

'Well, that makes a first,' I snort and ostentatiously fill my glass. This could be fun. 'Cheers!'

They all ignore me and one by one, put their glasses down.

Guy's face has crumpled. He peers out, his little eyes the image of tragic remorse. 'Did you know this was Zionist wine, Samuel? I guess not,' he says gently.

'Well, I did buy it at Ben Gurion airport!' Sam says.

'You *bought* it?' shrieks Ginny, not whinnying now. 'In Israel?'

'Look, we all make mistakes,' says Guy hastily, his fat seal face crinkling into folds of reproachful kindness. 'But I cannot drink it. I'm sorry, dear boy.'

'You were in Israel recently?' says Alan who has now put the glass as far away as his arm can reach.

'Yes,' says Sam, visibly shocked. 'Two weeks ago.'

'On some journalistic investigation?' says Josie.

'Not really,' says Sam 'though I did do a couple of interviews.'

'I suppose as a journalist you have to go to all sorts of places,' says Antony. 'I was in Saudi not long ago. Part of a House of Lords visit. Dreadful place. Utterly opulent—but dreadful.'

'Big mate of Israel now!' says Ginny, now whinnying again. 'Massive mates!'

'I was doing a piece on water,' says Sam, taking a slow, deliberate sip of wine.

'They're stealing Palestinian water,' says Ginny, back to shrieking.

'That's rubbish, Ginny,' says Sam quietly.

'I've seen it with my own eyes. With my own eyes!' She's pointing at her eyes. 'We were there, Sam. Right bloody there!'

'Well, you may have been, but it's bollocks. Most of the water in Israel is reclaimed from the sea. It's desalinated, dear girl—a technology that could save the whole Middle East, actually, if Israel's neighbours would only act normally and follow its example.' He takes another sip of wine. 'But I was mostly there on holiday. I've been going every year for a few years now. Tel Aviv is lovely and, unlike just about everywhere else in the Middle East, one can be a gay man there without having one's hands cut off, or one's feet, or one's head.'

'You visit Israel … for pleasure?' says Guy, incredulous.

His little eyes are popping out of his fat face.

'Every year, dear boy. Twice last year.'

Yves is waving his fists and incanting something about Zionism being the product of a death-wish Holocaust instinct to brutalise but runs out of puff, allowing Alan to slip in.

'Samuel—really, at the very least, the *very* least, you ought to have given us a choice … .'

'This is an assault!' says Lydia.

'Exactly,' whinnies Ginny. 'I am so offended.'

'I can't believe you forced me,' Lydia is saying, but Antony has got to his feet and has spread his magisterial hands.

'It's a mistake,' he says reasonably. 'We all make mistakes.'

Throughout this increasingly unsettling exchange, I keep looking at you. You have been resolutely staring at the table, your chin tucked in but listening to every word.

Then suddenly you look up. 'May I say a word?'

Your voice is firm. It's a surprise: you've been so quiet until now. Everyone hushes as you get to your feet. And you start with that beautiful smile, the way you always do when you speak at events.

'Samuel, you've given us the most marvellous meal. The food: out of this world! And I couldn't help but notice the care you took in providing vegan alternatives of equal quality. You're a beautiful and conscientious host, Sam. You always have been and we're very lucky to have you—aren't we, everyone?'

216

You put your hands together in a gesture intended to encourage applause. There's a murmur of agreement and a couple of guests join in.

'This evening, Samuel, under your roof, something occurred to me. Every person around this table has spent a lifetime committed in some way to truth and honest enquiry. Right? That's why we used to argue so much when we were younger. Do you remember? We had rows that went on for days. They were thrilling, weren't they? And fun. And sexy! Searching for answers and exploring the unexpected.

'Now pause for a moment and consider what's just happened. The moment the question of Samuel's wine came up, you were all of one mind. Suddenly there was no argument. It was all black and white. Israel is bad—and not just bad but exceptionally bad, uniquely bad, inherently bad. A criminal, apartheid, illegitimate, genocidal occupying power, the worst oppressor on Earth, the puppet of America's military-industrial complex and yet somehow also America's puppet-master, the tail that wags the dog. That's a funny bit of conspiratorial doublethink, isn't it! But you all buy into it, don't you?'

You stop and look around. Some of the guests focus on their laps.

'You all work in the media and education,' you continue, 'and the rest of us rely on you for your balance and impartiality—and yet, when it comes to Israel, you become an echo chamber of cliché and cynicism. There's not a flicker of doubt in your minds, not a spark of scepticism about all the excitable little rumours that you swap between you, the journalistic morsels, the falsities and deceptions that Israel's sworn enemies put out and that you gobble up. The mere repetition of the things you repeat turns them into incontrovertible truths, and they must be truths because your friends all repeat them, and you couldn't not repeat them because that would make you deeply suspect.

Antony is rousing himself to talk over you but you shut him down with an imperious finger.

'One moment, Antony. I know how bored you all are being reminded that half of Israel's Jews came from families that were wiped off the European map eighty years ago. That's sad, you say, but it doesn't justify their moving to the Mediterranean. Well, maybe it doesn't and maybe it does. But the other half of Israel comes from families kicked out of Arab countries when those countries "cleansed" themselves ethnically of their Jews, and that's not something that you have any trouble with. Interesting double standard, don't you think? And you're okay with that.'

It's the way you're standing—shoulders back, eyes blazing —that gives you this terrifying power. My darling, I have never seen you like this before, and it is a privilege to watch.

'And here's the nastiest thing,' you go on. 'When we Jews started returning to the homeland the Romans expelled us from two thousand years ago, our semitic cousins didn't say, "Welcome back, welcome back! You've been away so long!" Or some did, but their friends murdered them. The rest of them sided with Hitler, so that the principle of racial exclusivity that the Nazis had tried to impose on the German Reich could be imposed also on that thin strip of Israel, at some points only nine miles wide, that we have always regarded as our natural home.

'You know, because you're not ostriches, that Nazi-inspired filth is still being routinely published in Arab children's colouring books and in United Nations-funded school books, and that the people brought up on this trash are not just demanding racial purity for their precious land, they're also calling for us Jews to be wiped out, not only in Palestine but across the world. And you say nothing!

'But worst of all, for me, is the callous way you deny our relationship with Israel. This was the place that shaped our nationhood and our national consciousness thousands of years ago, and that gave us our name—*Israelites*. This is the place that the pious among us have prayed, three times a day, to return to, for two millennia. And you airily tell us that we're nothing more than settler-colonialists with no real ties to the land. And to make us sound more offensive and yourselves more incisive, you repeat lies about us having a "secret agenda"—of being imperialists intent on dominating more and more territory and exploiting other people's assets.

'By contrast, those mean people who can't bear the idea of our owning just 8,000 square miles of the 1.2 million square miles that make up the Arab lands—they're the oppressed, you say, and the oppressed can bomb and kill and kidnap and do what they like—because they're oppressed! What a great cop-out! And you lovely liberal, educated, humanitarian people are all okay with that.'

There's a sudden storm of protest, led by Guy, shouting 'Oh, come on!'

'Oh, I'll come on,' you say. 'You think Israel oppresses Arabs? Do you know how many active synagogues there are in the Arab world today? Apart from Morocco, fewer than ten and they're all empty. And how many mosques do you think there are in Israel? I'll tell you: over 400—in a little country the size of Wales. And you lecture Israel on intolerance and racism? I don't see you lecturing the Arab world about intolerance and racism. In fact I don't see you lecturing anyone except Israel. You're utterly obsessed and it's utterly irrational. And you're okay with that?

Ginny has finally stopped eating and started bleating and flapping her hands. You shut her up with a laser look.

'I wish you'd look at yourselves and see what you've become. You used to be so bright and discerning—and it's all gone. You pride yourself on thinking that Israel is tough on its enemies because it's inherently brutal, and you won't acknowledge the inherent brutality that its enemies have lined up against it, because … because what? You're afraid of stigmatising them? You're not afraid of stigmatising us. You're not afraid of alienating us. In fact, you rather enjoy getting the boot in. Oh, but I forgot: there aren't so many of us. We don't count. And we're mostly doing all right, so stigmatising us is okay. What an ingenious moral inversion.

'I'm so disappointed in you. You work in sectors that reward you for sowing hatred and division, rather than using what you know to solve conflicts and bring people together, and you're never called to account by your peers. You're a nasty, hypocritical, intellectually vacuous lot and I don't expect you to join me but I'm going to raise this glass of excellent Golan red and invite you to drink a toast to

Samuel, on his birthday, and to hope, with me, that he is able to keep going back to the only true liberal democracy in the Middle East and enjoy its extraordinary achievements and openness and sense of joy.'

And with that, you raise your brimming glass to your ruby red lips and take a long draught. 'Beautiful!' you say, as you take your seat again in the golden Caravaggio light.

'To Israel!' I cry out, in the strange silence that descends, euphoric at your daring, amazed by your defiance, grateful to have been there to witness the heroism of your stand. A year ago you were indifferent to Israel, Olivia, even perhaps a little hostile: this evening, you've focused your hostility instead on the phenomenon of mob mentality, of band-wagoning, and you've done so in a way that might, just for one tiny moment, have got through to them.

And the reason? I'd like to think it's because we've both had enough of the clichés and groupthink of our craven media-driven culture but I suspect there's another reason: Boaz.

That *Fickenfotzer*, Boaz.

Thrilled by you but now also feeling crushed and beaten, I withdraw into what is left of my fine, sombre Yatir Forest Red —feeling, for the first time in my life, a little proud to know a Jew; and perhaps (I cannot believe I am saying this, Olivia) a little proud to be one, too.

Your remarks have of course been devastating. There are a few quiet attempts at conversation around the table but they sputter out and it's not long before everyone's heading for the door. After some mumbled apologies and muted hugs, everyone's gone and we're alone.

You, me and Sam.

I pour us all a valedictory drink.

'Happy birthday, birthday boy!' I say, holding out my glass of wine to our host.

'Yes, a very happy birthday,' you echo. Then you get up to give Sam a hug. He gets up too, to accept the embrace.

We are not expecting the response that follows.

Samuel Springs A Surprise
20 May, 3:15 am

Samuel remains on his feet, which strikes me as unusual and suggests that he is about to impart something significant. Is that possible—our dear Sam, the mastermind of deflection, ready to reveal something of his secret world?

You and I exchange a quick glance. We are mesmerised

'Why do you think I visit Israel?' he asks.

'Tel Aviv?' you suggest. 'The night life? The freedom? Like you said.'

'There is that,' Sam says 'but those are not the main reasons. Can I tell you something important, something you have never known about me?'

We exchange glances of enquiry.

'I think you're going to tell us that you're Jewish,' I say. 'Now it all makes sense!'

'You're getting ahead of yourself, dear boy,' says Sam, in his urbane, ironic way. 'Now let me tell you my story—and help yourself to some more Yatir Forest Red, or whatever you like.'

We each pour ourselves a fresh glass and settle back in our chairs, entranced.

'I think I've told David a little about my mother: that she was a concert pianist and hanged herself in Buenos Aires when I was thirteen. The story made the papers at the time. It was tragic. But there's a lot more to it than you'd imagine. A few years ago, I became a little obsessed and did some research on her. She was born in a town called Antakya—Antioch in historical times—which was part of Turkey, near the Syrian border.

'Fourteen years before World War Two began, a revolt broke out in Syria against French colonial rule. Ultimately, the revolt was unsuccessful. The French military suppressed it, brutally, but, to my astonishment, I found out that the

221

families of both my parents had taken part in it—and enthusiastically. Lots of people got arrested and mistreated, and a few were actually executed. Others, like the Sultan al-Atrash, the leader of the Revolt—a rather fine-looking chap with a magnificent moustache—were forced into exile, and among them were my grand-aunt and uncle who escaped with my orphaned mother to Buenos Aires.

'It was there that she grew up and learned to play the piano. Apparently she was a prodigy, sight-reading Bach by the age of nine and eventually becoming a concert pianist. My father was also an exile from Antakya, and what they'd experienced as little children, especially the loss of their parents, must have been deeply damaging. In any case, I think they were both depressives. And one night, after a concert, my mother took her own life—in our garden.

You squeeze his hand. Your eyes are brimming. He acknowledges your kindness with that inimitable Samuel smile, and continues.

'What does this have to do with Israel? Well, after my mother died, my father sent me to boarding school in England and I never saw him again. He seems not to have been able to recover from my mother's death. So although I knew I came from a refugee family, I knew nothing about it, or about my background. Neither of them had told me anything. But when I started researching the family, it turned out out that while a few survivors of the Revolt had gone to Argentina, others had gone to Israel. Or what is now Israel.'

'I knew it,' I cry, triumphant at my clairvoyance. 'He's a Jew!'

'Quiet, David,' you say, always wiser and more reflective than me. 'I think there's more to come.'

And there is.

'Olivia, my darling, you are right,' says Samuel. 'My family went to Israel, not because they were Jewish but because they were Druze. The Druze had had a long history of resistance to foreign occupiers: they'd fought against the Ottoman Empire; now they put their efforts into seeing off the French. In fact, the leader of the Great Revolt was himself a Druze—so, inevitably, lots of other Druze signed up for it. It was a disaster for us.'

'Funny,' I quip, a little drunkenly, 'you don't look Druzish.'

'Happy to be bringing you the latest Druze,' he quipped back.

'All the Druze that's fit to print.'

'No news is good Druze.' He's heard them all before.

'Wait, Sam: have you been in a fight? That's quite a Druze you've got.'

'Dear boy, do you want to hear the rest of the story?'

'Sorry!' I say. 'The thing is, I'm confused. Who even are the Druze? I honestly don't have a clue.'

'It's not surprising. We're a tiny people, just over a million of us worldwide. Way back, we were a strange offshoot of an offshoot of Shia Islam, absorbing a mix of other religious influences—Judaism, Christianity, Gnosticism: syncretists, in short. And because we jettisoned various Islamic practices—ritual prayers, fasting, the Haj—in favour of lots of mystic stuff, it left us exposed as heretics. In short, we're not liked by hardline Muslims, and we've suffered frequent periods of discrimination and suppression in Muslim Syria and Muslim Lebanon, which are our main bases of population.

'One place we've never had a problem with is Israel. Although there are only about 140,000 of us there, mostly up north in the Golan, we've become a valued part of the Israeli state—in the Army, where our kids are celebrated for their courage, but also in education and science and technology and the arts. In short, we've become successful, proud Israelis—in fact, we're a role model for how life could have been for all the Arabs in Israel; and that's another reason why Israel's neighbours hate us. Because we've got a *modus vivendi* that works.

That's why the Golan is precious to me and why I bought this wine: it carries the taste of my home. It's odd: I almost feel proprietary about this tiny sliver of land, because it's the one place in the world where my people, the Druze, can feel safe and where we have a sense of ownership. Our high-minded friends at the dinner party tonight don't get it, of

223

course. All they can bring to the table is moralistic abstraction. They haven't got a clue what life is like for real people: for non-Muslim, independent communities in the Middle East.

'You know, I have cousins who live just across the Golan on the Syrian side and every day they live in fear that rival Arab militias or religious fanatics—or both—will take over in Syria and turn on them again. What will it mean if they do? Oh, the same as last time: slaughter, rape, torture, imprisonment, banishment. You tell our friends this, though, and they look at you as if you're insane—or worse: as if you're the gullible dupe of scheming, malevolent Zionists! And if and when the terror breaks out—and it will!—they'll ignore it entirely, because it doesn't conform to their view of Arab virtue and victimisation. And who will protect us then? Only Israel, if we're lucky.

'Of course, I knew nothing of all this as a boy growing up in England but the more I've found out about it recently, the more I've wanted to know, which is why I now go back to Israel whenever I have the time. And every time I go, I feel a stronger bond with the country. Does it bother me that it's a Jewish state? Not in the slightest, any more than it bothers me that Britain is Christian. And that, dear friends, is my story and the reason I came back with a crate of Yatir Forest Red!'

We sit for a long time, taking in these details of Sam's mysterious, fractured life, and its telling intersection with the events of the evening.

'You know what else?' says Sam with a grin. 'I also found out that I'm not exactly Samuel. I only became Samuel when I came to England as a boy. I'm really Sami! It's a Druze name—or Arabic, really. I can even spell it: *Seen, Alif, Meem, Yaa*. Different etymology from Samuel, which is Hebrew for "God has heard". Sami has an Arabic root: it means "high-ranking" or "elevated" or "sublime". I think that just about describes me, don't you think?!'

We laugh: it does indeed, Sami.

He takes a sip of the Yatir Forest Red. 'I really don't regret tonight. The wine was a sort of test, I think. And they failed.'

'Exactly,' you say. 'They really failed.'

'Dear friends, thank you for coming,' he stammers, tears in his eyes. 'What a night. What a night!'

Ronny Finds The Nazi
21 May, 9:05 pm

After you leave Sami's flat, I stay behind and sleep on his couch. When I wake up it's past midday and my head is pounding like a sledgehammer. My first thought is to dive into Boaz's Facebook wall—and there he is, the stupid fuck, in his cover photo, having breakfast in some tosser cafe, pointing toothily at a stupid cup of coffee.

So I'm staring at your war hero, hoping he gets some penis-related disease, when a message from Ronny pings onto the screen.

> —*got news. office at 4?*

I type back.

> —*Yes*

It has to be about the Nazi, I decide, and resolve, once and for all, to put an end to this stupid adventure of his.

I CREEP INTO MY OFFICE BUILDING AND AM AT ONCE STRUCK by the silence. It's Sunday and nobody's there. Not a single infant. Normally the most fanatically-committed babies keep the machine ticking over at the weekend but today it's deserted—until, after a few minutes of unnerving peace, Ronny the Runner scuttles into my room.

'Ronny, where is everyone? Did the kiddies eat each other?'

'You weren't invited? No, of course you wasn't, sorry.'

'I wasn't invited where?'

'The Awayday Cum. The Big One. The one in the fancy hotel in a forest for the weekend.'

'And why aren't you there?'

'Dude, can you keep a secret?'

'If I told you, it wouldn't be a secret any more.'

Ronny looks shifty. 'I'm here to get Ariella's shit.'

'You are?'

'She's out, Man. She's had enough.'

'You had a fight?'

'Not us, Man! This place. She can't take it no more. She don't like what's going down. How the company's exploiting people's data, screwing with their lives, making profit out of tension.'

'Good for her!'

'That's not all. Between you and me, Dude, the Fatties also creep her out.'

'So she's forgiven you?'

'One more chance, that's what I got.'

'Excellent news.'

'Got on my knees, Dude: swore I would never lie to her again. Dude, I was crying.' He sounds so proud. 'That's what did it. And it had to be done, 'cos this is the lady I'm gonna spend my life with, the lady who's gonna have my babies.'

'Ah, the hook-nosed babies, of course.'

'Yeah, Man.'

'How many hook-nosed babies?'

'Four. Eight. Ten. Who knows? Many as possible!'

'Does she know that yet?'

'Nah, course not.'

'Why don't you introduce me to her, Ronny? I want to meet her properly.'

He looks puzzled. 'Dude, sorry to say this but she really don't like you.'

'Maybe that'll change when she gets to know me a little.'

'I doubt it, Dude. To be honest, most people dislike you before they've met you, then dislike you more after they've met you. That's what I've noticed. Sorry to be so honest.'

I assure him it's okay, then ask why he wants to see me.

'Dude—I got news! My girl found our Nazi!'

'Really?' I say, disappointed.

'Yeah, Man. Found a shopping list in his trash with exactly the right handwriting. It's him, no doubt about it.'

I feel weary with trepidation. 'Who is he?'

'He's called Ernest Blackwell. Here, I can show you what he looks like.'

227

He takes out his phone and flicks to a photo. An oldish, bespectacled man, bald and grey, hunched into a blue anorak, sheltering from the drizzle.

'That's our Nazi?'

'Yup.'

We stare at the picture.

'I was expecting someone bigger.'

'Me too.'

'Blonder.'

'Yeah.'

'Meaner.'

'Yeah.'

'So who is he?'

'Lecturer at the local college.'

'What does he teach? Politics?'

'Accounting.'

'Accounting? That's distasteful.'

'Yeah. Like Eichmann.'

'Anything else?'

'He has a dog.'

'A dog?'

'Yeah. Like Hitler.'

'German Shepherd?'

'Schnauzer. And he collects stamps.'

'The dog collects stamps?'

'No, Man. The Nazi.'

'So what do we do now?'

'We pay him a visit.'

'Just like that?'

'Just like that.'

'You and me?'

'You and me. You okay with that?'

'Honest Injun? No.'

'I'm thinking, Sunday night.'

It's now or never. 'Listen, Pal. I've thought about this and it's not gonna happen. I'm pulling the plug. Leave it to the police.'

He stares at me for a long time with big moist eyes.

'Never again, Dude,' he says quietly. 'Never again.'

'Oh for God's sake, Ronny! What if he's just some regular guy who doesn't like Jews? Believe me, I know the feeling.'

'Dude, a man who poisons someone's cat because it's Jewish will eventually poison someone's babies because they're Jewish.'

'My cat wasn't Jewish, Ronny!'

'It was, Man, it was.'

'Does Ariella know about this?'

'I'll tell her when it's over. She wouldn't get it.'

'Oh, for fuck's sake, of course she'll get it Ronny! She's Jewish and she went to Cambridge!'

'Exactly,' he says grimly.

'And what are we going to do when we meet him face to face? Beat him?'

'Exactly,' he says calmly.

'He's an old man, Ronny.'

'You think he'd give a shit if it was my babies on the slab?'

'Oh, those fucking babies!'

'Dude, please.'

'We can't beat an old man, Ronny.'

'I agree that the violence has to be symbolic—mainly,' he says disarmingly. 'No punching. Just a bit of a tapping. Just hard enough to remind him not to fuck with us Jews.'

'Ronny, you're not a fucking Jew!'

'My babies are, Dude.'

'Your babies don't exist.'

'They do. They're just waiting to show themselves.'

Ronny, you're dreaming.'

'If you will it, it is no dream, Man. That's what Herzl said.'

'You do realise, we'll both go to prison?'

'Dude, listen to me: there is no alternative.'

'Of course there's an alternative! We just ignore him.'

'Like we ignored Hitler.'

'A part-time accountancy teacher will not be the next Hitler.'

'Never again, Dude!' This time he says it with a shaking fist and moist, enraged eyes.

'Ronny, you're not a Jew!'

'My babes, Dude. They are one-hundred-per-cent Jewish.' He's waving his fist again. 'Fear is not an option. Sunday ten o'clock. Meet here. Wear black. *Am Yisrael Chai!*'

'I'm not doing it, Ronny!' I yell as he makes his way to the stairs.

'Your choice,' he says, and disappears.

More Beeboid Fun

22 May, 11:05 am

And then, minutes after Ronny leaves, my neurodivergent Fate Fairy delivers me an unusual treat, in the form of a mystifying text from Marc Shapireau.

> —*Hi David, Marc here from the bbc. Me and a colleague were just passing and we're outside your offices (great offices!) and wonder if ur up for a quick friendly chat*

To be honest, Olivia, the prospect of flicking elastic bands at my Oscar while antagonising Shapireau and another brand new Beeboid seems appealing, so I send him ten smiley faces, a dozen red hearts and stroll to the front lobby to meet them.

Marc and a pale young man with a nose ring are outside, grinning uncomfortably.

'Oh, hi David,' says Marc. 'So glad you took the call! This is Benedict Fraser-Johnson, Manager of Specialist Arts and Zeitgeist Gender Projects in the Religious Programming Editorial Conflict Resolution Division.'

'It's a new department—part of the Overall Programme Legal Division rationalisation,' says Benedict in a voice that's half Ministry of Justice, half Ministry of Sound. It's exactly how Shapireau sounds, I suddenly realise. It's as if these woke little kiddies have all been at Eton or Roedean then gone to finishing school in Barking or Basildon.

'You mean there's more than just one of you?'

'Well, only five in my little team,' he grins.

Marc takes over. 'Benedict's department is there to resolve conflicts in programmes that involve race, religion or gender. It's a massive growth area.'

'I'll bet it is,' I growl, and lead them to my office.

Once installed, I offer them the tiny chairs and flick my first elastic band at Oscar.

'So why are you boys here?'

'Straight up? It's about Killa-Jah,' says Marc.

'Ah, the talentless Aryan Norwegian pretending to be black?'

'We'll agree to disagree,' says Marc, stoically. 'The truth is we need your help.'

The Beeboids clear their throats. Benedict's the first to speak.

'We find ourselves in a tricky situation,' he says.

'Has the Norwegian ski jumper knifed someone?'

'Oh no!' they laugh.

'Has his child knifed someone?'

As Marc makes a big deal of being offended, Benedict chokes on a stifled laugh. 'Nothing as simple like that. Thing is, Killa-Jah has taken the *shahada*.'

There is a long pause.

'What's a *shahada*?'

'He's become a Muslim,' says Marc sombrely.

'A devout Muslim,' says Benedict respectfully.

'And why should this interest me?' I ask.

'Well, it's good that you ask,' says Benedict reasonably. 'I've always thought that Judaism and Islam were very close —closer to each other than either of them to Christianity, yes? I did my final-year paper at Oxford on this very subject. Got a first. But I'm sure your rabbi would tell you the same.'

I examine Benedict for a while and decide I may loathe him even more than Marc. 'I don't have a rabbi. I don't identify with Judaism.'

'He doesn't have a rabbi,' Marc confirms. 'He doesn't identify with Judaism.'

'Well, if you did have a rabbi, I'm sure he'd tell you that Islam and Judaism are very close in respect to their strict monotheism.'

The posh voice trails away under my wide-eyed, comic-book gaze.

'So tell me, Benedict, is part of your job to pester people with snippets from your GCSE religion crib notes?'

'No, no, no,' he laughs. 'This is purely about Shahid.'

'Who the heck is Shahid?'

232

'Killa-Jah.'

It sinks in. 'I see. Killa-Jah has become Shahid.'

'That's right!' they cry joyously.

'And why should I care?'

'Because his new religious conviction has forced a major change on him. He's leaning into something quite new and very, very exciting.'

'It's brilliantly exciting!' squeaks Marc. 'And inventive.'

'Like yah, it really is,' says Benedict. 'Sort of Grunge meets Garage meets Ganges—'

Marc leaps in '—meets Rap meets Ragga—'

'—meets Grime meets Drill meets Jazz meets Muezzine—'

'—and it's gonna be big,' says Marc portentously.

'Muezzine is actually gonna be huge!' echoes Benedict.

'Congratulations,' I say. 'And I should care because … ?'

'Because we need your help,' says Benedict.

'You amaze me,' I say. For a highly deceptive moment, I suddenly feel valued by the kiddiewinkies. It's a not-unenjoyable sensation, I am ashamed to say, even if I'm not sure where it's headed. 'In what way do you need my help?

'Ah, well, that's where it becomes *culturally* interesting.' Benedict pauses to tug his thin beard. 'You see, Shahid wants to know whether you, David Britton, still have any influence over our project. It's important to him, you see.'

'Influence?'

'Yes,' says Marc. 'You know? Influence.'

They're looking shifty.

'You see, Shahid needs proof,' Benedict says, now taking the conversation in a much less promising direction. 'What we need from you is a signed letter from your lawyers to our lawyers and his lawyers, confirming that you no longer have any influence in the making of this programme. That's all.'

'Which of course we shall pay for!' Marc says brightly.

They're both looking even shiftier.

'Tell me what he said,' I say. 'Word for word. And how religion comes into play here.'

They swallow nervously.

'I don't think that will be helpful,' says Benedict, reasonably.

233

'Word for word.'

He pauses. Then: 'He texted us that your being of the Jewish persuasion—and we don't agree with him on this, we really don't—may put you in a state of conflict with his art and his newly found religious commitments.'

'Show me the text or fuck off.'

The Beeboids look at each other anxiously, then Benedict offers a tiny nod and Marc takes out his phone.

'I'll read the important bits.'

'Either I read it whole or you can fuck off.'

Another nod and Marc hands over the phone.

'Of course you have to decontextualise it,' he says.

I read the message, which is long, illiterate and insane.

'Why does he think I'm a Khazar and part of the Rothschild family?'

'Oh that. It's nothing, just a kind of shorthand,' laughs Benedict.

'Like using Smith, if one's English,' says Marc.

'Or Seamus, if you're Irish,' says Benedict.

'So what he's saying is that he's worried that my Jewish Zionist influence will corrupt his art, right?'

'Of course we don't agree with him for a minute—and nor does the BBC,' says Benedict hurriedly, 'but he's the client.'

'Fair enough,' I say.

'Really?' they both cry joyously.

'Sure. But I'm not prepared to do it by letter. Too formal. I'll speak to him directly.'

The Beeboids exchange nervous looks. 'A letter would be better,' says Benedict. 'That's what his lawyers have asked for.'

'Alright,' I say, 'but I also want to speak to him.'

The Beeboids exchange another nervous look.

'I'm not sure that's a great idea,' says Marc.

'Relax,' I say. 'I'll call him.'

I press the button on Benedict's phone. The Beeboids are panicking and snatching for the phone but I fend them away and retreat to a well-protected corner.

Killa-Jah picks up. 'Yo.'

I put the phone on speakerphone.

'Ah Killa-Jah,' I say pleasantly, smiling at the panicking

Beeboids. 'It's David here. You know, David Cohen-Rothschild from the BBC. Yes, yes, that's right. I hear you've become a Muslim? You have?! Oh, jolly good! Mazeltov! Yes, yes, Marc just told me. He's here and we're both on our way to the synagogue.' I pull a thumbs-up sign to the frantic Beeboids. 'That's right, Marc's with his rabbi. Yes, yes, lovely chap from Israel. That's right. Did he really? He said that? Well I'm just calling you to let you know that I'm afraid we do control your music, of course, because we control all of the media. Yes, yes, every bit of it. In fact my boss, also called Rothschild but Abe Van Warburg-Sassoon-Oppenheimer-Rothschild, he's handling your case. And he loves your music. One thing though—no don't hang up! Please don't hang up!—you're there? Good. One thing we want is a new chorus, like this ...'

And I start singing *Hava Nagila*. Loudly, even though I don't quite know the words and loathe the tune more than any other tune in the world. This goes on even after Shahid has hung up.

'You're a spiteful shit,' spits Marc.

'That was jolly unfair,' says Benedict.

I'm still singing loudly—so loudly, in fact, that Ronny the Runner has come up to my office to find out what's going on.

'You alright Dude?'

'Ronny, please throw these people out.'

'Out!' says Ronny.

They're gone within seconds. Ronny follows them, menacingly. I crash into the Hollywood chair, drop my head into my hands and try to make sense of what's just happened. Then I hear a quiet scratching at the door.

I throw the door open exuberantly, expecting Ronny.

But it's Emily.

She's so small, so reduced, like a tiny geisha folded in fear and grief.

'It's only me,' she says, weeping.

I tell her to come in, and close the door.

Olivia Meets The New Lodger
23 May, 3:05 pm

I'll admit it, I'm embarrassed. I've been swinging a rolling pin in front of the mirror, and you've caught me, and now I'm dying a million deaths—not least because you really don't seem surprised.

'What are you doing?'

I decide to tell the truth. 'I'm training to fight Nazis.'

'With a rolling pin?'

You disappear into the bedroom. I follow you.

'Ronny and I are visiting the Nazi stalker next week and I need an appropriate weapon. Ronny says this is perfect. "Legal and lethal".'

'What, you're going to teach him how to roll out pizza dough? Look, I've got some promising news. I've just had a coffee with Moose and the moron and you are right: they're going for a termination! *And* they had a stonking argument while I was there!'

I haven't seen you this happy in years. 'I presume the argument was about the baby?'

'No, it was actually about Foucault and the future of political street theatre but it doesn't matter. They're going for the abortion! She's at the clinic now.'

Olivia, that crushes me. I jump up, arms outstretched. 'She's having the op now? What, today?"

'No, just the initial consultation.'

I'm gritting my teeth.

'Oh stop it, David, please! Don't be so melodramatic! It's a normal, modern procedure. Think rationally! You don't really think the two of them could actually look after a baby, do you?'

'We managed.'

You ignore this entirely. 'It's good news, really good news. Good for you, good for me and good above all for

Moose. One day, I'm sure, she'll realise it and feel lucky to have avoided life tied to the village idiot.'

'I'd love to be a grandfather.'

'Oh for God's sake, it's not about you!'

'You've become a hard bitch.'

'Excuse me? Excuse me!' You're yelling now. 'You're right. I have become a hard bitch and you want to know why? Because I have a pregnant daughter with an imbecilic boyfriend and an infantile husband who can't stop sticking his prick into other women's hands, especially those of bloody Janice Toybeen! Do you understand? And don't dare tell me that her hand never touched you!'

I'm about to offer a desperate homily on the urgency of truth when a tiny voice penetrates the silence like a Buddhist bell.

'Sorry,' the voice says.

Emily is standing in a bathrobe with her hair dripping. 'It's only me.'

I was about to tell you, Olivia: promise.

You're standing there, frozen, blinking. 'Who are you?'

'I'm Emily but I used to be Emile,' Emily says.

'I was going to tell you about Emily,' I say. 'Olivia, she's staying here for a few days. Emily, this is my wife Olivia.'

'Oh hi!' says Emily. ' Nice to meet you. Can you help me? I really, really, REALLY need a hairdryer.'

Your squawk scares Emily, which scares me. 'Relax, Emily: it's okay. My wife hates me at the moment. It's not your fault.' I ignore your stare because it's unbearable. 'Olivia, this is Emily.'

'Sorry to be a pain, Olivia—proper posh, that name! I love it!—but my hair really needs it. Honestly, if I don't deal with it within a few minutes of washing it, it just goes off, like Nagasaki. You know, the big bomb thing?'

'Olivia,' I say. 'Where's the hairdryer? I'll get it.'

'Who is this … person?'

'She's a friend. I'll explain. Where's the damn hairdryer?'

'It sort of goes like wire, if you get me,' Emily's saying. 'Really, I have to wet it again and sometimes even use conditioner. I don't know why but my hair gets so … angry.

I think it's about family stuff. And I'm a Gemini.'

'In the bathroom, in the cupboard, under the sink,' you snarl.

'In the bathroom, in the cupboard, under the sink,' I repeat.

'Thanks,' Emily says and vanishes.

'I had no choice,' I whisper.

'Who the fuck is that?'

'Emily. She's here for protection. People are trying to chop her penis off.'

'Is that some sort of Ronny the Runner saying?'

'No. There really are people who want to chop her cock off. And her balls'

'And how precisely do you know all this?'

'I just do.'

'Who wants to chop her things off?'

'Her boyfriend Madden. And his giant lawyer, Tina.'

'And what on Earth has any of this got to do with you?'

'It's a long story.'

'It always is, David. But all I really want to know is why, at this very difficult time, you have chosen to bring this creature into our home?'

You retreat to the couch, drop down and start to wail.

'To save her. I had no choice, They're taking her to the doctor next week.' The wailing grows louder. 'I'm sorry, Olivia. Really. From the bottom of my heart.'

'So, let me see if I've got this right. Emily is a woman with a cock?'

'And balls.'

'Of course. And someone wants to chop them all off next week which is why you've brought her home?'

'Yes.'

'Is this some sort of game to make me die young and in pain?'

'No, I love you. I want you to live painlessly and forever. I just have to offer her a haven because nobody else will.'

'Are you also offering her your cock at the same time as she's getting rid of her own? A sort of compensation package?'

'Oh come on, Olivia!'

'Alright, I'll rephrase that. Are you putting your cock next to her hand but without actually touching it because you think that that would make it somehow more acceptable?'

'Of course not!'

'Then why is she here?' You're actually shrieking.

'Please! Be quiet! I just told you! She's a sweet confused kid—a tranny—' this I whisper '—and people are trying to turn her into a political icon by chopping her bits off. Okay?'

Now you're screaming into the cushion. 'How do you get into these situations, David?'

'I don't know.'

'And why now, with everything else going on?'

'I had no choice. '

I'm timidly advancing to join you on the sofa. The prospect does not please you. 'If you come anywhere near me I will stab you.'

'Okay, okay.'

In Emily's haven, the hair dryer is starting up.

At the same time, the doorbell rings.

You and I share a moment of terror that I find exquisite. I reach out to touch you but you make your way to the front door. It can only be Masaai and Moose.

You reach the door, then stop abruptly and turn to face me. 'Please, David! Tonight, please forget about your trannies and Nazis and penis choppers and everything else, and concentrate, really concentrate, on our poor daughter! I beg you!'

'Okay.'

You march to the door, rehearsing a smile.

'Coming darling!'

The Abortion Is On
24 May, 11:03 am

Moose rushes past you without a word. Masaai comes shuffling in close behind, ear speakers buzzing and tissing, shrugs a sorrowful hello in my direction and morosely follows her into the bedroom, firmly closing the door.

Behind the wall, their voices rumble in sharp waves. Neither of us is breathing much.

Then Masaai emerges for sandwich fodder.

'Food hunt, Man. The Girl's hungry. Anything, Man: that Bovril shit, onion, chocolate milk, Turkish delight, olives, seaweed … anything, Man, anything.'

'Great!' I cry, rushing off to prepare a tray.

'Is everything okay, Masaai?' you ask, obstructing his route to the fridge.

'No, Man, not at all.'

'You talking about the baby?' I ask.

'Don't call it that!' It's the first time Masaai's raised his voice.

You're nodding wildly. 'You're right, Masaai! Exactly!' You shoot me a furious warning glance. 'You have made the right decision. Well done!'

'Yeah, Man,' he says disconsolately. 'Gotta be done.'

'And you and Amelia are both sure?' I ask.

'Yeah, Man.'

'Absolutely sure?'

'He just said they were sure,' you snap.

I ignore you. 'Is she okay Masaai?'

Masaai's cocking his head in that cartoony way which I think indicates he's thinking as hard as he can. 'Yeah, I guess, but then she's started getting this mother thing, you get me?'

'I get you!' I cry, and feel like dancing.

You sigh in loud disgust, walk over to Masaai, and grab

240

him by the hand. 'When's the procedure? You know, once it's done, you'll soon have forgotten about it.'

'Tuesday, Man. Less than a week.'

'Well, you're both welcome to stay and we'll make you very comfortable,' you say, and hug him tightly. He looks scared. 'Well done, Masaai!' Now he looks terrified, like he's about to cry.

'We ain't ready for a baby, Man. Seriously: we can't even keep a hamster alive.'

'Exactly!' you say warmly.

'I'm sure you could,' I say.

'No really, we can't. We tried it twice. One of them we starved and the other we fed to death.'

You hug Masaai again.

'I saw a baby in the shops today—' I start.

'—No, you didn't,' you growl. 'You didn't even go to the shops today.'

'It was chortling.'

'Chortling?' Your eyes are murderous.

'Chortling.'

Masaai grins. 'You know what I'm thinking? Is the baby going to be white or black? If it's black, Man … .' His voice trails off tragically.

'It's not a baby,' Olivia says. 'Just cell tissue.'

'Goes through the father I think—' I try again.

You shut me up with a hand and take a deep breath. 'I agree with you, Masaai. I don't think you or Amelia are ready for a baby. Think of the hamsters: they're the test. As for the future, who knows?'

Masaai's about to say something important but stops when we all hear sobbing. It's Moose. She's walked in, wrapped in a sheet, a huge chocolate and Bovril sandwich in her fist.

'I heard all that and I've got something to say,' she announces. 'Mom. Dad. Masaai. I've thought about it. I mean I've really thought about it. I've discussed it with my therapist, and my other therapist. I've also read my stars and —you're right. You're right. We're not ready. It's okay. We'll kill him. Yes, him. It's a boy. I'm pretty sure.'

Then she dissolves into sobs.

'Oh darling,' says Olivia, and is about to hug her when there's an explosion. We all shut up and peer at where the blast came from.

A door opens and Emily steps out.

She looks amazing, you have to admit. Hair piled high in elaborate whorls, her face a delight. And the hair drier still smoking.

'It's just me,' she says. 'I think the hair dryer died. I'll get another one just like it tomorrow. Sorry!'

I feel I should say something. 'This is Emily, everyone. Emily, this is Masaai and this is my daughter Amelia.'

'Oh my God: you're Moose!'

'Oh my God: you're Emily!'

'Yeah! You're so pretty!'

'You're prettier!'

'But you look like shit. You okay?'

'No!' Moose says, choking up, ''cos, like next week, I'm gonna murder my baby, you know?' Then she starts weeping.

'Wow,' says Emily. 'Yeah, I heard your folks talking about it. Tough!'

'Yeah!' she sobs.

'Murdering your baby! That's so sad!' Emily says, and goes over to Amelia with her arms open.

The two girls hug.

'I also got a terrible week,' says Emily. 'I'm having my penis chopped off.'

Moose's eyes are popping. 'You got a penis?'

Emily nods. 'And balls, the lot. They're all going.'

'Wow,' Amelia whispers. 'Balls.'

Me And The Baby
26 May, 9:39 pm

When we're back in 'our' bedroom, after we've all had
supper together, you predictably fling yourself onto the bed
and vibrate with rage for four minutes and thirty-nine
seconds (I timed it) before turning on me.

'You do realise that your pretty little tranny weirdo is in
the process of destroying our daughter's life?'

'Oh come on, Olivia: don't exaggerate.'

'They were practically naming and dressing it by the end
of the meal!'

'Moose is just being kind—being herself, at last. I
thought she was lovely.'

'Are you kidding? Listen to them!'

We can hear them through the wall alright, a rolling hum
of lively chatter punctuated by laughter.

You throw yourself face down in your pillows and sob
with renewed vigour, coming up for air only to tell me once
that I'm the reason everything is going wrong. Just as I'm
about to protest, the rumble of laughter in the next room is
suddenly amplified by the sound of soft bongos and singing.

You resume sobbing.

'I just can't believe how destructive you are, David. How
you wreck everything. I'm going to wash, then bed. Don't
talk to me or come anywhere near me for any reason.'

You vanish into the bathroom.

I need some space too, so I put on my shoes and exit the
house quietly for a walk in the cold night air.

My walk's about two miles: to the Edgware Road,
through Marylebone, then back via the canals and the
estates. It's a cold, foggy night but I'm warm in my old Irish
tweed coat, my beanie and my black wool scarf. I'm alone
on the frozen street and when I get to the old iron bridge, I
halt. I breathe deeply, exhaling rich plumes into the still,

frozen air. And something happens, Olivia. A calmness suddenly enfolds me.

I feel happy, Olivia—happier than I've felt for a very long time. And why?

Because tonight I saw Moose at her finest—kind, naive, curious, attentive, funny, insightful—and something became clear. I think she needs the baby as much as the baby needs her. I think the baby will make her into a whole person, and if she destroys it, she will never be healthy.

So I think you're wrong, Olivia. That child is our daughter's only hope. And maybe our's too.

That *fickungsfotze* baby has to live.

The Shit Hits The Fan
27 May, 7:49

I owe you an explanation and probably an apology.

After I get back from the walk, I sneak in quietly, slump onto the sofa and fall into a disjointed sleep. I reasonably ignore two calls from Angela—because why not?—and then turn off the phone to avoid being disturbed by a third. At that point I have the most beautiful dream: you and me on a walk, swinging our grandson between us. This comes to an abrupt end when Ronny the Runner starts banging loudly on the front door, yelling stuff about the police, sexual assault and kidnap. At this point I once again abandon all hope and prepare to endure another surreal day at the Crazy-Fate Crash.

An hour later I'm alone in the boardroom, none the wiser, my head pulsing like a radioactive bomb and the Pain Fairy making her presence known by occasionally grasping my brain in her talons and rattling it. They're coming in fifteen minutes, according to Natalie.

Trouble is, I'm still not sure who 'they' are. Ronny, however, seems very sure. 'The police, Man,' he chides. 'You should never take a crazy chick home, Dude. Never, never, never.'

I'm about to explain it all over again when I hear Natalie's heels clicking down the stairs. She knocks quietly and the door creaks open. She's brought me a cup of coffee, the darling, and looks terrified.

'Always a troublemaker!' she coos, swaying on her gold five inchers but not spilling a drop. 'I thought you might need this.'

'Morning, Sweetheart. And I do. Thanks.'

Then she whispers. 'In truth, David, what have you done? They're saying you kidnapped Emily! You silly sausage! Why on Earth?'

I laugh. 'No darling. What I've done is save Emily from being mutilated by ideological terrorists.'

'Mutilated?'

'Natalie, there are people who want to chop off Emily's cock against her will, and some of them work for this company.'

Natalie's hands have flown to her face. 'Eeek!'

'Very eeek. And her balls. And she doesn't want the op. They want her to have it because it gives credibility to their craziness. And after going along with it, she finally asked for my help, so I offered her my home as a haven and she readily accepted.'

'So she's safe!'

'Of course she's safe! Call her yourself, if you like: why not?'

'I'm so relieved. They were saying you'd taken her as … a sex slave!' Natalie mouths the last words histrionically.

'Sweetheart! Trannies aren't my thing. Nor are slaves.'

'Thank goodness,' says Natalie. 'It didn't sound like you —but you do get up to some odd things sometimes, don't you!'

Outside we hear footsteps and angry snatches of conversation and the door bursts open. Angela's on the attack even before she has sat down.

'I don't want a row with you, David, yeah? Things have gone way too far for that sorta shit now, yeah?'

'*Ja*, it is really definitely serious now,' adds Matilda, flapping in the slipstream but managing, at last, to crash land in a chair beside Angela.

'I gotta be honest with you, Mate, but we might not be able to keep you outta prison this time which, to be honest, is probably what you deserve.'

I'm about to defend myself, yet again—explain my concern, yet again—when Angela fires a vast broadside at me.

'Now listen, Mate, 'cos I'm only going to lay this on you once and that's it. You're not getting this Emily thing, right? You're really not. You're stuck in your old stupid, fascist, binary world. So let me explain. Emily's in distress, right? But why? Because her body's at odds with her gender identity, so she feels out of phase, and she wants to feel authentically herself, right? She wants to be seen as what she really is by other people, because she's lived her life on the receiving end of misgendering and discrimination, and that's screwed her up proper: are you hearing me, Mate? It's called gender dysphoria and it's a real medical condition, and it hurts, got it? And she's exercising her free will and her right to choose a solution, and what she's opting for is a surgical intervention that will make her feel better and improve her mental health and fight the stigma and hatred and ignorance from your lot. You get me? Right? And if you'd suffered the pain that she has suffered, you'd wanna do the same. So stop being a fucking fascist, David: stop trying to control people when you can't even control yourself, and stop making trouble for all of us when you don't have the imagination or intelligence to understand anyone who isn't you. Okay?'

It's weird to hear Angela talking like this because it's almost coherent. I think my jaw has dropped. This encourages her to continue.

'And while I'm at it, Mate, maybe you should also examine your baby-boomer luck franchise and its own fucked up moral compass—'

'*Ja*, *zis* is so,' Matilda murmurs sadly.

'—and who knows, maybe one day you'll grow enough to see that you owe us all an apology for the way you treat us. Me especially.'

Up to this point, The Woman Who Will Resuscitate The Dodo has mounted a surprisingly impressive counter-blast, but as she flips from excusing her own narcissism to attacking mine, I decide that I've had enough and I explode.

'Shut the fuck up!'

I'm suddenly aware that I have just shouted at the top of my lungs and both women have jumped back about a yard and are holding their mouths. Natalie is watching keenly but saying nothing. It seems a good time to plunge in.

'Listen to me, because I'm telling you facts, not theory. They want to cut off Emily's penis and testicles. She does not want them to. She wants to keep her penis. And her testicles. How do I know this? Because she told me. She's

247

too intimidated and frightened to tell anyone else because she's shy and because you horrible people, who want her to go through with this, have an agenda of your own—but she told me, because she trusts me and asked for my protection. It's that simple. Do you fucking get it?'

Generation Moron is staring at me, crazily.

'In fact, I'll tell you what. I'll draw it for you,' I say, and I go over to the large presentation flipchart, take a thick black crayon and draw a huge cock and balls with a crude knife advancing on the easel. And then, with a red crayon, I draw torrents of blood. Tell you what, Olivia: I can still draw.

'There you go! That's what you all want to do to poor Emily. And why? Because you've got the top-rated tranny franchise in the world, and you want pretty little Emily, who works for the company, to be your poster girl. She's easy meat for your ratings. She's staff. Which means she's cheap. You're not doing this for her: you're doing it to build your following at her expense.'

Angela hasn't heard a word I've said because she's shivering with disgust at my drawing on the flipchart. 'That's … so … gross!'

'*Ja, zat* is very gross David,' echoes Matilda.

At which point, the door swings open and in walk the huge Tina and the tiny Madden, both looking pantomime fierce.

Everyone freezes. They're staring at my artwork, which I have titled, *Emily's Penis and Scrotum and the Advancing Knife.*

'Incredible,' says the giant lawyer, getting out her phone.

'Fucking incredible,' spits Madden, getting out his phone.

They film it all from every available angle, especially after I add my signature and give the giant the old trademark studio-guest welcome wink.

'What do you think?' I say, adding a cartoony hair on the left side of the scrotum. Just can't stop myself, Olivia. You know how I get. And from there, predictably perhaps, things go downhill.

Not Good At All
28 May, 3:59 am

Olivia, I know you think everything is my fault and, yes, I know a lot of it is, but before you judge, you must understand the surreal nature of my world. This is why I am making such an effort to relay all the relevant facts.

Word for word, this is what happened.

After Empress Tina has finally finished filming *Emily's Penis and Scrotum and the Advancing Knife*, she announces that she's feeling violated.

'Me too!' Angela yells back.

'*Ja*, me too' says Matilda.

An entire boardroom of violated people stares back at me.

'This is offensive,' The Tina says, indicating my handiwork.

'It's beyond offensive,' mutters Madden in a tiny warlike voice.

'But not as offensive as having your cock and balls cut off,' I sing. I'm now up and shading the scrotal sack with a blue marker. You know, Olivia: I really can draw.

'First, sexual abuse, then sexual assault, then kidnap, and now victim humiliation,' shouts the Goddess of the Law. Madden squeals outraged assent.

'I'm calling the police,' Angela announces. 'Emily has to be protected.'

'Fine,' I say. 'Do it! But first, let's call Emily and hear what she has to say.'

I take out my phone and call her number.

'I warn you, do not do that!' cries Tina-Megaera, leaping to her feet.

'No!' shrieks Madden.

The lawyer's pounding on the table. 'It is our belief that because of the abuse and kidnap, Emily is wholly unable to make a free statement and indeed that asking her to do so would compound the offence.'

I'm laughing, Olivia. They're terrified.

'Stop it, David!' shrieks Angela. 'For once in your life, listen and shut up.'

'*Ja, ja*, David, just listen now, please,' begs Matilda, and I feel so sorry for her that I sit down.

'Go on. Fire away.'

It's deadly quiet. Tina-Atropos lumbers to her feet.

'As to the facts of the case, these can be broken down into the following charges. One, that our client Emily has been subjected to a constant regime of bullying and intimidation—'

'Yeah, by that little freak there.' I point at Madden.

'He used the word "freak"!' shrieks Madden. 'And the word "little"!'

'I noticed,' says Tina-Tisiphone. 'These words are proof of prejudice and bigotry—' she angrily gestures to his phone '—and we're recording it all!'

'Excellent!' I cry.

Olivia, I feel exhilarated.

'Two, that by calling Emily a chicken-foxer on frequent occasions—you don't deny that, I presume?—'

'Not at all,' I say exuberantly, 'I call everyone that.'

'—by calling Emily a chicken-foxer, and especially during her transition period, you have behaved in a mocking, bullying, prejudicial and discriminatory way that has seriously impacted our client's ability to do her job and live a normal life.'

'Normal life!' I laugh. 'You wouldn't know normal if it stood up and squeezed your nipps.'

The word 'nipps' provokes pandemonium.

'*Nein*, David, you can't say *ze* nipps!' cries Matilda, horrified.

'I've recorded that too!' cries Tina-Sardina.

'Me too,' breathes Madden, orgiastically.

'Three, that as a result of the intimidation and mockery, you have constructively dismissed my client. And four, that you have frequently subjected my client to physical and sexual abuse—' I'm back on my feet, adding another hair to the right side of Emily's scrotum for symmetry '—and fifth, that yesterday afternoon you kidnapped my client and are holding her against her will.'

She sits down.

I dial a number and put it on speakerphone. 'Do not do that!' The Grand-Duchess of Revenge has got to her feet, a six-and-a-half-foot giant pawing wildly at me across the table. 'I warn you, put the phone down: you're at risk of a committing further abusive intervention.'

Damn it, the number's engaged.

The High Queen of Justice is hastily opening a large file with red legal binding. 'Here is our deposition which we shall be lodging with the courts. On Emily's behalf we are demanding her immediate release and are making a claim against the company for £25 million in damages—'

Angela's reeling. 'That's ridiculous, Tina—'

'—and we demand Emily's immediate release into our care, to attend her costly pending medical appointments—'

'You can just piss off!'

'—and we reserve the right to ask the police to conduct an immediate search of these premises and start a prosecution.'

I start drawing another knife, closing in on the balls.

'I know what you're trying to do,' growls Thyphoea. 'You're trying to get me to confront you physically and, believe me, there is nothing more I'd like to do than smash your racist, sexist, fascist face to a pulp—'

'Yeah!' shrieks Madden.

I begin work on a foreskin and press again.

'—but I won't do it,' shouts the Princess of Principle, packing her things away. 'I came here to serve you with the signed witness statement and other documents that will be used at trial.'

Everyone hears the ring.

'Stop it! Stop it!' booms Great Clytië.

'Hello.'

Emily's lovely, faint voice.

'Emily!'

'Oh hi, David. You okay?'

'I am, Honey, I am. Are you having fun?'

'Me and Moose are making clothes and Masaai's so cool!'

My heart leaps with joy.

'Listen, I've got some of your friends here: Tina, who's just served the company with some legal documents, and Madden.'

'We're leaving,' the Cailleach is shouting. 'Come on Madden, quickly. We have to go.'

'I don't wanna talk to them or see them ever again!' Emily yells.

'Emily, Honey: do you want to have your genitals removed by surgery?'

'No!' she cries. 'I really, really don't! Tell them to leave me alone!'

Madden and Clíodhna are halfway to the door, and Natalie, with her usual initiative, steps to one side and blocks their route.

'And who has forced you to have this surgery?'

'My ex-boyfriend Madden. And that horrible lawyer. Oh, and I want to break up with you, Madden!'

That does it. I feel Madden's little fist swinging into my face. The phone goes flying as blood salts my mouth and I feel a wave of delirious joy.

'You provoked that deliberately,' Putana is yelling, as she drags Madden past Natalie and out into the corridor.

Exultantly I spin round to face Angela and Matilda, blood issuing from my mouth, howling with laughter, spitting with joy. 'How good was that!'

Angela's weeping.

'No, David, *zat* was not good,' says Matilda. 'Not good at all.'

Matilda Comes Good
29 May, 8:03 pm

I clean my mouth in the bathroom, wind down my joyous rendition of 'I Will Survive' and dance my way back to Angela and Matilda in the boardroom.

Natalie and Angela have already gone but, weirdly, Matilda is waiting for me.

'So what do you think? Total victory, I think.'

'David, *zis* did not go well,' she says in an exhausted way. 'You got hit in *ze* face. *Zis* is not a good meeting when someone in *ze* face gets hit and blood everywhere is.'

'But we won. Why aren't you happy? They no longer have a legal case. Emily told those dicks to leave her alone. That means she's safe, and free, and so are we. And Madden attacked me, so that's a free Get-Out-of-Jail card.'

'*Ja*, but Angela sees it from a business perspective. We have a huge Trans Community, and they're often, you know, angry? Emily was going to be our gift to them. When *zis* hits *ze* social media, it's going to be *ze* suicide for us.'

'Well, I think we've done the Trans community a good turn. Like anyone else, what they want is truth, not media coercion.'

Matilda looks at me and shrugs. 'You know, David: I like you because you're crazy and talented and ... ridiculous, *ja*, but you don't understand business and that makes you a very—' she's struggling for the right word '—a very annoying person'?'

'Matilda, I know that. Sometimes it's bad. But sometimes, like just now, it's good.'

'*Ja*,' says Matilda. 'I don't like to hurt *ze* feelings, but your naivety annoys people, *ja*? Lots of people. So many people.'

'I know. I'm sorry. I'm glad we've cleared that up.'

'*Ja*, but everyone. You don't see things as *zey* are. And *zat*

253

is annoying for people who do see things as *zey* are. Especially in business.'

'And in my home life too, Matilda. Believe me, my wife and daughter remind me of it every day. But maybe I just see things differently. I promise you, you'll see things differently as you get older.'

'*Ja*, but I think you *try* to annoy, David. You enjoy it. And *zis* makes you a liability in the company.'

'I know. I've annoyed Angela a little.'

'*Ja*! O *ja*! A lot!'

'More than once, to be honest.'

'O *ja*! Much more than once! David: every day! Every second! Angela can't stand your guts!'

'Really? Well, I don't blame her,' I say confessionally. 'I even feel a bit sorry for her.'

'*Ja*? I don't think so.'

'I do. I think'

We sit in silence for a while, and then Matilda clears her throat. 'So we need to move forward David. And *ze* only way is to, how you say, "edge you out". You have to leave. *Ja*?'

'That sounds like a sensible solution, Matilda. And I agree.'

'You do? *Boah! Das ist sehr gut. Sehr gut.* So, I have come up *wiz* a settlement: something that protects you and us. Here it is, David.' She hands me the paper. 'Under *zese* terms, you must be gone by the end of *ze* week. Everything out. Okay? Because things cannot go on as *zey* are, *ja*? Please read it carefully. Show your lawyer. Okay?'

I put the document in my bag. 'I promise. Today. And I'll get back to you. You know, I actually hope you do well.'

'*Zank* you, David. I know you'll much happier not being here will.'

'I'm sure I will. But, in truth, Matilda: won't you at least miss me, just a little, when I'm gone?'

'No, David. At *zis* moment I feel sorry for you. But you are very annoying and I shall not miss you.'

'Fair enough. I'll read the papers and get back to you asap.'

She's standing up.

'Goodbye, David.'

We shake hands in a rather formal, German way, and I, equally formally, see her to the door.

'You've got to admit, that was a good meeting,' I say.

Her eyes stray miserably to my revised masterpiece, *Emily's Penis and Scrotum, with Two Knives and a Foreskin*, and she departs, shaking her head.

Olivia, I really can still draw!

I Finally Get It
30 May, 8:35 pm

I'm hurrying home to see you. It's early in the morning, marble-cold, and I'm buried in the Irish tweed we bought together twenty-seven years ago. My heart lurches when I remember how you loved it. It smells of you, Olivia. But it's no protection from your most recent text:

—we need to speak asap I'm home

I know from this morning's Facebook snoop that you've been with Boaz all day and you're probably going to break the news that you're going away, perhaps by helicopter, with Dr Eyeball.

I knew something was up this morning from the moment you awoke. As usual I was spying on you through my fingers. Your meticulous toilette, the necklace, the emerald scarf, the sassy red skirt and the tight amethyst top with the gold-spun coat as iridescent as your hair, all the way down to the dazzle of those new black boots with the big brass buckles. And worst of all, the lethal little travel bag.

That *Fickenfotzer*, Boaz. Today's photos were so awful that I've decided to stop stalking you on Facebook. I can't take any more of the man's shining teeth and stupid grin. In an ideal caveman world, I would slay him—and yes, before you even think it, I do realise how pathetic that sounds, given that Boaz could swat me like a fly, probably while saving a million Africans' eyes. In short, I know I will never be able to compete with this man, doctor, soldier, saint and lover.

I reach Tottenham Court Road station to get my train home and a flood of misery overcomes me. I realise:

- That I'm a ridiculous, annoying, ageing man with nothing to offer, and that my betrayal justifies your

hatred of me.
- That you are right to leave me and should have done so decades ago.
- That in a few days, our daughter is going to kill her baby and with it the last filament of hope that could keep us together as a family.
- That there is nothing, but nothing, I can do.
- That it's over between you and me.

It all hits me like a tsunami, Olivia. I crease up into a smelly, much urinated-into corner of the concourse, turn my face to the tiles and weep.

A Tiny Ray Of Hope
30 May, 9:08 pm

This is how I remember it, Olivia. Of course, you'll have a version of your own.

You're on the big sofa pretending to read when I arrive. You clock me quickly but barely glance up. 'You look like shit.'

'Sorry about that,' I say. 'In fact, I'm sorry about absolutely everything to do with me, Olivia. My appearance. My manner. My humour. My blood group. My lack of sophistication. My soul. My nature. Have I missed anything?'

You ignore me for a beat, and then say 'plenty'. A flaccid cock on the point of being received into another woman's hand and a lifetime of betrayal is what I think you're suggesting.

'What are you reading?'

You peremptorily show me the cover. A new David Grossman novel.

'Suggestion from Boaz?'

You look at me with distaste. 'Get yourself a coffee, David. And maybe wash your face and brush your teeth.'

I obey and return with combed hair, a double black espresso and a determination to have what I am imagining will be the final chat. I sit down and stare at you. You stare back, daring me.

'So he's arrived?'

'Last night.'

'Did you spend the day with him? I mean, we're still technically married, so I think I still have the right to ask whether … '

'Yes.'

This knocks the breath out of my lungs.

'Yes, I have the right to ask or yes—'

'Yes, I spent the day with Boaz.'

'In his bed?'

'David,' you say, your voice corrosive with pity: 'as it happens, we didn't have sex. I don't know why I'm telling you this but maybe because I want you to understand something. This is no longer about Boaz. It's no longer even about you. It's about me and what I've decided. Are you listening?'

'Of course.'

'David, you and I are separating.'

I'm feeling a wave of delirious relief. 'You didn't fuck then!'

'Oh, for God's sake: is that all you can think about?'

'It's important.'

'It's not important. It really isn't.'

'It really is!'

And then something changes in your face. Fury, again. 'You know: you're right. It is important and you know why? Because even if I did have sex with him, who the hell are you to say anything?' I start to speak but you shut me up with a forefinger. 'I have always been honest with you. And faithful. And loyal. I haven't sneaked around like a criminal, lying and deceitful. Do you know what infidelity means David? It means the breaking of trust—' your voice has dropped to a searing whisper '—and the truth is, you've made it impossible to love you.'

'What about Moose?' It's all I've got left.

You sigh, from the heart. 'I told you. After the procedure, when she's strong enough, I'm going to tell her we're splitting. It won't surprise her, will it? She's known it since she was in nappies. She has to grow up, David, and as long as she isn't burdened with a baby and an idiot, she'll make it. I believe that.'

'And if she marries The Idiot?'

'We can't protect her all her life, can we? She fell in love with an idiot. She got it from me, I guess. So this is what's going to happen. After the procedure I'm moving in with my sister. And let me repeat for probably the fiftieth time: Boaz is not the reason I'm leaving you. You are. And under no circumstances are we going to allow our daughter to have that baby. Right?'

And before I can say a word, they're back, Masaai and Moose, banging through the front door, slamming chairs, huffing and puffing, sneaker headphones buzzing and thumping, bottles, bags and coats being swung and stashed and Moose, our beautiful Moose, her stricken face bathed in beautiful ringlets, looking at me with tears running down her face and flying into my arms.

'Daddy, I'm going to kill my baby!'

Moose Loves Her Daddy!
31 May, 3:48 am

She folds into my arms and we stand there cocooned, just like the old days. Moose and her daddy. 'I'm here, Darling,' I whisper.

You advance quickly, don't you, Olivia, to rob me of this primal moment. 'Can I get you something, Darling? Coffee? Juice? Muffins?'

'Water, please,' Moose says, tempted but not wholly won.

You don't go. You hover.

'Coffee and muffin, yeah!' says Masaai. Actually he kind of shouts it. 'Or a sandwich, Man. Yeah, a sandwich. I'll go and choose.'

Moose and I are inseparably comfortable. 'You know I love you, Daddy?' she whispers.

'Course. You know I love you?'

'Course.'

Then Moose gets impatient, as she always does, and slips away. She grabs a bottle of water from her bag, then sits down to face us. 'I've got something to say to you both. I've made my decision. I'm having an abortion.'

'Oh Darling!' you cry, laughing and weeping. 'What a painful decision that must have been, but I think it's the right one. We'll support you in every possible way, Darling.'

'We will,' I say, more mutedly.

I feel like weeping. You probably didn't notice.

'See, I've done a lot of thinking,' Moose is saying.

'Great!' we both say.

'We've talked a lot, Masaai and me.'

'Great!' we say and, right on cue, Masaai is back with a monstrous multi-layered sandwich. He flops into a chair.

'Yeah, Man. Lotta chat, lotta chat, lotta chat.'

'And I know what I've gotta do,' Moose is saying. 'For my career. For my life!'

'Exactly!' we exclaim, both wondering what exactly this career might be.

'So that's why we need the procedure,' Moose says in a quiet voice.

'Yes, Darling!' you say, and hug her again.

'And anyway, it's not really a baby,' Moose continues. 'Not yet.'

'No, it certainly isn't,' you confirm.

'Yeah, I read it up, Man, and it's just a mass of cells,' opines Masaai through a jawful of mush.

'That's right,' says Moose.

'Exactly,' says Olivia.

'And I have to be responsible and mature,' Moose says.

'Yeah, Man,' says Masaai.

'That's right,' says Olivia. 'And one day, when you're ready, you'll have a beautiful family of your own.'

The word 'family', unfortunately, makes Moose howl.

'Are you alright, Darling? I didn't mean to—'

'I'm not stupid you know!'

'Of course you're not stupid,' we all cry, even Masaai.

And then, out of the blue, she drops the bombshell. Stopped us in our tracks, didn't it?

'I know what's happening between you two. I know you're not sleeping in the same bed.'

We freeze. Busted.

'And it's okay,' says Moose, as if she means it. She pauses and cocks her head in that way she's done since she was a kid, 'because life is like a river. There are twists and turns and rapids and shores. And there's always light at the end of the night.'

'That's really lovely, Darling. Who said that?'

'Masaai.'

'There's always light at the end of the night,' chants Masaai and blows her a slobbery kiss before sauntering off to the kitchen for a sandwich refinement.

'He's not as dumb as you both think, you know. And I'll tell you this: he's always, but always, there for me. I'd be in pieces right now if it wasn't for him. It's because of him that I'm here today. But I'm right about you two, aren't I?'

You sit beside her and take her hand. Inside, I'm blubbing too much to move,

'Yes, Darling, there have to be some changes.'

'You alright Dad?'

'I'm fine, Darling,' I say, and head off to the bathroom.

Inside I collapse onto the floor. I run the tap loudly, pull the toilet chain and bawl until I'm exhausted.

My phone buzzes. I yank it out.

—*David Shalom! Just a reminder about next Wednesday we'll be at you at 3 and I've got you a very nice mezuzah it's from Jerusalem which is a gift from me and Hymie to you Olivia Moose and Masaai don't mention it and I'm bringing my family cos they want to meet you we'll bring our own kosher food and plates don't worry. Menachem*

I See My Doctor
1 June, 2:43 pm

I have to go to my doctor today because my drug supplies are running low. My doctor is a Dr Kwame, a handsome, gloomy, Christian Ghanaian who, I am sorry to say, is no pushover when it comes to scoring drugs.

Peering through his tiny spectacles at yet another X-ray on an illuminated screen, Dr Kwame crinkles his eyes and says "uh-huh" again. He has methodically uh-huhed his way through the large pile of medical reports that lie scattered on his desk, every so often lifting his eyes to ask me a question: Am I sleeping (no)? Do my ankles swell (sometimes)? How are my waterworks (pisspoor)? Erections (you kidding)? Bowel (strangely, fine)?

Problem is, Dr Kwame has become too careful, ever since he discovered my minor TV celebrity status.

He takes a deep breath, removes his spectacles, leans back in his chair and regards me through the morbidly amused squint he's been deploying since he found out about Oscar.

'There's good news and bad news,' he says, which is what he said last time.

'Goody. Let's have the bad news first,' which is what I said last time.

'It's the same as the good news.' This is a new one. He's pleased with it.

'Fire away.'

'There's nothing there. Again.'

'What, nothing at all?'

'According to the pathology, the radiology, the haematology and the neurology, you're fine for a man of your age, I'm afraid. Sorry.'

'Sorry? That's good news, surely?'

'Well it isn't, because you still feel sick.'

'You think I'm a hypochondriac?'

'Do *you* think you're a hypochondriac?'

'Yes, but a sick one. Maybe even a dying one.'

'You're not dying.'

'Didn't you say last time that we're all dying?'

'Yes, but it takes time. According to these results you're not even sick.'

'Pain doesn't lie. It's most days. Like there's an evil spirit orchestrating it all, you know? My pain fairy, creating fresh new tortures from a little bag of torture gimmicks, always inventive and so expertly calibrated that I still—just—want to go on living.'

'Yes, you told me. Mr Britton I think you need to see a psychiatrist. Have you considered it?'

'I saw a shrink for years. Only stopped last year.'

'Why did you stop?'

'I stopped believing her. Look, I need painkillers. The most vicious painkillers available. Pure heroin if you've got it.'

'You shouldn't talk like that. It's not funny.'

'Neither are my pains.'

There's a long pause.

'Tell me about your life, Mr Britton.'

He's not looking as if he'll budge on the drugs so I decide to tell him everything.

'Have I told you my wife's leaving me?'

'No, you haven't.'

'You don't look surprised.'

'I'm sorry to hear she's leaving you.'

'She's running off with an Israeli war hero who saves the sight of blind Africans.'

'Uh-huh. Maybe that's why you're getting headaches.'

'She's doing it because she caught me with my penis on its way into the hand of her arch-rival. But it wasn't erect. Just, like, sitting there. Kinda for old times sake. Nothing sexual, really. Hard to explain, really. But she's leaving me because of that. And also because she thinks I'm a prick.'

'I see.'

'And I love her and I don't want her to leave me.'

'Uh-huh.'

'Also, my beautiful daughter has shacked up with a retard and is about to have her first abortion, which will almost certainly result in a serious mental breakdown—for us all.'

The doctor's nodding. 'That doesn't sound good either.'

'And my company is at risk of being sued £25 million for kidnapping a transsexual whose boyfriend is trying to chop off her genitals.'

He's too stunned to say a word. Victory.

'And to cap it all, I'm being stalked by a rabbi who's blackmailing me and a Nazi who poisoned my cat. In fact, pretty soon, I'm going to join a friend of mine, and we're going to go round to the Nazi's flat in balaclavas, to threaten him.'

After a moment's reflection, the doctor says, 'There's a lot going on in your life, Mr Britton.'

'There is. That's why I need really good drugs.'

'Assuming, of course, that what you have told me is true.'

'I'm sorry, doc. What are you finding difficult to believe: the wife, the Israeli, the affair, the daughter, the retard, the abortion, the breakdown, the flaccid cock, the tranny, the kidnap, the legal case, the rabbi, the Nazi, or the balaclavas?'

'All of them,' he says. 'Any of them.'

'They're all true. Can you give me some pills?'

'Yes. And would you like me to refer you to a psychiatrist?'

'Forget it. The drugs will be fine.'

'Alright, then. But I'm also arranging for a scan of your brain, Mr Britton. I'll be in touch.'

We Take On The Nazi
2 June, 3.45 pm

Ronny the Runner's in his dirtiest leathers, picking insect splashes off his helmet and looking like murder.

'It's a bad idea,' I say for the fourth time.

He looks up, theatrically indifferent. 'I told you, Dude: you don't have to come.'

'I do. I can't let you go alone, can I? I feel responsible for you. It's my fault we're in this ridiculous situation.'

He shrugs. 'Your call, Man. I'm going in.'

'You think there'll be violence?'

'Maybe.'

'For Christ's sake, Ronny.'

'Focus, Dude. The key is being prepared, like I explained. You follow me. We walk quickly. I knock, lids on. When he opens the door we force our way in. Quickly. No shouting, no violence. Gentle, if possible. You close the door, we talk in soft voices. We tell him why we're there and warn him that if anything happens again to you, we won't ask no more questions: we'll just break every bone in his miserable Nazi body. We may have to slap him once, hard but with an open hand—you get me, an open slap—to shut him up. Then we leave quickly. And that's it. Job done.'

I feel like fainting. 'Ronny, I can't do this.'

'Then don't.'

He says it with a shrug. Like a Jew.

'And nor should you.'

'This is for Ariella, Man. And our babies. And Mordecai.'

'Mordecai? Who's Mordecai?'

'Mordecai Anielewicz. Warsaw Ghetto fighter. Ariella's from Poland.'

'She's from Hampstead!'

'Her grandparents.'

He hands me a helmet and starts up the bike. It roars with the tiniest twist of the throttle.

Ronny snaps shut his visor and waits. I have no choice. I climb on behind him. When we arrive, I will try once more to stop him and, if it all fails, I can explain to the police later that this was a journalistic recce that just went wrong.

As soon as I'm settled, Ronny glides the Ninja into the flashing London night. He surfs the traffic to perfection and in no time at all, we're swooping off the Goldhawk Road and rolling soundlessly into a dark space behind the target building.

Ronny kills the lights. We dismount in silence.

'No talking until we're inside,' he whispers.

He leads me to the side entrance and up the service stairwell to the second floor. On the corridor, he points and walks quickly to the target flat.

We're outside the flat, ears to the door.

I'm a journalist, I tell myself.

Inside there's the sound of a radio.

Ronny squares up and knocks loudly. Three raps.

We hear movement. The door swings open. It's an old man in a worn dressing gown blinking into the light. He says 'hello' in a strangely polite way. Him, without a doubt.

We burst past him and shut the door.

'Oh my God!' screams the man. 'What do you want?'

'Just need to ask you a few questions,' I say, BBC-style.

'Are you Reginald White?' Ronny barks.

'I am,' says the old man, terrified. He's taking off his thick greasy glasses and clumsily cleaning them with the sleeve of his dressing gown.

'Are you a fucking Nazi?'

'No.' The old man looks affronted, then adds, with some embarrassment, 'I'm actually a Liberal Democrat.'

'I don't believe you, Mate,' says Ronny feebly.

'Well, I used to be Labour, to be honest, but then I got disillusioned with the local council,' he says. 'Hammersmith and Fulham. If you knew the mistakes they've made with road routing and buses and general traffic management. Or mismanagement, really. There has to be dirty money behind it, but there's nothing you can do, is there? You can't appeal. And then there a few other things—like the problems we've had with rubbish collection but I'd never think of voting Tory because of it.'

'Shut up,' Ronny commands, grabbing him by the collar. 'You're a Nazi! Admit it.'

'Look, okay: I did once think of voting Tory when the Leader of the Council used his casting vote to allow private taxis to use bus lanes,' the man sputters 'but I never did. Like I say, I'm a Lib Dem now; have been for ten years.'

'Did you poison my cat?' I yell.

The man twists his head and stares into my helmet.

'Did I what in your mat?'

I open the visor wider. 'I said, did you poison my cat?'

'Did I poison your flat?'

'My cat.'

'Did I poison your cat?'

I nod feverishly.

The man looks astonished. 'Why would I want to poison your cat? I don't even know you.'

'You did, you lying Nazi thug!' I say unconvincingly and the old man starts babbling about the local council's problems with pet cats, strays and urban foxes.

As he is talking, we hear a door open and we look up.

A younger, corpulent man, also in a dressing gown, has left the kitchen and is standing with an open carton of ice cream and a spoon, watching us.

Ronny lets go of the old man and advances on the young one.

'Who the fuck are you?'

'Brian,' says the young man. 'I'm his son.'

There's something about Brian, something about his fleshy face and sorrowful little brown eyes, that I recognise. So I pat the old guy on the shoulder and hasten towards his son.

'I know you, don't I?' I say.

The young man nods his head, a little bewildered.

'What's my name?' I say from behind the helmet.

'David Britton,' he gasps. 'The film-maker.'

'Oh shit,' says Ronny.

I rip off my helmet. 'It's you, isn't it? You killed my cat.'

'I was only trying to make it sick, you know? So it would vomit on your carpets.'

'You're a filthy Nazi!' I say, grabbing him in a choke hold.

'Actually, he also votes Lib Dem,' says the old man.

'That's true,' gasps Brian. 'Though I quite like Jeremy Corbyn.'

'Why'd you poison my cat?' I shout.

'I don't know. Let go.'

'And why've you been threatening me?'

'Because of the gate,' he wheezes.

'The hate?' yells Ronny.

'The gate.'

'What did he say?'

'Hate. He said "because of the hate", I think,' says Ronny.

'I thought it was mate,' the old man says.

'Did you say gate, mate or hate?' I cry.

'Gate,' he pants. 'I said gate!'

'Gate,' says Ronny.

'Did you say "gate", you piece of Nazi shit.'

'Yes,' blubs the man. 'I said gate!'

I look at the father, who shrugs. 'Can I make you some tea?' he says. 'You can drag him into the lounge and strangle him there. It's more comfortable.'

My stalker is starting to turn red.

'Do I know you?' I ask.

'Yes,' he gasps.

He does look familiar. 'Where do i know you from?'

'I'm Brian. Your dubbing editor for *Criminal Natures*. The gate. Don't you remember the gate? I dubbed the gate.'

'I'll make tea,' says the old man. 'You can take your helmets off. My son's a bit of an idiot, to be honest.'

I drag the son into the lounge and dump him into a chair.

'Nobody takes dubbing seriously any more,' he complains. 'Not as a craft skill!'

'What the heck is he talking about?' Ronny asks me.

'It's audio mixing,' I explain. 'When you've made a film, you try get the audio levels right so the sound complements what you're seeing. Sound quality is just as important as video quality; sometimes it's more important.'

'That's right!' says Brian, getting his breath back. 'But you laughed. You laughed at me.' He's pointing at me.

'Why did I laugh at you?'

'Because of the gate!'

'What gate?'

'Tell him what gate or I'll break your nose,' Ronny growls.

'I went out and sampled the sound of a gate, a real gate, one of those big ones that farmers use to keep cattle in a field, you know? A country gate. It took a whole day. In my own time. At my own expense. I found one that made a beautiful creak, just perfect, with cows in the background too, and I dubbed it over the shot ... and then I showed you ... and ramped it up to foley levels, you know, so it really stood out ...'

He's gasping again.

'And?'

'And you laughed!' he shrieks.

'Yes, well, in the middle of a film, there's suddenly this deafeningly loud creaking gate? Of course I laughed. Anyone would have laughed.'

'It took hours to do that sound. And it worked really nicely! But you made it almost inaudible. After all my hard work.'

Now I'm laughing again. And Ronny's laughing. Even the old man is laughing.

But Brian isn't finished. 'And then,' he splutters, 'to add insult to injury, you got my name wrong in the credits! You called me Brain!'

I scream with laughter, wondering if Adolf Hitler hadn't dreamt up National Socialism all because a teacher had misspelled Schicklgruber.

But Brian isn't finished. 'You didn't check. You should have checked. I'm an artist too! We get so little recognition in the production team. You could at least have cared enough to get my bloody name right.'

I look at Ronny. 'Can you believe this?'

'"The Socialism of Fools", he says. 'That's what August Bebel called antisemitism.'

'August Bebel?'

'Dude, he was one of the founders of the SPD in Germany. Bismarck put him in prison for being a Marxist.'

'I'll get you a new cat,' Brian says sulkily.

I slump into a chair and glare at him.

'I told you he's an idiot,' says the father. 'More tea?'

'Why the Nazi shit?' Ronny growls.

''Cos he's a Jew,' Brian replies, as if the question didn't need asking, 'and Jews run the world. We have to fight back somehow.'

I get up, walk over and slap him open-handed as hard as I can across the face.

I look at Ronny.

'Again.'

I oblige.

'Ouch!' says the old man.

'Let's get out of here,' Ronny says.

My Life In A Box
3 June, 7:48 pm

Olivia, I can't tell you how happy I've been since I beat up The Stalker! I feel fantastic! So happy that this morning I felt brave enough to sneak a peek at Boaz's dreaded Facebook wall.

Bad idea, as you know.

It opens like an artillery barrage. A whole page of new snaps, with you in every one of them, grinning your head off, and bovine Boaz with that keyboard smile. In one photo you've linked arms but thank heavens that's all. And who's that third guy, the ferociously handsome lurker? No doubt the guy who Boaz dragged out of the flaming tank before pleasuring you and saving five hundred African peasants' eyes, right?

But it's you I can't take my eyes off, Olivia. You look so beautiful. Even worse, you look so happy. Happier, I think, than I've ever seen you. That hurts.

I close Facebook, swearing never to look at it again, and return to my task, freshly crushed. As usual, this is no ordinary day, Olivia. I'm packing up my life in a box. It's been about four hours since I saw Matilda, signed the contract, shook hands with her again and parted from my company. I'm now sitting on my Hollywood chair, the one with my name on the back, surveying the detritus. What to rescue, what to discard? I scour the shelves, the open cupboards, the rows of bookshelves and at every turn my memory is ambushed.

Mostly it's old VHS films with grand BBC labels yellowing on the spines. The Bafta-winning *Tomorrow I Die*, the twenty-four-hour vigil filmed inside five death-row prisons across the United States; my recidivist series *Payback!* and its bleak cast of Newcastle ne'er-do-wells: boys and girls fated to spend their lives behind bars; *The Socrates of Winson Green*, whose dashing young star, Ronald Boyton Smith, would later find fame and friendship with me as the one-and-only Ronny the Runner. And many others: my panel discussions, my appearances on *Newsnight*, and *This Week*, and TV-am, and *The Jury*. Passionate, handsome, suavely liberal me with my lustrous black curls, my fine Roman nose, piercing black eyes and sensual, ironic mouth. Honestly, it's like a comedy sketch now. Every one goes into the trash.

In a folder in a box in a cupboard I retrieve my *Love in Purgatory* material. An old ad in *Variety* about the crazy cast of likeable cripples and madmen. Wads of citations, awards and praise. The Oscar announcement. An editorial in *The Daily Telegraph* calling on Britain's ambassador to intervene on a murderer's behalf. And there on the shelf above, resplendent and dominating, the old gold dildo himself. He goes in the box.

And the photographs, dozens of them. Boozy smiles at award ceremonies; assignments abroad; epic lunches in Notting Hill, Bulawayo, Amman, Delhi, Baton Rouge, New York, L.A.; shining hair and smiling faces; all those pretty young fixers, researchers, presenters and producers; and the old disgruntled, envious competitors. Everything, in the bin.

And now it's 6 pm and I've finished. All crammed into a single cardboard box, Oscar peering magnificently out of the top. And that's when you call, the call I've been dreading.

'You're late.'

'On my way. Is Boaz there?'

'No.'

The phone goes dead before I can ask why not.

Boaz And His Massive Surprise
5 May, 11:49 pm

The taxi halts outside the cafe. I clamber out with the cardboard box, which is tearing and spilling. You're sitting by the window, watching me and shaking your head.

I stumble to the table. Thanks for your help.

'What's that?'

'It's a box that's falling to bits, with an Academy Award Oscar sticking out the top.' You nod your head, which I take as a sign that I may continue. 'The remnants of my life. Be as gentle as you can, Olivia. I've had one hell of a day.'

'I'm sure you have, David,' you sigh. 'You and your box.'

'So where's Boaz?'

'He's not coming.' I feel exhilarated but deflated. I was looking forward to telling him about my hand-to-hand stuff with the Nazi. He'd understand.

You spot what's coming. 'Not in the mood, David. He's not coming. That's all you need to know.'

Buoyed by this intriguingly ambiguous news, I decide to show off. 'I sold my company this morning,' I say. 'Hence the box. One of the conditions was I had to get out of the building as quickly as possible so as not to traumatise any more young people.

I touch Oscar suggestively. Our old Dildo gag.

'Remember him?'

'I remember. Please put him back.'

'So where's the war hero? Couldn't face me, huh?'

'Zip it. Go get your coffee.'

'Want anything?'

You shake your head and there's something in your expression—a bleakness, a resignation—that lifts my soul. Problems with Boaz. I can smell it, so I jump up, almost levitating with excitement, and when I return you're finishing a text and happily still looking gloomy.

'How's it going with Boaz, then? Sorry, but I need to know.'

'None of your business.' But it's the way you hesitate that gives it away. I want to yelp with joy but manage to sit quietly and say nothing for a very long time, while looking both mature and compassionate.

'I'm sorry,' I say, eventually.

'The hell you are.'

'I want your happiness, Olivia.'

'Could have fooled me.'

'Is he seeing someone else?'

'Yes.'

As you stifle a sob, I find myself shivering with joy.

'That's disappointing for you.'

'He's going back to Israel tomorrow,' you say. Then you halt, look at me fiercely and blurt out the magical words: 'He's getting re-married and if you laugh at me I'll never talk to you again because I feel a little heartbroken, okay?'

I want to jump on the table and start singing celebratory songs but, since I can't do that, I sigh loudly and sympathetically instead. I sound asthmatic. 'Oh, that's terrible! You deserve better. Better than me. And better than Boaz.'

'You're damned right there.'

'If it's any consolation, the woman who gets him will suffer. Of this I am sure.'

'No, she won't.'

'Oh, she will—' I'm shaking my head gravely '—she will.'

'It's not a woman, you idiot. It's a man.'

It takes me a while to process this but, when it lands, a bolt of ecstasy sends me reeling. Now I want to scream. I want to grab the pensioners at the next table and start a hokey-cokey around the cafe and through the door, joining with every driver, pedestrian and worker in all of London, all of England, all of the world, a huge hokey-cokey embrace of joy and love.

'Ari!' I yell.

You look up sharply. 'How do you know about Ari?' You're fixing me with a livid stare. 'How do you know about Ari and Boaz?'

276

'Facebook. I've been stalking you through Boaz. Sorry.'

Oddly you don't seem to care. 'The name means "lion",' you say witheringly.

'Oh. Decent chap?'

'A bit of a prick, actually,' you snarl. 'Twenty years younger than Boaz and the vainest man I have ever met.'

To stop myself ululating, I say the first thing that drifts into my head. 'Can't be easy being gay in a prejudiced world. I guess one should always remember that.'

You are now looking at me with unbridled hatred. 'David, I know you're delighted. I know you're amused. I know you think this will force me back to you but listen to me: it won't. Not in a million years. That's why I'm here. To tell you that. So you'll understand that.'

'I love you, Olivia,' I say. And I do.

You wipe your mouth, take another sip of coffee.

'What's wrong with me, David? Why do I always fall for inadequate, childish, vain, stupid men? Are there no responsible, faithful, heterosexual adult males left in this world?'

'I know one,' I say.

'No you don't.' Then you remember. 'Now remind me: what nonsense do I have to go through this evening as a result of your assaulting a rabbi? Not your rabbi, you'll hasten to add.'

'They're installing an amulet on the doorframe of our house.'

This prompts a fresh expression of loathing. 'It's a mezuzah. How do you do it, David? How do you always get us into these situations?'

'Fate, I keep telling you. There is a demented minor deity with a Kafkaesque sense of humour who has taken a particular dislike to me. But I have good news.'

'No you don't.'

'I found the Nazi who poisoned our cat.'

'Oh my God. No, this is not good news.'

'And I beat him up.'

You stare at me a long time before saying: 'I suppose on Planet David, that does count for good news. Are you being literal?'

'Yes. His name is Brian Wilson and he was my dubbing editor about ten years ago. He hates Jews and me, because we all run the world—you too—and he killed our cat because I hadn't given pride of place to a sound effect he had made, and then misspelled his name in the credits.'

'He poisoned the cat because he felt snubbed?'

'Brian had produced a very loud squeaky gate sound, which apparently I laughed at and lowered in volume.'

'So he decided to run a one-man Gestapo operation?'

'Yes. After he'd explained why he'd done it, I slapped him. Twice. Once in each direction.'

'You know, David, only you can do that.'

'Do what?'

'Turn a mild-mannered dubbing editor into a cat-murdering SS volunteer.'

'That's not fair.' I check the time. 'We'd better go. The Jews will be waiting.'

You're looking at me weirdly, fists balled. 'Wait! Look, I've changed my mind. I'm not coming. I've had enough of your nonsense. And I don't care what your rabbi thinks.'

'He's not my rabbi.'

'Whatever,' you say wearily. 'I'm exhausted. Drained. I'm sure your rabbi won't mind me not being there on this one occasion.'

'He's not my rabbi.'

'I'll be at my sister's,' you say, halfway to the exit. 'Don't forget your little box.'

A Lot Of Children
6 May, 10:06 pm

I open the front door.

'Who invited you?'

Peter Dent, his handsome face creased into an amiable smile, holds out a spray of flowers. 'Ah, David!' He says it as if he's surprised to see me in my own house.

'Who, I repeat, invited you?'

'Well, Menachem actually,' he chuckles.

'Menachem? Sorry: is Menachem your client? Because for some weird reason, I thought you were being paid by me, and quite handsomely too, rather than by Menachem, and that that single fact, oddly enough, made you *my* lawyer, and not his.'

'Of course I'm your lawyer, David, and naturally there's no charge, because I'm Menachem's guest,'

As Dent indulgently parries my rebuffs, he cannot help sneaking glances over my shoulder into the living room, where shoals of small Victorian-looking Jewish children are spilling toy animals noisily onto every available surface.

'Ah, so you *are* my lawyer—'

'Of course David!'

'—which makes me not only your client but also, way more importantly, your ongoing box-series entertainment—'

'Now, now, David, you're just being silly.'

'—*David and the Jews!* A Netflix family favourite!' For some reason, the idea that Dent is deriving amusement from the demented soap opera that has become my life annoys me more and more.

'Now come on—'

'Subscribe now and watch extra episodes in the comfort of *their* own home.'

Dent dismisses my riff with an elegant wave. 'I haven't missed the ceremony have I?'

'Tell me, are you as attentive as this with all your clients?'

He looks past me and marvels. 'Gosh. So many kids! What's that? Dear boy, of course I'm just as attentive with all my clients: that's why I'm so rich.' A flock of children suddenly gathers around us, then as suddenly congregates elsewhere, like starlings. 'How lovely!'

'So when you take on, I don't know, a shipping line, say, do you visit the engine room to inspect the bilge pumps?'

'Very funny, David, very amusing.'

'Or, say, when you're preparing leasing contracts for a private hospital, are you the guy who checks on the colonoscopy tubes?'

Dent dismisses me with another fragrant wave. 'Can all these children possibly be Menachem's?'

'No, just two hundred of them,' I growl. 'The rest belong to Hymie.'

'Well I never!'

And before I can tell Dent of my plans to sell them to Afghan slave traffickers, he's off, striding towards the colony of kiddies now turning our sturdy mahogany dining room table into Noah's ark.

Never before have I been so consumed with hatred, Olivia. And not just for Dent. At this moment I hate you, Masaai, Hymie, Hymie's wife, Hymie's children and all their stupid toys. But mostly I hate Menachem. You should have seen his arrival. He rang the bell loudly for about thirty seconds and then, when I let him in, he came striding into the house with a proprietorial smile and a ludicrously pretty, pregnant wife in tow, followed by their cargo of weirdly serious children gaping as though they were on the wrong side of the glass in an aquarium.

As I am wondering how one gets in touch with Central Asian child trafficking gangs, I am interrupted by a rabbinic cheer from the living room. I hurry inside to investigate. It's Masaai and the Menachoids, excitedly comparing family trees in San Francisco.

The only person I don't hate at the moment is Moose, our pale daughter, who has emerged from the bedroom. She's hiding in the shadows, gripping the remains of yet another Bovril, carrot and chocolate sandwich, while blinking incomprehensibly at the menagerie of children who suddenly go silent to stare at her, with a kindly, anthropological curiosity. I want to rush to her side, hold her, and protect her against this invasion but as soon as I start forward the Two Matriarchs are upon her. They corner her with fearsome hugs and before the poor kid can say 'please let me go so I can hurl myself out of the window,' the women have lined up about four hundred children and are reciting their names, apparently from memory, since they seem to have no prompts to hand: Yosele, Yossi, Yankoyv, Avraham, Moyshie, Menachem Mendel, Yitzie, Yitz, Dov Ber, Levi, Yosif, Chaya, Chaya Mushka, Mushie, Nechama, Dina, Nechama Dina, Sorah, Rivkie, Sorah Rivka, Esther, Rochelleh, Channah … after which I start to lose track, but am amazed to see each child offering a shy smile and a nod, and Moose reciting each name, with an equally shy smile and a nod.

As I absorb this worrying sight, I am intercepted by the ever-nimble Menachem. 'Ah, *Dovidl*, we never got a chance to talk at the door: how are you?'

'The name's David.'

I'm straining to escape but he's barred my way. '*Dovidl* is David,' he laughs. 'So how are you? I asked a question.'

I'm considering whether to use brute force to crash through the eight-inch gap that has opened between Menachem and the door frame when Hymie suddenly materialises out of thin air and seals that last remaining route.

'*Sholom aleichem, Dovidl*,' he singsongs.

'Supercalifragilistic,' I say, as offensively as I can.

The Jews look at each other and cackle. Hymie says something in Yiddish and they cackle, Menachem says something else and they cackle, and then Menachem dips his hand into one of the cavernous inside pockets in his black jacket.

'Well, here it is,' he says gleefully. He hands me a transparent plastic envelope and a small silver tube about six inches long.

'Your new *mezuzah*. Go on, take it: have a look.'

The envelope contains a small square of parchment covered with tiny handwritten Hebrew lettering. The silver tube has a single embossed Hebrew word on the casing.

'*Azoy*, we're going to take out the *klaf*, roll it up, put it into the tube, and then nail the tube to your doorpost.'

'Sounds too easy,' I say. 'I'm thinking there's a downside. How much is this going to cost me? I'm guessing four figures.'

'No, no, no: it's a gift—from me and Hymie, in honour of your father.'

'Really?'

'But if you want, you can make a nice donation to a charity we've set up—'

'Ah, the Hymie and Menachem Grabathon Appeal.'

'—and about £200 would be a lovely gift to give in your beloved father's name—a real *mitzvah*. Thank you, David.'

'That's all? I can get away for just two hundred quid?'

'Alright, alright: £300 then, and thank you. You're a *mensch*, just like your father. It's a charity for Torah-learning for poor Jewish kids in Israel—a very good charity, so thank you again. So, tell me, *Dovidl*: do you know what a *mezuzah* is? Do you know why we put it on our door frames?'

'I don't actually but I'm guessing it's a kind of celestial doorbell that you ring, so God knows the guy from Amazon's arrived with the parcel?'

'Yes, yes, very funny, *Boychik*' says Menachem 'and weirdly, as usual—and this is the really funny thing—you're always about one tenth right with your gags but always in the wrong way, missing the big picture, so let me explain. On the parchment scroll, the *klaf*, a scribe has written the first two verses of the *Shema*, with every letter perfectly formed, in indelible ink. Do you know what the *Shema* is?'

'A football chant?'

'*Ach*, *Dovidl*. Always the joker. No, *Shema* is the most important prayer a Jew can say, or has to say, and what it reminds you is that there is only one God: *Adonoi Eloheynu Adonoi Echod*.'

'*Adonoi Eloheynu Adonoi Echod!*' repeats Hymie, excitedly.

282

'*Expialidocious!*' I cry.

Menachem's scowling. 'It's the most fundamental declaration of the Jewish faith, David: that the Lord is our God, that the Lord is unique! No more mockery, okay?'

Under the mournful, scorching gaze of two bearded Jews, I nod grumpily.

Menachem's off again in singsong, Hymie rocking at his side. 'And then the *Shema* tells you what you have to do about it. Love God with all of your being! Teach it to your children! Recite it when you wake and lie down! Bind it as a symbol on your body—you remember? The *tefillin?* And you know what David? If you do all this, your life will be good, *Boruch Hashem!*'

In the living room I spot my lawyer, on his knees, holding a tiny plastic pelican against a flock of other birds controlled by a commando unit of small but determined children.

Suddenly a panic. Where is Moose? To my horror I find her still being mugged by the dramatically pregnant matriarchs. Oh, and Masaai is drifting around with an insane, unrelenting grin on his face. I think he may be high on heroin.

Time to get a move on, I think.

'Okay, Jews,' I say loudly in my biggest BBC voice: 'let's get this *mezuzah* show on the road!'

But Menachem's not budging. He wants to know where you are. I tell him you're not well and that you can't come.

'Not well? I'm sorry to hear that,' he says 'No problem: we'll come back another time.' He snatches back the envelope and the tube.

'You can't do that, Guys!' I cry. 'People get sick. Life goes on.'

The Jews stare at me for a moment, then resume packing up.

'Fuck this, I'm speaking to my lawyer.'

I fight my way through a herd of hyperactive but pallid children to find Dent discussing a toy he's holding with an earnest child with two long ringlets on either side of his otherwise shaved head, and wearing a black velvet *yarmulke*, as do all this brothers and quasi-brothers.

283

'I need to talk to you.'

'Oh David, it's you.' He seems surprised I'm there.

'Of course it's me! Who else would it be?'

'One second.' Dent picks up a toy bird and hands it to one of the girls. 'Her name's Yocheved,' he says, straightening up with an athletic grace. 'The name of Moses's mother. Quite charming. How can I help you, David?'

I explain that you can't possibly join us because you're unwell and that the rabbi is therefore refusing to go ahead with the goat sacrifice.

'The *mezuzah* consecration,' he says, passively scolding me.

'Whatever. Now you have to tell them that we cannot and will not delay the ceremony because someone happens to be ill. You will insist and, if they disagree, you will break their children's legs, one by one.'

Eventually Dent yields to the fanatical determination evident in my eyes and my balled-up fists. 'I'll see what I can do,' he says.

The Jews are waiting for him. When he arrives they exchange great bear hugs. They then talk for what seems like hours. When it's over, he returns. It is evident from his slouch that the shruggers have triumphed.

'The thing is,' Dent tells me in a lawyerly way, 'I don't feel we have any room for manoeuvre. As Hymie points out, there is no specific exclusionary clause and no scope for assuming any right to be represented *in absentia*, especially when it's the mother who is, in Jewish juridical terms, the head of the house, whether *de facto* or *de jure*—or even *de Jewry!* Ho ho! He also says the terms are specific and agreed to, irrespective of any jurisprudential latitude, and I fear he's right. Rather elegant formulation, actually.'

'Hymie told you all this even though he doesn't speak a word of English.'

'Menachem translated.'

'Are you joking, Peter?'

'No. They've got us over the proverbial barrel I'm afraid.'

'What if we take this to court?—because I am prepared to fight this all the way. With a new lawyer. Preferably a

German. An unreconstructed German. Ideally, the legal adviser to *Alternative für Deutschland*.'

'Now don't be rash, Dear Chap, because you'll lose. They will simply terminate the process, invoke the assault charges against you and cut you out of your father's will.'

'It's fucking worth it!'

'Oh, stop it, David!' There's something in Dent's tone that stuns me. For the first time, I'm looking at a genuinely angry Peter Dent. 'For God's sake! Something good can happen here, if only you'll allow it. Stop being such a prig. Call your wife. Tell her she has to come her now, and make it clear that if she's really too ill, it will all simply get bounced to another day. This is not something any of us can get out of.'

I look at Dent sideways.

'Are you a secret Jew, Peter?'

'Of course not!'

'Well, you sure as hell sound like one.'

I look away and there's Moose, helping the giant matriarchs to lay the table. They are opening a hundred plastic bags, taking out plastic plates and plastic cutlery, and unleashing enough pre-wrapped food to feed a small nation.

I really, really want you to see this, Olivia. 'Alright already,' I say to Dent. 'I'll call her.'

Alright already? Olivia, I am starting to talk like a Jew.

285

The Mezuzah
7 May, 11:11 pm

An hour later, after the visiting Jews have had a long lunch of sugary, fatty and over-processed kosher food, complete with loud singing, praying and assorted mumbo jumbo, the doorbell rings and I pounce on the handle.

I open the door to reveal Martin looking happily anguished.

'David, David, David,' he intones with a huge disappointed-headmaster frown. 'I must tell you this has not been convenient.'

I ask him where you are and he tells me that you're coming with Ruth and that you're on your way. He tells me again that this has not been convenient.

He's loving it, the prick. 'I know this has not been convenient, Martin. I know that better than anyone. Believe me, if there is any man alive who understands how *fickenfotze* inconvenient this is, it's me, okay?'

The '*fickenfotze*' floors him. 'Ah. I see.'

I ask him how you are and he tells me they're worried about you and that you need their support. Then he springs inside the house, spots some Jews and gets excited. But his reprimand isn't over. 'Ruth has actually taken a day off from the hospital to be here. At very short notice.'

'There was no need. You and Ruth did not have to come.'

'It's a big thing, her coming, let me tell you. She works in ICU.'

'I know, Martin, and I know that people can and do die there very often, and that Ruth's work is invaluable. I know all of that, but there was no need for you to come.'

We hear footsteps. You and Ruth are approaching quickly with a shared rictus of sisterly fury.

'Thanks for coming,' I say to you, hand on my breast.

You grunt.

'And hi, Ruth. Wasn't expecting you and Martin, to be

286

honest, but the more the merrier, I guess. Come and meet the Jews.'

'We came because we're a little worried about Olivia,' says Ruth. 'We think she needs our support. I must tell you, though: this has not been convenient.'

You quieten your sister with a squeeze of her arm. 'This is ridiculous, David,' you snarl at me. 'Ridiculous!'

Suddenly a wave of silence sweeps across the house. I look up.

Emily has emerged. And wasn't she incredible, Olivia? Halting on the red carpet so everyone can see her, swathed in a glittery diaphanous thing with a flower tiara and that utterly resplendent smile. Everyone is hypnotised. Even the Jews.

In fact, especially the Jews. I've never seen them so quiet.

'Would anyone like a smoothie?' Emily is saying. 'I'm going to make a batch.'

'Not now, Sweetheart,' I say. 'Maybe later. But you make one.'

'Did you know smoothies are kosher?' she says. 'I didn't know that. It's so cute. I thought to be kosher you had to kill a pig. Or not kill it. Anyway, bye.'

As Emily drifts into the kitchen, Ruth advances on me with an angry grimace. 'So that's the one you dragged off the streets?'

'I didn't drag her off the streets. I kidnapped her from work.'

'He didn't actually, literally kidnap her,' you're saying to Ruth.

'Are you sure?' replies Ruth. She turns to me. 'I see a lot of that in my work, David—'

'I'm sure you do, Ruth.'

'—and I've got a very good idea of what people are capable of.'

I resort to the truth. 'Well, I did kind of kidnap her, to be honest, because people were trying to cut off her penis.'

My reply hangs in the air until you cut in. 'Said so. Obsessed.'

Martin is pleasurably horrified. 'Honestly? Cut it off?'

'Yes. And her testicles. And the whole scrotum thing, which then gets made into an internal cavity.'

'A cavity? Well I never!' he exclaims.

'Yes, because the scrotal skin is elastic and very similar in texture to vaginal tissue, so it becomes the basis of a neovagina. Of course, if the neovagina needs to be lengthened, and the scrotal tissue is insufficient, grafts may be taken from abdominal or thigh tissue to extend it.'

'You're saying she has balls?' Martin repeats.

'I'm saying she *still* has balls, and a cock, and the rest, thanks to me and Olivia.'

'David, why is our flat full of strange children?' you ask.

'Because Hymie and Menachem brought their kids along for the fun. About 385 of them.'

'Unbelievable,' you sigh.

'Do they all have balls?' says Martin.

'I don't know!'

Ruth snaps. 'David, this isn't funny! You have to grow up!'

Martin is shaking his head in his sternest, most headmasterly way, to lend his support to the view that it is no longer funny and that I have to grow up. He's so happy, I want to slap him.

'It never was funny, Ruth,' I say. 'In fact I'd go so far as to say that your ICU, on a bad day when everyone's flatlining simultaneously, which they do, would be happier than this.'

'That's not funny either, David,' sniffs Ruth.

'That's what I'm saying, Ruth. It's not funny.'

'No, but that's really not funny.'

'Nor is this Ruth. I promise you, nor is this.'

'Have you ever seen someone die in ICU, David? No? Because I have. Many times.'

'Yes, I know your shifts are busy, Ruth.'

'Will you two stop it!' Your hands are crossed across your breasts, and it makes me want to hug you. 'Can we just get on with this please!'

'Look at this way,' I whisper. 'If you hadn't come now, I'd be on my way to prison and we'd be cut out of my father's will. And believe me, it's a will worth suffering a little for.'

'How's Moose?' you whisper, terrified.

'Playing with children.'

'Oh God, no!' Your hands fly to your mouth. You crane your head to look but your view is blocked by the sudden appearance of the cheerfully wild-eyed Menachem.

'Olivia! *Bruchah haba'ah!* Welcome. Thank you so much for coming and even better for bringing your whole family. I hope it wasn't such a nuisance. Look, I know you're important people with busy lives, thank God, but to be honest, a *mezuzah* can help you through things, you know? Through it the miraculous power of *Hashem* is channeled, and this has been demonstrated many many times. In fact, remind me, when there's time, to tell you the story of the Rebbe and the poor cobbler, *nebbich*. Lovely story. You know it? So the cobbler's *mezuzah* got damaged during the plague of Vishniezska, which was a little village in Ukraine—'

Martin is staring with his mouth wide open. Ruth jabs him, then abruptly steps forward to square off with the rabbi, her hands balled and her shoulders curled as if she's about to start a hakka.

'My sister was very busy and so were we. Is this really necessary, Rabbi?'

'Of course, of course, of course. So you're the sister, Ruth? Very nice. It's good you came all this way to join us in putting up the *mezuzah*. It's a *mitzvah!* And you are—?'

Martin is gasping like a landed fish. 'Martin.'

'Martin, fascinating name. Roman. You're like the god of war! Nice to meet you, Martin. So I guess we can begin.' He looks at Ruth. 'Do you know what a *mezuzah* is?'

'Of course. I'm Jewish.' Her defiance withers under his probing smile. 'Culturally.'

'Very nice, very nice. Always a *metsiyah* to meet cultural Jews. Funny thing: I used to be one, but that's another story. So you know what an important thing the *mezuzah* is and how it can change lives. I'll go and get everyone and we can start.'

He swings round to face you. 'Lovely you could come, and be here with your daughter and husband, and I'm sorry if it was inconvenient but I promise: you won't regret it.'

And before you can respond he's off, careering into the other rooms like a cyclone, chanting and clucking as he goes.

I'm lurking in a corner. In the commotion I spot Hymie, within range and alone. He's got a pair of tiny twins buried in his arms and a demented smile under his massive beard. 'Ah, Hymie!' I say, relishing the prospect of some intense guerrilla mockery. 'You're a stud, Old Chap, you know that? A jolly good stud!' Hymie mutters something in Yiddish and looks puzzled. 'If you were a bull, Hymie, your farm manager would send you off to agricultural events all over Britain and you'd come away with lots of big rosettes and silver cups, you know? Hymie, the Gold Medal champion stud!' Hymie surrenders with a grin. 'Also old chap, how on earth have you managed to avoid speaking English? And how the fuckety-fuck do you manage to raise sixty-four children without a job and with your only skills being an ability to sway while mumbling, procreate, and do an occasional authentic blue whale sound?

Suddenly Moose is there, holding hands with two pretty little girls. You are in hot pursuit.

Hymie pinches the kids' cheeks and vanishes quickly.

'Daddy, I don't know what to do with these children,' Moose says.

'Amelia, Darling!' you cry. 'Who are they? Shake them off!'

'Mom, they won't let go. I don't know what to do.'

The girls look up at you, puzzled.

'Have you tried shaking hard?'

'Yes. They just laughed. I don't want to hurt their feelings'

Another child with a rosebud mouth and bright blue eyes arrives and offers Moose a toy rhino, and then all three children vanish in a collective giggle.

You flash me the dagger look. Yes, I know it's my fault, naturally, but there is no time for me to fall on my sword because suddenly, the entire entourage is being shepherded by Menachem, Hymie and the two matriarchs towards the front of the house.

'I like your rabbi,' Martin tells me. 'Knows what he's doing. Fine beard.'

There are so many things wrong in that sentence that it takes me a while to answer. 'He's not my rabbi, Martin.'

'Well, he gives a jolly good impression of it,' Martin giggles. I'm about to deploy the expression '*fickenfotzen*' on him again, to shut him up, but there's no time because Menachem has marched up, grabbed me round the shoulders and frogmarched me to the front door.

'Please, put this on.' He hands me a skullcap.

I look back and see that you are being bullied into position by the matriarchs. Behind them, Masaai is still grinning in a heroin way and the sweet, maniacal twins have once again apprehended Moose. Hymie appears with a large hammer and presents it to Menachem.

'Why are we doing this?' Menachem asks me in that loud sing-song voice.

'I ask myself the same question,' I respond. 'How about, because it's part of the deal my lawyer agreed to.'

'That's not why,' laughs Menachem. 'The reason we put a *mezuzah* on the right doorpost of a Jewish home is to fulfil the *mitzvah* of writing the words of God on the doorposts and gates of your house … which is a quotation from where?'

He's looking at me. '*The Hobbit?*'

'It's from Deuteronomy. And the *Shema*. And where do we put it? Here? Two thirds up the doorway. And do we put it straight or crooked?'

'Crooked!' I yell, wanting to get the thing over.

'Correct!' says Menachem. 'And why?'

This time he doesn't allow me time to answer and instead directs his reply to Masaai, who is standing next to Moose and wearing a large skullcap perched precariously on the apex of his huge mat of hair. 'Because the rabbis couldn't agree whether it should be straight or on its side.'

Masaai finds this very, very funny. So does Dent, which makes me silently promise to sack him when this ordeal is over.

'And what is a *mezuzah*?' Menachem continues. 'This silver container is just the case. This is the actual *mezuzah*.'

Hymie takes the small piece of parchment out of the plastic envelope, so everyone can see the handwritten Hebrew writing.

'This is the *klaf*. Say it: *klaf*.'

I am about to try and say *klaf* with as much guttural mockery as possible but am stopped by the sound of Masaai, whose own resonant '*klaf*' silences the room.

'Yaakov! Very good' says Menachem to the beaming Masaai.

'Yaakov?'

'My Hebrew name,' Masaai tells me.

'And what's written in this *klaf*?' booms Menachem.

'"*Hear, O Israel! The Lord is our God, the Lord alone. You shall love the Lord your God with all your heart and with all your soul and with all your might. Take to heart these instructions with which I charge you this day. Impress them upon your children. Recite them when you stay at home and when you are away, when you lie down and when you get up. Bind them as a sign on your hand and let them serve as a symbol on your forehead; inscribe them on the doorposts of your house and on your gates.*"'

And with that, he hands me the hammer, positions the mezuzah on the doorpost and commands me to fix it, sloping, with a nail at the top and a nail at bottom, which I do. I refrain from then using the hammer on either of the rabbis, though the thought does occur.

'Now repeat after me,' commands Menachem. '*Borukh atoh Adonoi—*' I murmur the words '*—Eloheinu Melekh ho'olom, asher kideshonu bemitzvosov, vetzivonu, liqboa mezuzah.*'

When my tongue has finished getting itself round Menachem's tangle of words, the two Jews, the huge wives and the battalions of children start to sing. I'm searching you out when, from nowhere, there's a penetrating cry.

It's Hymie's wife. She's holding her huge stomach and backing into the wall, yelling and laughing.

Ruth comes pounding past me to the stricken woman.

'The baby's coming!' she says. 'We've got to go to the hospital! Now!'

A Melodramatic Night
Dreamtime 1

How on earth did we all get to the hospital, Olivia?

All I remember is that Rivka's waters broke on our old Turkish kilim carpet—the carpet you and I bought and made love on twenty-five years ago on a beach by an azure lagoon in a then-unknown Fethiye, on Turkey's south-western Turquoise Coast, after which you got pregnant with Moose and we quickly got married.

Then there was a giant howl and everything exploded.

This is what I recall. Menachem waving his arms about like a pantomime Moses. Moose retreating into a corner, with her hands over her mouth. Masaai and his saucer-eyed grin. Ruth barking orders. Martin loving it. You looking at me with new versions of loathing. And that's about it. And then you were off, bringing fresh supplies of towels as ordered by Ruth, while Rivka lay groaning, smiling, laughing and reciting psalms on our carpet.

Then what happened? Oh yes: then there were people screaming, shouting, praying, singing, reciting psalms and climbing into cars, and, before I knew it, there I was, pressed into a cramped car with a chattering child on each knee and smiley Hymie squeezing my arm and muttering incantations in Hobbitspeak.

We get to the hospital—I remember the sign—and who should arrive with us? The Pain Fairy—but this time, the Pain Fairy on steroids. She has been threatening to put in an appearance all day, sending tiny titillating sprays of acid down the spine. I've experienced this before, but this time it's different. This time, the Pain Fairy means business. I'm slumped in a creased plastic chair with my eyes closed to fight the gathering intensity of pain in my head when I feel a hand on my shoulder.

'You okay, Old Chap?'

Dent. Unruffled, uncreased and repulsively jolly. 'She's had a boy!' he cries. 'Her sixth. What a *simcha*!'

I force my eyes open. 'Come again?'

'I said Rivka has had her sixth boy.'

'No. After that.'

Dent looks embarrassed.

'Come on. What did you just say?'

'I said, "what a simcha".' He looks ashamed. 'Did I mispronounce it?'

'How would I know?' I'm about to tell Dent he's been fired but the pain's pressing me further into the creaking chair.

'But just so you know,' Dent's saying, 'I do understand what the word "*simcha*" means. Menachem explained. It means joy or joyous event. But interestingly, joy is different from happiness, in that it can only be expressed and experienced socially, with other *Yidn*, which is fascinating.'

'*Yidn*'?! That's it. I've had enough. I am about to tell Dent that he is not only fired but that I will also be making an official complaint to the Law Society when the Pain Fairy makes her move.

A crack in the middle of my head sends a thudding shock-wave across my body. Everything's blurred. And echoing.

'Are you alright, David? You look terrible,' says Dent.

'Never been better,' I groan.

'Never been better?' Dent is placing his palm on my forehead. 'I don't think so, Old Boy.'

'I was hoping you'd infer ironic intent but I realise now that since you've became a Hasidic Jew, you've probably abandoned irony and western humour,' I shout.

Even to me my voice sounds funny, Olivia. Like a vinyl record spinning too slowly.

'I'm going to get someone,' Dent says and vanishes.

In no time at all I'm surrounded. Ruth's in the lead, reproachfully shaking her head, The gleeful Martin springs to her side. I can see you and Moose, poor kid, who looks terrified. And here comes Menachem, his tassels waving, and Masaai with him, no longer grinning and moving more decisively than I've seen him before.

'David, are you okay?' Ruth at her bossiest, her face so close I can feel her hot breath.

'I want to sack my lawyer,' I say. 'I want someone who interned in their youth with the Third Reich or BBC Verify.'

'What? David, please repeat that.'

'I want to sack my lawyer!' I shout. 'In fact I want to sue him. He's joined the Jews. He's undermined the whole of our professional working relationship. He has been coopted into the world Jewish conspiracy and I can no longer trust that he's on my side.'

'David we can't understand you.'

'I think he's speaking Yiddish,' Dent says.

'You would think that, you Jewish idiot!' I scream.

'He seems agitated,' Ruth says. 'Where's the emergency neurology team!'

'That's not Yiddish,' says Menachem, breaking through to the front and breathing hotly into my face. '*Dovidl*, can you hear me? Yes, I think he can. Listen: you heard the wonderful news! Hymie just had another son, *Boruch Hashem*, and I need to consult you. They've chosen a name but they want your permission, *tucker*. I can't say this loudly because we usually keep the name private until the actual naming ceremony, but Hymie has a name and wants your permission.'

'Call him Christopher!' I shout, hoping that's an insult.

'What did he say? What did you say, David?' yells Ruth.

'"Patrick",' says Martin. 'I think he said "Patrick". Did you say "Patrick", David?'

'*Azoy*, they don't want to call him Patrick,' says Menachem. 'They want something much more special and they need your agreement. And by the way, it's the boy's *bris* in eight days' time, and Hymie wants to give you the honour of holding the baby while the circumcision is done: it's a big honour—you'll understand why when I explain. You see, Hymie wants to name the boy in your family's honour, and it will bring joy and *naches*.'

At that, Menachem indicates to everyone around that they should back off because he needs to speak to me privately.

'*Dovidl*, Hymie wants to name his boy after your beloved father, *zichrono l'vrochoh*. They want to call him Binyamin.'

He pauses to see if I register what he has just said. I don't.

'My father's name is Ben, you moron,' is all that I can think.

Ruth, in her role as medic-in-chief has not backed away as far as Menachem had wanted. 'What did you say to your rabbi, David?' Ruth's whispering now.

'He's not my rabbi.'

'Binyamin was the youngest, most beloved son of Jacob,' Menachem goes on. 'Benjamin. Such a beautiful name and such a beautiful meaning, because it means "son of the south" or "son of the right hand" from the Hebrew words "ben", meaning "son", and "yamin", meaning "right hand" or "south".'

The others have stepped back from my chair but I can hear them still arguing.

'It was "Brian",' Martin is saying. 'I heard it loud and clear.'

Ruth's back in my face, whispering. 'David, did you say "Brian"? Nod if you said "Brian".'

Then suddenly, in the sea of faces, you're there! Almost close enough to hold. Almost close enough to kiss. 'David, can you hear me?' you say. It's like music.

'Yes!' I scream. I am broken with love and when I cry 'I love you,' the exertion shoots a sulphurous bolt into my brain, but I carry on. 'Olivia, I'm sorry about everything. Sorry for being such a shit father to Moose. Sorry for being such a terrible husband. Sorry for Janice Toybeen. Sorry for not being there when you needed me. Sorry for being elsewhere and for being so vain and only thinking of myself and never taking you into account. You're an angel and I'm an idiot and I don't deserve you, not for a moment, but please, please, please, please give me one last chance: just one more chance.'

'He's hallucinating,' says Ruth. She's grabbing my wrist and placing her ear over my heart. 'Where are they? Someone get on the phone! Now!'

'Daddy!' Moose's cry cuts through the air. As Ruth steps

back, she throws her sobbing face on my chest. I can feel the fragrant embrace of her hair, delight in her fingers tracing the contours of my face. 'Daddy!'

'Darling girl,' I sing. 'I beg you! Don't abort your baby!'

'Wake up Daddy! Say something!'

'Don't kill your baby!'

Then they arrive. The doctors are kneeling before me.

'David,' says the bigger of the doctors, holding my head. 'I'm here.'

'Me too,' says the smaller one loudly.

The Boys!

'Brian! There, you see! He said "Brian" again!' shouts Martin.

'David, can you hear me?' Big Boy says.

'We have some news. Important news,' yells Little Boy, who isn't smiling but desperately looks as though he wants to. He's about to speak when Big Boy shoots Little Boy a look and shakes his head, and I see you spot it.

'What?' you demand. The boys look at each other. 'What's the news? I'm David's wife.'

Bravo! I yell. My wife!

'"Brian"!' shouts Martin. 'He said it again! Clear as day!'

Moose, who has been observing mutely, suddenly speaks up. 'It's about Grandad isn't it?'

'It is,' Dr Patel says. 'I'm sorry to say he passed away an hour ago. But now we have get your Dad to Emergency. I think he's having a stroke.'

'I meant good news about the paper,' says Little Boy.

A World Of Sound
Dreamtime 2

I'm tumbling, Olivia, plunging through an infinite black vortex. It has no start and no end. It is neither pleasant nor unpleasant. It goes on for what seems like years but I have no sense of time.

Then it stops.

Around me, a still-black world. No light at all.

I prise open my eyes as wide as they will go but there's nothing: just black.

Then I realise that I'm thinking. Talking in my head. I must be alive!

I try to communicate with my body, my legs, my tongue, my toes, my fingers. But there's nothing.

But I'm alive!

I scream it as loudly as I can: *I am alive!* And after long hours, days, weeks, maybe years, I get used to the fathomless black. And I start to make a life.

And this is how I spend my days: I make up games. I count to a hundred, do sums and memory tests, practise the times tables, spell the prime minister's name backwards, recite the registration numbers of all the cars I've ever had, repeat my mobile number, and my email and my online passwords. I meditate. I recite poetry. I breathe mindfully. And frequently I scream.

I'm alive! I'm fickenfotze alive!

Then, a huge breakthrough. I awake one day, or night, and realise, at first with panic and then with joy, that I can hear. Sounds. Hundreds of them. I am back in the world, Olivia: this magnificent aural jungle, this universe of beeping, whooshing, purring, scraping, of doors opening and closing, of cupboards and wheels. And of course, voices!

And because of these voices, many of which I recognise, I know where I am, Olivia.

I'm in the hospital. In the ICU.

Let me tell you about today. It's morning when I wake up (the nurses have just changed shifts) and outside my room the voices are getting closer. It's The Boys. I recognise them instantly.

They come often and, as usual, Little Boy is getting on Big Boy's nerves, but then they go quiet because the door has opened. I hear someone entering the room. It's a woman. I can tell from the quiet tread and breath.

She greets The Boys and, as soon as she speaks, I know who she is.

Olivia! It's you! You're beside me. I recognise your perfume.

'Sorry gentlemen. Have I got this right?' you're saying. 'You want to remove his brain?'

Pardon?

'Well, I wouldn't put it quite like that,' Big Boy replies.

'But you mean actually, physically, remove his brain? Take it out of his skull?'

What??!!!

'It does sound rather mediaeval,' giggles Little Boy, 'but we put it back neatly afterwards. You'd be amazed how tightly a brain re-fits. Honestly, you wouldn't know the difference.'

I'm not liking this, Olivia.

'You see, it's the only way to access the area we need to get to,' says Big Boy hurriedly.

'Oh, I see,' you say.

You see? You see what?

'And of course this includes the spinal column and nerves,' says Little Boy in a mature voice.

'The nerves too?' you say thoughtfully.

'Well, they're really part of the brain,' says Little Boy.

'I suppose they are,' you say. 'And you want me to give you permission to do this?'

'We need your consent,' says Big Boy.

'I can't answer that straight off,' you say. 'I've only just got here. I need a moment to think about it.'

You need a MOMENT to think about it, Olivia? No, you don't. They want to remove my brain! You're not going to let them do that!

'Of course,' says Big Boy. 'Take as long as you like.'

'Why do you want his brain?' you ask.

Are you kidding me? Does it matter?

'Well we think this study could lead to critically important advances in genetic medicine,' says Big Boy. 'It's an area of medicine we've both been interested in so we need reliable resections—'

'—Dr Patel did his Masters in Neurogenetics at Nottingham,' says Little Boy. 'I was at Addenbrooke's in Cambridge—'

'—and we've seen a correlation in David's father's genetic make-up which apparently matches David's—'

'—which signals a pathway for genetic-marker identification—'

'—which could help map out a pathway for preventive intervention—'

'—and our proposal for another article has already been accepted by the top journal,' squeals Little Boy.

Olivia, will you please tell these infants to piss off!

'I think it's useful to think of it as organ donation,' counsels Big Boy gravely.

You say Oh.

'Have you considered that?'

'No, no of course not. This has all been such a shock.'

'Of course it has,' says Dr Patel. 'A terrible thing to have to deal with. But organ donation is a surprisingly positive way of dealing with the death of a loved one.'

'I guess that makes sense.'

Makes sense? What sense? They're *my* organs, bitch!

I'm screaming with every bit of my strength, Olivia, and finally—finally!—a machine beeps in response.

'What's that?' you ask.

'Oh nothing, just the monitor,' says Little Boy. 'His heart rate is erratic. A common sign of neural as well as cardiac stress. It's like—' he pauses for a simple explanation '—a chicken, you know, that's been—'

'Have you any questions, Mrs Britton?' says Big Boy, firmly cutting in.

'Yes. Is my husband actually dead?'

No!

Little Boy starts to reply but Big Boy shuts him up. 'Of course, before we do anything, we'll run a full battery of tests to ensure irreversible brain death. These haven't been done, but it's been nine days now, so we have to at least anticipate the worst. At the moment, all we can say is that your husband is in a deep coma and we have reason to fear he may not emerge.'

I have emerged, you scumbag! You piece of crap! You shit!

'Oh David ...'

Olivia! You're weeping!

'I'm so sorry,' Dr Patel says. 'We'll leave you now to be alone with him.'

'Thank you.'

As the door closes, I can feel you drawing closer.

You're sobbing. Sobbing!

That makes me so happy, Olivia.

Screaming Into The Black
Dreamtime 3

I hear the squeak of your chair drawing closer.

'You bastard!' A searing rasp. Like you mean it with every fibre of your being.

Olivia! My darling!

'You fucking bastard!'

You're here! You've come! You're crying!

'You fucking, fucking, fucking, fucking bastard.'

Your fists and sobs crash like fragrant waves on my chest and I don't want you ever to stop.

I love you! I scream.

'I hate you.'

I adore you!

'I hate you!'

Olivia listen to me—

'You fucking, fucking bastard.'

But you're here. You're crying!

'I don't know if you can hear me, David—'

I can! I can!

'—but if you can, I want you to know just how ... how angry I am with you.'

You and me both, but listen to me ...

'Because you never gave us a chance, David. You never took me seriously, did you? You never respected me. And you betrayed me. And now ...'

I'm so sorry.

'Even as a mother, you belittled me.'

That's not true, Olivia!

'Every time I raised a worry or a doubt, even a thought about Amelia, you'd brush it away like it was of no value.'

That's so not true!

'Which is why she's so uncertain, David. So doomed to make mistakes.'

Are you blaming me for Masaai?

'Which is how she ends up pregnant with that fool Masaai.'

Now you're blaming me for Masaai?

'It was always so qualified with you. You were never there, never content, never …'

Her voice trails off into small sobs.

Masaai is not my fault.

'She was never pretty enough, never clever enough—'

She absolutely was pretty enough! Clever … well …

'—and why? Because it was always about you, David. All our lives had to revolve around famous you and your needs.

I know, I am so sorry.

And you think I didn't know what was going on?'

Masaai is NOT my fault!

'Even on holiday! You were never there! Always tearing off in search of some … story.'

That bonehead Masaai is NOT my fault, Olivia!

'Remember that time we went to America?'

Oh come on, Olivia! That was the *Death Row Incest* film! I had no choice!

'You were gone the whole time. The whole two weeks!'

I had to! The film literally landed in my lap.

'Moose was three. And where were you? Chasing bloody perverts.'

That film won two Baftas!

'And what did you do? Sent me two fucking tickets to Disneyland—'

She loved it! Mickey Mouse!

'—so you could run around with murderers and rapists and perverts.'

I was working. I was making a great film.

'The great stupid Oscar winner.'

That's not nice, Olivia.

'Even in your work, you exploited people, didn't you?'

Now your sobs are angry, breaking my heart.

'Oh, David! You know the doctors want to take your brain out of your head and do tests on it. They want to break your skull apart and take out your brain.'

I know, I know.

'And you know what? I still can't get my head around it, to be honest—'

Literally in my case.

'—the idea that they literally want to rip your brain out of your head. And your nerves ...'

Okay, okay: I get the picture.

'When the doctors told me that just now, you know what I thought? I thought, okay. I'll give you a bloody hand!'

Olivia!

'Because at this moment, that's how much I hate you.'

You'd help them?

'And not just your brain, David.'

You'd really help them?

'I hate you so much, I'd like to rip your balls off and donate those to medical science too.'

Aw c'mon.

Now you're sobbing so deeply, you have to stop for breath. 'Or better still, give them to fucking Janice Toybeen!'

Shave them. She's squeamish.

'And you know something? Even now, I just know, David, that if you were here you'd make a stupid joke about it. Something about mounting them on a plinth, or polishing them, or making them look bigger, or some stupid, childish shit like that—'

Olivia, please.

'—so this is how it ends, David. This is how twenty-eight years of my life with you ends. In a gift to medical science.'

No! Don't give them my brain! Olivia, I beg you!

'By signing away permission for someone to break your head open and tear out your brain. And hating you while I sign. And wishing I'd never laid eyes on you in the first place.'

Ah come on!

'Because that's what I feel: that my whole life with you has been one huge fatal error of judgement.'

No! We had so much love!

'So that's what I'm doing. I'm giving my permission, David. I'm allowing them to use your organs for transplant, research or whatever the hell they want to do.'

No, Olivia. Please! I beg you! I'm alive!

'Maybe, for once, you'll do some good in this world. And the little doctor chap will get his paper.'

And with that, you get up and walk out of my life.

I scream and scream into the silent black until I fall asleep, exhausted.

Locked-In Life
Dreamtime 4

I have lost all sense of time, Olivia. The days and weeks slide past uncalculated.

But it's still so busy! What might be hours and what might be minutes are calibrated by a medical soundscape: the snatched conversations of the staff, the morning and evening check-ups, the machines being wheeled in and out and turned on and off; the never-changing wheezing in my trachea … . This is the joyless, clicking, pumping soundtrack of my life.

Yet even in this liminal world, I live. I have friends. The nurses who wash and change me. The cleaners, especially the old Jamaican guy who sings and whistles like an angel and always makes me cry. The doctors, of course. I know them all individually, their names, their footsteps, their jokes, and some of their secrets.

And of course there are The Boys, whom I now love, except that every time I hear their unmistakeable tread, I wonder if this is the occasion when they will gently change my cannula, introduce the deadly fluid into my veins and then, when I'm unconscious, saw open my skull and retrieve that marvellous trophy, this *fickenfotze* brain of mine that's caused us both so much grief. But, to be fair, as Little Boy pointed out some indeterminate time ago, it's this troublesome brain that has also yielded no less than four important medical papers—with the big one yet to come. So that's something.

You know, Olivia, in the first few weeks, if weeks is what they were, I fought. Fought like a lion. Maniacally protested my right to exist at every waking hour. Wept and screamed and railed at the cruelty of my locked-in fate. But you know what? Even that anger has faded. I'm too exhausted to protest any more.

So this is my locked-in and soon to be locked-out life. Let's be frank: it is self-evidently not a life worth living.

One thing though: it has entirely robbed me of my fear of death. I now genuinely welcome death and wish I could speed its arrival. My heart lifts when I hear The Boys' soft footfall, and every time they stop by—and it's pretty much every day now—I pray that they will prepare the saw and begin their final work of liberating me. How odd that, in my teens, we used to talk about liberation in terms of doing what we liked. Now, half a century later, liberation puts me more in mind of freedom from damnation for having done what I liked, of *Libera Me*, of the Office of the Dead—a Catholic sentiment, admittedly, but now's not the time to be fussy.

Ooh, it's still so busy in this head of mine! Never a minute's peace, Olivia. Every waking moment thinking thoughts, scouring my soon-to-be-relocated brain, scavenging for memories, reviewing how much I wanted to do and what I am leaving behind undone. I trawl over every place, country, lover and friendship, every disappointment, betrayal and quarrel. I recall moments of shame: the little researcher I yelled at in Rio, the office cleaner I blamed for losing a tape, the nervous dental hygienist I called Mengele. Janice Toybeen. And a thousand others. So many apologies to make.

But most of all you, Olivia. I am so sorry.

I am still getting visits. Peter Dent is a frequent visitor. Every time he visits me he cries, the soppy git, and tells me in excruciating detail of his ardent return to Catholicism, for which he blames—or rather, praises—Menachem. He, more than anyone, would understand the Office of the Dead.

Menachem's here all the time. He's probably my most loyal visitor. Doesn't say much, just sits down purposefully, says hello, pointedly, *in Yiddish*, shakes my arm, then mumbles prayers. Every time he comes I implore him to tell me my father's final message but, frankly, I've pretty much lost hope. I'll never find out.

Best of all are the visits from Moose. In the beginning she came in every day but now it's more occasional. She greets me with a huge hug and a sloppy cascade of kisses on my face, her hair trailing between the pipes and pumps across my shoulders and chest. She used to bring stuff to read—newspapers, magazines, quotes from famously idiotic leftists, little poems and snippets from various morons on social media—but she no longer reads to me. Instead she just sits there, holding my hand and chatting. And on her last visit she told me the terrible news, Olivia, that the abortion was booked for the following day. That could have been three weeks ago or three months. I have no sense of time.

So it's over. There will be no baby. I knew eventually she'd visit to tell me herself, so it wasn't a surprise when I heard her entering my room today.

Moose! I scream.

'Hi, Dad.'

She leans over me, scented hair caressing my face. 'It's me, Moose.'

Hello darling! How are you? Are you okay?

She pulls the chair close, takes my hand and squeezes it. 'I know you can't hear me. I wish you could. I so wish you could!'

I can. Every word. Are you okay? Have you had the op?

'God, there's so much to tell you, I don't know where to start. It's weird without you, 'cos you're kind of here and kind of not. Kind of alive and kind of dead. It's really hard, Daddy. So hard.'

Daddy. My heart weeps.

In her sobs I hear her as a little child. Ah Baby, I'm so sorry I was such a shitty father. And I'm so sorry for putting you through all this. I'll be dead soon, and that will be a relief for you.

'Mom told me yesterday about the brain thing. She wants me to give my permission. Of course I went off the deep end: screamed and shouted.'

Good. Very good.

'I hate the idea of someone hurting you like that … breaking open your head—'

You hate it?! It's my head!

'—to take out your beautiful brain—' she pauses here to catch her breath—

308

Excellent. Excellent.

'—but I can see that there's no other way and that maybe, just maybe, some good may come of it.'

Whoa. Steady on, there.

'That's what Mom says.'

Yeah, I'll bet that's what Mom says.

'And Masaai thinks so too.'

Ah, the genius thinks so too? I'm glad young Einstein wants the scientists to take my brain out of my skull and play post-doctoral football with it. You know what? I hope Little Boy's big paper bombs!

'Daddy, I know you don't really like Masaai but, really, it's just cos you don't know him. And he's changed so much lately.'

What, since he became black?

'You know, he's no longer a black man.'

What?

'Well, that's not quite right. He's still a black man but he sees his blackness differently. He's joined an Igbo synagogue. Now he's a proud black Jew.'

A proud black Jew who also happens to be a moron.

'And I've got important news.'

I brace myself. This is it.

'We went to the hospital for the abortion last week. It was so hard.'

I know, Baby, I know. She sobs and I'm crying with her as her tears spray lightly on my face.

'Where to start? Okay, first thing: Masaai has changed his name. He's now Yaacov Ben Nahman.'

Oh, come on.

'Named after some very important rabbi who lived hundreds of years ago in Ukraine—'

Oh for heaven's sake.

'—and when Menachem came to visit—'

Menachem? What's that thieving conman got to do with this?

'—and said that the baby we were about to murder could change the world—'

Oh, screaming Jesus.

'—because our little baby could be the next Messiah, and we'd be killing the Messiah—anyway, that night, Masaai had this dream—'

Oh, Mother Mary and Joseph!

'—and the next day he changed his name—'

He's a moron!

'—and said there was no way on Earth we could go through with the abortion.'

This takes a while to sink in. Huh?

'He said we can't kill this Jewish child. Not after the Holocaust. And what if our baby really was the next Messiah? We just can't do it. That's what Masaai said.'

Masaai! You big bad black beautiful Jewboy genius!

'But I'm so scared, Daddy, and I wish you were here, 'cos I know how much you wanted this baby, but I'm so frightened that I won't be able to look after it properly. I mean: suppose it *is* the next Messiah, I dunno how to look after a Messiah, do I? Where do they teach you that? They don't offer it at GCSE.'

As our daughter leans over me and wails, I feel a rush of joy and hope, like nothing I've ever felt before, Olivia.

I want to assure her that it will be fine, just fine. Because hardwired within her I know she can do it, and do it brilliantly, for any baby—even the Messiah. I'm just so sad that I won't be there to see her do it.

'I've got to go, Daddy,' she says, gathering her things, 'but someone's already here to take over from me. I'll come again tomorrow.'

She gets up and leaves. I am weeping with joy for the grandchild I will never meet (it's a boy) and it's the happiest moment of my life.

Then, shortly after, a new set of footsteps enters my room. The sounds are heavy and big-set. I hear what is obviously a man sit down laboriously and grunt. Then the unmistakable sing-song sound of Hebrew prayer.

It's Hymie. Hymie, the Champion Bull.

'*Mi Shebeirach avoseinu Avraham, Yitzchok v'Yaakoyv, hu y'voreich es ha'choleh Dovid ben Rivkoh—*' he sings.

Oh, go home, you hypocrite, you fraud!

'—*Hakodosh Boruch Hu yimalei rachamim olov, l'hachlimo ul'rapoiso l'hachaziko ul'hachayoso. V'yishlach lo bimheiroh r'fuah shleimah, r'fuas hanefesh ur'fuas haguf, besoch she'ar cholei Yisroel. V'nomar: Omein.*'

Then Hymie places his clammy hand on my forehead.

Nurse! Nurse! I'm being attacked! I'm being molested!

'Ah, David, David, David,' Hymie says. 'What a shame, what a terrible shame! *A shod.*'

What? What did you just say?

'It's so sad. Especially now that you're going to become a grandfather.'

You're speaking English? In an American accent?

'So I've come because Menachem's busy and he really wanted someone to come and pray for you, and I said I'd do it. In fact I wanted to anyway because, in a funny way, I think of you as a friend: you know that? For some reason Menachem loves you very much too. I think it's because your insults are so funny—I mean, they really are!'

He's sniggering, the phoney.

'And you are funny! Very funny! I've loved your insults too, you know, and I so often wanted to come clean and just talk, you know, in English, but Menachem thought the disguise was necessary. That night you suffered your stroke? That night I was going to come clean. And now I can't. Too bad.'

Conman! Liar!

'But you know what I most like about you, David? It's your *chesed*. Your kindness. You talk hard and act soft. All the stuff you do for those weirdos, that crazy Ronny who pesters me every day now with complicated questions on Jewish Law; and Emily, that crazy mixed up kid—I hear she's doing well—and Natalie, that pretty lady at work. And I know that your wife wants to leave you and that you still love her. What can I say? Life can be unkind. Maybe next time I come, I'll read to you from the *Book of Job*.'

He pauses and sighs. 'The funny thing is, we have so much to talk about. You know, I was a film producer like you. In LA, before I became a Jew. I made movies, cop shows: *LA Sheriff*, that was mine. And *Booty Jack*, that was mine too.'

I do not believe this.

'Not just that. I was also a Deadhead, you know, because my dad was a Deadhead, tripping every weekend at the Golden Gate Park, all that *meshuggeh* hippy stuff. He used to record bootlegs, you know. I've still got a couple somewhere but I don't listen to that music now. *Azoy*, it would have been nice to talk about this, you know: which album you liked most. Me? Probably *Workingman's Dead* or *Steal Your Face* but the bootlegs are the best—nothing like them. Actually, I once met Jerry and Bob and I knew Bill Kreutzmann, you know? We came from the same neighbourhood. I heard he became a proper Jew, but that's another story. Hell, I even once held Phil Lesh's electronic bass guitar: you know, it had this computer-like thing in the fretboard?'

For the first time since my awakening into consciousness I am utterly lost for words. And then something happens.

I feel it deep in my skull—an unfamiliar stirring. So I open my eyes and, just like that, the world is forming before me. And there is Hymie the Bull's sad, magnificently-bearded face looming above me.

'You know you look a little like Jerry Garcia,' I say.

Hymie reels back. His hands have flown to his mouth and his eyes are popping.

'What did you just say?' he cries.

And I hear my own BBC voice, as clear as day. 'I said you look a little like Jerry Garcia, Man. Hymie, am I reaching you?'

Boruch Hashem!' Hymie cries.

'I think I'm talking to you about Jerry Garcia in English, right?'

'*Boruch Hashem! Dovidl*, you've come back from the dead!'

He's shouting, yelling, rushing madly into the corridor.

'*Boruch Hashem! Boruch Hashem!* Nurse! Nurse!'

Boruch Hashem, As The Yids Say
17 August, 9:45 pm

Olivia, I hope you didn't mind me sending you this, my book, my apologia, my confession—whatever it is. I can only think of it as a true account of my failures, my treachery and my undying love. Maybe you'll read it, maybe you won't. But at least now you'll know how it looked and felt from my side.

I was hoping to see you today. I was crushed when I heard you wouldn't be coming. But I understand.

Still, I feel strangely content, proud that I've been able to drive alone and walk unaided from the car park. And now, as I make my way to one of the prayer halls at the new Bushey Jewish Cemetery, all surrounded by ornamental grasses and reed beds, I feel confident. My new, ornately-carved Senegalese walking stick, a gift from Masaai, is doing an admirable job and every day I feel a little stronger. And when I identify the Hebrew lettering that spells out my own ancient name—*Dovid*—on some of the graves I pass—the *Daled*, the *Vav*, the *Daled*—I feel strangely happy and proud that my Hebrew lessons with Masaai are going somewhere. *Boruch Hashem*, as Menachem would say.

I spot our group. By the way, it was Moose who told me that you wouldn't be coming. She gave all sorts of reasons but she didn't have to. I understand. Of course I'm sad but, you know what, Olivia? In the grand scheme of things, it doesn't really matter. I have finally accepted that I have to let you go, and that you will get on with your life and that I will get on with mine, whatever the pain.

Losing you still hurts though. Literally hurts. That's why I stop in my tracks, every so often, to exhale a lungful of grief. And each time I recover, I breathe in the spring air and luxuriate in the gentle gusts of warmth that fall upon my face. I was dead and now I'm alive, Olivia—with a grandchild on the way. Maybe that's why I can accept the loss and move on.

Moose, visibly pregnant, sees me, yelps, and sprints over.

'Stop running for goodness' sake! Think of the baby!'

'Daddy, stop! Wait for me!' she cries.

'Walk! Don't run!' I yell.

How beautiful she looks, Olivia. Pregnant and 'glowing'— such a cliché but so true. 'You gotta be careful!'

She laughs. 'Relax, Daddy, I'm fine. I'm only seven months gone.' Then she throws her arms around me and puts on her cross face. 'Why didn't you wait for me like I told you, like we agreed?'

'Because I've got to learn to walk on my own three legs. Really, it's getting better every day. Is everyone here?' I'm peering at the group. A large wall of grinning black-hatted Jews smiles and waves enthusiastically in my direction. 'Lotta Jews this time of year.'

'Yup. Menachem and Hymie sure know how to draw a crowd. Come! And Daddy, please be nice today.'

'Aren't I always, Darling?'

She laughs.

'I'm guessing we're certain your mother isn't coming?'

She stops laughing. 'Daddy, I explained why. Really it's better this way.'

We fall silent for a moment. Then I tell her how beautiful she looks.

'I'm fat as a horse. And still two months to go. Ah look, here's Yaacov.'

And it is indeed Masaai, bounding down the pathway, a garish skullcap perched on his springy mop of bouncing hair. 'Yaacov. Just as I was getting used to Masaai.'

'It's crazy,' she laughs.

'I sort of miss the old Masaai.'

'I'm surprised to hear you say that.'

'He was a character, that's for sure.'

'Believe me, so is Yaacov. Your rabbi has a lot to answer for.'

I laugh. 'He does.'

Masaai joins us. 'Duuuuude! How's the stick? Looks good, Man, looks proper good.'

We shake hands in a vaguely ethnic way.

'The best gift a man could get.' I tell him. 'Thank you. So, who are all those Jews?

'I dunno, Man: Menachem's Jews. It's for the *minyan*. That means ten male Yiddles; without ten we can't say *kaddish*. And a few came just to gawp at you, I think. You're big news in these parts, Dude. You're leading the *kaddish*—you know that, right?'

'I know, relax. Been rehearsing. So what exactly's happening today? Exhuming my father? Reburying him? I dunno.'

'I heard that,' says Menachem. He and Hymie are leading a posse of Black Hats towards us.

'He's done better, to be honest,' says Hymie.

'Ah, *The Guns of Navarone*,' I say, by way of greeting. 'Or is it *The Good, the Bad and the Ugly*?'

'Good morning, *Dovidl*,' says Menachem.

'Perhaps *A Fistful of Dollars*.'

We all embrace.

'How are you, *Dovidl*?' says Menachem.

'Walking, Breathing. Living. Can't complain.'

'That's right,' says Menachem. 'Thanks to the *Aybishter* for life!'

'Been a busy few weeks for Him, I can tell you,' I say. 'And for me.' It has. The grim, exhausting legalities of initiating a divorce.

'Long, strange trip,' says Hymie.

'When life looks like easy street—'

'Danger at your door.'

'Okay, enough Grateful Dead already,' says Menachem in a big voice. 'You missed your father's funeral David, so today's stone-setting ceremony is especially important.'

'Very important,' says Hymie.

'And you're going to tell me why, right?'

Menachem launches in. 'Consecrating the gravestone is a physical act of memory, okay? You weren't able to attend the funeral or *shiva*, so the unveiling of the stone provides one more opportunity to grieve and acknowledge your loss.'

'Menachem, there is no loss. I didn't love my father,' I say quietly.

315

'Daddy, please don't say that.'

'It's a fact. It's true.'

'You didn't love him because you didn't know him,' says Menachem—

'—and maybe you didn't know him because you didn't allow yourself to know him,' says Hymie.

'I wish I'd known him,' says Masaai.

'And maybe he didn't want you to know him,' says Menachem, pulling his beard. 'It can work both ways.'

'Maybe he couldn't,' says Hymie, pulling his own beard.

'That's right,' says Masaai, pulling the beard he didn't have the first time we met.

'How true!' exclaims Peter Dent, who has infiltrated our little huddle with a reptilian elegance. 'And how are we all today?'

'Oh fuck,' I say. 'You.'

'Now, now. Morning, David. May I wish you "long life".'

I look at Masaai. 'What did my ex-lawyer just say?'

'He wished you "long life",' says Masaai. 'That's what English Jews do after a death.'

Menachem has adjusted his position so he's near enough to lick. 'You see *Dovidl*, during the ceremony, you get to see the name of your beloved father etched in stone and there's a realisation of the finality of death; so the ritual forces you not just to face death and loss realistically, and to affirm a commitment to life and the living, but also—and this is vital, so try and concentrate—to recall the memory of the departed and reflect upon the significance of that person's life and accomplishments—and your father had many accomplishments, believe me—and in this way to etch his memory permanently onto the collective memory of the Jewish community.'

'My father hated me,' I say.

'No!'

Menachem's cry, from the heart, with all his might, leaves everyone stunned. He turns on me fiercely.

'Do you remember that I have a message to you from your father?' he intones, his voice shaking

'I do.'

'I was going to give it to you privately after the service, but instead, David, I'm going to give it to you right now, in public.'

'Epic!' says Masaai.

Menachem's got his biggest sermon voice on. 'As you know, David, your father desperately wanted to see you before he suffered his stroke. *Nu*, you were busy; it happens. And your father knew that. He said to me: 'Menachem, don't blame my son. I was a terrible father'. And he had this message for you. He made me promise I would give it to you if he couldn't. And that's what I'm going to do right now. Tell you the whole message. Without notes. How can I remember? Because it's very short. In fact, just one word. And do you know what that word is, *Dovidl*?'

No,' I say.

'That word is: "Sorry".' He repeats it in a huge voice. '"Sorry"!'

And suddenly, it all makes sense. There is nothing to add or subtract. For the first time, I see my father's face and there is no fear, no anger, just a catch in my throat.

'He wanted your forgiveness,' Menachem explains. 'And now, *Dovidl*, it's over to you. Come, let's go over to your father's gravestone.'

He takes my arm and we walk slowly up the path. Up ahead, my father's grave comes into view.

And there you are, Olivia. You've arrived alone, hidden, from the other side. Your hair is shining under your black hat. You've been waiting for me by the graveside. I can see it in your eyes.

'You came?' I say when I come alongside you.

'I did.'

Boruch Hashem, as the Jews say.

THE END

Acknowledgements

There are many people to whom I'd like to register my thanks. Friends from my childhood and youth, scattered around the world, who enjoyed my short stories and encouraged me to write at greater length. My nearest and dearest, who bravely read my early drafts, told me they were horrendous and inspired me to make essential changes. Judy Nussbaum for her advice. Shane Mackay for his constant, kind support. Philman, for his advice on Brummie bikers. Joanna, to whom I entrust my body and soul on Planet Earth, book or no book. And the brilliant Dr Stephen Games, editor and publisher of EnvelopeBooks, who improved this book in too many ways to count.

The Green Man | Dan Jones

After humiliating a fellow inquisitor at a trumped-up witch trial in Northern Italy, Brother Jacobus of Vienna is intrigued by rumours of strange events in Northern England. In defiance of the cardinals in Avignon, Jacobus travels to Berwick where he finds a land in disarray, beset by Scottish raiders, eccentric Franciscan friars and talk of demons in the woods. Can he solve the mystery and keep his faith and reason intact?

Mrs Woodbine's Prejudices | Michael Ladner

Prof. Arthur Lash, born Artur Lasch in pre-war Austria, takes his American wife and three sons back to Vienna, in 1960, to see how well his father is rebuilding a life interrupted by Nazi Germany's annexation of Austria in 1938. For Arthur, the journey helps re-establish his links with the city he was brought up in; for the rest of his family, other emotions are awoken—all watched over by Mrs. Woodbine, their needy, disregarded but loyal nanny.

Belle Nash and the Bath Soufflé | William Keeling Esq.

In the first volume of *The Gay Street Chronicles*, bachelor Belle Nash attempts to navigate bigotry and corruption in 1830s Bath without compromising his boyfriend, the nephew of Immanuel Kant, or his best friend, the widow of Bath's greatest lawyer. Intrigue and whimsy overflow after—horror!—a soufflé fails to rise.

The Train House on Lobengula Street | Fatima Kara

An anguished, folksy and life-affirming novel, set within the Indian community in Bulawayo, Rhodesia, from the 1940s to the 1960s, about female empowerment and the capacity of women to gain the same advantages as men in the modern world while remaining faithful to traditional Muslim values. Affectionate and passionate.

Mustard Seed Itinerary | Robert Mullen
Po Cheng falls into a dream and finds himself on the road to the imperial Chinese capital. Once there he rises to the heights of the civil service, then finds that in addition to the ladders that helped him ascend, there are snakes facilitating his fall. An object lesson to all ambitious young men and a case study in Carrollian satire.

Frances Creighton: Found and Lost | Kirby Porter
Love demands trust, but trust is a lot to ask for from a victim of abuse. Having been bullied in Belfast as a boy, at his school and at his church, Michael Roberts suppresses his childhood pains until a girlfriend's death years later forces him to revisit lost memories. A Northern Ireland reply to Sally Rooney's *Normal People*.

A Sin of Omission | Marguerite Poland
An emotionally intense novel, set in 1870s South Africa at a time of rising anti-colonial resistance. The book examines the tragedy of a promising black preacher, hand-picked for training in England as a missionary, only to be neglected by the Church he loves. Winner of the 2021 *Sunday Times* CNA 'Book of the Year' Award in South Africa.

The Hopeful Traveller | Janina David
A collection of short stories about—and told by—single women who have put the past behind them but are still looking for their anchor in the present. It includes bitter-sweet accounts of the freedoms of postwar life, of foreign travel, of the rekindling of old friendships and of the search for new ones.

A Girl's Own War | K.J. Kelly
Flt. Lieut. Oliver Carmichael and Baron Julius von Stulp-nagel had been living together in Berlin, trying to sell forged paintings. Why are they now in run-down Ballingore, in wartime neutral Ireland in 1940, and how will ex-convent-girl Mary Collins and her devoted red-headed sidekick Niamh Slattery play into their hands? Hilarious Irish farce.

Belle Nash and the Bath Circus | William Keeling Esq.

In Volume Two of *The Gay Street Chronicles*, bachelor Belle Nash returns to Regency Bath from Grenada, inspired by a new love that leads him into pretences that may compromise the ambitions of black circus impresario Pablo Fanque.

Lagos, Life and Sexual Distraction | Tunde Ososanya

Twelve short stories, mostly focused on the struggle to survive in Lagos, Nigeria's commercial capital, illustrating the tensions that exist between the generations, the sexes and the country's different social classes and ethnicities. Honest, acute and with moments of unexpected humour.

The Attraction of Cuba | Chris Hilton

Chris Hilton went to Cuba to escape the boredom of everyday life and to make money, only to be entranced by the beauty of the country and of Yamilia, a street girl who brought him love and laughter but who could not help him from falling into an inevitable downward spiral.

Princess Brainy | Stephen Games

Raine couldn't help being hated for being clever, but it didn't help that her mother was modern and made her father (the king) ban the fairies. So what was she meant to do when disaster came to Rainland and the rivers dried up? Accept her fate or get sacrificed to the revolution?

Cigars Occasionally | Anthony Motley

World-weary Detective Jake Miller has seen everything that Florida's Pinellas County can throw at him, but just as he's wondering whether to take early retirement—and maybe get a divorce—in favour of a new life and a new partner, a series of incidents renews his sensitivity to his real mission.

The Lost Woman | Karen Mulvahill

When then Nazis invade Paris, Nicole's parents' art gallery is raided and their best art looted. Years later, living in New York, she hires an art historian to find out if anything has survived, especially the portrait of her mother by Matisse.

How to Rescue a Tiger
When Roger Allen began his career as a photographer in South London, he sometimes covered funny local-interest stories about animals. Years later, a national newspaper sent him to Borneo to photograph a rescue centre for orphaned orangutans. En route, he met Mely, once a pet for its owner, now a captive adult. He and Mely touched hands, and instantly he was converted into an impassioned campaigner for animal freedom. This wonderful picture book documents some of his most important assignments.

Wembley Speaks: A Year in the Life of a London Suburb
How do people talk to each other, react to each other, give and ask for advice, commiserate and laugh? In a modern reconstruction of Mayhew's landmark 19th-century social study, EnvelopeBooks turns to the *Nextdoor* social networking app to show a community engaging with itself on day-to-day issues. In the face of all the clichés, *Wembley Speaks* offers a heartwarming picture of online engagement.

Lost Levant: A Journey of Ideas | Rupert de Borchgrave
In the last thousand years, cultural innovation has moved inexorably westwards, leaving us with a poor grasp of the turmoil out of which our own civilisation grew. In 2003 Rupert de Borchgrave went on a journey of ideas to the much-disputed grounds where many of the issues that shape us now were formed.

Why My Wife Had To Die | Brian Verity
There is no known cure for Huntington's disease, a wasting condition that sufferers acquire from a parent. In this painful account, the author vents his rage at society, lawmakers, health services and the Church for not grasping the need, as he sees it, to legalise compulsory sterilisation and assisted dying.

A Question of Paternity | David Tereshchuk
As a TV reporter, David Tereshchuk traveled the world interviewing tyrants and their victims, but could never get his own mother to say who his father was. Her evasion led to his life of insecurity and alcoholism. And a quest.

The West and the Rest | Ian Ross
Having worked in the oil and tobacco industries, Ian Ross argues that trade is objectively more creative than democracy in bridging cultural divisions. Where diplomats are held back by caution and principle, business executives are incentivised to be adaptable, forward-looking and trusting.

A Road to Extinction | Jonathan Lawley
When Britain colonised the Andamans in 1857, the welfare of its African pygmy inhabitants was of no concern. Nine tribes died out. Dr Lawley now assesses the survival prospects for the three remaining tribes and weighs up the legacy of his grandfather, a former colonial administrator

The Martyrdom of Ahmad Shawkat | Michael Goldfarb
When Gulf War II broke out in 2003, Ahmad Shawkat became guide and translator to NPR-reporter Michael Goldfarb. After the fall of Saddam, Ahmad set up a cultural magazine, published eleven issues and then was killed for publicly decrying Islamic terror. This is his poignant story.

Artist Spy Prisoner | George Tomaziu
Artist George Tomaziu was imprisoned for monitoring Nazi troop movements through Bucharest in World War Two but thought that his efforts would be recognised once the war was over. He was mistaken. When Romania became Communist he was imprisoned again—this time for thirteen years.

From Bedales to the Boche | Robert Best
Bedales, the progressive boarding school founded in 1893, instilled values that sustained many of its pupils for the rest of their lives. Robert Best recalls its impact on him as an army recruit in 1914 and, from 1916, in the Royal Flying Corps.

My Modern Movement | Robert Best

London's Festival of Britain in 1951 marked the belief that Modern design was visually and morally superior. Robert Best, at one time the UK's leading lighting manufacturer, thinks the dice were loaded. This is his memoir.

For more information about
EnvelopeBooks titles,
visit
www.envelopebooks.co.uk

Visit also our sister magazine
Booklaunch
at
www.booklaunch.london

Printed in Dunstable, United Kingdom